Every belle époque has its end . . .

"Enough chatter," Florence said, standing slowly, tugging at the frilled cuffs of her springy blouse. "Cut to the chase, Wally. What happened to poor Vivienne?"

"Well, that's a problem; we don't exactly know."

Francis sat down, thudding into the nearest chair as if his legs wouldn't hold him any longer. He buried his face in his hands and moaned.

Wally glanced at him, then continued. "The medical examiner says if he was to hazard a guess, he'd say that Mrs. Vivienne Whittaker had been poisoned, either purposely or accidentally, by something she ingested in the minutes before her demise."

"You mean something she ate?" Thelma Mae loudly asked. "If that's what you mean, just say it plain, Wally; don't beat around the bush."

He met her grim stare. "All right then, yes, it appears it was something she ate or drank in your tearoom that killed her."

"You finally did it," Francis said, lifting his face and glaring at the senior owner of Belle Époque. "You finally *killed* someone with your awful food!"

10668594

Tempest in a Teapot

Amanda Cooper

BERKLEY PRIME CRIME, NEW YORK

THE BERKLEY PUBLISHING GROUP
Published by the Penguin Group
Penguin Group (USA) LLC
375 Hudson Street, New York, New York 10014

USA • Canada • UK • Ireland • Australia • New Zealand • India • South Africa • China

penguin.com

A Penguin Random House Company

TEMPEST IN A TEAPOT

A Berkley Prime Crime Book / published by arrangement with the author

Copyright © 2014 by Penguin Group (USA) LLC.
Penguin supports copyright. Copyright fuels creativity, encourages diverse voices,
promotes free speech, and creates a vibrant culture. Thank you for buying an authorized
edition of this book and for complying with copyright laws by not reproducing, scanning,
or distributing any part of it in any form without permission. You are supporting writers
and allowing Penguin to continue to publish books for every reader.

Berkley Prime Crime Books are published by The Berkley Publishing Group.
BERKLEY® PRIME CRIME and the PRIME CRIME logo are trademarks of
Penguin Group (USA) LLC.

For information, address: The Berkley Publishing Group,
a division of Penguin Group (USA) LLC,
375 Hudson Street, New York, New York 10014.

ISBN: 978-0-425-26523-9

PUBLISHING HISTORY
Berkley Prime Crime mass-market edition / June 2014

PRINTED IN THE UNITED STATES OF AMERICA

10 9 8 7 6 5 4 3 2 1

Cover illustration by Griesbach Martucci.
Cover design by Diana Kolsky.
Interior text design by Kelly Lipovich.

This is a work of fiction. Names, characters, places, and incidents either are the product
of the author's imagination or are used fictitiously, and any resemblance to actual persons,
living or dead, business establishments, events, or locales is entirely coincidental.

PUBLISHER'S NOTE: The recipes contained in this book are to be followed exactly
as written. The publisher is not responsible for your specific health or allergy needs
that may require medical supervision. The publisher is not responsible for any adverse
reactions to the recipes contained in this book.

If you purchased this book without a cover, you should be aware that this book is
stolen property. It was reported as "unsold and destroyed" to the publisher, and neither
the author nor the publisher has received any payment for this "stripped book."

*For Karen: mystery reader, tea drinker,
and most of all, wonderful friend!*

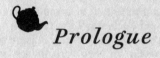

Prologue

"**S**o, you're a cook, right?" Sebastian DeRocque sat back in his chair in the dining room of the Eastern Star restaurant in Tribeca and crossed his legs. He pinched the knife-edge crease of his gray wool slacks and shot his white French cuff just enough to show one inch of white linen and a gold monogrammed cuff link.

"I'm a *chef*," Sophie Taylor corrected, lifting a dumpling from the dim sum plate with chopsticks and popping it into her mouth. She savored the flavor, head cocked to one side. What *was* that spice the chef had used?

"I thought that men were chefs and women were cooks," Sebastian said, signaling for another *tokkuri*, a ceramic carafe of sake.

Sophie stared at him for a moment, examining the supercilious curve of his lips. There was a chance he was teasing, but she didn't think so. As she'd suffered his snobbery throughout the meal, he had exhibited not a single shred of a sense of humor. He had regaled her with the wonder that was Sebastian, but this was the first time he had asked anything about her. She didn't really care if he was *trying* to be funny, anyway. Misogyny was rarely humorous. "No, a trained cook is a chef. Period. Gender, age, race and/or sexual orientation don't enter into it. I have a culinary degree and one in restaurant management."

"I see I've touched a PC nerve."

"I don't consider a refusal to discriminate being politically correct," she said. "The way I was raised, it was called politeness and respect." At least that was the lesson from her nana, in Gracious Grove, New York, though her mother didn't feel the same. *She* would say if you are clearly superior, you deserve to discriminate.

"*Anyway* . . . is that why your restaurant failed so badly . . . your, er, *degree* in restaurant management?"

His effort to irritate her made her wonder if perhaps she hadn't worshipped readily enough at the altar of his magnificence. As a surgeon of familial wealth and some fame, Sebastian was accustomed to adulation from women, she supposed. But she had known other doctors and many wealthy people, and most were not such snobs. No, his failings were *his* fault, not that of his situation in life. This blind date, set up by her mother, the ineffably lovely and cultured Rosalind Freemont Taylor, was not going to be repeated.

Sophie knew her mother *meant* well, which was the only reason she had agreed to the date. Her mom was convinced that her only daughter, having lost her livelihood—in other words, having lost In Fashion, the restaurant that was her reason for getting up every morning—should now give up, marry well, and retire to domestic bliss in Manhattan in winter, the Hamptons in summer.

That was not Sophie's plan, but to be fair, did she even have a plan anymore? The restaurant had failed, yes, but it was one of a hundred or more that failed every year in New York. The economy's nosedive had taken so many great eateries down with it that it was like some culinary Darwinian environment; only the strong survived. Sophie put her hand over her sake cup, so when Sebastian tried to pour, it spilled over her hand and onto the white linen tablecloth.

The long-suffering waiter was there in an instant. Sophie

smiled up at him, and he ducked his head while he mopped up the spilled rice wine.

"I'm sorry," she said, to the waiter, not Sebastian, as she wiped her hand with the linen napkin. "But I've had quite enough to drink. Could you ask the chef if that is white truffle in the dumpling? I'm curious."

He ducked his head again—his English was not very good, and he was unlikely to risk speaking much after Sebastian had savaged his inability to pronounce his name—and took away the soiled linen with him.

"Chef, cook, manager . . . you sweat in a kitchen for a living. I wouldn't have thought that *my* mother and *your* mother would have much in common, but apparently they belong to the same clubs." He sipped his sake, made a face and said, "We should have gone to *my* choice of a restaurant, but I assumed that you, as familiar as you should be with the Manhattan restaurant scene, would be able to recommend some place decent."

Sophie took in a deep breath, ready to let Sebastian have it, but instead a whiff of good black tea floated up her nostrils, the honey scent rolling across her in a wave. It took her away, to Auntie Rose's Victorian Tea House in Gracious Grove, New York. Auntie Rose's was her grandmother's establishment and where she had learned, as a kid on vacation, to make cranberry scones and strawberry compote. The tearoom was the genesis of her hunger for and knowledge of food.

And teapots! The adorable teapots that lined shelves and shelves of Nana's tearoom had been a source of endless pleasure as a child. If she was good . . . very, *very* good . . . she could take them down one by one and dust them. A teapot in the shape of a kitten on a cushion, abandoned by Nana because it was chipped, had been the start of her own sizable collection. Though she preferred art nouveau and art deco, now, over chintz and figural, it was something that bonded her and her maternal grandmother.

It was not even worth her while to chew out Sebastian for his presumption and arrogance. He wasn't going to have an epiphany and realize he was a giant, braying ass. Her grandmother had always said, *"Sophie, you have to choose your battles in life. Don't waste your time on folks who don't matter."*

Sebastian most definitely did *not* matter.

She took a deep breath and let it go, slowly. Sophie had made a decision regarding her future; she was going home. Not to her mother's Manhattan apartment, not to the house in the Hamptons, nor the South Beach condo, but to Gracious Grove and Auntie Rose's Victorian Tea House, her nana's tearoom. She would find herself there, as she always did, among the teapots and cranberry scones.

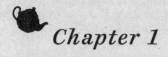

Chapter 1

Thelma Mae Earnshaw peeped through the lacy curtains that adorned the side window of La Belle Époque, her quaint(ish) inn and tearoom. She was trying to figure out what had her archenemy and business competitor, Rose Freemont, in such a fuss. Rose had already, several times that morning, gone to the front door of Auntie Rose's Victorian Tea House and paced the narrow sidewalk. She had scrubbed that front door, polished the teapot-shaped brass knocker and washed the windows as high as a woman too old to climb a ladder could.

If Thelma didn't know better, she would have speculated Rose was waiting for a visitor as important as Queen Elizabeth, with Philip, Charles, Camilla, Will, Kate, the baby and handsome Prince Harry in tow! But such a string of luminaries would never brighten the modest streets of Gracious Grove, New York, "Prettiest Town in All the Finger Lakes." Folks were always surprised to find out that it wasn't just pretty, it was "dry," and perhaps the ban on alcohol had a positive influence on the prettiness, who could judge?

But back to Rose: Thelma gathered her thoughts, which

had a tendency to scatter like chickens from a barking dog. It had to be someone important Rose was expecting. Who? Or was it *whom*? Thelma could never remember the right usage, and hadn't even seventy-some-odd years ago when she and Rose were pigtailed schoolgirls sharing secrets at Gracious Grove Elementary. That was years before the fateful Methodist Church pie social where Rose Beaudry had stolen Harold Freemont from Thelma.

Rose exited her tearoom again and this time walked right out into the street, wringing her hands and looking anxious. Well, now, what had her knickers in a knot?

That very minute a rattletrap van came tootling down Seneca Street. It screeched to a halt in front of Auntie Rose's, and a youthful figure leaped out of the passenger side and ran at Rose. It was like one of those home invasion attacks you heard of happening in Buffalo or Rochester, the ones that were so common on the news, Thelma thought, one hand over her heart and one on the telephone, in case the police were needed. But in another second she realized who the youthful figure was . . . Sophie Taylor!

While still watching the girl and her grandmother in a tight, long-lasting embrace—the proceedings were complicated by Pearl, Rose's gorgeous chocolate-point Birman cat, winding around their legs—Thelma quickly dialed a number she knew by heart. Her granddaughter answered the phone with her customary "Peterson Books 'n Stuff . . . Cissy Peterson speaking. How can I help you?"

"Cissy, you'll never guess who's come home to Gracious Grove!" Thelma kept watching out the window as Rose propped open the front door of the tearoom and some young fellow started lugging boxes labeled TEAPOTS out of the back of the van. Thelma might be old, but her far vision was sharper than ever!

"Who, Granny?" Cissy said, her voice sounding as bored as it always did nowadays.

"Sophie Rose Freemont Taylor, that's who!" Thelma stated. "And it looks like she's come to stay!"

* * *

Three days had already passed since Sophie arrived, Rose Freemont fumed, and still she hadn't so much as dipped her toe in the local friendship circles. Rose figured that's the first thing she would want to do, get reacquainted with all the kids she used to be friendly with when she came to stay in Gracious Grove every summer. She hadn't been back in years, too busy trying to shore up a dying business, her restaurant in the garment district in New York.

Rose stood at the door of Sophie's sitting room, one of three rooms in her attic apartment above Rose's second-floor quarters, which were, in turn, above the tearoom, her beloved business for the last forty years. Sophie, screwdriver in hand, was eyeballing a shelf she was mounting on the only straight wall in the room. As in most attic apartments, many of the walls were slanted, with dormer-style windows that had a gorgeous view of Seneca Lake, two miles distant.

"Nana, is this level, do you think?" Sophie asked, holding the shelf in place with one hand and trying to lean back to judge.

"Looks like it," Rose answered. As level as the other six shelves that held Sophie's collection of art deco, art nouveau and modernist teapots. But after twenty years, the white-Persian-cat-on-a-cushion teapot, which Sophie had begged to keep when Rose was going to reluctantly chuck it after it got chipped while cleaning, was still in the center, the heart of the collection.

Sophie bent all her strength to fastening the seventh and final shelf to the wall then stood back, eyeing the display. She unpacked her last box of teapots and began to arrange them on the shelf. The Silver Spouts, Rose's teapot-collecting group, would be fascinated by Sophie's collection. The next meeting was in just a few days, and Rose hoped Sophie would bring some down to the tearoom to show them off to the other collectors.

"I'm so happy to have you here, Sophie dear. I'm not

getting any younger; neither is Laverne," she said, of her only employee. "I was just saying to her the other day, I wasn't sure how we'd manage everything with the bridal shower season upon us and more reservations than I know what to do with. When you called and asked to come home to stay, it was like the answer to a prayer."

Lovely Sophie, twenty-nine, dark haired and blue eyed, was across the room in two long strides and hugged her. "No, you're the answer to *my* prayers, Nana. It was like a voice told me to come home to Gracious Grove! Well, I know it was never *really* my home," she said, squeezing and releasing. "Just my favorite place to be during summer holidays and at Christmas and Easter."

Rose gazed up at her gorgeous granddaughter, feeling a swell of pride. She was vivacious, smart, beautiful and . . . a little downhearted. She cocked her head to one side as she looked up at the child. There was a hint of self-doubt in her manner since the lingering death of her restaurant.

"This *is* your home!" Rose stoutly insisted. "Your brothers hated it here in Gracious Grove; nothing to do, they said. So I just let them go off and hunt and fish and wander the woods. But I could always count on my little helper to dust and polish and serve the guests. And now I really need you to do all that, and probably more."

"I'm happy to help, Nana."

Help. Hmm. Probably best not to drop the whole load of her plans on the child right away. Start small: "I had a teeny bit more in mind for you than just helping, my dear. You remember Cissy Peterson?"

"*Do* I!" Sophie said, fervently, crossing her eyes and making a face. She went back to placing teapots, talking over her shoulder. "What a pain she was! She never wanted to do anything fun. No tree climbing because she'd get her dress dirty. No mud pies, ditto. I kind of felt sorry for her, stuck with old Mrs. Earnshaw as a grandmother. Is she still as cranky as ever? I'll never forget her chasing me off her front porch when I came trick-or-treating that time I was staying here over Halloween weekend!"

"Thelma was born cranky," Rose declared. "She insists that I stole your Grandpa Harold away from her, when she knows I saw him first!" She shook her head, in disbelief. Thelma had married a lovely man who adored her, and they had a sweet daughter who had loved Thelma more than she deserved. Though her daughter had died too young, Thelma still had Cissy and Phil, her grandkids; both loved their grumpy grandmother.

Rose's supposed "snatching" of Harold Freemont away from Thelma during the Methodist Church pie social had driven a wedge between the former best friends that had never been removed. Despite living and working right next door to each other for all these years, they rarely spoke. It was sad, really.

"So, what were you going to say about Cissy, Nana?" Sophie asked, perching on the arm of the overstuffed armchair to bring herself down to her grandmother's eye level. Pearl wanted in on the conversation, and leaped gracefully up on the back of the chair, so she, too, was eye level with the humans. Sophie took the fluffy cat in her arms, cradling her like a baby. The cat purred, a throaty hum like a distant boat motor on the lake.

Rose smiled at the cat and girl; it made such a pretty picture, both of them so beautiful, both blue eyed. Pearl was a Birman, with a dark mask, ivory ruff and chocolate brown legs, and the mandatory pale socks required by breed specifications. Birmans were supposed to be one-human cats in their single-minded devotion, but Pearl made an exception for Sophie, perhaps sensing the bond between grandmother and granddaughter. She treated Sophie like she did Rose, with sweet adoration and affection.

"Nana? What about Cissy?"

Rose started. "What? Oh! My mind wandered for a moment. Cissy's engaged to be married, and nothing will do for the girl but to have her bridal shower here, in Auntie Rose's Victorian Tea House!"

Sophie gasped and said, "How does her grandmother feel about that?"

Rose reached out to scruff her cat's chin. "How would I know? The last time that woman spoke to me, Eisenhower was president." She was exaggerating, but she truly was not on friendly enough terms to ask Thelma what she thought of anything. "Cissy apparently informed her matron of honor, Gretchen Harcourt—she married Hollis Harcourt, the lawyer, and has only been in town a couple of years— that Auntie Rose's is where she wants it held. We're to *go all out*, I was told."

Sophie eyed her grandmother; what exactly was Nana trying to say? "I'll be happy to help," she said, slowly. "Do you need an extra hand in the kitchen? Making tea? Serving? Setting up? Cleaning afterward? I'll do it all, if you like."

"I want you to do the presentations."

"Presentations." Sophie's mind was a blank. She gently set Pearl on the back of the chair and regarded the cat; she squeezed her blue eyes shut then opened them wide. Sophie looked back to her grandmother. "Nana, what do you mean by *presentations*?"

"I guess you've never been to one of Auntie Rose's bridal showers. I do a talk about tea and the Victorian era, the history of teapots, highlights from the Auntie Rose collection, and the presentation of the 'tea-a-ra' to the bride. I would like you to take over for this one."

"Nana, I couldn't," Sophie said, horrified. "Mom says you've become famous for what she calls your 'tearoom shows.' She sent me a newspaper clipping! I couldn't do it justice."

"Now you listen to me, Sophie Rose Freemont Taylor," Nana said, her voice stern. "I don't want you to do *my* presentation, I want you to do your *own* bridal shower presentation! And don't tell me you can't do it. You managed In Fashion for three years."

"Managed it into bankruptcy," Sophie said, feeling the familiar tightening in her throat when she thought of her beloved restaurant, shuttered and auctioned right down to the carpets. She turned to Pearl and lifted her gently to her lap again, burying her face in the Birman's luscious mane of fur. Pearl nudged her hand and purred throatily.

"That's the past," Nana said, putting one warm hand on Sophie's shoulder and squeezing, while she gently petted Pearl's head. "I have faith in you. If you don't do it, I'll have to cancel."

"Cancel? Why?"

"I need to scale back, honey," she said, her shoulders drooping. "The showers just exhaust me. This last week we had a bridal shower, a birthday party and four bus tours, and the Silver Spouts meeting is coming up. I'm exhausted!"

Sophie was immediately stricken by guilt. She examined her grandmother's careworn face, the wrinkles more pronounced than in bygone years. While she had been puttering around, Nana had been overworking herself. But there was something more there than the workload bothering her grandmother. "Nana, is there some reason you don't want to do Cissy Peterson's shower? I mean, other than the work?"

The older woman looked off into the distance for a moment. She walked over to the shelves, adjusted an art deco round teapot with Bakelite handle and knob. "It's complicated. I know you see Thelma Mae Earnshaw as just an annoying old woman and she does drive me crazy. Did you know she has started serving a full-on cream tea, and is trying to start her own teapot-collecting club? I just don't understand the woman. I exaggerated about her not talking to me since Eisenhower was president, but our relationship is strained. Always has been. And yet . . . she was my friend once."

Sophie waited for her grandmother to get to the point. Pearl jumped down from Sophie's lap and headed downstairs, perhaps to beg treats from Laverne, Nana's only employee in the tearoom.

"It's about the wedding," Nana finally said. "Cissy is marrying Francis Whittaker Junior. Remember him?"

"Frankie, that . . . that putz? I sure do."

"Honey, don't call him Frankie. Or a putz. Frankie . . . uh, *Francis* is now an architect and still lives in the Whittaker

house his daddy built. Vivienne—his mother—moved out to
a modern home up in the hills. But you know what Thelma
is like; she thinks that the Whittakers aren't up to her standards. Thelma Mae Earnshaw has always stood on the dignity
of her mama's family being the first to settle Gracious Grove.
She's bad enough now, but you would not believe the way she
put on airs when she was Thelma Mae Hendry!"

"What do you mean, the Whittakers aren't up to Mrs.
Earnshaw's standards? They're the richest family in the
whole area."

"The Whittakers are *nouveau riche*, if you listen to
Thelma tell it. After all, the Whittakers' money came from
grocery stores. She's always claimed that Vivienne, Francis's
mother, was born in a hootchy-kootchy traveling show, back
in the fifties. I guess that's why she's so dead set against
Cissy marrying Francis." Her forehead wrinkled. "I *guess*
that's what it is."

"What do you mean?"

"I don't know, honey. I've been listening to Laverne too
much; you know how she likes to gossip."

"If something is worrying you, tell me."

Nana scrunched up her face. "Laverne has some idea that
there's trouble at the company Francis works for, Leathorne
and Hedges Architecture. Her niece works there, and she's
heard rumblings."

"Nothing really to do with him, is it?"

"True . . . not worth talking about. Gossip is mostly fancy
and frills put on speculation."

Sophie watched her grandmother's face, but she wasn't
saying anything else. "Let's go down to the tearoom and
discuss this. If you want me to do Cissy's shower, I can try."
Her stomach twisted. It was silly; she had managed *and* been
the executive chef of an eighty-seat restaurant in the trendy
garment district of New York, the youngest to do both jobs,
she had been told. Surely she could do a little bridal show
presentation and talk about teapots for twenty minutes. So
why was she so uptight about it?

Maybe because she had failed so miserably in her last job.

* * *

Laverne Hodge was already setting up the tearoom for the expected afternoon guests. Auntie Rose's Victorian Tea House was a forty-year tradition in Gracious Grove, popular long before the rage for tearooms peaked as baby boomers aged. Part of Auntie Rose's popularity could be explained by Gracious Grove being a "dry" town, conducive to civilized discourse over tea and scones, rather than boozy confessions over whiskey and peanuts. But mostly it was because Rose and Laverne excelled at providing the true tearoom experience, with refreshing tea, soothing decor and good food.

Sophie remembered Nana's favorite joke . . . guests came for the tea and stayed for the experience, but spent their money on the pretty doodads! The Tea Nook, a small room off the tearoom proper, was responsible for much of the profit, and so was carefully tended. Fresh offerings of tea-scented candles, teacups, complete tea sets both for children and adults, packaged tea—including a blend called Auntie Rose's Tea-riffic Tea—books on tea with bookmarks, and "tea-shirts," which were T-shirts with teacups and teapots emblazoned on them, were added weekly.

The tearoom itself was pretty, if a little too frilly for Sophie's taste. White wainscoting lined the main room, with rose-toile-papered walls above. Antique sideboards and buffet hutches filled with teapots in various themes lined the walls. An ornate Eastlake buffet held floral teapots, while a heavy Victorian held chintz designs. On floating shelves in between there were animal shapes, people, royal family tributes, Red Hat Society teapots and too many more to name.

Scattered around the room—it used to be a living room and dining room, but a wall had been removed and supporting pillars had been added to make space for the tearoom—were white-linen-covered tables with comfortable chairs, about eleven tables in all, enough space to seat forty-four guests or so. Nana threaded through the chairs and tables, straightening as she went, toward the cash desk at the front.

Sophie followed, tentatively, realizing why she had avoided the tearoom for three days: She was afraid of the responsibility her grandmother seemed eager to foist upon her.

Was that what she had been left with since her restaurant went belly-up, this crippling lack of confidence? It hadn't really occurred to her why she had been floating along, listless and directionless, but fear explained a lot, even why she let her mother cajole her into the awful date with Dr. Sebastian-the-Repulsive. A part of her had bought into her mom's belief that she ought to just give up and marry a rich dude.

That wasn't exactly what Rosalind Taylor had said, but it was the thrust of her argument. Sophie squared her shoulders. Nana needed her and she was going to help however she could. If that meant hosting Cissy's bridal shower, then she'd do it. Maybe it would be fun.

Right, like tooth extraction or taxes. Fun or not, she'd do it.

She hustled across the room to relieve Laverne, almost as old as Nana, of a heavy tray of tea things. "Let me," she said, hefting the tray.

"Sophie!" Laverne said, her black eyes glowing with fondness. "My sweet godchild. Rose told me you were in town, but until I saw you I didn't dare believe it." Without the burden of the tray, she reached out to gather Sophie into a hug.

Laverne Hodge, whose ancestry dated back to the Seneca Indians and an African-American trader, was honorary godmother to Sophie, adopted as such long ago at a tea party for her fifth birthday. Little Sophie was teary-eyed because her mother had called to say she couldn't make it to Nana's for the party. Laverne had said she would stand in as Sophie's "godmother," and ever after had showered Sophie with goodies, handmade quilts and all of the homey goods a "mother" could think of.

Sophie set the tray down and was enveloped in the woman's suffocating hug. "Auntie Laverne," she mumbled, her voice muffled by Laverne's aproned bosom, "I've missed you so much!"

The woman held Sophie away from her in her strong grip. Head tilted to one side, she squinted at her godchild. Laverne was tall and strongly built, so she met Sophie eye to eye. "Now, don't you say that. You've been here three days and I haven't laid eyes on you 'til today."

"I know. I'm sorry."

Laverne exchanged a glance with Rose, who counted bills at the cash desk, put the float back in and stashed the extra money in a canvas deposit bag. The two women had been friends for so long they didn't need words, communicating with shared looks instead. "If you're here to help," Laverne said, turning back to Sophie, "we need to set the tables with silverware and dishes so I can get a batch of cranberry lemon scones in the oven. We got a three o'clock bus tour coming in, and it's near two now."

While the three women worked they talked, of course. Sophie caught up on all the news that was fit to spread, as Laverne called it.

"So Cissy is getting married," Sophie mused. "And to Francis Whittaker! Why does Mrs. Earnshaw *really* not like the Whittaker family?"

Laverne looked over at Nana, who was now busy in The Tea Nook filling up the candle display, then bent toward Sophie. "There was quite the scandal back in the day. The Whittakers all belonged to the country club, you know. I worked there as a waitress for a while, and was working the night of the big dustup!" Her dark eyes sparkled.

"What happened?" Sophie asked, patting the wrinkles out of a tablecloth.

"Everyone was well oiled, as you can imagine." The country club, being outside the town limits, served alcohol, one reason memberships were sought. "Alcohol loosened a few tongues and Vivienne Whittaker, she up and threw a glass of champagne in Florence Whittaker's face and accused the woman of sleeping with her husband!"

"Really? Was it true?"

Laverne shrugged. "Always was bad blood between those two sisters-in-law, ever since Vivienne snagged the

Whittaker brother who didn't gamble and drink his money away, and Florence got stuck with the Whittaker that ended up penniless."

Nana, who had silently approached, said, "Are you two gossiping about all that old water under the bridge?"

"Mucky water still runs dirty, you know that, Rose," Laverne said, dropping a wink in Sophie's direction. "Those two just barely tolerate each other to this day."

"So *that's* why Mrs. Earnshaw doesn't like the idea of Cissy marrying Frankie—I mean, Francis—because of the old scandal?"

"I'm sure I couldn't say," Laverne said, with a bland expression on her face. "But I *will* say, with both those Whittaker brothers in the grave, you'd think the sisters-in-law would be better friends."

They continued to work, but when Rose left the room to check on the scones, Sophie said, "Laverne, can I ask you something?"

"What's troubling you?"

"Nana wants me to do the presentation for Cissy Peterson's bridal shower. Is there some reason *she* doesn't want to do it?"

Laverne's dark eyes shifted away, to the door that led to the tearoom's kitchen. "No mystery, child. She believes Cissy's shower will help you get your feet wet. Pun intended."

"I don't need her propping up my wobbly self-confidence," Sophie grumbled. She followed Laverne, folding napkins, laying out silverware and setting the centerpieces in place. They were small crystal vases of fresh white tulips today, a pretty reminder of spring.

"She's just worried about you. You're her favorite grandchild."

"I know. My brothers hardly ever get to Gracious Grove anymore." Sophie stood back and looked the room over with a critical eye. A bus tour at three, and it was two thirty now. The tables always looked so pretty, the fresh white linens a backdrop for the eclectic mix of china Nana used. She didn't go for clunky restaurant dishes, instead hitting yard sales and antique markets for mismatched china that made the tables bloom with color. Sophie liked setting the tables in themes . . . blue willow pattern on one table, roses on another, spring flowers on yet another.

They chatted and finished setting the tables. Laverne told her there was talk of annexation of local farmland, an extremely divisive issue among Grovers, as locals called themselves, and the ever-present issue of liquor or no liquor. There weren't many dry towns left in New York State, Gracious Grove being one of only a handful, all but a couple in the western half of the state.

"That talk was during the last mayoral election, though. A local developer, Oliver Stanfield, ran briefly, so there was some discussion about annexation and the liquor laws, and all that folderol, but he dropped out of the race for some reason or another. From then on it was another smooth sail to victory unopposed for Mr. Mayor Blenkenship."

"I hope the town doesn't change too much," Sophie fretted. "It's charming and doesn't need an influx of big box stores and crowded suburbs." And now she sounded more old-fashioned than her forward-thinking grandmother!

"What will be, will be," Laverne said.

Just as Sophie was straightening the last place setting of silver, a young woman came in the door, setting the bell over it jangling. She was slim and thirtyish, perfectly coiffed and nicely dressed in a form-fitting D&G charmeuse floral dress, carrying a Marc Jacobs bag. She looked like the kind of women who came to In Fashion for cocktails. Sophie was immediately on guard. "I'm sorry, we're not quite open yet. Are you with the bus tour?"

"Certainly not," the woman sniffed. "I'd like to speak to Rose Freemont."

"She's busy right now. May I help you?" Sophie asked, approaching her.

"I don't think so. I need to speak to her about Cissy Peterson's bridal shower."

Sophie straightened her shoulders. "I can help you with that. I'm Sophie Freemont Taylor; Rose Freemont is my grandmother. I'm taking over the organization of Cissy's shower for my grandmother. And you are . . . ?"

The woman had gone on alert as soon as Sophie announced her name. "I've heard about you. You're the failed restaurateur, right? I'm Gretchen Harcourt. Welcome to Gracious Grove."

She stuck her hand out and Sophie took it even as the insult sank in. It went beyond the *failed restaurateur* dig; *Welcome to Gracious Grove*? This was her home away from home, so to be welcomed by a woman who had married into the town, so to speak, stung. But she would take the high road. She barely touched the other woman's chilly hand and released. "How can I help you regarding Cissy's shower? You're the matron of honor, right?"

Gretchen Harcourt's beautiful face had a frozen look, like *botox meets bad temper*. "I need to cancel. We're switching the venue to the country club."

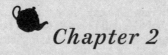

Chapter 2

"**I**sn't it a little late to be deciding that?" Sophie was familiar with country club calendars and doubted they would be able to fit in a bridal shower that was just a couple of weeks away.

"We're members, Hollis and I," Gretchen said, straightening her back and standing, one toe pointed, the other foot behind it, like a model. "It'll be fine."

Laverne hovered in the background, not adding anything, but her eyebrows raised and shaking her head.

Sophie thought for a moment, observing the other woman. "My understanding was that Cissy specifically said she wanted her shower to be here, at Auntie Rose's Victorian Tea House," she said. "Has she changed her mind, or are you doing this on your own?"

Gretchen licked her lips and adjusted her expensive watch on her slim wrist. "I'm just . . . it's . . . to be honest, it's her future mother-in-law's idea, and frankly, I agree. Tearooms are so yesterday."

Whenever anyone said, *to be honest* or *frankly*, Sophie suspected them of lying. A spark lit in her belly. So *yesterday*?

"I'll have you know a *New York Times* financial reporter wrote an article last month about a study that said that tearooms are *the* up-and-coming type of eating establishment, and the only one that was truly recessionproof."

"Really?"

"Yes. The study was done by a doctoral student at Harvard Business School; she said in her thesis that because of the aging demographics in the USA and an increase in disposable income in women age fifty-four to seventy-five, tearooms are not going away. There is a new tearoom opened every thirty-three-point-five hours in the United States. *That* stat is from Wharton." Sophie nodded, sharply. She moved forward a step, invading the other woman's space. "And younger markets are increasingly interested; the trend toward elaborate birthday parties for young children, destination bridal showers and Sweet Sixteen Parties has caused a surge in tearoom bookings. I've done a *lot* of research on the subject."

Gretchen Harcourt nervously pleated the short skirt of her dress, stepped back and babbled, "All right, then, we'll reconsider."

"You do that. You reconsider. Tell Mrs. Whittaker *everything* I said."

The young woman hustled out the front door just as Rose came out of the kitchen with a tray of warm scones. "Who was that, dear? I thought I heard voices in here."

Laverne, still staring at Sophie, said, "It was that Gretchen girl, Rose, and she was going to cancel Cissy Peterson's shower here, but missy pulled out a bunch of statistics—just rhymed them right off—and told her some percentage of people are going to tearooms, and some ages . . . I don't know what all she said."

"So did she cancel or not?" Rose asked, setting the scones down on the servery and approaching the two.

"She did *not*!" Laverne said. "Little Miss Business Woman, here, talked her out of it."

"Where did you get all those statistics, Sophie?" Rose asked, a frown wrinkling her forehead.

"I made them up."

"All of them?" Laverne asked.

"Every last one of them, right down to the *New York Times* article."

The afternoon was busy, with a gaggle of drop-in visitors touring the Finger Lakes as well as a second unexpected bus tour. One of the tourists decided on the spot to book a Red Hat Society event and another a tea party for her granddaughter's Sweet Sixteen. Sophie manned The Tea Nook for a while; she sold a pretty chintz child's tea set, several boxes of specialty teas and answered questions about holding a tea party for a group of six-year-olds. Midafternoon Sophie had to hustle back into the kitchen and quickly whip up a batch of butterscotch scones to satisfy raging sweet tooths.

As she brought it out, she was struck by a secretive-looking tête-à-tête that was taking place in one of the more protected tables near the front window. A distinguished-looking woman had her head bent toward a well-dressed older fellow, and they were heatedly discussing something. Curious, Sophie moved nearby and caught only a few words before the woman gave her a cross look. All she overheard was the ferocious comment that her son was the most important thing in the whole mess.

Sophie retrieved a bus tray from the servery at the back of the tearoom and cleared the dirty tables. All the vintage china would have to be washed by hand, but the cutlery and some of the serving pieces could be done in the dishwasher. Someone had left a nice tip; cool! It would go in the tip jar and Nana would see that Laverne got it, and Laverne would hand it directly over to her church, where it would go to dental work or glasses for needy seniors, or schools in Africa, or something else that needed doing in the world. Such was the Auntie Rose way; Laverne often paraphrased from Luke: From those to whom much is given, much is expected.

There were three tables near the distinguished-looking couple and all needed clearing; Sophie edged toward them, not wanting to interrupt.

The woman stood, shook the wrinkles out of her skirt and said, in a firm tone, "I hope we understand each other?"

"I'll see what I can do, Viv, but you know it may be too late. Word has already gone out."

"I don't believe it's too late. I *know* you have the mayor's ear, Holly––you and your cadre of busy buddies—and you had better bend it but good. Things look shady and it will come back to haunt him if anything goes wrong." She bent closer and growled, "I will make it my personal quest to make sure that everyone involved will suffer in the public eye if my boy is in any way implicated in monkey business!"

Wow . . . ferocious Mama Bear!

The rest of the afternoon was uneventful but busy. Finally the tearoom closed, the three women tidied up and put dishes in the dishwasher, washing the cups, saucers and plates by hand and stacking them back in the tearoom in the service area. Pearl, as always, watched the action from her perch on a high stool near the counter.

Laverne headed home to take care of her nonagenarian father, Malcolm Hodge, and then would attend an evening prayer meeting. She was the eldest of a large family and had never married, so looking after them all had been her life's work. She said that now, with just her father to look after, she felt like she was on holiday. Her "vacation" was her church evenings, knitting and crocheting, and the Silver Spouts, Nana's teapot-collecting society.

Sophie did some prep work in the kitchen, then vacuumed, picking up the random bits of paper and items forgotten or dropped by visitors: a lipstick, a photo, an umbrella hooked on a chair armrest, all of which she deposited in the lost and found. She then wiped down the tables, finally turning out the lights around seven. Nana had already climbed the stairs, followed by Pearl, to soak her feet in Epsom salts, but Sophie was restless. She grabbed a sweater and walked out into the sweet springtime evening air.

She turned right instead of left so she didn't have to pass Belle Époque, Mrs. Earnshaw's inn and now tearoom. It was troubling that the old woman was trying to not only compete with Nana, but defeat her. The two had been dueling for decades, right back to the oft-referenced theft of Harold Freemont by pretty, genteel Rose Beaudry, as Nana was then. It seemed silly to Sophie, but it would be wrong to dismiss the other woman's feelings.

Still . . . a sixty-year grudge?

The spring air enfolded her, the scent of lilacs and freshly turned earth drifting on a light, moist breeze as the sky turned gloomy, the purple dusk signaling rain to come. She had been avoiding this walk, this rediscovery of her old stomping ground, but why? Maybe she loved Gracious Grove too much. She liked the city, too; it was exciting, fun and fast-paced, just like her restaurant, In Fashion. But Gracious Grove was different. While New York was *hurry up and hustle*, Gracious Grove was *slow down, put your feet up, rest awhile*. Split down the middle as to which was best for her, she decided that after over ten years of *hurry up*, both in school and work, and then her restaurant, she'd enjoy the *slow down* part for a time until she knew what she wanted out of her life.

Gracious Grove was as familiar as a pair of favorite jeans, the kind that slip on and are so comfortable you know you're going to love them forever. When she described it to city friends, she told them about the Finger Lakes region as a whole, the native lore of the Senecas and Cayugas, and the natural beauty of the area, hilltop vistas and lush green valleys. But that didn't speak of the sense of home that hit her whenever she arrived at Nana's.

Staying at Auntie Rose's was like living in a teapot museum, some thought. Sophie had brought a few girlfriends to Nana's during school break, and all were awed by the rows and rows of teapots . . . hundreds of them! It was as if time had stopped in Gracious Grove, others said, around the middle of the last century. That wasn't true and Sophie knew it, because she had listened to Nana's stories.

As much as nostalgia for a simpler time made some long for the "good old days," Nana was a clear-eyed realist. She told Sophie about the good, the bad and the downright *ugly* things that happened in the "good old days."

Change was necessary and good and inevitable, and had not missed the town except for the liquor ban, which seemed an immutable part of Gracious Grove's charm. The town endured, and so did Nana's tearoom and her teapot-collectors society, The Silver Spouts. Nana was not getting any younger, though, as she put it herself. What would happen to the tearoom when she couldn't look after it anymore?

The breeze stiffened. Sophie folded her arms over her chest, hugging herself as she strolled downhill, passing the gracious homes that lined Seneca. The boulevards were wide, and clapboard houses were set well back from the street. Most had a deep porch with clematis or morning glories winding up a trellis to shade the veranda from the summer sun. But in early May everything was still kind of sparse-looking, beds of tulips and daffodils giving color but everything else green. Many lawns had blooming lilac bushes, and not-yet-blooming rose of Sharon.

Once she got down to the center of town, there were neo-Gothic buildings, red brick, with Roman arched windows and ornate cupolas. Unfortunately a few old buildings had been torn down to make way for uninspired modern utilitarian designs, but *fortunately* the town had never been prosperous enough to do much damage. Old buildings were repurposed, so a mansion too big for a modern family now held a dental practice, a chiropractor and a doctor's office. The town hall was still a New York Gothic monstrosity of red brick and limestone, as was the post office.

The center of town had been redone as a pedestrian mall, with red brick walkways lined by coffee shops, a florist, a gift shop, a sandwich place, a patisserie and many more small stores and cafés. Sophie loved the recent change. At the center of the meeting of Seneca Street and State Street was an open area with a large clock and carillon that chimed the hours. There were wrought iron tables and chairs where on warm summer nights folks gathered to enjoy coffee or tea—it was a dry town, after all—and buskers played to happy tourists and locals alike. Life was lived at a civilized pace.

Sophie adored everything that her mother hated about Gracious Grove, and maybe there was a *because* in there somewhere. Rosalind Taylor enjoyed the hustle and bustle of Miami in winter, spring in New York, London for shopping, summer in the Hamptons, Milan during fashion season and Paris in April. Sophie liked Gracious Grove all year round.

Gracious Grove, despite its name, which made it sound like it was in a green valley, was on a hillside that sloped gently toward Seneca Lake. From the cemetery on the edge of the town proper—set high on the hill to honor the dead, among them the veterans of too many wars—she could see all the way to sparkling Seneca Lake, in the valley. One of Nana's own sons was in that cemetery, laid to rest among the spreading oak trees and stately cypresses. Sophie had never met him, since he died serving in Vietnam, and her mother rarely talked about the brother she had lost; but as a child Sophie had loved to climb the hill with her Gracious Grove friends and trace the names on the pale marble slabs. They raced among the graves and climbed the ancient ornamental plum that had stood guard for at least a century over the townsfolk who had passed on.

Gracious Grove was home in a way no place else on Earth was for Sophie Rose Freemont Taylor.

A misty rain started, so she turned back before reaching the far edge of downtown, but she still didn't rush. Robins, grateful for the drizzle and the worms it would bring up from the hard-packed earth, began their throaty warbling love song to rain. At one with the world, Sophie didn't even mind getting wet. She strolled, passed occasionally by a car swishing along the blacktop.

Someone was walking toward her and she had to stop that jolt of fear she automatically felt, left over from walking home alone from a day at In Fashion on a New York street.

She had been threatened once, though she had never been mugged, but it had left her a little skittish. The guy seemed familiar, even from a distance. She peered into the half light of the hour after twilight, frowning through the mist. When they were close, she suddenly said, "Jason . . . Jason Murphy! It *is* you!"

The man stopped, lifted his black umbrella and squinted through the rain at her. "Sophie? Hey, I'd heard you were back in town. Isn't this cool?"

Jason Murphy . . . he was a buddy of her older brothers. She'd had a crush on him until he finally noticed her when she was fifteen. The past flooded back to Sophie, the memory of that long hot summer when they finally dated, their hands constantly clasped, days spent on the lake as he piloted his dad's boat. She recalled a wooden raft moored a hundred yards out and their towels spread on it to dry, evenings on the shore with a fire blazing within a circle of rocks, other kids roasting marshmallows and kissing. They were a gang of friends: Cissy Peterson and her ne'er-do-well brother, Phil; local beauty queen Dana Saunders; Frankie Whittaker; Wally Bowman; Sophie's brothers Andrew and Samuel; and last but not least, her and Jason Murphy.

"Sophie? Are you okay?"

She blinked once and examined his face in the light of the streetlamp. "Yes, I'm fine. How are *you*? It's been ages."

"You haven't been back for a few years. I've heard all about your doings, of course. Your grandmother makes sure we all do!" He laughed.

He had always been a nice guy and that hadn't changed, but there was a bit of a bite behind his comments. He'd be . . . what, thirty-one now? He looked good, his dark hair a little long, a hint of scruff along the jawline, tall and still lanky. "It's been a busy few years, but with my restaurant going under it seemed like a good time to come back to Gracious Grove for a while." The wound of her failed restaurant was a sore she just couldn't help picking at. It would never heal that way, she knew, just like long-ago skinned knees hadn't healed while she picked at the scabs.

"New York's loss, our gain. So you're staying for a vacation?"

"I don't know what I'm doing," she admitted, shoving her hands in her sweater pockets. "Helping Nana, for sure. I didn't realize how hard taking care of the tearoom is getting for her with just Laverne to help."

"It's tough watching them get older. My grandparents are all gone now. Grandma Murphy just died two months ago."

"I'm so sorry, Jason," she said, as she reached out and touched his arm. She felt a flush of heat rush over her, but when she looked up into his eyes there was no matching spark. She backed away. "I think I'd better get back home. It's starting to rain harder."

"Let me walk you," he said. "You can stay under the umbrella that way."

"I don't mind getting wet," she said.

"I insist."

She laughed, chanted a bit of the old Rihanna song "Umbrella," and then they headed up the street. "So what do you do now?" she asked.

"I teach English Lit at Cruickshank College," he said, naming a community college that was set in the pastoral countryside between Gracious Grove and Ithaca. Cornell might be the most famous institution of higher learning in the Finger Lakes region, but there was a rich tradition of post-secondary-school establishments in the area. Cruickshank, which had started out as a religious school, was old and well-respected, with a beautiful campus set in rolling green hills. "I'm the junior professor, so I get stuck with all the first-year students, but that's okay. I love their enthusiasm!"

"Really? That's great." She tried to imagine the beau of her youth, who was more interested in girls and cars and fast boats, teaching Shakespeare and Walt Whitman to college kids. "But why English Lit?"

He chuckled, a warm sound that drifted down to her as she felt the heat from his body, so close to hers. He always was good-looking, but now he had the assurance of maturity to make him more attractive. "Why English Lit? This from the girl who used to read Blake to me by moonlight, when all I wanted to do was kiss her?"

"Touché," she said, smiling up at him. "Do you like it? Teaching, I mean." Not kissing her! At least it was dark enough now that he wouldn't see her blush at her own gaffe.

"I do."

Was he going out with anyone, she wanted to ask, but that was off-limits. She had broken his heart at the end of that long-ago summer, or at least he told her she had. She had broken up with him and gone back to her private school in Connecticut for her final year of high school, while he headed off to back-pack around Europe for a year before college.

They were already at the side door of the tearoom, the one that led straight up to her and Nana's apartments.

"It's nice that you're here, Sophie," he said. He leaned down and pressed a friendly kiss on her damp cheek, then turned and walked away, black umbrella bobbing along jauntily in the light of the streetlamps.

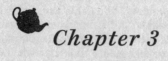

Chapter 3

It was midmorning. **Thelma Mae Earnshaw** roamed the tearoom she had created in what was once the grand dining room of the family home she had converted into Belle Époque. She moved ponderously, like a steamship, her granddaughter Cissy Peterson said, but since Thelma had broken her hip two years ago that was the best she could do, slow and steady. It was a miracle she could move at all without the aid of a walker, but no one seemed to care that she had constant pain and was much braver about it than anyone noticed.

Irritation surged through her as she viewed her employee Gilda Bachman's latest attempts at "brightening the place up," as she called it. Silk flowers on the tea tables? Silk flowers did not belong in a tearoom. Real flowers only! Gilda should know that by now. She complained about not having enough money to do it, but that was too bad. It was Gilda's job to make do on the money Thelma gave her to decorate. Thelma's grand scheme—to outdo Rose Freemont's tearoom, steal all her customers and put her out of business—had so far failed, and most of the blame could be placed squarely on Gilda's slumped shoulders.

Yesterday had been a good day, especially for a weekday in early May, but Auntie Rose's had done much better; Thelma knew because she had spent most of the afternoon looking out the window while Gilda worked. All Thelma had done, then, was to tell Gilda where she could have improved, how she needed to sell more to the customers and encourage them to make future bookings, when Gilda out of nowhere blew up. They had it out and her only employee had threatened not to come to work today. If that happened, Thelma was in trouble, but it was all Gilda's fault.

Aha, there was the woman now, Thelma thought, hearing a key in the door. She moved to a spot where she was semi-hidden so she could catch Gilda off guard—any employee worth her salt had to assume she was being spied on—and waited.

But it was not Gilda, it was . . . who *was* that? Thelma peered through the gloom, and watched her grandson Phillip tiptoeing through the dining room toward the storeroom door. He paused, glanced around, then slipped another key into the storeroom door's lock and opened it. What on earth was he up to? And how had he gotten a key to the storeroom? Gilda didn't even have one. Thelma couldn't risk moving, because she didn't do anything quietly anymore, but she could stay where she was sitting by the front cash desk and wait for her grandson to come out.

When he did, he had a big—and from the look of the strain on his face—heavy box in his arms. He pushed the door shut with his butt and crouched, wedging the box between his body and the wall while he struggled to get the key back in the lock.

Thelma briefly considered what to do, then flicked on the light switch and yelled, "Surprise!"

The box crashed out of Phil's hold to the ceramic tile floor and there was the tinkle of broken glass. A moment later, there was the unmistakable smell of alcohol. Booze, right there in dry Gracious Grove.

"Phillip Alfred Peterson, what in tarnation have you been up to?"

S ophie was spending the morning in the tearoom with Nana going over the teapots with a dust cloth and refamiliarizing herself with every one of them, from the quaint figurals of hats and animals and people, to the chintz and floral, right on through the classics and oldest, some as valuable as a pricey Caribbean cruise. It was a busy morning. An order of teapots and cups had just arrived and had to be unpacked and displayed on the shelves of The Tea Nook. There were also Auntie Rose postcards, fresh packets of Auntie Rose's Tea-riffic Tea and lots of other souvenirs. But much of the work was automatic and didn't require all of her concentration. "Nana, can I ask you something?"

Her grandmother was at the cash desk preparing the float for the day, as Laverne set the tables. "You know you can, my Sophie," she said.

My Sophie. It had always made her feel warm inside to hear her grandmother call her that. It was good to belong to somebody. "Do you remember Jason Murphy?"

Laverne looked up and glanced between grandmother and granddaughter. The older woman gave her employee a raised-eyebrow look, and Laverne nodded.

"I think I'd better get some of the scone batter mixed up," she said, and headed off to the kitchen.

"I remember Jason," said Rose. "Weren't you and he going together at one point?"

"You know we were, Nana. Do you happen to know if he's seeing anyone?"

The woman stopped counting money and stared at her granddaughter. "Now what made you think of him, I wonder?"

"You've been bugging me for days to get in touch with some of my old friends and he was a friend."

Her grandmother's attention was caught by something outside the window, and she frowned. "Now, speaking of your old friends, I wonder what in heaven's name Cissy Peterson is running into her grandmother's place for?"

"Why wouldn't she go to her grandmother's place?" Sophie joined Nana at the window, just as Cissy, wearing a springy skirt and blouse, dashed in the front door.

"It's my understanding that she and her grandmother haven't been speaking lately, since Cissy insisted on having her bridal shower here. She's hustling pretty fast; that girl never runs anywhere."

Sophie frowned. "I hope everything's all right. Maybe I should go over and see."

"You do that, honey," Nana said. "Poor Thelma! When she broke her hip two years ago, she was lying there for an hour before Gilda came to check on her. And me right next door! I felt so awful."

Sophie exited by the side door and circled around to the front of Belle Époque. The front door was ajar, so she slipped in past the entry lobby and into the tearoom, where she could hear loud voices. It was gloomy because the curtains had not yet been drawn back, but the unmistakable smell of alcohol hit her like a wave.

"Phil, how *could* you use Grandma's place like this?" That was Cissy's high, childlike voice; it hadn't changed a bit. Sophie remembered it well from whispered confidences and lingering jokes.

"Hey, is everything all right?" Sophie called out, cautiously moving forward. "Cissy? Mrs. Earnshaw?"

Silence. As Sophie crept forward Cissy came into view along with her grandmother and brother. They stood by an open door that led off the tearoom, staring down at a cardboard box on the floor, and shattered glass among a pool of dark liquid that seeped in a stream toward the carpet. The smell of alcohol was even stronger now and seemed to fill the room. Years of restaurant work meant Sophie had a refined nose, and could even tell different types of alcohol. That was whiskey . . . whiskey, in Gracious Grove?

Mrs. Earnshaw moaned and rocked back on her heels. "We're ruined!" she cried, putting one hand over her eyes and the other to the bosom of her flowered dress. Her grandson, Phil, sullenly stared down at the mess, poking at a broken bottle with one sneakered toe.

"Sophie!" Cissy shrieked, staring at her. "You should go back to Auntie Rose's and forget about this . . . *please*?"

"She's not going to do that," Phil muttered. "She'll be happy to spread it around. Probably call Wally Bowman herself!"

Sophie figured it out in a minute. Since the day he became a teenager, Phil had been trying to sneak booze into dry events in Gracious Grove. It appeared that he was now trying to sneak them into his grandmother's establishment. Or maybe just using it as a storage depot.

"She's not going to do that, Phil," Cissy said. "Just because *you* don't care about anyone but yourself—"

"You're a real prig, Cissy, you know that?" her brother said. "Ever since you got engaged to that jerk, you've got no family feeling at all. Am I right, Grandma?"

Oblivious to her grandson's plea, Thelma moaned, "What am I going to do? I have a bus tour coming in four hours and the whole place reeks of alcohol! A *tea*room, stinking like a distillery!"

"I'll call to cancel the bus tour," Cissy said, turning toward the cashier's desk.

"Wait!" Sophie said, casting one dirty look at Phil, then dismissing him from her mind. "I'm here to help, Cissy. One thing I know from running a restaurant, you can get the smell of alcohol out of carpets. Nana has an extraction carpet shampooer and lots of shampoo, and I know how to run it. Besides, most of this liquid is on the tile, and only a bit on the rug. If we work together, we can get it done in an hour. And if we open all the windows, the odor will be gone and the carpets dry by the time the bus tour is due."

Cissy's eyes watered up, gleaming palely in the dimness. "Thanks, Sophie. We . . . I appreciate it."

Thelma Mae harrumphed, but nodded and quietly said a semi-gracious thank you as Phil slunk out the back door, ignoring Cissy's commands that he come back and help.

An hour later it was done. Doors and windows were thrown open to dry and air the place out. The two sets of guests in the upstairs bed and breakfast rooms had vacated Belle Époque, and were off touring the beauties of the Finger Lakes. Sophie saw an opportunity and invited Cissy back to Auntie Rose's to talk about her bridal shower.

She took her directly up to her attic room. Cissy dropped into one of the overstuffed chairs in the sitting room, settling with a sigh. Sophie made a pot of tea in a good old-fashioned Brown Betty, one of the best all-round tea-making teapots, and set it on a tray with pretty teacups and a couple of left-over scones and butter. She added a pot of Nana's preserves, a luscious pear conserve dotted with maraschino cherries that glowed in the pale jam like rubies. A soft *thump-thump-thump* indicated that Pearl was on her way up the carpeted stairs to Sophie's apartment, alerted to the potential for a snack. Buttered scones were her favorite.

"You don't look like you've eaten a thing in days, girl," Sophie said, setting the tray down in front of her former best "summer at Nana's" friend. While growing up she would spend most of every summer in Gracious Grove, and would reacquaint herself with many of the kids who lived in the town year-round. Cissy was one of them, always there, always the same, always glad to see Sophie despite her best Gracious Grove friend Dana's snide remarks to the contrary.

Cissy took her time making a cup of tea, stirring in sugar and milk, answering Sophie's questions with brief replies. Yes, she should be at work managing her bookstore, but Dana, who worked for her, was there and could handle it. Yes, she was terribly, *terribly* excited about getting married to Francis Whittaker. Her expression belied the emphasis, but Sophie set that thought aside for later.

Pearl jumped up on the chair arm and Cissy patted her lap. The Birman prettily stepped onto the young woman's lap and sat waiting for a treat, her blue eyes wide and unblinking. Yes, Cissy continued, she knew her grandmother was hurt by her decision to have the bridal shower at Auntie Rose's, but for just one day she wanted what she wanted. Silence fell between them. As the sun moved across the sky it beamed through the skylight in the sitting room ceiling, sending a block of light marching across the floor.

"I know Gretchen paid you a visit yesterday," Cissy said, glancing up at Sophie over the rim of her teacup. "I'm so happy you talked her into staying with the plan."

"Why did she want to cancel with us? Really? She said that Francis's mother ordered it, but I wasn't sure."

"It wasn't Vivienne." Cissy set down her cup and—being careful not to disturb Pearl—pulled off her pale-blue sweater, slinging it over the back of the chair. The pool of brilliant sunlight, was directly over her chair now, setting her reddish-blonde hair aglow, like a corona. She stretched out in the sunlight, closing her light-blue eyes for a moment. Pearl did the same, lolling in the patch of sun that now hit Cissy's lap. "Mostly, I think Gretchen just doesn't like tea-rooms. If I caved in and we had the shower at the country club, she could have martinis, since it's outside of the town limits and isn't dry. She's too *sophisticated* for tea."

Why did Cissy have that kind of woman as her matron of honor, Sophie wanted to ask. But that would be impolitic, so she held her tongue.

"I guess you're wondering why she's my matron of honor?" Cissy asked, straightening and picking up her tea-cup again as she stroked Pearl with her free hand.

Spooky. When they were kids she'd do the same thing, sometimes, just pick Sophie's brain effortlessly. "Uh, sure."

"Francis wants to run for state senate in a few years and Gretchen's husband, Hollis Harcourt the Third, is an attorney with connections in the senate." She shrugged and drank the rest of her tea. "It was a small price to pay. I don't really care who's standing next to me at the altar. Does it matter?"

Sophie considered her words; it almost sounded like she was saying it didn't matter who her groom was, but of course she *meant* it didn't matter who her matron of honor was. "I've had friends who were willing to go into battle to secure their spot as maid of honor."

"I don't understand it, myself. It's a pain in the neck. The

maid or matron of honor has to do all this stuff, like organize
the bridal shower." She shuddered. "I'd rather just be a
bridesmaid. Dana's nose is out of joint. She just assumed
she'd be my maid of honor. If I could go back . . . but she's
still one of my bridesmaids, so . . ." Cissy shrugged, one of
her customary gestures. "That's the best I can do. You have
to make sacrifices, you know?"

She took a scone and nibbled on it, but set it down mostly
uneaten. She was so very thin and pale. She broke off a
good-sized buttered piece and held her hand out flat, with
the crumbling chunk on it. Pearl daintily lapped at her palm,
then jumped down, licked her paw and began to wash.

"I'm just being pulled to pieces," Cissy finally confessed,
her gaze on the cat. "Francis's mother, Vivienne Whittaker . . . do you remember her?"

"Uh, not really," Sophie said. She knew *of* the woman,
but didn't think she'd recognize her if she saw her.

"Well, she and Florence, Francis's aunt, are just pulling
me this way and that. Those two compete over everything,
including this wedding. They're going to drive me right
around the bend."

"Why is any of this his aunt's business?"

"Everything is Florence's business!" Cissy said.

"What does Francis say?"

"Nothing, that's the problem! And now with Gretchen
trying to take over the wedding, too, and Phil acting up . . ."
She shook her head, tears welling in her eyes. "I'm really
looking forward to the bridal shower here. It's like . . . it's
like this little tiny piece of my wedding that is just for me,"
she said, putting up her thumb and index finger a millimeter
apart. "And no one can tamper with it."

Sophie swallowed hard. Nana had buffaloed her into
doing the shower presentation, and now Cissy was saying
how important it was to her. Seemed like she'd better take
it more seriously than she had so far. She had two weeks.

"We're going to make it the absolute best shower that any
bride has ever had at Auntie Rose's," Sophie said, with

feeling. "While you're here maybe I can ask you a few questions, so we do this right!" She got a clipboard and some paper and began a series of lists, beginning with who to expect. "I know I should get this from Gretchen, but I'd rather talk to you." She didn't mention that she now didn't trust Gretchen to tell her what Cissy really wanted.

Cissy rattled off a list of people, including Dana Saunders, Gretchen Harcourt, Florence Whittaker, Vivienne Whittaker and five other friends. "Phil wants his sleazy girlfriend Tanya there. I haven't decided yet."

"So ten or eleven."

Cissy snuck a look at Sophie. "And Grandma, too. I just can't have my bridal shower without Grandma there."

"Oooh, yes. Well. That'll make it interesting."

"And poor old Gilda, Grandma's helper. I feel sorry for her because she gets nothing but abuse from Grandma."

"Okay, Gilda, too. That's twelve or thirteen. Now, Nana has always done some traditional elements, like talking about Victorian tea traditions, a tea tasting, with a sweet or savory tea luncheon and gifts for everyone."

"I want exactly that," Cissy said, her eyes beginning to brighten. She bounced up in her chair. "Do you remember your sixteenth birthday party, Sophie?"

Her birthday was in the middle of July, so she had always celebrated it at her grandmother's. "Of course! We did a full-on tea party at Auntie Rose's, then had a beach party at Seneca Lake." It was at that party that Jason had asked her if she'd be his girlfriend. When she looked back on it now, there seemed to be a golden haze over that summer.

"Well, I was *so* envious. I was born in January, so my sixteenth birthday was a trip to the movies with my mom and Phil."

Sophie reached out and touched Cissy's arm. "I'm sorry, Cis."

"Don't be," she said. "It's just the way it was. Our family never went in for big birthday parties. I didn't realize it at the time, but Mom was already sick, and—" She broke off, shaking her head. "I felt like such a creep afterward, when I realized how awful she felt, and yet she made time to take me to dinner and the movies, and all."

Sadness flooded Sophie as she remembered the rest of the tale, how later that year, in the autumn, Cissy's mom ended up in the hospital and never came out. She passed away just before Thanksgiving. Sophie was back in school in Connecticut by then, but heard about it from Nana. She had sent Cissy a card and a note, but never received an answer. "We'll have a proper shower for you, even better than my Sweet Sixteen, a great send-off into married life for you and Francis."

Cissy's watery smile faded a bit. "Yes, for . . . for me and Francis."

Sophie frowned down at her sheet. Why did the mention of her fiancé not bring a radiant smile to Cissy's wan face? "I remember Francis from back in the day. My brothers always picked on him; I felt bad about that. What is he like now?"

"He's a good guy," Cissy said. "He wants to take care of me."

Ringing endorsement of a future husband. As Sophie doodled on the clipboard list, she said, "I was out walking last night and ran into Jason Murphy."

"Yeah, he likes walking."

"Is he . . . I mean, did he . . ." Sophie looked up into Cissy's light-blue eyes.

"Is he married?" Cissy said, with a secretive smile. "No. He was engaged a couple of years ago but broke it off."

"Why?"

"No one knows."

"Who was he engaged to?"

"No one you know." Cissy stood. "I really have to go. Dana will be fuming by now, even though I texted her I'd be late. So are we good with what we need for the bridal shower?"

"We're good for now," Sophie said, standing, too. She followed Cissy down the stairs and let her out the side door.

Cissy turned back and awkwardly grasped Sophie in a hug. "It's good to have you back in GiGi," she said, calling the town what they all had as kids.

The next day Sophie realized she should be working on the shower invitations with Gretchen but she didn't know her address, phone number, or anything else about her. Since she had to go out to buy supplies, she decided she'd stop off at the Peterson bookstore to check in with Cissy. She didn't relish the thought of working with Gretchen, but had decided to woman up and see it through to the bitter end.

She took Nana's SUV and drove down toward the common, turning left before she got there so she could head down to Cayuga Street, where the Peterson bookstore was located. It was in an old house, the one Sophie remembered from childhood as Cissy's home, when her mom was still alive, a gracious old red brick Queen Anne too big for the smaller modern family. Like Nana's establishment, Auntie Rose's Victorian Tea House, the bookstore took up the whole main floor of the former Peterson residence, the big picture windows—sheltered by the wide porch that fronted it—filled with a stained-glass sign that proclaimed it to be Peterson Books 'n Stuff.

Sophie parked in the drive, hopped up the four steps and entered, a string of silvery bells tinkling a welcome. She stood for a moment, letting her eyes get used to the dim lighting. The different rooms of the main floor—what used to be living room, den, dining room and spare room—now had no doors and were labeled as KIDDY LIT, MYSTERIES & ROMANCE, NONFICTION and MAINSTREAM. The large foyer was the reception area and cash desk. A wooden counter near the front held the cash register and the usual stacks of pamphlets, bookmarks and sale items. Hanging over the desk was a polished branch that had strung from it crystals, necklaces, ribbon bookmarks and bracelets that flashed in the pin spot halogen lighting. This main room also had a table in the center piled high with teddy bears, kids' books, sale items, mugs with cute sayings and boxes of all-occasion cards. One large bookshelf was filled with best sellers.

The serene sounds of harp music filled the air, along with the scent of potpourri. She turned, and saw that she was being studied by a Persian-looking cat, sitting alone on the cash desk, unblinking in his calm observation. "Well hello, gorgeous. And what's your name?"

"Beauty," came a voice.

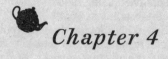

Chapter 4

Dana Saunders was sitting behind the cash desk, her feet up, a hardback novel in her lap.

"Hey, Dana," Sophie cried. "Long time no see!"

"It's been a few years."

"Is Cissy here today?"

"She'll be in at some point. She's meeting with her wedding planner this morning, and then she's going to some do at her grandmother's. Thelma is capable of holding a grudge about the bridal shower—as you well know—so to placate the old biddy she's doing tea there this afternoon with Francis's mother and aunt. I'm not invited."

"She didn't mention it to me when I saw her yesterday, so I guess I'm not invited, either." Sophie approached the desk. Dana still sat, her finger holding her place, a cup of steaming coffee on the windowsill beside her. "Cissy told me you worked here. Do you like it?"

"Suits me. The work's not hard and all the books I can read."

"How is it, working for Cissy?"

"It's fine. She's too easygoing, but I try not to take advantage."

Sophie rested her arms on the cash desk counter and Beauty came to her, sniffing her breath, rubbing against her tentatively. She scratched along her chin and behind her ears; she was almost as pretty as Pearl!

Dana was still striking, Sophie thought, though she'd gained some weight. It suited her; she looked lush and gorgeous in that effortless way some women have, dark haired and dark eyed, her skin olive and her coral-lipsticked mouth full. She wore tangerine cropped pants and a cerulean embroidered tunic, not a color scheme that every woman could wear but on her it was stunning. "Dana, can I ask you a question?"

"Sure." The woman set her book aside and stood, stretching, languid as any cat. She approached the counter from the other side and rested her arms along it. Beauty abandoned Sophie and made a beeline for Dana, rubbing against her face and purring. "What gives?"

How to start? "Cissy and I talked about her wedding yesterday."

"Right, to the wonderful Francis."

"I remember him as Frankie," Sophie said, reaching out and stroking Beauty. "I called him a putz, and Nana disapproved. Is he some kind of big shot now? What's up with that?"

"He's an architect. Went to Cornell, graduated top of his class."

"Aha!" Sophie said, understanding immediately how that made Francis a respected local-boy-makes-good kind of guy.

"Yeah, *aha*. His mom doesn't let anyone forget it, either. He's recently made a big score, some huge development that he's the chief architect on. Since the news broke, his mom has been parading around town, mentioning 'her son, the architect' at every turn."

"His mom . . . Vivienne Whittaker, right?"

"That's right." Dana's laconic manner was soothing.

"The Whittakers . . . they own a grocery store in GiGi."

"Used to. When Francis Senior and his ne'er-do-well brother were killed in an accident five years ago, they sold to some out-of-state conglomerate that has been lobbying to break the 'dry' statute ever since so they can sell wine and beer."

Sophie smiled. "Like that'll ever happen!"

"I know, right? I've heard they're giving up and have sold to someone else now."

"I guess Cissy is lucky, in love, marrying a successful guy?"

"Hah! Lucky? If she listened to me, she'd break it off."

"Why?" Sophie asked, smelling a good story.

"I shouldn't say," Dana murmured.

Sophie leaned forward. "I won't tell a soul, Girl Scout's honor," she said, crossing her heart and her eyes.

Dana grinned. "You're a lot more fun now than you were back in the day."

"Was I that bad?"

"Man, you were a prig. I envied you *and* disliked you at the same time."

"Envied me?" *And* disliked?

"Oh, come *on*! You attended private school in Connecticut. You lived in New York and had a house in the Hamptons. You shopped at friggin' Bergdorf Goodman! I was stuck at Gracious Grove High with Phil Peterson and Wally Bowman as potential boyfriend material. Ugh."

Sophie shifted, uncomfortable with the direction the conversation was taking. Her privileged background, bought by her mother's marriage to a man with money, was only one part of who she was and not the most important, she hoped. "And all that time I would have given *anything* to be going to GiGi High with all of you. I tried to talk my mom into it, but she wouldn't budge. Nothing but the best for her little girl."

Dana looked at her in disbelief for a long minute then laughed, tossing her dark hair back and combing it with her fingers. "I think I believe you. Who would have thought it?"

"So, about Francis Whittaker . . . what's wrong with the guy?"

Rolling her eyes, Dana said, "Not much, I guess. Sometimes I wonder if I just haven't given him enough of a chance. He was such a tool in high school. But this development is apparently a big deal, as much as I make fun of it. And I know he really wants to marry Cissy; I don't think it's just her 'little girl lost' routine, though a lot of guys dig that."

"He's successful and he's not a bad guy and he really wants to marry Cissy, but still, you don't think she should marry him," Sophie said, summarizing, trying to make sense of it.

"I know. Sounds lame."

"No, Dana, there has to be some reason."

She sighed. "Not necessarily."

"Okay. What I really came here for today was to get Gretchen Harcourt's phone number or e-mail address or something. We have to get together to plan the bridal shower."

"Gretchen. Another on my top ten 'yuck' list." Dana grimaced, but shuffled some papers aside on the cash desk. "I've got her number here," she said, pulling out an address book and thumbing through it. "Just be careful; that witch with a *b* will tell you anything, and it won't necessarily be what Cissy wants."

"She already tried that on me," Sophie said, and related the tale of Gretchen's visit to cancel the shower and what Sophie had done about it.

"Good going!" Dana laughed out loud and high-fived Sophie, while Beauty leaped from the cash desk down to Dana's chair.

As she typed Gretchen's contact information into her cell-phone contacts list, Sophie, curious about the liquor confrontation at Belle Époque, asked, "So how is Phillip doing now?"

"He's still the same old Phil the Pill."

"I thought you dated him once?"

"For a millisecond. Selfish to the bone, that's Phil."

"What does he do? I mean, for a job."

Dana smirked. "What do you think? Not a damn thing."

S ophie tried to call Gretchen but just got her voice mail. She was hoping the matron of honor would know what color scheme the shower would be so she could order the flowers for the tables ahead of time, but that was a no-go. Too bad she hadn't thought to ask Cissy the day before. Sophie headed to the store that used to be Whittaker Groceries—there was indeed, as Dana had indicated, an UNDER NEW MANAGEMENT sign in the window—picked up tearoom supplies and headed back to Auntie Rose's in time to help set up.

As she parked the SUV, she noted the cars lined up at Belle Époque. According to Dana, Cissy had caved in and had some kind of familial tea party going on to placate her grandmother. It was family; you did what you had to do. As Sophie made her way to the side door, arms loaded with groceries, a Lincoln pulled up and eased into a parking spot. A gorgeously dressed woman got out of the driver's side, as a younger fellow in a suit and tie emerged from the passenger's side.

That, if she was not mistaken, was Vivienne Whittaker and her son, Francis Junior, the mother-in-law-to-be and groom-to-be. With a start, she realized that Vivienne was the well-dressed woman at Auntie Rose's two days before, the one who was arguing with a gentleman about something or other. Small world. Wait . . . wasn't the argument about her *boy*, in other words, Francis? Hmm. Gretchen pulled up just then in a silver Prius. So she was around, just not answering her voice mail. Sophie would give her until the next day and call again. They all went into Belle Époque.

What Sophie wouldn't give to be a fly on *that* wall. She bit her lip to keep from laughing as she noticed Phil Peterson skulking out the back door, getting on a motorcycle and tearing off down the road, away from the tea party that was about to commence and to which he was probably not invited, anyway.

"Supplies, Nana," Sophie called out. Nana came into the kitchen trailed by Pearl, who jumped up on the counter, only to be shooed down by Sophie. No cats on the food prep area, she believed. Sophie started unloading plastic wrap and cupcake liners.

"Sophie, I was going through the lost and found and wondered about this photograph," Nana said, holding out the picture Sophie had put there the night before.

"I know. I don't know who dropped it. It was under the table in the front window. What is it of? I couldn't see last night; it was too dim."

Nana handed it to her. "It's just some land with a signboard on it."

"Weird," Sophie said squinting at it. The sign was there, but it was blurry, impossible to read what it said. She handed it back to her grandmother. "I don't know who dropped it. There were two or three changes of table here that afternoon."

"Okay, I'll put it back in the lost and found."

It was a quiet day at Auntie Rose's, so after putting the groceries away and helping to set up, Sophie retreated to her sitting room to try to plan out the bridal shower presentation she'd give. Nana, Sophie knew, would give a little talk on the history of teapots with selected examples from her own collection, then she would explain various tea ceremonies around the world. There would be a luncheon—a generous cream or savory tea—and the presentation of the "tea-a-ra" to the bride-to-be, a handmade tiara fashioned of cute teapot trinkets. She would wear that while she opened gifts, and then everyone would play games; in other words, typical bridal shower stuff, but with a tea theme.

She lolled back in her chair with a clipboard and package of color-coded file cards, trying to figure out what to say and how. She had always believed in being prepared, but this was out of her comfort zone, for sure. A scratching at the door indicated that Pearl wanted to come in, so Sophie bounced up, set the door ajar to let the cat come in, then dropped back into the chair. "What should I do, Pearlie-girlie?" she said, thinking out loud. "I want to make this the best shower; Cissy deserves that. But how?"

She thought about Dana's uncertainty over Francis. She wouldn't say what she had against him but Sophie would swear there was something more than just leftover dislike from the old days. "It's getting a little warm in here, Pearl. If I'm going to be here all summer, I'm going to have to get an air conditioner."

She set the cat aside on the other chair and roamed, opening all the windows, trying to get a cross breeze going in the attic apartment. She stood looking out the dormer that overlooked Belle Époque. The tearoom windows were open and she could hear Thelma's stentorian voice as she held forth at length. Nana had told her all about how the woman had tried to re-create the Auntie Rose experience, the tea talk, the showers and Red Hat Society luncheons, though nothing quite worked.

For one thing, Thelma Mae Earnshaw was just not a good cook, nor was Gilda, her employee. They used frozen food, popped into the oven and overbaked. If Thelma spent half as much time on being original and using fresh ingredients rather than copying Auntie Rose while skimping on the food, Nana said, she might get somewhere. Instead, she had spent the last few years on dirty tricks—waylaying packages meant for Auntie Rose's, starting rumors about the food used at the tearoom, even going so far as inserting an ad in the local paper saying Auntie Rose's was closing for renovations—but nothing had dulled her nana's popularity.

Pearl rubbed against her ankle. Just as she bent over to pick up the cat, Sophie heard a loud scream, and a ruckus broke out in Belle Époque—shouts and a woman's wailing voice. Sophie put Pearl down and raced for the stairs, clattering down the two flights and out the side door and over to the inn next door. It was like déjà vu from the other day with Phil's busted liquor bottles. She raced in the front door and saw a ring of women, some weeping, all looking down at someone or something. "What's going on?"

Five faces turned to regard her, then turned back to the matter at hand, which, Sophie saw, as she pushed through, was Vivienne Whittaker on the floor. She looked a ghastly yellowish color, but Sophie realized in a flash that that was just the frosting smeared on her face. Her eyes were wide and she was making an eerie sound, like air being let out of tires.

The moment froze in time and Sophie saw Gilda Bachman, Thelma's underpaid assistant, with the phone in her hand. She was babbling about a sick woman, while Thelma fell back on a chair, hand clutched over her heart. Francis was on his knees by his mother, yelling in her face, asking what was wrong, cake crumbs grinding into his trousers. Cissy clutched at Francis's suit jacket sleeve, the fabric bunching in her fingers. Others clustered in a group, watching, horrified, but she couldn't manage individual faces, just a blur of female figures.

"Is she choking?" Sophie cried, bending over them. "Can anyone do the Heimlich? Or . . . or is she having a heart attack?"

Cissy screamed, "Do *something*, Francis!"

A heavyset, handsome woman was standing nearby moaning, hand over her mouth, her heavily mascaraed eyes wide. She slumped down into a chair and covered her face with her hands. The wail of sirens in the background alerted them that the ambulance was on its way, and Sophie ran to the door just as it screeched into the parking lot. "This way!" she shouted, as it pulled to a halt.

Two paramedics jumped out and opened the back doors, working together to get a heavy case out. A police car screamed to a halt, too, and Wally Bowman threw himself out of the car and hustled to the door. "Sophie, I heard you were back. What's going on?" Paramedics pushed past them carrying their emergency kits.

"I don't know, exactly," Sophie said. "I was in my apartment and heard a scream. When I came over, I saw Vivienne Whittaker on the floor, sick or choking or having a heart attack . . . or something!"

Wally strode in and Sophie followed, hanging back but

still able to see, since the paramedics had cleared the way. They knelt by Vivienne, whose eyes were now closed, her face red. The convulsions had stopped; Sophie couldn't decide if that was a good thing or bad. The paramedics, two young guys, worked to rescue the distressed woman, initiating CPR and hooking up a heart monitor. Their dialogue was terse and cryptic.

The guests, knotted together, watched the scene, the attitude of the group one of disbelief mixed with shock. One paramedic fired a series of questions at Francis, who replied with what little he seemed to know about his mother's health. No, she had no heart ailments that he was aware of. Yes, she had allergies but only to a few foods, none of which had been served that day that he knew of. No, no history of stroke, and no, she was not on blood thinners. He thought. He wasn't sure. They finally strapped Vivienne to a gurney and wheeled her out to the ambulance; moments later they screamed away toward the closest hospital.

Wally Bowman cast one long glance around the room. "Francis, you want to tell me what happened here?"

"My mom . . . she's sick. I need to get to the hospital," he said, his voice choked. He straightened his tie and jacket, then started toward the door.

"Wait!" Wally said, putting out his arm to block the way. "Francis, it's okay, she's being taken care of. Cissy, *you* want to tell me what happened?"

Francis paused, then turned toward his fiancée.

Tears stood in her eyes, but she responded well to Wally's command. "We were having a little celebration for our engagement. Everything was real nice," she said, nodding toward the table arrayed with a tea set and trays with the remnants of finger sandwiches, scones and frosted red-velvet cupcakes. "We were just having some snacks when Vivienne started up out of her chair, then collapsed on the floor." She waved her hand at the mess—tea spilled, crumbs and yellow icing smeared around.

The florid, heavyset woman moaned. Everyone turned to look at her.

"Aunt Florence?" Francis said, looking worried.

"It was *her*," Florence Whittaker said, pointing one shaky finger at Thelma Mae Earnshaw, still collapsed on the chair but now with both hands over her eyes. "It was her cooking that caused this! Poor Vivienne. She'll probably have to have her stomach pumped. What was it, cheap chicken with sal-monella in the sandwiches?" she screeched, working herself up. "Or . . ." Her voice trailed off and she just stared, shak-ing her head. She leaped up from her chair and grabbed her big purse. "We need to get to the hospital. Francis is right. We need to *go*."

"I agree," Cissy said, her tone calm. "Before it's too late."

Sophie stared at her childhood friend. Cissy's high voice was calm, her gaze level, her face as pale as always. Wally was watching her, too. His cell phone chirped and he answered it, his expression becoming grave. "Okay," he muttered. "All right, I'm on it. Immediately." He cleared his throat. "This room is now off-limits to anyone. We'll need to move you all out of here."

"Wally, why?" Cissy asked.

"What's going on?" Sophie asked, moving toward Cissy.

Wally adjusted his uniform tie, then surveyed the group, his gaze settling on Francis. "I'm sorry, Frank," he said, his tone grave. "Your mother didn't make it. She's dead." He paused, and his glance took them all in. "Until we figure out why, I have to secure this scene for the detectives and the forensic investigators."

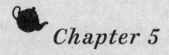

Chapter 5

"**D**ead?" Francis paled and staggered back. "Impossible!" His voice sounded thin and raspy.

"No!" Florence screeched, her pouchy eyes wide.

"What did it?" Sophie asked Wally, who was watching them all with squinted eyes. "Did she have a heart attack? Or . . . how did she . . . ? I don't understand, Wally."

"All of you will have to . . ." He paused and looked around. "Let's go next door. Sophie, can we go over to Auntie Rose's?"

"Why?"

"We need to vacate this place, but I don't want folks to go too far," he said, raising his voice over the scream of sirens now filling the air. Another car screeched to a stop outside, and doors slammed.

"Wally, you need to tell us what's wrong." Her voice sounded strange to her, quivery and trembling. "I mean, I *know* what's wrong, but why . . ." Sophie didn't want to think about what his concern implied.

"You need to just do as I say," he said, steel strengthening his tone. He glanced over at Cissy, who was pale but

composed. "Take Cissy and the others over to your grandma's and I'll explain as soon as I can." He walked to the
door and motioned for them all to follow.

Thelma Mae Earnshaw stubbornly refused to go. "I have
not set foot in that woman's home for forty years, and I'm
not about to go now!"

"Grandma, *please*," Cissy pleaded. "This is not the time."

Gilda Bachman, Thelma Mae's only employee and general factotum, had already exited, and Florence Whittaker
had taken her nephew by the arm and was tugging him
toward the door.

He resisted. "Wally, what the *hell* is going on? I need to
get to the hospital. My mom—her purse is still here with
her insurance card and—and . . ."

Sophie watched Francis's face. He clearly had not taken
in what Wally had said, that his mother was dead.

"Francis, it's too late," Florence said, tears clogging her
voice, making it thick with emotion. "She's . . . she's *gone*.
The only sister I ever had!" She grabbed her nephew's arm
and squeezed, her knuckles white from the pressure.

He wrenched his arm away from Florence and seemed
to crumble in on himself, his shoulders slumping, his whole
body shuddering. "That's not possible. She just *can't* be
gone! How could this have happened? You have to tell me!"

Florence grabbed him in a hug, her gigantic handbag
whacking against him. "I don't know," she said. She forced
his head against her shoulder so they were bound in a tight
embrace. "But right now we have to do what Wally says and
go next door."

"Thanks, Aunt Flo," Wally said.

"Aunt?" Sophie looked between them.

But her implied question was ignored as Wally waggled
his fingers to get everyone moving as outside car doors
slammed shut. They trooped out into the early May sunshine, where just a few minutes ago life had seemed so
normal. Sophie blinked at the transformation the parking
area had undergone. Two Gracious Grove police cruisers
were parked at the curb and a mobile forensic unit was

pulled into the drive. Neighbors were coming out of their houses and watching; they clustered in small groups, heads bent toward each other as they chattered. Whatever had killed Mrs. Vivienne Whittaker, leading socialite of the Gracious Grove social scene, it seemed the police weren't convinced it was natural, or they wouldn't be making this much of a fuss, Sophie thought.

Her grandmother took everything in stride and set about, with Laverne's help, to organize. A half hour later the last customer had left Auntie Rose's and the only folk sitting at the tables were those who had been at the tragic engagement tea, as well as Sophie's nana, Laverne and Sophie herself. As long as there were customers no one had said a word about the tragedy next door, though there was a lot of whispering and covert glances by those who had just dropped in for tea and scones.

Tea had been made and served to those who had come from Belle Époque, but silence still reigned. Sophie surveyed the party. Cissy sat next to Francis, but they weren't talking. Gretchen Harcourt flanked Francis on the other side; she was playing with her bracelet in between texting. Wally should have barred them from communicating, because Sophie had a feeling the news would be all over town with Gretchen Harcourt's own spin on it before the police had done any investigating at all. A young blonde woman, waved hair as stiff as a 1950s beehive, wept quietly into her hands and blew her nose on a cloth hankie.

Gilda Bachman sat alone at a small table for two as did Thelma, who had a sour look on her wrinkled face. Nana had tried talking to the woman but had been ignored. Laverne, standing by the serving hatch at the back of the tearoom, busied herself with folding linen napkins for the next day's trade. Florence Whittaker sat staring at the wall, a frown etching wrinkles into her high forehead. Sophie wondered how she felt in light of what Sophie now knew about the bad blood between her and her sister-in-law. Had they buried that decades-old hatchet, or was it still sharp and hurtful?

Florence had moaned that she had just lost the only sister she ever had; perhaps that was how the tragic death struck her on a personal level. What happened if you lost the one person you shared both a family and an enmity with? Was she feeling bereft in more than one way?

"I wish I knew what was going on over there," Nana whispered.

"Me too," Sophie murmured, reliving the moments of horror, watching Mrs. Vivienne Whittaker's patrician face, yellow-smeared and contorted, turn red. The memory left her light-headed and nauseous. How *awful* to die like that, confused, scared, sick. It was terrible that her only child had to witness it, too. Tears welled in her eyes but she refused to give in. The others needed her to stay strong. "I know everyone here except for one . . . who is the blonde girl, the one with the inappropriate hairdo?"

Nana looked over and smiled gently. "She's Mayor Blenkenship's wife."

"The mayor's wife? But I had the impression he was older . . . at least in his fifties or so?"

"He is, but this is his third wife, newly minted. They just got married, oh . . . not even a year ago? It was big news at the time, got a lot of coverage. What is her name?" She frowned for a moment, then her expression cleared. "Belinda, that's it! Poor girl. I've seen her photo in the society pages—and before you ask, yes, the local newspaper still does have such a thing—and I got the feeling she is trying to make herself over into a trophy wife."

"I think she's been watching too many reruns of *Mad Men*," Sophie muttered, eyeing the skirt suit and blue eyeshadow.

"She's young," Nana said.

Sophie settled in to wait. Trying to take her emotion out of it, she replayed the scene in her mind, her restaurateur's experience making every detail jump out. Belle Époque, like Auntie Rose's, was a large house turned into a tearoom, and like Nana's, the front rooms had been renovated into one larger space. The tearoom had been closed for the afternoon to other patrons because of the engagement tea, so the big center table was the only one in use. Trays of the leftovers of unevenly cut finger sandwiches and salads had been discarded on nearby tables. A few crumbling pastries were on large plates, and vanilla-frosted red-velvet cupcakes formed a spotty half ring around a platter, while a tiered tray of pale, dry-looking scones filled the center of the table, a silk flower in a milk glass vase the only decoration.

The trays were almost empty, as were the partygoer's plates, so they must have almost finished their food. Three large teapots cluttered the table even more, accompanied by an array of lemon wedges, milk pitchers, sugar bowls and packets of artificial sweetener. Was there anything there she should remember, any little detail Wally would need to know about?

Cissy had been sitting so still for so long that Sophie was startled when she jumped up. "Oh, this is awful!" she cried, wringing her hands, tears streaming down her pale, narrow face. She turned to her fiancé. "Francis, can't we *do* something? They can't keep us caged up like animals."

Francis, his expression blank, shook his head.

"Cissy, please; I know this is terrible, but we have to wait until Wally tells us more," Sophie said, taking her friend by her wrist and leading her to sit in a chair near Mrs. Earnshaw. "I think Francis is in shock right now," she murmured. "He doesn't look well at all."

Gretchen was watching Sophie and Cissy with a cool, evaluating stare. Why wasn't she helping her friend, Sophie wondered, irritated by the woman's detached behavior. Searching her mind for some distraction, Sophie picked at a detail that puzzled her. "Cissy, why did Wally call Mrs. Whittaker . . . Mrs. *Florence* Whittaker . . . his aunt?"

"She was Florence Bowman—Wally's dad's sister— before she married a Whittaker," Cissy said. "I thought you knew that."

"I may have," Sophie admitted. "But I only spent summers here, remember, so some of the finer points of Gracious Grove intermingling may have eluded me." That meant that Francis and Wally were practically related; funny that she had not known that before.

"Right," Cissy said, her tone weary. She put her head down on the table. "I wish this was all over," she muttered, and it wasn't quite clear to Sophie exactly what she meant by *all*.

Wally Bowman entered that minute, and it interested Sophie to see how his gaze went directly to Cissy. He looked concerned, but his expression blanked as he caught sight of Francis Whittaker eyeing him. "Frankie . . . Francis, may I speak with you alone?" They disappeared outside for a few minutes and when they came back in, Francis appeared paler, shock etched on his face. He leaned, palms flat, on a table.

"What's going on, Wally?" Thelma Mae said, her voice loud enough to fill the room. "I've got a right to know!"

The police officer strode to the center of the room and gathered everyone in his gaze. "I know you're all wondering the same, exactly what Mrs. Earnshaw just asked. I understand that you're frightened and upset. Especially those of you who were in the room when Mrs. Vivienne Whittaker was taken ill." He eyed Cissy.

"Enough chatter," Florence said, standing slowly, tugging at the frilled cuffs of her springy blouse. "Cut to the chase, Wally. What happened to poor Vivienne?"

"Well, that's a problem; we don't exactly know."

Francis sat down, thudding into the nearest chair as if his legs wouldn't hold him any longer. He buried his face in his hands and moaned.

Wally glanced at him, then continued. "The medical examiner says if he was to hazard a guess, he'd say that Mrs. Vivienne Whittaker had been poisoned, either purposely or accidentally, by something she ingested in the minutes before her demise."

"You mean something she ate?" Thelma Mae loudly asked. "If that's what you mean, just say it plain, Wally; don't beat around the bush."

He met her grim stare. "All right then, yes, it appears it was something she ate or drank in your tearoom that killed her."

"You finally did it," Francis said, lifting his face and

glaring at the senior owner of Belle Époque. "You finally *killed* someone with your awful food!"

"It wasn't *me* that cooked it," she said, her face going a blotchy red and her cheeks puffing out. "It was Gilda! Don't go pointing your finger at *me*, young man."

"I didn't do anything wrong! *She's* the one who buys expired produce and past-date chicken," Gilda Bachman said, pointing a shaky finger at her employer. "I told her she's got to get fresh, but she never met a corner she didn't want to cut!"

"Enough!" Everyone turned to look at Sophie, who hadn't even realized she had spoken out loud. Her nerves were frayed. "This is not the time to be making accusations." And besides, food poisoning or salmonella wouldn't have resulted in an immediate death. If Vivienne Whittaker was poisoned, it had to be deliberate. Sophie knew that, but didn't see the point in sharing. "Wally, how can we help?"

He nodded and cast her a grateful look. "Thank you, Sophie. Glad to see someone has some sense. We've got a team of investigators who are going to take you somewhere one at a time to answer some questions. We need to figure out what happened and when. Mrs. Earnshaw, since it's your place, we'll take you first."

"You want to use my kitchen, Wally?" Nana asked.

"I was hoping you'd say that, Mrs. Freemont. I already showed the detective in there." He took Thelma Mae's arm, helping her out of the tearoom toward the back.

They were going to try to pin it all on her, Thelma Mae thought, busily taking in every detail of the spotless kitchen beyond Auntie Rose's Victorian Tea House as she lagged, making Wally haul her along step by step. Gilda had to go and open her big fat mouth when all Thelma had been doing was pointing out that she *herself* was not the one who cooked the food. Besides, everyone knew the "best before" date on food was just a guideline, not a hard-and-fast rule!

She had been doing the same thing for years and never made anyone sick. That she knew of. Yet.

That woman's red face and wide-eyed stare were going to haunt her for some time to come. Maybe—just maybe—she'd stop buying past-date chicken and produce. Not that she believed it was her fault, but it could be her bargain with God; he'd get her out of this mess, and she'd stop trying to cut so many corners. She muttered a quick prayer that nothing she had done had caused Vivienne Whittaker's death.

She eyed the detective, a woman, older and with craggy features, some wrinkles around the eyes and mouth. Who was she? Did Thelma know her people? Or was she new in town, one of those feminists come to take jobs away from Gracious Grove men? Women should not take jobs from men; it wasn't right.

Take Wally Bowman, for example . . . now, how old was Wally? Just a year older than Cissy, so thirty. He had grown up, though. He wasn't broad shouldered and big bellied like his daddy, Florence's brother; instead he was slim and tall, kinda gangly. Shouldn't he be the detective and the woman the officer? Or maybe she should be a meter maid, like they had back in the old days.

As Wally guided her to a seat opposite the detective at the little table in the corner, where Laverne Hodge and Gilda sometimes sat to have their morning coffee (both employees chattering like magpies, exchanging all kind of secrets, probably), Thelma Mae had a few seconds to think about what she would tell them. Not everything. Oh, no, certainly not everything. Not about the booze Phil had stored in her stockroom, nor about how that boy kept at it, trying to turn dry Gracious Grove into party central, as he called it. Nor her fears about Cissy marrying Francis Whittaker. Everyone kept congratulating her: "Such a successful boy!" "Such a good match!" "Cissy will be well taken care of; those Whittakers sure know how to make money."

And how to lose it, Thelma Mae thought, her foreboding about the marriage clouding everything else. Ever since Cassandra, Cissy's mother, died fourteen years ago . . . was it fourteen years already? No, not quite. Thirteen and a half or so. Since then Thelma Mae had done nothing but worry about her only granddaughter, and now to have her marry into *that family*!

"Mrs. Earnshaw!" Wally Bowman said loudly.

"All right, Wally, you don't need to shout," she said, eyeing him with irritation. Why were young people all so loud? She wasn't hard of hearing, no matter what Gilda hinted.

"You haven't answered Detective Morris, so I just thought you didn't hear the question," he said.

"Question? Nobody's asked me anything yet. How can I answer if you haven't asked anything?"

He sighed and compressed his lips, then said, slowly and clearly, "Ma'am, please listen carefully."

The woman, supposedly a detective, looked like she was going to smile, but instead said, "Mrs. Earnshaw, can you tell me in your own words what happened?"

"Well, now, who else's words would I use? Stupidest thing I ever heard." She let her gaze drift over the kitchen. My, it sure was clean. Almost *too* clean! Like a hospital. That was Laverne Hodge's doing. She was a hard worker, that one, not like Gilda. Maybe Thelma could steal Laverne away from Rose. She grinned. Wouldn't that just be the cat's pajamas, to be able to steal Laverne Hodge away from Rose Freemont!

What would it take, she wondered?

"Ma'am?"

"Oh, right. Give me a moment." Now, what did she want to tell them?

"Ma'am, all I want is your account of what happened at the engagement tea for Miss Peterson!" the detective said loudly. She wasn't hiding any smile now; she looked as grim as a Bible-thumper in a casino.

"Well, now, you don't have to raise your voice," she said. Why were folks so impatient? Nobody had time anymore for—

"Ma'am!"

"Okay, keep your knickers on. Let's see . . . that snoot, Vivienne, suggested I have that darn tea party, but then she got all in a tizzy about something, all worked up about money and worrying about her precious Francis, and . . . well, anyway, Cissy is my only granddaughter and if I can't have a tea for her then who can? But that Vivienne had the nerve to say—"

"Mrs. Earnshaw, just today, okay?" Wally passed one hand over his eyes, like he had a headache or something. "Detective Morris wants to know exactly what happened starting from the preparations today for the tea to the moment when Mrs. Whittaker became ill."

"Why didn't you say so? If folks would just say plain what they want, I wouldn't have to go through so much trouble all the time."

He drummed his fingers on the table, but then the detective woman cast him an irritated look, and he stopped.

"Mrs. Earnshaw," the detective said, her tone gentle now. "I can only imagine how upsetting this had been for you. I'm sure it will really help things along if we solve this quickly."

Now that made sense! Thelma told her most of what happened as Wally scratched down notes. But only most; a little trimming here and there was necessary, right? She wasn't about to tell them anything that made her or her establishment look bad. That would get all over town in a hurry, then no one would come! And she loved her business. It was going to be so much better, too, once she had a chance to use the million ideas she had gotten just from coming over to Auntie Rose's. Belle Époque was going to beat it hands down this summer.

She added a few choice words about Rose Freemont and Auntie Rose's Victorian Tea House, and how jealous Rose had always had been. She may have embellished just a little bit, and she may even have told a fib or two. But it sure did feel good to complain, for once, to people who were listening instead of to those with their ears closed, like Gilda and Cissy.

Once she was done, the detective seemed satisfied enough, though Wally kept giving her that fishy-eyed stare she remembered so well from his father, and, come to think of it, Florence Whittaker! Two of a kind, those siblings were, Wally's papa and Florence Bowman, as she was then,

Florence Whittaker now. Not like Cissy and Phil; now those two were as different as chalk and cheese.

"Okay, ma'am, you can go back to the tearoom," Detective Morris said.

"Back to Belle Époque? Good. See what kind of mess your people made, and let me tell you—"

"No, ma'am, not there yet," Wally said. "Just back out to Mrs. Freemont's tearoom. And send Cissy in, if you would."

She harrumphed. "Well, you could have said that. Auntie Rose's is not the *only* tearoom in town, you know, though some people act like it is." As she limped back out to the tearoom—her hip was giving her trouble today, probably all the work she had done to get ready for the ruined engagement party—she eyed the folks out there as she passed each table, moving toward one near the door.

It was clear as a bell to her that Wally and the rest of the police believed Vivienne Whittaker was done in. It was no accident and she knew who she hoped was responsible. *And* who she hoped it wasn't. She sure hoped it wasn't Phil, who had hated Vivienne since long before the engagement was announced and he was told by the snobby hoity-toit that he would not be welcome at the wedding. 'Course, you couldn't blame the woman after the trouble Phil had caused, even though Thelma would never admit it out loud. That boy . . . sometimes he was a handful. His problem was he had no patience. Revenge was not best taken on an impulse, it was something to be planned, like any event you looked forward to.

But Phil . . . he got mad when he suspected Vivienne Whittaker had turned him in to the police once, and so had taken it out on her foreign car, which explained her trying to ban him from her son's wedding. Had his dirty tricks gone beyond the foolery he had done with Vivienne's car, those words scratched in the paint? Thelma almost didn't blame Vivienne for that, but Phil was basically a good boy; he wouldn't have done anything on purpose to kill her.

However . . . what if it was an accident? What if he had only meant to make her sick?

All Thelma knew was, Phil had been right there in the kitchen of Belle Époque taking a particular interest in everything that was being set out for the party just minutes before the guests arrived. And Thelma was in and out, not thinking anything about it. He could have done something. She would *never* tell Wally Bowman or any other police officer that. She only had two grandchildren, and she would die before she let one be carted off to jail, guilty or not guilty.

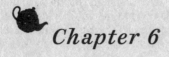

Chapter 6

As much as she tried, Sophie could not stop wondering: What did the police know that led them to think Vivienne had been murdered? Because for all Wally tried to talk around it, it was clear that was the thrust of their fears and beliefs.

Mrs. Earnshaw whispered something to Cissy as she made her way to a table, and Cissy jumped up and headed to the kitchen. She came back out a few minutes later, telling Gretchen she was next. When Gretchen emerged, she went to Belinda Blenkenship and said stiffly, "They want to see *you*."

Gretchen sat alone and stoic after talking to the police, but her eyes darted all around the room, resting on each person who had been at the tea. What was she thinking? Sophie wondered.

After a lapse of a few minutes, Wally came out and said, "Mrs. Florence Whittaker, the detective would like to see you next."

Where did the mayor's wife go? There was only one other way out of there and that was through the side door. It seemed like special treatment.

When Florence Whittaker emerged, teary and sobbing, she sent in Francis, who came back out fifteen minutes later, red eyed and pale, but composed. "They want you and your grandmother in together," he said, without looking at Sophie. He slumped down into a chair and put his head in his hands. Cissy moved to sit next to him, but didn't touch him.

Sophie and Nana headed back to the kitchen, where they found Wally sitting with a woman in a black suit jacket and gray slacks.

"Sophie, Mrs. Freemont, this is Detective Morris. Detective, this is Sophie Taylor and her grandmother, Mrs. Rose Freemont, owner of this establishment."

"I've actually been here for tea with my mother and aunt," Detective Morris said, the timbre of her voice husky but pleasant.

"I thought you looked familiar!" Nana said. "You had the escarole salad and iced tea."

"Please sit down, ladies," the detective said. "I understand, Sophie, that you ran over to Belle Époque even before the police and paramedics arrived. Did you hear something?"

She told the detective about the scream she had heard through her open third-floor window. "I don't know who screamed, but it was loud."

"That would have likely been Florence Whittaker," Wally said, checking his notes.

The detective cast him a look and he shut his mouth. "Did the scream sound frightened to you, or . . . how *did* it sound?"

Sophie eyed the woman. What exactly was she fishing for? "It sounded, I don't know . . . like a scream. I didn't think about it, I was just in a hurry to find out what had happened."

"What did you see when you entered?"

"I saw folks standing around and Mrs. Whittaker . . . Mrs. *Vivienne* Whittaker . . . in trouble. I rushed over to them, but I didn't know what to do."

"What did you think was happening?"

"At first I thought she was choking. I said that someone should do the Heimlich maneuver."

"But you didn't volunteer."

Sophie paused, but then said, "No. The last time I did it, I almost got sued."

"I didn't hear about this, Sophie, honey!" her grandmother said, one hand on her arm.

At the same moment, Wally blurted, "Sued? Why?"

Sophie covered her grandmother's hand and squeezed. "I ran a restaurant in New York called In Fashion," she told the detective. "I was the manager and executive chef."

"Aren't you a little young to run your own restaurant?" Detective Morris said.

Sophie shrugged. It was the criticism most leveled at her when talking about the failure of In Fashion and maybe there was some truth in it. She had trusted people she shouldn't have. It was a humbling experience, being so sure of herself when she started, knowing every step of the path to success, and then failing so miserably anyway. Some folks, including former instructors, told her she had not been entirely responsible, but she beat herself up anyway.

The detective made a note on a pad of paper and said, "What happened that caused you to almost get sued?"

"I was making the rounds of the tables, like I did every night after the first rush, just making sure people were enjoying the food. A woman started to choke on a piece of lobster, and I . . . I did the Heimlich."

"And? Didn't it work?"

"Oh, it worked all right. The hunk of lobster popped out into the clarified butter bowl and the butter splashed on her breast. The dress she was wearing was an Ungaro original, silk, and worth a lot of money."

"So you saved her life and she sued you?"

"She was going to until one of the financial partners ponied up for the money to pay for the Ungaro."

"So since then you don't do the Heimlich," the detective said.

"I would have tried, but when I got a good look at Mrs. Whittaker, I didn't think she was choking."

The detective narrowed her eyes. "Why do you say that?"

"I don't know, it just . . ." Sophie shook her head. "I can't explain why I thought it, but it didn't *look* like she was choking, exactly."

"Interesting," the detective said, her gaze fixed on Sophie's face. "How did she look to you?"

"She was getting red in the face, and her eyes were wide open, like she was scared." Sophie shivered and forced back tears. "But it wasn't like she was choking, it was more like . . ." She thought for a moment. "More like she was *suffocating.*"

"Did you notice anything else? Anything out of place, or odd?"

Sophie pondered that for a moment, but shook her head. "I don't think so. I don't know. It feels like there's something there, but I can't say what it is."

"If you think of anything, please let me know." She turned to Sophie's grandmother. "Ma'am, I understand you and Mrs. Earnshaw don't get along."

"Who told you that?" Sophie asked.

"Why?" the detective shot back.

"Sophie, every Gracious Grover knows the state of my relationship with Thelma Mae Earnshaw. It's no secret." Nana looked the detective square on. "Thelma, bless her heart, is a cranky soul. She always thinks that someone else has the only thing that would have made her happy. She's like that dog that has a bone, but suspects that every other dog has a better bone. So she snaps and snarls and tries to steal every other bone she sees, disregarding the one right in front of her nose."

"That's funny, Mrs. Freemont, because Mrs. Earnshaw said much the same thing about you, that you were jealous of her success and always had been."

Sophie gasped. "That is *so* not true! She's the one who has tried to sabotage my grandma! You just ask around town; ask folks about Mrs. Earnshaw trying to ruin Nana's business. *She's* the one who badmouths Grandma every chance she gets."

"Sophie!" Nana said, warning in her tone.

The detective sat back in her chair. "So it is your considered opinion that Mrs. Earnshaw would go out of her way to harm Mrs. Freemont's reputation and livelihood. And that there has been bad blood between them for decades?"

Startled, Sophie said, "Well, kind of. I guess. But mostly on Mrs. Earnshaw's part."

"Interesting. And immaterial, I suppose." The detective closed the notebook in front of her with a slap of paper on paper. "Is she the kind who would hide things?"

"What kind of things?" Nana asked.

"Information, or even her suspicions."

"If it had to do with Phil, she would," Sophie muttered.

Wally jumped up. "Do you think Phil could be involved with this?"

"With killing Mrs. Whittaker?" Sophie regretted her impulsive muttering. "He would *never* do anything like that. He's an idiot, but he's never hurt anyone, right?" The boy she remembered was mischievous, not malicious. But what had the intervening years done to him?

"There is bad blood between Mrs. Whittaker and Phillip Peterson, though, isn't there?" the detective asked.

"Look, I just got back in town," Sophie said. "I don't have any idea about bad blood."

"Would it surprise you to learn that Phil Peterson uttered threats against Mrs. Whittaker?" the detective asked. "And that he vowed in public to stop the marriage between his sister and Francis Whittaker no matter what it took?"

Wally looked away, toward the window. He must be the source of that information, and Sophie was irritated at him for turning on his former friend until she remembered that this was a murder investigation, not a time to worry about being a snitch. And it was his job. Once upon a time they had all three been best buddies, Wally, Frankie and Phil, but that, she heard, had ended badly. "He'd never kill anyone," Sophie said. "Come on, Wally, you *know* that! You guys were friends!"

"You can't protect Phil, so don't even try," Wally said.

She frowned, her gaze slewing between the two police officers. "I'm not trying to protect anyone, least of all Phil

Peterson. I really can't help you. Like I said, I've only been back in town a week."

"Look here, you two," Nana said, squinting at the detective and Wally. "I don't like the tone you're taking with my granddaughter. She doesn't know anything, and neither do I."

After a long wordless pause, the detective nodded, as if satisfied. "Okay, you can both go," she said, standing. "If you think of anything, Sophie or Mrs. Freemont—anything that seemed *off* to you—please let us know. Officer Bowman will be keeping an eye on things."

The detective followed Sophie and her grandmother back out to the tearoom and stood by the servery. She cleared her throat, successfully gathering everyone's attention. "I know you're all concerned and I'll make it official. At two forty-three this afternoon, Mrs. Vivienne Whittaker was pronounced dead at Cruickshank Memorial Hospital."

There was a startled outcry, then the hum of subdued conversation. Sophie watched as Gretchen Harcourt tapped away at her phone screen. Live updates, no doubt, announced on every social network there was. Francis groaned and buried his face in his arms, while Cissy patted him on the back and frowned off into space. Gilda Bachman narrowed her eyes and stared at someone, but she was slightly cross-eyed, so Sophie couldn't tell who exactly she was staring at from among Gretchen, Cissy, Francis, Florence, or Laverne.

"You can all go home. Mrs. Earnshaw, are you expecting any new guests today?"

Thelma ran Belle Époque as a bed and breakfast, but it was struggling, to say the least, from what Sophie's grandmother said.

"They've all gone and I don't have a soul coming today. I'm going broke and this mess is going to just kill me!" She sent an accusatory stare around at all of them. "I'd think you all would be trying to help me, instead of gossiping and treating me bad. Especially you, Rose Freemont! After what you did to me, you should be trying to help me!"

Everyone stared. Nana said, her voice trembling, "Now that is just *enough*, Thelma Mae Earnshaw. I saw Harold Freemont first, and don't you *ever* forget it!" With that, she turned and retreated, climbing the stairs to her second-floor apartment.

Wally whispered something to the detective, probably clearing up that reference. It would seem obscure to someone who didn't know the history between the women.

"Really, Granny, can't you just let it go?" Cissy said, in a low tone. "It was, like, sixty years ago already, and you got Grandpa, didn't you? There are more important things going on, you know. Come on, Francis, we have things that have to be done. Or . . ." Her expression stricken, she turned and looked at the detective. "We can't . . . can we plan . . . ? I guess not, I mean . . ."

Sophie felt horrible for her old friend. She turned back to Detective Morris and said, "I think Cissy is wondering, will the family be able to plan a funeral for Mrs. Whittaker?"

"Not yet," she said, her husky voice holding a neutral tone. "I'm sorry, but you'll all have to just wait until we figure things out. Mrs. Whittaker's body will not be released to her family until we are satisfied we have all we need." She turned to Thelma. "But the scene has been cleared, Mrs. Earnshaw, so you can go back to your place."

"Poor Vivienne!" Florence moaned. "She'd despise all this fuss."

E veryone had gone home. Sophie stood in the tiny kitchen of her grandmother's upstairs suite looking out the window toward Belle Époque, wondering how everyone was coping. She desperately wanted to rush in and ease people's suffering. That part of her personality had made both life and work difficult at times. She had tried to fix problems at the restaurant alone instead of using the resources her partners could offer simply because she *never* asked for help if she could avoid it. Nana told everyone that

when Sophie was little, standing on a stool at her grandmother's elbow, her favorite phrase was *I can do it myself!*
when stirring a stiff batter.

"What are you thinking, my Sophie?" her grandmother
said, from behind her.

"Truthfully?" she asked, turning and eyeing her nana,
who had already changed into a nightie and slathered lotion
on her face, though it was only about six thirty. "I was wondering why I have a sudden urge to try to figure out what
happened to Vivienne Whittaker so everyone can begin to
heal."

"You always were the kind who needed to take care of
everyone, smooth things over, make it all better. That's
because of the way your mom handles things, I've always
figured. Rosalind is an avoider. *And* it's because you were
the mediator between your brothers, between your mom and
dad, between me and your mom . . . between everyone!"

"I guess that's true," she said. Her older brothers Andrew
and Samuel were supercompetitive with each other, rocket-
ing between estrangement and being each others' best buddies. She had tried to be the buffer between them at family
gatherings. Her father was a distant, difficult man and her
mother a needy, clinging woman. Reconciling the two had
been a constant battle in her teenage years.

That was one of the many reasons Gracious Grove was
home for her more than anywhere else; it was a serene,
untroubled place where all she had to be was herself. It
occurred to her in that moment that she had carried her
family's crazy behavior into her business life, trying to solve
things between her financial partners, among staff, between
the front of the house and the kitchen at In Fashion. How
had that served her? Not so great.

She plunked down in one of Nana's retro chrome and
aqua plastic kitchen chairs and sent her grandmother a
searching look. "Nana, why do you and Mom not get along?
And why doesn't she like Gracious Grove? When I was a
kid, she would plop Sam, Andy and me down here and then

leave. I can't remember her staying more than a night or two in Gracious Grove my whole life."

Her grandmother looked conflicted for a long minute, then appeared to make up her mind. "Come sit down on the sofa for a minute, honey. I have something to show you."

Sophie moved to the sofa in the tiny living room space that adjoined the kitchen and sank into the softness. Like all of Gracious Grove, that comfy powder-blue sofa was a soft place to land. When Nana came back from her bedroom, she was carrying a photo album, and she plopped down with a groan beside Sophie, setting the album on the polished-wood coffee table in front of them. She opened it to the first page. "Now, who do you suppose that baby is?" she said, pointing at a black-and-white photo of a chunky little toddler holding a Christmas gift up toward the camera.

"I have no clue," Sophie said, eyeing the other photos on the page. It looked familiar, the house and even some of the furniture. "Is that downstairs before you turned it into a tearoom, Nana?"

"It sure is. That toddler is your own mother, my little baby Rosalind. There's her older brother in the background." Her voice choked. Losing her oldest son to the Vietnam War had been a horrible blow.

"Why have I never seen these photos before?"

Nana waved one hand dismissively. "I knew it would cause no end of trouble with your mother if I showed them to you, so I didn't. Chickened out, I guess. But you have a right to them. They don't belong to Rosalind, they belong to her children. It's *your* heritage, just as Gracious Grove is, if you want it to be."

Sophie avidly scanned the page and leafed through the rest, watching her mother grow up (along with her two brothers, Jack and Harold Junior) before her eyes into . . . wow. Her mom had been a heavyset, unhappy-looking, spotted teen. "This explains a lot."

"What do you mean, honey?"

She stared down at a photo of her mother, a teen in the

disco era, with wild, blowsy curls and too much tummy squeezed into a polyester disco dress. "It explains Mom's attitude toward food, and even why she didn't want me to become a chef." She considered her next words, not wanting to offend. "Was Mom ashamed of being heavy?"

Nana nodded, a thoughtful gleam in her pale eyes. "Yes, she was. And I see what you mean about your mother's attitude toward your chosen career. I never thought about it before. She was a chunky girl when she was a kid, but so pretty! I told her she was being foolish when she worried about her weight. Told her it was just baby fat and that she'd grow out of it."

"Did she?"

Nana shrugged. "She went on this wild diet, cabbage soup and grapefruit. Wouldn't eat anything else, no matter that I tried making all her favorites, chicken and dumplings, Spaghetti Bolognese, macaroni and cheese. How I worried!"

It was weird how generations flailed around, coming up against issues time and time again, masked in different costumes but always the same. Her mother didn't cook at all, so Sophie had grown up with a chef in their home who had been ordered to prepare the most minimal of meals—a chicken breast with a spinach salad, or a filet of salmon and *salade frisée*—and had hated every minute of it. When Sophie had stayed with her grandmother, she reveled in the home cooking Nana offered and that her mother abominated. Now Sophie understood and felt bad for all the times she had railed at her about her obsession with eating only the simplest, smallest meals. Weight loss had been a great triumph, probably, for a Gracious Grove teen, and she had been determined not to see her own daughter struggle with the same issues.

But Sophie was not elegant, perfect Rosalind Freemont Taylor and would not feel bad for wanting something different. Her mother had found what *she* wanted: wealth, status and security. It was Sophie's turn to figure out her own life. She closed the photo album with a slap and said, "Nana, do you think Mrs. Whittaker was really murdered?"

Her grandmother started and Sophie realized she was dozing, the events of the day too much for her. "I'm sorry, honey, what did you say?"

Sophie repeated her question.

"The police must have some reason for thinking so. Did you notice anything?"

"Nothing important," Sophie said.

"Tell me about it."

Sophie described the scene, the attendees all sitting around the one large round table in the center of the room and the leftovers from their tea crowding the space, some platters set aside on nearby tables. She viewed it all in her mind's eye, the half-empty trays of misshapen finger sandwiches, the scones studded with nuts and the vanilla-iced red-velvet cupcakes in a semicircle on a plate. "It looked like a flower with some of the petals missing and the center gone," Sophie mused. "Like some weird game of 'he loves me, he loves me not.' That poor woman, Vivienne Whittaker . . . she was on the floor, yellow frosting smeared on her face." Sophie shuddered. "Her face was all swollen and . . . and red. She was writhing, but no one was *helping* her." Tears welled up in Sophie's eyes and she pressed her shaking hands to her mouth. "Including me. It was terrible!"

Nana patted her back. "You couldn't have done anything, sweetheart. What about the rest of them? What were they doing?"

Try as she might, Sophie could not bring to mind some of the faces. Francis, certainly, had looked shocked, down on his knees trying to soothe his mother. Cissy appeared frightened and elderly Mrs. Earnshaw horrified. But was there someone whose expression did not go with the scene? Was it Gilda Bachman's ghoulish curiosity? Florence Whittaker's blank expression? Gretchen's distaste? Belinda Blenkenship's quivering lip?

She talked all this out, only to realize when she was done that her grandma was slumped over, snoring slightly. Pearl gracefully jumped up and cuddled against her mistress. Sophie got up, covered her grandmother and the beautiful

Birman with the granny-square afghan that was flung over the back of the sofa, kissed her grandmother's soft cheek just beyond the face cream and ascended to her own space to ponder the day's events.

As she got ready for bed herself, exhausted and aching from the events of the day, she picked up her cell phone and checked her messages. She had a text, all in caps, from Cissy, and it said, CALL ME . . . I'M SO SCARED!"

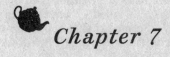 *Chapter 7*

"**C**issy? I got a text from you; what's wrong?" she demanded, as her friend gasped out a weak "Hello?"

"I'm so *scared*!" Cissy said, her voice trembling.

"What's going on? Are you okay?"

There was silence for a minute. "Vivienne was *murdered*!" Her tone was like, *duh . . . how do you not know this?*

"I know that," Sophie replied. "But there's no cause for *you* to be scared, is there?"

"What if the killer was really after me?"

"Why would you think that?" Sophie remembered how her friend had always been a drama queen wannabe, constantly hoping and wishing that the inevitable teen angst swirling around Gracious Grove circles was about her, when it never was. Cissy was the kind of girl that nobody felt strongly enough about to murder, Sophie thought. Or was she wrong?

"I just *know* someone is out to get me," she muttered, her voice muffled. "They don't want me to marry Francis."

"Cissy, who is *they*? Has anyone told you that to your face?"

"Phil told me he'd rather see me leave town than marry Francis Whittaker."

Sophie was taken aback at the mention of Cissy's brother. "Are you saying that Phil killed Vivienne to keep you from marrying Francis?" Seemed kind of a roundabout method of keeping her from marrying a guy, to kill the fiancé's mother, but who knew?

"Of *course* not! Phil wouldn't kill anyone."

Sophie recalled Phil sneaking out of the Belle Époque moments before the engagement party was to begin, even as the guests came in the front. She was about to ask Cissy about that, but her friend said something to someone in the background. She wasn't alone.

"I have to go," she said.

"But Cissy, wait! You said you were scared!"

"I have to go. I'll talk to you tomorrow, okay?"

"Sure." Sophie tried to quell the annoyance that welled up in her. Cissy had freaked her out over nothing, just more of her drama queen stuff.

"We'll go over plans for the bridal shower, right?"

The shift from life-threatening situation to normal everyday was weird. "Okay. But I *should* be getting together with Gretchen about that. You're not supposed to be planning your own shower."

"I know, but . . . all right. I'll talk to you later." She hung up.

Sophie sighed, flung her clothes off and pulled on a long T-shirt and went to bed.

Over at Belle Époque, Thelma Mae Earnshaw, in the kitchen with her feet in a basin of hot water and Epsom salts, pondered the horror that had happened just beyond the big double doors, in the tearoom. How it could have come about was beyond her. Those police were acting like it was something in the food and had searched her place top to bottom before letting her back into her own kitchen. They had taken away a lot of stuff, too.

It just couldn't be her food. Every scrap of that food had been hand prepared by Thelma or Gilda. Well, pretty much all of it, anyway. Or . . . to be *completely* honest, at Belle Époque there just wasn't time to do everything fresh so they did buy frozen rolls, scones, tarts and cream puffs and thawed them out. She defied anyone to tell the difference! At least the finger sandwiches were fresh, made right in her own kitchen, except for the fillings, which she'd bought at the deli. The ham salad at the Tastee Mart was the best, and the egg salad wasn't too shabby, either.

She sat back in her chair as the water cooled. It was just plain easier to buy frozen, pull it out of the freezer, thaw it and bake it, or buy ready-made from the grocery store or bakery. So those police folks wouldn't pin this awful thing on her just because it happened at Belle Époque, no sir! It was impossible that anyone could have tainted any of the foods that were put out for the guests.

Or *almost* impossible. Folks had brought stuff, too, and they all said the same thing; someone told them to bring a dish, like it was some potluck or something instead of a professional tearoom! She harrumphed and frowned down at her feet, wiggling her arthritic toes. She should take her feet out of the water or they'd get cold and crampy, she thought, but then forgot about it as she tried to recollect what all had happened.

It had been terribly busy, an awful rush right before the tea party. She closed her eyes, trying to remember; let's see . . . Gilda was being her usual slowpokey self, whining that she only had two hands and couldn't be expected to do everything, Thelma thought. People had brought a few containers, cookies, cupcakes, some strange thingies that looked like little whole-wheat blankets with grass sticking out of them; wraps, they were called, she had been told. Looked uneatable, to Thelma, but they went faster than the finger sandwiches she had taken so much trouble over. No accounting for taste.

Then some of the guests (a couple who Thelma didn't even know and didn't like much, anyway), who had been waiting out in the tearoom for luncheon, wandered back to the kitchen, probably to see what was wrong and what the holdup was. Francis, Vivienne, some woman with stiff hair that Thelma had had to put in her place, a blonde girl, Florence Whittaker, that hoity-toity Gretchen girl and even Cissy had all wandered around, "helping," which translated to sampling, suggesting, plopping things on plates, looking in the fridge, checking out the oven and generally making nuisances of themselves.

And she had to shoo Phil out of the kitchen just as folks were arriving in the front door. But no, there was not an ounce of evil in that boy's bones. All the trouble he had been in had been other people's faults, folks who had led him astray, like that Francis Whittaker. That confounded boy had done everything Phil had done and *still* come out smelling like a rose while her poor grandson ended up in trouble. Francis's mother was behind that, her and her money.

This tragedy was like a divine judgment on Vivienne Whittaker for putting on airs all these years when she had been born plain-old Vivienne Crenshaw, daughter of a hootchy-kootch dancer who got lucky by marrying up. And even that wasn't a real love match or nothing. No, that woman had tempted poor, unsuspecting Francis Whittaker Senior, heir to the Whittaker grocery fortune, into bed where she got herself pregnant so he'd marry her. Most folks had forgotten about that, but not Thelma!

It wasn't as if Thelma had wished this on her, but it did seem that the good Lord was removing thorns from her side. Maybe Cissy would see what kind of family she was preparing to marry into and back out before it was too late. Thelma decided she had better watch what she wished for. It was dangerous to have so much power. She would most definitely not wish for Rose Beaudry Freemont to break her hip in a fall. She wouldn't wish that on her worst enemy. She clutched at her hip, the constant ache a reminder of a difficult period of recovery.

But wishes didn't make something happen, after all; human hands performed the Devil's work. Someone had wanted Vivienne out of the way, but who? Fear shot through Thelma; could it have been Francis himself who killed his momma? And if that was so, how could Thelma convince sweet, naive Cissy that he was an evil mother-killing monster?

She'd have to start the very next day. If she could just get those police officers . . . not that there was a pair of brains to choose between them. Take Wally Bowman, *please*! Thelma snuffled at her clever variation on her favorite old Henny Youngman joke. But she had known that boy since he still required an hourly change of diaper. There was no way he was qualified to investigate a murder. And that woman, Detective Morris . . . well, everyone knew policing was a man's job; no woman was fit to be a police officer.

Okay, now, what on earth had she been thinking?

Francis Whittaker. Right; if Thelma could just get one of them to arrest Francis, then Cissy would be safely free of him. She could give the police a good stern warning that he could be the killer, but too often folks didn't listen to her like they ought. She didn't know why. She told folks all the time what was good for them, warned them about the dangers lurking behind every smiling face, but no one paid attention.

It was all a part of getting old, she guessed, because everyone ignored old ladies no matter how much they demanded help or attention or sympathy. Getting old was a pain . . . a pain in the back, a pain in the hip, a pain in the feet. She lifted her feet out of the now-cold soaking water and dried them off as best she could, given that she couldn't bend over very far without getting vertigo. The *plop-plop-plop* of dripping water echoed in the empty kitchen; the old house sure felt lonely with no guests, no Gilda and no Cissy.

She pushed her feet into warm slippers. Ah! That was better. Now, what had she just been planning? Right . . . how to get one of the police people to arrest Francis, so at least *he* would be out of the way. Maybe she could get them to think Francis was capable of it, first. Wally was the one she knew, but he had never paid her any mind even when he was a scrawny little brat playing Hacky Sack in her driveway. He sure wouldn't pay attention now.

But that woman . . . she wouldn't be too logical. Women, except for Thelma herself, just weren't. Maybe she would believe an anonymous note, or a whispered phone call. A thrill shot through Thelma as she remembered the old mystery movies she loved, like *Dial M for Murder*, or *Strangers on a Train* . . . a black-and-white movie, her in a glamorous fedora and trench coat whispering in the phone receiver that so-and-so ought to be looked at more closely because they had dark secrets to hide.

She'd do it. She got up suddenly, knocked the plastic basin and water sloshed all over the floor. Darn it! She'd have to make sure Gilda cleaned that up first thing in the morning, but right now she had a phone call to make.

P urring awoke Sophie. She opened one eye to find Pearl staring into her face, blue eyes set in a chocolate mask and almost crossed with the intensity of her stare. The sun was already up, and so should she be.

"Hey, Pearlie-Girlie, Nana's up, right? And you're my wake-up call?" The cat purred and murmured something, then jumped off the bed and headed downstairs with a soft *thump-thump-thump*. Sophie had stayed up late trying to figure out how Vivienne Whittaker had been killed and who would have done such an awful thing. She felt enormous sympathy for Francis, losing a mother like that. He and Cissy would bond even more now, perhaps, with the mutual loss of parents to link them.

After a shower, some hair and makeup fussing and a cup of coffee drunk while she did all those things, she descended to find Laverne and Nana communing over tea in the kitchen.

"It's about time you made your star appearance," Laverne said, tilting her head for a cheek kiss. It was a greeting almost twenty years old, a private joke between her and her godmother.

She kissed both women good morning and poured a cup of tea out of the big urn on the stove. "So what's on tap for today?"

The two friends exchanged glances.

"After yesterday, we weren't sure what you wanted to do," her grandmother said.

"What do you mean? I'm going to help here, and plan Cissy's bridal shower." She told them about the weird phone call between her and Cissy the night before.

"Things may be a little different now, though," Nana said. "Wally Bowman showed up here first thing this morning and told us some news."

Had they found the killer so quickly? "What's up?"

"They got an anonymous phone call last night. Someone told them something very interesting. The caller said that Francis had been seen in Ithaca last week asking someone about undetectable poisons."

Sophie stared, open-mouthed. "Francis? But . . . but . . . why would he want to kill his own mother? That's *horrible*!"

"Good lord, honey, where on earth have you been hiding?" Laverne asked. "There are a hundred-and-one reasons to kill someone, even your mother. Maybe she has a fat insurance policy on her. Maybe she knew something he was doing that he oughtn't have. Maybe she disapproved of his upcoming marriage and was trying to stop it, or maybe—"

"Okay, *okay*! You watch too many crime shows. Still . . . I just can't see Francis killing his mother."

"No, I agree," Nana said.

Just then they heard a throaty motor roar up to Belle Époque next door, then stop.

"Wonder what's going on?" Sophie wandered to the

kitchen window, which looked over on the inn next door. She watched for a moment, and gasped as she saw a sight no one could ever have expected.

"What's wrong, Sophie?" both older women chimed.

"They're . . . good heavens! They're arresting Mrs. Earnshaw!"

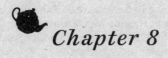

Chapter 8

"**W**hat?" Nana sprang to her feet with a swiftness that belied her age and hustled to the window. "What do they think they're doing?"

"I don't know," Sophie said, giving up her spot so her grandmother could see. "But I'm going to find out." She raced to the front door and then outside. This was getting to be a habit, one she'd just as soon break.

A police officer with a grim expression had Thelma Mae's arm in a light grip. "Please, Mrs. Earnshaw," he pleaded of the elderly woman, "don't make this any harder!"

"Billy Anderson, you ought to be ashamed," Thelma wailed, "arresting a woman the same age as your grandma!"

Sophie, alarmed, dashed toward them, hands out. "What's going on? Why is Mrs. Earnshaw being arrested?" It was too ridiculous and shocking a statement even to believe, but as he guided her down the path toward his cruiser, what else could she say?

"Miss, please go back to your home. There's nothing to see here."

At that moment Gilda Bachman, Thelma's long-time

employee, trotted out of Belle Époque weeping. "Sophie, what are we going to do?" she wailed, wringing her hands. "They're arresting Thelma!"

The police officer, a fresh-faced fellow of about twenty-three, was pink with agitation as he gently tried to convince Mrs. Earnshaw to sit in the backseat of the police cruiser. "Ma'am, we are *not* arresting Mrs. Earnshaw," he said over his shoulder to Gilda. "She's coming to police headquarters to . . . to help us in our investigation."

Gilda wailed even louder and put both hands to her head. "*No!* I know what that means. You're gonna get her down there, torture her into a confession, then throw her in the hole!"

The young officer rolled his eyes. "Good grief!"

Sophie took a deep breath and grabbed Gilda's arm, feeling her trembling all through her body. "Calm down, Gilda. Officer, Mrs. Earnshaw is in frail health and clearly very upset. Why don't we go back to Belle Époque and talk about this?"

"I'm sorry, miss," he said, and he genuinely looked like he'd rather be anywhere but there, his cheeks burning red with embarrassment and his gaze darting around to eye the neighbors out on their lawns watching the drama unfold. "I was told to bring Mrs. Earnshaw down to police headquarters and that's what I'm going to do. None of this would have been troubling except she told me she wasn't going and threw a plate of flapjacks at my head. Now, I'm not going to arrest her, but you see my dilemma? If I report what she did, she could be arrested for assaulting an officer of the law."

"But you don't want to do that," Sophie guessed, noticing the sticky residue of syrup on his otherwise pristine uniform. The sugary smell was intensifying in the warm spring air.

His face got even pinker as he shook his head. "No ma'am," he said, with feeling. "Do you have any clue what kind of ribbing I'd take for arresting an old lady for assault with a plate of pancakes? I'd never live it down."

"Mrs. Earnshaw, please don't worry," Sophie said, approaching the inn owner, who stood by the open cruiser door, tears rolling down her lined cheeks. She put her arm over the woman's shoulders. "This police officer says he only wants to take you to police headquarters to ask you some questions. Do you know what this is about?"

She shook her head, but it was clear from the way her glance slid away and her shoulders trembled that she did. Sophie turned to Gilda. "Do you know what this is about?"

The woman shook her head. Sophie turned back to Mrs. Earnshaw. "Ma'am, I think you should go with him, but . . . can I call Cissy for you? I'll make sure she meets you at the police department, and . . . and if you want a lawyer . . ." Sophie calmed her mind and sorted through all the scrambled thoughts. "You don't *have* to talk to them, that I know. She doesn't *have* to talk to anyone, does she officer?"

"No, ma'am, she doesn't have to talk to anyone. But if they only want to clear up a misunderstanding, it might be better for her if she does." He shrugged. "It's your call, ma'am," he said, looking down at Mrs. Earnshaw.

Her watery eyes squinted, and she glared around. "All right, I'll go. Seems like no one is on my side, anyway, I may as well get it over with. Bring on the rubber hoses and waterboard, Billy," she said, as she climbed into the cruiser with some difficulty.

The officer shut the door gently and turned back to Sophie. "They really do just want to ask her some questions." He paused and glanced over to the cruiser, where the woman sullenly folded her arms over her bosom. "I think, anyway."

"I'm calling her granddaughter to meet her there."

As the cruiser drove away, Sophie took Gilda's arm. The woman was in her sixties, but appeared older. She wore a matronly dress and her frizzy hair was confined atop her head by a neon-pink scrunchie. "Come and have a cup of tea with Nana and Laverne," she said, curiosity burning in her gut. Despite Gilda shaking her head, Sophie thought that she knew something, and they would pry it out of her with tea and sympathy.

Laverne and Nana had been watching the proceedings from the tearoom windows, and both hustled out to help a shaky Gilda back to the kitchen. Gilda knew her way around at Auntie Rose's. Over the years she and Laverne had struck up a friendship, and Gilda even attended Laverne's church now.

The odd little train made its way back to the kitchen and soon the two women had Gilda ensconced in a sunny window seat with a cup of strong tea and a lemon cranberry muffin. It appeared to Sophie that Gilda was enjoying being at the center of a drama, but there was no doubt she was shaken. Sophie went into the tearoom and made a quick call to Cissy. There was no answer, not that strange since she was probably comforting her fiancé, who, after all, had just lost his mother. She called Peterson Books 'n Stuff, got Dana and told her what had happened to Cissy's grandmother.

"You're kidding, right? They've arrested Granny Thelma?"

"Not arrested, Dana, taken in for questioning."

"There's a difference?"

"Of course there is! But she wasn't too happy about it and refused to go at first."

"I'll bet that's a big fat understatement," the other woman said, her tone wry. Everyone in Gracious Grove knew about Thelma Mae Earnshaw's temper. "Why are they questioning her? What could she *possibly* know?"

"The death did happen in her tearoom," Sophie said, chewing on that thought. Did she know more than she had told the police at first? It was possible. With Mrs. Earnshaw you could never be sure. "They were bound to want to talk to her more after some investigation."

"True. I'll call Cissy and have her call you, okay?"

"Don't worry about having her call me, just make sure she gets to the police station as quickly as she can!" Sophie returned to find that the three women were deeply into the topic. Her grandmother brought her up to speed.

Her expression perturbed, she said, "Gilda tells us that Thelma, in her infinite wisdom, decided to turn in Francis Whittaker by calling the police anonymously last night and telling them that he had poisoned his mother."

Sophie plunked down in a kitchen chair. "She called the

police anonymously from her *own phone*? Didn't she realize they'd know who phoned?"

Laverne bit her lip, but a snicker escaped.

"It is not funny, Laverne Hodge," Gilda said, her lined face twisted in anguish.

"Of course it isn't, dearie," Nana said, shooting her friend and employee a quelling look. Laverne settled down, but there was still a glimmer of mischief in her dark eyes.

"Why does she think Francis did it?" Sophie asked.

The woman sighed and stared out the window, over to Belle Époque. "Who on earth understands that woman's mind? I've known her for years and I still don't."

"Does she really know something, or did she see something?"

"I don't think so. She can jump to a conclusion faster than a cat can jump on a mouse."

Laverne took Gilda's hand and patted it. "I don't know how you put up with everything Thelma puts you through!"

Gilda's eyes shone with gratitude at the kind words. "We manage most of the time, but . . ." She paused and guiltily looked around. "I just feel so bad when she makes me do something to you folks."

"What do you mean, *do something*?" Sophie asked.

"Well, like the phony ad saying Auntie Rose's was closed for renovations."

"That was *you*?" Nana asked, her lined face expressing astonishment. That had to be acting, because Nana had suspected all along who was behind the dirty-tricks campaign, and in fact her eyes twinkled with humor.

Gilda nodded. "And the misdirected teapot shipment, and the rumors of food poisoning and . . . I've been so *awful* and you're being so nice to me!" She broke down and wept.

Nana and Laverne exchanged looks over her head. "So why do you do it, dearie?" Nana asked.

"I *have* to!" Gilda whined. "She keeps threatening to fire me. Who else would give me a job at my age?" She was silent for a long moment, still staring out the window, the tears drying on her capillary-threaded cheeks. "She said she was going to make me a partner. Do you know what that would mean to me? To actually own a piece of something?"

The phone rang and Sophie got up to answer it. It was Dana Saunders.

"So I got ahold of Cissy and she's over at the police station now, but I thought I'd let you know some stuff I found out."

"Cool! What's up?" Sophie was surprised at Dana's help— they had never been close friends—but glad to have it.

"So listen to this: The cops think it was a poisoned cupcake that killed Vivienne Whittaker."

Sophie was stunned. "A poisoned *cupcake*?" She remembered the platter of cupcakes; death by red velvet? "Do they . . . oh my gosh! Is that why they've asked Mrs. Earnshaw in for questioning?"

"Wouldn't that just be too fabulous if it was true, if Thelma had finally gone off her rocker and did someone in?" The malice in Dana's voice dripped like the poison they spoke of.

"I wouldn't want to see Mrs. Earnshaw up for murder," Sophie said, reprimand in her voice.

"Careful now, or you'll start climbing up on that priggish pony again," Dana warned. "You've not had to live in the same town as that woman. Do you know she had the police investigate me because she said I *must* be stealing from the bookstore?"

"Really?" Sophie was appalled. "What is up with her?"

"I don't know, but whatever it was happened too long ago for even the dinosaurs to remember."

"Dana, you know a lot about local gossip . . . do you know anything about Belinda Blenkenship? The girl who married the mayor?"

She chuckled, a throaty warm sound. "Do I? Oh yes, I surely do. Gracious Grove's own local Miss New York State."

"She's a beauty contestant?"

"Among other things."

"I was surprised the police let her go the way they did," Sophie said.

"Doesn't surprise me. There was a hubbub locally when she and Mayor Mike married, and he ordered several blog posts and gossip sites taken down over his dear little wifey. He sued a couple of others who refused to retract, including one shock jock on satellite radio. They know darn well they better handle her with kid gloves or His Honor will come down on them."

"What's so controversial about her?" Sophie was trying to get at the implication behind Dana's *among other things* remark.

"Let's see . . . where to start? Her title was taken away from her when a sex tape emerged. She was caught in a cocaine den but was released for lack of evidence. She told the cops that she had been tricked into going there, and I guess when she batted her long lashes they just believed her and let her go." Dana paused, and then said, with great emphasis, "Oh, and she despised Vivienne Whittaker with a white-hot passion."

"What? Why?"

"She was one of the legions of dumb blondes our own Francis 'dated'—and I hope you can see the air quotes around that word—and who Vivienne chased off from her little precious. Word on the streets was, she was pregnant when Frankie broke up with her, but I can't confirm that."

"Pregnant with Francis's baby?" Sophie blurted out.

"So I've heard, but rumor is . . . oops, customer . . . I gotta go," she said.

"You can't leave it at that!"

"I'll tell you more later, but I really have to go."

Dial tone. Her head spinning at what she had heard, Sophie went back to the table to find the women still talking over what had happened the day before.

"So, you and Thelma were setting stuff on platters," Laverne summed up for Sophie's sake. "But then everyone came into the kitchen and began helping willy-nilly?"

Gilda nodded, misery and guilt in her eyes. "All of 'em at once! I guess someone heard me just mentioning quietly that I didn't have any help. Thelma says she does it all, but she's usually just telling me what to do then going off to look out the window."

"But you didn't see anything?"

She looked down, hesitated, but then nodded. "I *did* see something. I saw Phil pour something into the fruit punch."

"Phil? When was he there?" Laverne asked.

"Before the party began," Sophie said, watching Gilda's face. Nana turned to stare at her, but Sophie didn't elaborate.

The woman nodded. "That's right. Thelma knew he was there, but she was off doing something, or getting ready. He didn't know I saw him, but I was peeking at him out the door of the back bathroom. Thelma is always blaming me for food missing, but I think Phil sneaks in and takes it, so I watch him every chance I get. That's when I saw him lookin' around and pouring something out of a bottle into the punch bowl."

"Did you tell the police about him being in there and what he did?" Sophie asked.

"Turn in little Philly, Thelma's grandson? Might as well slit my own throat," the woman grumbled.

"And he actually put something in the punch?" Nana asked.

Gilda nodded. "I saw it, plain as day."

"You *should* tell the police, Miss Bachman." Sophie circled to stand behind Laverne and watched the woman's face. "Did he do anything else?"

She shrugged. "Not that I saw."

It didn't seem like she was lying or being evasive. "What about the cupcakes? Who made those?" Sophie asked, sliding into a seat beside her grandmother.

"I don't know, they just appeared."

"The red-velvet cupcakes?"

Gilda nodded. "I didn't see who brought 'em. I'd bought some other cupcakes that never got put out. Got 'em at the bakery and decorated them real nice with buttercream frosting we buy by the tub."

"You picked those ones up yourself?"

"Honey, what is this about?" Nana asked, eyeing her. "Why the interest in the cupcakes?"

"Okay, this doesn't go beyond this room, but the poison was apparently in the cupcakes, the police think. Or in *one* cupcake, anyway. But the question is, what kind, and where did it come from?"

T helma sat, stoic, in the barren police cell. Torture could not break her. Not even if they pulled out her nails, or whacked the bottoms of her feet with whips. Even the tears of her only granddaughter wouldn't work.

"But Granny what were you thinking? Why did you tell the police that Francis did it?" Cissy was weeping, her lovely pale-blue eyes, so like her mother's, drowned in water.

Thelma stared at Cissy and prayed that by the grace of God Cissy would never know the pain of losing a child. Yes, the girl had lost her *mother* at sixteen and it had been a mighty blow; she'd never take that away from her. Poor Cissy, little more than a child, had wept and then gone downright sullen. It had taken months of coaxing to get her to eat almost anything at all, much less normal meals. So much work had gone into Cissy that Phil had been forgotten and had run wild. Their father was in his own fog—he took off shortly after that for the coast, and hadn't been heard from in years— and everyone else was too busy to do what was necessary except for Thelma Mae Earnshaw. She had done *everything* for her grandchildren and would never regret that.

But her choices had come with a price. While she tended to everyone else, Thelma's own bitterness at losing her daughter had grown like mold in a closet. *You don't even know it's there*, she thought, *but every day that misery gets blacker and takes up more space.* After a while even the church folk started ignoring her. She couldn't really blame them after she about bit their heads off whenever they asked how she was doing. There was no pain like the burn of losing a child at whatever age, and she hoped no one she knew ever felt it. It was like part of her heart had been amputated.

She asked the Lord to make sure that Cissy would never know the depth of the burning hole in her heart. Thelma had pictured her and Cassie, her only child, getting older together, watching Cissy and Phillip grow up, find jobs, marry and become parents themselves. They would sit on the porch dandling Cassie's grandchildren on their knees. Instead Thelma had been thrown back into the awful terror that was raising a teen—*two* teens—motherless and angry, both of 'em.

It had been a trial, one that she had not always managed well. At the same time, she had started up Belle Époque because the medical bills left after Cassie passed had been atrocious, and Thelma's pension wasn't enough to even begin to cover it all. Cassie's husband had sent a little money back east at first, but then he disappeared and Thelma was left to take care of it all. And she did. Now no one would ever come between her and her grandchildren. Phil might be what everyone called a screwup, but he was *her* screwup. And Cissy . . . she would not waste her life on a drip like Frankie Whittaker. She just knew deep in her heart that the boy was not right for her precious granddaughter, but how to tell her that? So maybe he didn't kill his mother, but who knew, after all?

Cissy was staring at her, tears streaming down her hollow cheeks, waiting for an answer to her question. Thelma opened her mouth, then closed it again. But she just couldn't stay silent. "Francis Whittaker . . . bad blood, there, you know. Are you so sure he *didn't* do it?" she finally asked her granddaughter, hoping the seeds of doubt were planted and would grow.

Laverne and Rose got Gilda calmed down and sent her back to Belle Époque. Gilda would have to close up the place and put a sign on the window that they would not be open today because of "unforeseen circumstances." That wouldn't fool anyone because word—warped by repeated telling—was surely speeding through town that crabby old

Thelma Mae Earnshaw had finally done it, gone and killed someone and gotten herself arrested. There would even be some church folks who would sniff approvingly, hoping the gossip was true. That couldn't be helped. Belle Époque would stay closed; Gilda couldn't run the place alone or at all, since she hadn't even been trusted with the keys to the cash register.

Sophie then told her grandmother and their friend what she had learned about Belinda Blenkenship.

"I did hear some kind of gossip like that," Laverne said. "That girl's auntie goes to my church, and she asked for a prayer intervention."

"What's that?"

"We all pray for the Lord to work his might on someone's life." Laverne sighed. "Too often the one asking uses it as an excuse to air their grievances. Woman last week stood up in church and asked us all to pray for her neighbor so-and-so that he might change his wicked ways and not cheat on his wife with the widow across the road."

"Good grief, that was a little pointed, wasn't it?" Nana said.

Sophie said, "So if this auntie asked for a prayer intervention for the girl, she may have revealed a little too much of what was going on in her life."

Laverne nodded. "Still . . . two months later she was marrying the mayor, so Belinda's auntie takes all the credit for getting her right with God."

Knowing Laverne, and her no-nonsense relationship with the Lord, she didn't hold with that. "So much drama right here in Gracious Grove. What about her dating Francis and supposedly being pregnant by him at some point?"

"That must have been a while before all of this," Laverne said. "That girl has never had a child, that's all I can say."

Sophie dashed off upstairs and Rose and Laverne looked at each other.

"This is not good, Rose, all of this trouble with Thelma Mae." Laverne made a noise between her teeth and took a sip of her cold tea.

"She's really gotten herself into it this time. Why did she have to call the police on Francis? She always did rush in where she oughtn't." Still, Rose had a deep well of sympathy for Thelma that she drew on constantly when the woman tried her patience. Thelma's miserable disposition had soured forever the day she lost her daughter. Rose had ached for her on that day and the many difficult ones to come after, but didn't know how to get past the frosty divide between her and her old friend. A card expressing sympathy, a sincere offer to help in any way, offerings of food: All had been brushed away with a short "Not needed."

"Who do you think really did it?" Laverne mused.

"I don't know, but Sophie's got a bee in her bonnet about trying to figure it out. She always was the kind of girl to try to solve folks' problems."

Laverne cast her a sly look over the teacup. "You did want her to get more involved in Gracious Grove doings, right? So she'd stay?"

Rose chuckled, but then became serious. "I never thought it would take a murder for her to get involved. But she's a smart girl. She's not going to interfere, I'm sure."

Laverne looked skeptical. "I don't know. That girl never could leave a problem alone. She'll worry at it like a knot until she unravels it, if I know our Sophie."

Up in her apartment Sophie dressed in what she thought of as going-out-to-the-grocery-store clothes—something a little better than yoga pants and a T-shirt—then headed back downstairs. She heard voices as she entered the kitchen and found Phil Peterson, of all people, standing by the back door talking to Laverne and Nana. She paused and watched for a moment. Phil was an acquaintance, of course, from the old days. He was one of their group, but had chummed around mostly with Francis Whittaker. It had been common knowledge among the teens that he was hung up on Dana Saunders, but that she had little time for him except when she needed a date to the prom or someone to drive her around.

His enduring legacy was a stubborn determination to

smuggle booze into Gracious Grove gatherings. He had spiked every liquid anyone drank, and by Gilda's account, even the punch for the engagement party yesterday. Why, no one knew. He was hell-bent, it seemed, on getting dry Gracious Grove very wet, and very drunk.

But that didn't make him a murderer. The poison was in the cupcake, or so Dana said the *police* said. But how did she find that out? That was something Sophie wanted to know firsthand.

"If Granny says that Francis did it, then he did it!" Phil was saying to the two women.

"But does she have any proof? Did she *see* anything?" Nana asked.

"How am I supposed to know?" Phil whined. "I wasn't there!"

"But you *were* there, just before the guests arrived," Sophie said, approaching.

Phil whirled around and watched Sophie, fear in his eyes. "I . . . no, I wasn't. Why would you say that?"

Typical Phil . . . when caught at something, deny and lie. She wasn't about to bring Gilda into it, so she said, "I saw you sneak out the back door just as the guests were arriving at the front."

He didn't meet her gaze, instead his eyes shifted back and forth, as if he was examining everything in the kitchen but her. "Grandma knew I was there. I didn't do anything. I wasn't really in the kitchen, I was just in the storeroom."

That was a lie, but she couldn't very well confront him about it without saying what Gilda saw. "What were you doing, hiding more booze? What's the story with that, Phil?"

"God, Soph, you are such a little snob! Always were."

"Enough, young man," Nana said, using her no-nonsense voice.

"It's okay, Nana," Sophie said, tilting her head and eyeing Phil. "It's not the first time I've heard that since coming back to Gracious Grove. Phil, why don't you just move to a town that's not dry, if it's so important to drink?"

He rolled his eyes. "You just don't get it. I don't give a

damn about the booze, but we need to loosen up this town, take it back from the puritans! We're young; why do we have to live like a bunch of tea-drinking old fogies?"

"Nice thing to say in a tearoom and next to your own grandmother's tearoom." She was so over Phil Peterson. So Gilda saw him spiking the punch; that didn't make any difference. It was the cupcake that killed Vivienne Whittaker, after all. "Whatever. Nana, I'm going out. May I take the SUV? And do you need anything while I'm gone?"

"Silver Spouts meeting tonight, honey. Can you pick some things up at the grocery store for me, and my special tea at the tea blender?" She handed Sophie a list, along with the keys.

"Sure." She watched Phil for a moment. Maybe he knew more than he was saying. On an impulse she said, "Can I give you a ride anywhere?"

He shoved his hands in his jeans pockets and hunched his shoulders in a defeated stance. "Yeah. To hell, because that's where I'm going, according to local busybodies."

"I'll need to fuel up for that," she said, with a slight smile. "It's a long trip, and the road there is paved with good intentions, or so I've heard."

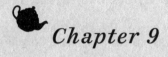

Chapter 9

Phil was sullenly silent despite several conversational attempts from Sophie until they pulled up to Peterson Books 'n Stuff. "What the hell?" he said, whirling in his seat to glare at her. "I thought you were heading downtown. I can't go in *there*!"

"Why not? It's your sister's store, and your house. Didn't your mom leave it to you both?"

"I don't live there anymore," he grumbled. "And I can't go there during business hours. Cissy banned me, and Dana always gets on my case, anyway."

"I thought you two dated once?"

"We did," he grumbled, glaring out of the SUV window. "She said I was selfish and a jerk. I said she was needy and too much like a girl."

"Did she slug you?"

He gave her a quick look. "She did."

"You deserved it. She isn't 'like' a girl, she *is* a girl . . . a woman, now."

"Well, anyway, I can't go in there. Plus, Cissy has *Francis* upstairs babying him since he lost his mommy dearest."

Just the way he said *Francis*, with a mocking tone, reminded Sophie that he and the other man had been best buddies once. To draw him out she asked, "You didn't like Vivienne Whittaker?"

"Who did? She had balls, I will say that, though. More than Francis."

Again, the way he said Francis's name revealed a level of disdain that was worrisome. "What do you mean by that?"

"Everyone in town knows that he got where he got because of his mother. She pushed him. Back in the day, when we were friends, she was always trying to get rid of me. Said I wasn't good enough for her Francis to be seen with."

"Yeah, so?" Sophie privately thought most of the parents in town felt the same way about Phil the Pill. "His mother couldn't make him *not* associate with you."

"Oh yeah? Let's just say, she *found* a way to make sure we didn't hang out anymore."

"What do you mean?"

"Never mind. I gotta go."

"But Phil . . . wait! I wanted to ask—"

Too late; he had gotten out and slammed the car door on her questions. He slouched off down the street, hoodie pulled up over his bristly hair, looking the very essence of a thug up to no good. Maybe he was fulfilling everyone's expectations. Sophie got out and entered the bookstore. Dana was on the floor shelving some children's books as Beauty rubbed up against her back. The kids' section was centered in a play area, the books on low shelves with seating areas on top. Cozy, Sophie thought, and very inviting.

"Hey, Dana. How are you?"

"Peachy keen," she said, clambering to her feet. Beauty curled around her legs, eyeing Sophie with disdain.

"Any news?" Sophie asked.

"What do you mean?"

"The investigation . . . you seem to be in the know."

"Why do you say that?" Dana asked, circling behind the cash desk and rearranging some of the bookmarks and trinkets displayed for sale on the counter. Her bangles glittered in the pin spot halogen lights.

"Otherwise how could you know that the poison that killed Vivienne Whittaker was in the cupcake she ate?"

Dana made a show of looking around, then leaned over the counter. She put one finger to her red lips. "Shhhh! Don't tell anyone, but I'm a secret agent."

Sophie laughed, as she knew she was intended to, and said, "No, really . . . how did you find out?"

"I have a friend on the force," she said, tidying a stack of books. She twirled a postcard rack that showed various scenes of Gracious Grove and the surrounding areas, including Cruickshank College, which made Sophie think of Jason.

"A male friend?" Sophie asked, setting her mind back to the problem at hand.

"Well, yeah."

"A boyfriend?"

"Not really. Not now, anyway. He's married."

Dana Saunders was the kind of woman who could get men to do things for her, Sophie thought. She had a lush, curvy figure, what had been called a *Coke-bottle figure* in another era. Today she wore turquoise capris, high heels and a filmy, white chiffon blouse with a low décolletage. A turquoise pendant dangled in her cleavage, drawing the eye. But besides all that she had a subtle charm when she chose to use it.

"Did he, this married police officer, say anything else?" Sophie asked.

"Aren't you the curious little Nancy Drew?"

"Just wondering."

Dana eyed her for a long moment, and then said, "He didn't really say anything, but I got the impression that they're investigating if Vivienne Whittaker was really the intended victim."

Sophie started . . . now *that* was an interesting question, wasn't it? It took her back to Cissy's hysterical fears; maybe she wasn't just dramatizing herself. But there were other possibilities, she supposed. Who else was at the engagement tea? Florence, Francis, Cissy, Belinda, Gretchen, Thelma and Gilda. She opened her mouth to ask Dana who the police might think was the intended victim if not Vivienne.

"And if you're going to ask me who that could be," Dana said, one hand up, "don't bother, because I don't know."

Disconcerted, Sophie said, "Uh . . . thanks for telling me that, though."

Dana sat down in the chair behind the counter and put her feet up. "Seriously, are you trying to figure out who did it?"

Beauty jumped gracefully up to her lap, and then up to the counter. The cat eyed Sophie with unblinking interest.

"Isn't everyone?"

Dana nodded, as she took a novel off the shelf behind the desk and opened it to where a bookmark held her place. "You have a point. Every single person who has come in here today has asked first thing, 'So, who do you think killed Vivienne Whittaker?' "

"Like murder mystery theater, only real. Hey, you were going to tell me more about Belinda Blenkenship, that she was pregnant and it was supposed to be Francis's baby."

"So some said, but it could well have been just a rumor."

"Laverne goes to church with her aunt and says for sure that Belinda never had a baby."

"She could have lost it, I guess. She disappeared for a couple of weeks and could have been recovering."

"Vivienne seems to have had a history of breaking up Francis's love affairs," Sophie mused, eyeing Dana.

"No comment," Dana said sourly. She fluttered the pages of her book. "Cissy got along with her just fine—I don't know how—but then, our little Cissy would be the perfect unquestioning wife for a man on the rise, wouldn't she?"

Dana looked down at her book and Sophie got the hint that the inquisition was over. "Is Cissy home? She still lives upstairs, right?"

"Yeah, she's up there. So is Francis."

"Good. Thanks, Dana."

Sophie knew she had to go back outside, down off the porch and around to the side to access the steps that ascended to Cissy's converted apartment. She climbed the wooden steps and paused at the blue door, but then knocked. To her surprise it was Florence Whittaker who answered. She stared at Sophie blankly.

"Hi, Mrs. Whittaker. I'm Sophie Taylor, Rose Freemont's granddaughter."

"Oh, yes, the Taylor girl . . . come in!" She stepped back and Sophie entered. Mrs. Whittaker looked like she hadn't slept, her sweep of dark hair in a tangle, and who could blame her? Her sister-in-law was dead and no matter how they had gotten along, it was still a shock. But as Sophie turned and regarded her, she wondered how much the two women had really disliked each other. Enough to kill? And if so, why now? Or had Florence Whittaker been the intended victim all along, and she knew it? How would that feel, if you had cheated death by so little, and someone else close to you had died in your place?

So many questions, no answers. "Is Cissy available? I'd like to see her."

"She's looking after my nephew right now. This has been such a terrible shock." Her voice was hoarse, her tone despondent.

"Aunt Flo, who is that? Is it the police? Have they found who did it?" Francis's voice sounded thick with unshed tears. A soothing murmur followed . . . Cissy, no doubt.

"No, Francis," Mrs. Whittaker called out. "It's just that Taylor girl, Sophie, here to talk to Cissy."

Cissy emerged from the next room and ran to Sophie, giving her a hug. "Oh Soph, it's so nice to see you!" She turned to Florence and said, "I just want to talk to Sophie for a minute about poor Nana. We're going to go down to the store porch. Can you get Francis a cup of coffee? And can you make him eat a few spoonfuls of soup? He hasn't touched a thing, and I'm worried."

"I'll make sure he eats, don't you worry. You run along.

That Thelma! What possessed her to tell the police that poor Francis killed his own mother? Your grandmother is her own worst enemy."

"I know, I know," Cissy murmured.

It sounded like old ground. People had probably been saying the same thing about Thelma Mae since she was a girl in pigtails, if she ever was. When they were all kids, Sophie's older brothers used to tell her that Mrs. Earnshaw had sprung up out of the earth fully formed and breathing fire. The woman's personality was such that it gave the young Sophie pause before she dismissed it as just her brothers' idiocy.

The two friends descended. When they got to the bottom of the steps, Cissy paused and took in a deep breath. She fished around in her little clutch purse for a piece of gum. "I know I shouldn't say this, but I'm so grateful to be out of there for a few minutes!"

"Don't feel bad," Sophie said. Cissy looked like she could use a break. "I saw a patisserie downtown that I really want to try while I'm in Gracious Grove. Can you come for a cup of coffee and a pastry?"

"I don't know," Cissy said, looking back up the stairs. "Francis is in a bad state. He's so upset he won't sleep, won't eat . . . I can't even get him to talk."

"It won't hurt if you come out. Maybe if you're gone for a half hour he'll sleep. His aunt looks like she can manage him."

Cissy shivered. "I'm surrounded by domineering old women."

"Come on; it'll be good for you."

"Okay, I'll go!" As they got in the car, Cissy pulled her phone out of her clutch and tapped in a message. "I just let Francis know where we're going. He's so frightened right now, afraid to let me out of his sight. But I can't stand to be watched all the time, to be hemmed in and fussed over. Grandma did that after Mom died. Drove me nuts."

"What is he scared of?" Sophie asked, backing out of the drive.

Cissy shrugged. "I don't know. I feel like he's worried about something but he won't tell me what."

Maybe he believed *he* was the intended target, Sophie thought. Or Cissy! "Did your grandmother say why she tried to turn Francis in?"

Cissy sighed. "She just kept saying he isn't the man for me, and there was bad blood there. It goes back to the old days, I think. Grandma would never set foot in a Whittaker grocery store."

"But Mrs. Whittaker is only a Whittaker by marriage."

"I know. I've given up trying to make sense of Grandma's vendettas. You know how she's treated your nana. If she can hold a grudge over sixty years . . ." She sighed. "If I didn't know better, I'd suspect *her* of poisoning Vivienne."

Sophie pulled into the municipal parking lot closest to GiGi's French Pastries.

"You'll like this place," Cissy said, climbing out of the passenger side. "I know the owner. We both belong to the Gracious Grove Businesswomen's Association."

As they stood in line waiting for their order, Cissy perked up, pointing to the far side of the bakeshop. "That's the owner over there, at that table. I'd introduce you, but it looks like she's busy."

She pointed to a mid-forties woman wearing a baker's apron who was sitting at a table with a man in a suit, far from the hustle and bustle. Sophie's eyes narrowed; she had seen that man the day before. He was one of the plainclothes police detectives who had swarmed Belle Époque. When she mentioned that to Cissy, her friend paled, but just shook her head when Sophie asked what she thought they were talking about.

As they wove back through the crowded and noisy patisserie with their plates and cups, Sophie eyed the pair. The detective was showing the woman a series of photos. It had to be about the poisoned cupcake! The police had to be trying to track down who brought the cupcakes, every last one of them! Gilda didn't seem to have a clue. Sophie's stomach turned at the memory of the yellow frosting and crushed cake on the rug, and she averted her gaze.

Once they were seated with a cappuccino and piece of mille-feuille to split, as well as a couple of hunks of baklava and a few palmiers, Sophie devoted herself first to tasting the pastries, which were delicious. The mille-feuille was flaky, the baklava intensely sweet. Cissy picked at her food and Sophie wondered if that was her usual way, or if it was because she was upset about everything that was going on.

"I am so sorry about Vivienne. That poor woman! Francis must be in shock after such a sudden loss."

"He is. I wish Granny wouldn't make things worse. Why does she always do that . . . make things worse for me?" Cissy started eating, her cheeks suffused with blotchy red and her eyes filling. She took a big bite of baklava and chewed, little flakes of phyllo dropping on the white tablecloth.

Sophie watched her for a moment, then decided just to be as matter-of-fact as possible. "What on earth possessed her to call the police and tell them Francis did it?"

"She's never wanted me to marry Francis. She says—get this—that his family is low class." She took another bite of baklava and then moistened her fingertip, picking up the flaky crumbs from her plate and licking her finger.

"Is that all she has against him?"

"What else could there be? Francis has done so well for himself. We're all really proud."

"I was surprised to hear that he had become a successful architect. He seemed headed down the same road as Phil—no offense, Cissy."

"None taken," she said. No one knew Phil's proclivity for flouting the law better than his sister. "Francis got tired of getting in trouble, his mom told me. He went to Cornell, majored in architecture, then landed a great job. Just a month ago or so he was given a huge promotion because he got an investment group that is developing a tract of land outside of GiGi to sign with Leathorne and Hedges for the architecture. Vivienne was so proud." Her voice choked with emotion. The mother's pride was now a thing of the past, and no one understood how that felt better than Cissy.

"So how did he manage such a coup?" Sophie asked.

Cissy shrugged and dipped one finger into the cappuccino foam. "I don't know. He's only told me the barest details. It's going to be a big deal!"

"What . . . are they putting a Walmart in downtown Gracious Grove?"

"Right, like that would ever happen," Cissy said, with a faint smile. "Houses? Stores? I honestly have no idea what it's all about." And couldn't care less, from her tone.

It was puzzling to Sophie that she knew so little about such a major part of her fiancé's life. Shouldn't she be passionately interested in the details?

"How did you and Francis get together?" Sophie finally asked.

Cissy took a long drink of her cappuccino and licked the foam from her upper lip. "We always knew each other, from when he and Phil used to hang out."

Sophie remembered Phil's assertion that Francis's mother made sure the buddies were split up. "Why did Phil and Francis stop hanging out with each other?"

Cissy sighed and rolled her eyes. "Long story."

Curious, Sophie said, "I've got time."

"I keep forgetting that you haven't been around GiGi for so long. It was a few years ago, when Francis was at Cornell. Phil claims that Francis and he were in business to make alcohol in his dorm room and sell it here in town. It sounds like something Phil would dream up, but Francis? *He* says it's not true and I believe him over my brother any day. So Phil had moonshine in his pickup and Wally Bowman—he was just starting with the police force then, after college—pulled him over for a traffic stop. He had a brake light out, or something dumb like that. Typical Phil. Anyway, long story short, Wally busted him. Phil *claimed* he was moving the booze for Francis."

"Could that be true?"

Cissy shook her head. "No way. You know what Phil is like . . . always in trouble. Francis had cleaned up his act and was doing well at Cornell. I always thought that Phil felt abandoned by his buddy and tried to set him up when he got caught with the booze. Anyway, the police went easy on him and charged him with just a misdemeanor. He spent thirty days in County and got off without a record."

Sophie ate the last palmier; how could she raise the possibility that Phil, angry at the family and not wanting Cissy to marry Francis, had killed Vivienne? Or maybe intended to kill Francis?

Oblivious, Cissy stared off into space. "Can you do an all-white-and-yellow theme for my bridal shower tea party?" she asked, her voice strangely thick. "Vivienne would have liked that. Yellow was her favorite color."

"You got along with Vivienne?"

Cissy nodded, one tear trickling down her cheek. "She was really kind to me."

Sophie briefly thought about what she'd learned regarding Vivienne breaking up her son's romance with Belinda Blenkenship; she must have liked Cissy a lot, to be nice to her.

"You know, just before the party yesterday she gave me a box and told me it was a special present just for me and that I should tuck it away, then open it in private. She wanted to know what I thought about it."

"Have you opened it?"

"Oh, no . . . it makes me cry just thinking about it. She wasn't supposed to give me anything until the wedding shower! She was so sweet to me."

"I'm so sorry, Cissy, really," Sophie said, putting one hand over her friend's. "We'll make sure the color scheme is yellow and white." She shuddered, remembering the yellow cupcake frosting smeared around Vivienne's mouth; how was she going to go on with that image in her head? Especially if the cupcake was indeed what killed her.

Cissy turned her hand palm up and squeezed. "I'm so glad you're home, Sophie. I don't have a lot of friends, and we always were . . . friends, I mean."

Sophie squeezed back, tears welling in her own eyes. Maybe she had underestimated what a good friend Cissy could be. "I'm glad to be home. I don't have many friends either. There was never time, in New York. I had lots of acquaintances and work buddies, but not many friends." She took a deep breath. "I feel like I've been looking for something for a long time and now that I'm back in Gracious Grove I'll find it."

There was a watery pause, and both young women sniffed and smiled at each other through the tears.

"Who do you think did this awful thing?" Cissy said, reaching into her purse for a tissue. She blew her nose daintily.

"You know everyone a lot better than I do, Cissy," Sophie protested.

"I know, but I just can't imagine it. To purposely *kill* someone? I think it was some kind of dreadful mistake."

"Maybe." How did poison *accidentally* get into a cupcake? This was no mistake, but if Cissy needed to tell herself that, then Sophie was not going to interfere.

"Can I ask you a huge favor?" Cissy asked, eyeing her across the table.

"I'll try," Sophie replied, loath to commit without knowing what she was getting herself into.

"It's about Granny; she can be a royal pain in the butt, but she means well."

"I know."

"One thing she has just been *so* upset about over the years is that your grandmother never asked her to join the Silver Spouts. It's kind of like an honor in Gracious Grove to be asked to join, you know."

"You *know* how your grandmother has always been toward Nana," Sophie said.

"But it's time those two mended their fences, don't you think?" She looked off into the distance and said, her tone sad, "Don't you think life's too short?"

"Well, yeah."

"No, I mean, life's too short to hold a grudge for so long."

"I get you." And she really did. But there was no calculat-

ing Thelma Mae Earnshaw. Cautiously, Sophie said, "I'll
see what I can do."

Cissy stood and meticulously calculated the total and tip,
and laid a ten-dollar bill down on her plate. "Vivienne's
death is tragic, and just when we were going to be happy."
Cissy paused, staring down at the table, her eyes watering
again. "I think it was just an accident."

Sophie wasn't going to argue with her. "I'll drive you
back to the bookstore."

"No, you go on with your day," Cissy said, taking in a
deep breath and letting it out slowly. She held her head high
and looked up and down the pedestrian mall as they exited
the patisserie. "I could use a little fresh air. I'd like to walk
and remember that it's spring, and I'm getting married in
four weeks!"

"And *I'm* going to make sure you have the most wonderful bridal shower tea party in the world, no matter how
Gretchen interferes. Yellow and white and pretty."

Her dark eyes twinkling, Laverne slipped back into the
kitchen of Auntie Rose's.

"Well?" Rose said, her gaze fastened on her old friend.
Laverne had gone over to Belle Époque, supposedly to help
Gilda close up.

"*Well!* I've got news." After explaining that Thelma had
been delivered home by the police, but had gone directly
upstairs to lie down, Laverne said, "There *were* some store-
bought buttercream-frosted cupcakes in the fridge at Belle
Époque, just like Gilda said."

"*Were* . . . meaning that there aren't any there now?"

"Police took them for evidence," Laverne said. "But listen
to this . . . Gilda swears up and down that when the police
took those cupcakes away, the container was full, not a
single one gone out of it."

"Which means that the poisoned cupcake was probably
brought in by whoever intended to do Vivienne in."

"*If* it was Vivienne Whittaker who was the target," Laverne said.

Rose nodded, thoughtfully. "What about the container the red-velvet cupcakes were brought in?"

"That is a good question," Laverne said, her face wrinkled in thought. "One was empty and in the garbage, according to Gilda. But there's some confusion there. The way she remembers it, the red-velvet cupcakes looked homemade, not store bought, and yet she saw one of those cheap grocery store clamshell containers with a label saying RED-VELVET CUPCAKES."

"Hmm. But we don't know who made them or who brought them."

"No, we do not," Laverne said. "Do you think it matters?"

"Well, we don't think she ate a red-velvet cupcake, right? If that's so, then whoever brought the red-velvet cupcakes probably wasn't the murderer. In any case, we'll have to find out who brought them," Rose said.

"We surely will. Anything we can dig up will help."

Chapter 10

Sophie picked up a newspaper from a box outside GiGi's French Pastries, then went back to the SUV in the parking lot across the street. She sat at the wheel and watched Cissy walk away, window shopping at the gift stores along the pedestrian mall, then glanced down at the newspaper. The headlines blared ANNEXATION PLANS IN THE WORKS FOR GG, TWO ARRESTED IN KICKBACK SCHEME and CITY TENDER PROCESS CALLED INTO QUESTION below the fold, but above it was a full half page headlined by MURDER OF LOCAL SOCIALITE CALLED "TERRIBLE TRAGEDY."

There was a huge photo attached, and Sophie was reminded that Vivienne Whittaker had been in the tearoom before her death with a gentleman . . . what did she call him? Sophie couldn't remember. But they were arguing, and she seemed upset; she said something about her son being the only important thing. Sophie read the story.

"According to reliable sources, Vivienne Whittaker, club-woman and leading light in many local charitable concerns, was poisoned at a private event at Belle Époque Inn and Tearoom." The story went on to name those at the event, and even named the poison used, cyanide, before giving a history of her life and charitable involvements.

Sophie swallowed hard and felt her throat close. Cyanide! She remembered a little chemistry and a course in geology she had taken once. Cyanide was present in nature, especially in peach pits and cassava root. It had a lot of uses, including the refinement of gold and silver. Did all that mean it was readily available?

She also remembered a court case a few years ago where a man used a cyanide "suicide" pill to kill himself right there in the court after his guilty verdict was read. He had died quickly, just like Vivienne Whittaker. Sophie sat and pondered that; could someone have stuffed a suicide pill into a cupcake? How could you be sure the right person would take the right cupcake?

Or . . . Sophie's eyes widened. Had Vivienne maybe killed herself? No. That was the last thing the woman would do at the engagement tea for her son and daughter-in-law-to-be when she had been so looking forward to having Cissy as her new family. No loving mother would *ever* do such a thing in front of her son. Thoughts in a tumult, Sophie checked her mirrors and pulled out, driving slowly through town.

As she drove she turned her thoughts away from the awful death she had witnessed and focused on the beauties of Gracious Grove. She remembered each place she passed along the way and what it meant to her: the library where she had devoured cookbooks and biographies, the public garden where she and Nana had walked and talked, marveling at the roses that were her grandmother's favorite flower, the local high school all her Gracious Grove friends had attended, and where she had longed to go. The closest she ever got was attending a few school events during vacations, a Christmas concert, an Easter festival chorus. Maybe if she had spent all her life in this town it would not affect her the same way, but having been away for a few years, she saw it with fresh eyes.

Gracious Grove was lovely, gowned in pastel trees:

cherry blossoms bursting into flower, apple blossoms a shower of white and lilacs heavy and fragrant with flowers. Every corner she turned took her to a new vista, sometimes of gracious homes and two-centuries-old stone buildings sloping down the steeper streets, and then a view of the lake in the distance, sparkling in the sun, blue sky arching in splendor above. The lake . . . she would always remember it fondly, whole days spent on its shore, swimming, picnicking, then later a bonfire and marshmallows toasted, couples drifting off hand in hand to kiss and cuddle in the dark.

She thought about Jason Murphy, and how she would always see him as he was the summer she turned sixteen. He was already tall, skinny and as brown as an acorn from being out in the sun. He drove his dad's boat around the lake with all of them yelling and whooping it up. His hair shone with golden streaks in it, and as she watched him pilot the craft she had never been happier.

Until her mother descended on Gracious Grove for one of her brief, flying visits near the end of August. Jason was going nowhere, her mother insisted. He was lazy. He didn't even work. (That wasn't true; he did work in his dad's hardware store, but his hours were flexible because Jason's parents believed that he should be a kid while he could.) He had no future plans, goals . . . did Sophie really think he would amount to anything other than taking over the family hardware store?

The battering had gotten to her, and she reluctantly accepted the reality that she was going to go off to her last year of high school, then directly to a summer of prep courses, then on to university, the same one her two brothers were attending, if she kept her grades up. When would they ever be together again? So she broke it off in a weepy, stormy scene and allowed her mother to haul her back to New York.

And now he was, of all things, an English professor! That still wouldn't be good enough for her mom because he wasn't a professor at Brown, or Harvard, or Yale. It was disconcerting how often her mother's voice was in her head, judging, commenting, criticizing. It had taken a lot for her to break away from her mother's expectations and do what she wanted, to go to cooking school and earn her degree in restaurant management.

If she hadn't let her mother pull her away from Jason, who knew what would have happened? Instead, every man she met and liked, she judged by Rosalind Freemont Taylor's exacting measures. If she ever managed to erase her mother's voice from her head, maybe she'd be able to move on in other ways than just her career aspirations.

She had to go to a tea-blending store in Butterhill, so she headed out of Gracious Grove, hoping the drive would clear her head. She had only gone a quarter mile when a huge, shiny-new signboard set in a field made her pull over and stare in surprise. That was the signboard from the photo she'd found under the table where Vivienne Whittaker and that fellow had sat. The exact one! She could tell by the background, a farmhouse and big red barn in the distance, with a set of three silos, and an old oak tree right near the sign.

Now she could see what it read: COME HOME TO LAKEVIEW ENCLAVE; HOMES OF DISTINCTION, A GATED COMMUNITY. Lakeview? Not exactly; she had driven inland from Seneca Lake, but okay. It was illustrated with photos of a smiling, pale, blond family all wearing polo shirts and riding bicycles. Builders were listed as Stanfield Homes and Hammond Construction, and the developer was listed as GG Group. According to the billboard it was going to be a planned, gated community with a retail component along the highway so home buyers would have all the conveniences.

Maybe this was the development Francis had brought to Leathorne and Hedges, the reason he got such a big promotion. But even so, why did Vivienne Whittaker have a photo of the development with her? Or . . . was it the man she was with who had dropped the photo? Either way, it was odd that the photo had even been taken. Why was it of interest? And was Vivienne really concerned about Francis's part in the development, as it seemed from her words?

Sophie started up the SUV again and pulled back onto the road. She drove on, her path taking her past Cruickshank

College. On a whim, she turned around and pulled through the stone gates and up the long, crushed-gravel drive that curved past a grove of graceful white paper birch. The vista opened out to the college building itself, made of white limestone and originally used as a home by Cruickshank, a lumber baron in the Finger Lakes region. She stopped the SUV and sat for a moment in the visitors' parking lot, watching students lolling in the spring sunshine and one professor under a huge, old chestnut tree laden with spikes of fragrant white flowers.

Was that . . . she squinted and stared through the glare of the windshield. Jason was the professor teaching his class out under the spreading chestnut tree! Just then, the kids all got up, dusted themselves off and headed toward the building, while he put his briefcase on a bench and gathered the papers he had been reading from. She got out of the truck and crossed the grass to the shade tree, and stood before him.

"Sophie!" he exclaimed, looking up from his papers.

"Jason. How are you?"

"Good! That was my Introduction to American Poetry class. I thought an outside class would keep the students awake." He smiled, but then his eyes widened. "Oh, hey, I heard you saw that terrible scene yesterday . . . Vivienne Whittaker's death. So tragic!"

She nodded but didn't answer as he clicked his case closed. After a pause, she said, "I'm kind of trying not to think about that today."

He looked stricken for a moment, then stepped over to her and pulled her into a hug. She took a deep breath and relaxed. He smelled so good! Like aftershave, but not too strong, and fresh laundry and leather. She luxuriated for a long moment, but then a silvery voice said, "Jason, we have a meeting?" Sophie looked up.

A woman stood near them, smiling; she was slim and attractive, dressed neatly in a skirt suit and holding a sheaf of papers.

"Oh, sorry!" Jason said, with a start. He held Sophie's

arm lightly, still. "Julia, this is Sophie Taylor, an old, *old* friend of mine!"

This was the part of the romantic comedy flick where Julia should say "Not too *old* a friend," with a sarcastic, jealous edge, as she grabbed Jason's other arm, but instead the woman looked completely pleasant. "Julia Dandridge," she said, striding forward, hand outstretched. "So nice to meet a friend of Jason's."

Her handshake was warm but brief, a mere clasp and release. Sophie smiled at her, wondering what her relationship was with Jason.

"I do have a departmental meeting," he said, with regret in his tone. "Julia is the English Lit department head . . . medieval literature is her specialty. It's nice to see you again, Sophie. I hope you're doing okay? I'll drop in at your grandmother's on the weekend."

"I'd like that."

Heads together, the two professors walked off, comparing notes. Sophie and he were old, *old* friends, he'd said. She wasn't going to dwell on it. Jason was her past and it was pleasant to look back on that time in her life, nothing more. She had shopping to do, a tearoom to work in and a bridal shower tea to plan.

Thelma Earnshaw stared out her window over to Auntie Rose's. They had had a steady stream of customers and a lot of them were locals, *all* of 'em taking a gander at Belle Époque as they slowly entered the tearoom next door. Darned rubberneckers. It was an outrage, but did the police take an interest and stop those people from staring? No.

She had thought she ought to stay closed so folks didn't ask awkward questions or make a big deal about someone dying after eating something at her tearoom, but darned if she didn't think that was a bad idea. She was missing out on a whole passel of customers who would love to come and gawk, and she'd make them buy tea and food, too, whatever she could scrounge up from the freezers. They might not eat it, but they'd buy it. As she usually did, she ignored whispers in her brain; this time the whispers murmured that it was unfeeling to open so soon after her granddaughter's mother-in-law-to-be died in her establishment.

She hoofed it awkwardly over to the wall phone and dialed a number. "Gilda? Get your butt up out of your easy chair and come on down to work. We're going to open, and no one can stop me. Oh, and go pick up cleaning supplies at the dollar store. Darned flatfoots left fingerprint powder everywhere."

She hung up as Gilda squawked some questions Thelma wasn't about to answer, and went back to the window. Rose would just love to lord this over her, *if* they were speaking, which they weren't. While it wasn't exactly true that they hadn't spoken at *all* in the past sixty-some-odd years, they hadn't spoken much. But it wasn't her fault that Rose had the audacity to claim she didn't know what she was doing when she stole Thelma's beau back . . . how long ago was it, actually? Let's see . . . she did some quick math, which turned into confusion. What year was it right now? Lord, it did not seem possible that she had lived past the millennium, and here it was . . . how many years later?

She got confused and gave up. The important thing was, never once had Rose apologized for stealing Harold Freemont away from her, all those years ago. Not to say she lamented marrying her own gone and regretted hubby; he was a good man and he did his best, even though his best was often second rate.

Gilda, who lived in a rooming house five doors down, slipped in the back door wearing a silly scarf and big sunglasses.

"Good lord, what kind of getup is that?" Thelma said, lathered that Gilda hadn't bothered getting the cleaning supplies she'd asked for.

"I can't believe, Thelma Mae Earnshaw, that you intend to open the tearoom up after everything," Gilda whispered, peeking out the front window. "A murder here, you being hauled off to the police! All those people . . . oh!" She fanned herself. "It gives me palpitations."

"You're not having one of those hot flashes again, are you? You're too old for that nonsense. It's all just mind over matter anyway," Thelma said.

"It's not right; it's just not right! Someone *died* out there in the tearoom!"

"But *I* didn't kill her, and by staying closed it pretty much says I did. So we're going to open for late tea. Now, get down in the cupboard and see if we have any ammonia and bleach. Gotta clean up the mess those cops made."

S ophie was surprised to see Belle Époque open for busi- ness when she got home. Nana and Laverne were busy in the tearoom, but both said they could handle it because they had Laverne's niece Cindy helping out. Cindy was just fourteen, but tall for her age, and with a big, broad gorgeous smile that folks clearly warmed to. Sophie liked the girl on sight and knew that any relative of Laverne's would be help- ful and polite, as well as sharp and quick.

She put the supplies away in the kitchen, and looked around. It wasn't quite In Fashion caliber, but the commercial-grade ovens were spotless, as was the large glass-doored fridge. The counters were clear of all clutter. At first she had thought there was little she could do at Auntie Rose's Victorian Tea House. Nana and Laverne worked together in perfect harmony after many years, so what could Sophie add?

But her mind had started wandering, as it was wont to do, and she had reimagined the tearoom without the chintz drapes and floral wallpaper. If it was her establishment, she'd get rid of all of that in favor of a simpler decor. It wasn't a matter of improving the place, just updating it. Or if Nana was still stuck on the typical tearoom look, maybe they could go in the other direction and make it more opulently shabby chic, with cabbage roses and white-painted chande- liers, aqua walls and worn white furnishings.

She stared out the window. Maybe change would be a mistake. After all, Auntie Rose's was doing great without her input. Were her ideas any good at all? Look what had happened with In Fashion; they had started out great guns, but after the first while customers had dropped off. It wasn't the food, because that was always top notch. But it took something more to beat the competition in New York, home of some of the greatest restaurants in the world. Still, they could have gotten by, giving her time to find her way, but the investors got nervous and began to pull back. It was almost as if they had wanted it to fail, because every suggestion she had for improvements and upgrades had been met with a *We can't afford that* or *There just isn't money in the budget.*

A software-designing friend had floated the idea of "planned failure" on the part of her partners. Planned failure in software design was putting flaws in a program for beta testers so they could toil through problems and see how things worked. But that was not appropriate to the business model of a restaurant, she argued. No one went into business to fail. Did they?

She awoke from her memories and looked around the kitchen. Okay, so her restaurant had failed. But she was still a darned good chef, and she had a tearoom right there. Food wasn't cheap but it didn't cost the earth, either, and she could afford to experiment a little. Nana had wanted her to get involved, so she would, starting with food. Auntie Rose's offered luncheons and tea, the usual expected light fare like finger sandwiches and salads.

But there was no reason that soups couldn't be added, and maybe even some pasta dishes. Everyone loved Italian food; maybe they could add a little Italian fare to the other more traditional English tea offerings. Why offer only what folks could make at home in ten minutes when you could give them taste challenges? She rolled up her sleeves, put a net over her abundant hair, washed her hands thoroughly and set to work. First she would make some things for the

Silver Spouts meeting that evening. It would be good to test her creations on non-customers first, to get reactions.

Then she would have some fun, really go overboard with the inventiveness, on new dishes for the tearoom lunch crowd. Zuppa Maritata, first, a traditional Italian wedding soup, and maybe a nice bread pasta for the soup, a *passatelli*. It was good to be in a kitchen again.

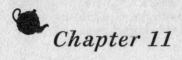

Chapter 11

The tearoom was closed, but it needed to be set up for the weekly Silver Spouts meeting, which meant rearranging the chairs and tables. Sophie did the hard work of moving tables and chairs, with her grandmother's direction. When Nana tried to help, she shooed her away.

"You've done more than enough. It's my turn to do this stuff." She stood back and eyed the arrangement, a semicircle of chairs pointing toward the servery and two tables behind the chairs with serving pieces ready for all of the treats they would eat after the meeting. "I was surprised to see Belle Époque open when I got back today."

"Thelma couldn't resist. I know they *were* going to stay closed because Laverne went over to help Gilda lock up. But Thelma came home and I guess later she called Gilda back to work."

"Mrs. Earnshaw couldn't pass up all the money from the curiosity seekers."

"Oh! Speaking of curiosity seekers . . . when Laverne went over, it was with a purpose." She told Sophie what Laverne had discovered about the cupcakes.

"So there were two *different* sets of red-velvet cupcakes?" she said.

"Sounds like it. One set homemade, one set store bought. So if we find out who brought the red-velvet cupcakes, we can eliminate them from the possible murderers."

"Why?" Sophie asked.

"If they brought red velvet, then they didn't bring another type of cupcake, right?"

"You mean because the yellow frosting on Vivienne's face was clearly not from the red-velvet cupcakes," Sophie said. "But maybe bringing red-velvet cupcakes was a cover-up."

"Oh. You could be right. You are the bright one, my Sophie!"

"But it would still be interesting to find out who brought the cupcakes, right? And we can't assume that just because the bakery clamshell said red velvet, that there were red-velvet cupcakes in it. Nor does it mean if there *were* red-velvet cupcakes in it, they were necessarily store bought."

"This is getting more complicated by the minute!" Nana exclaimed, one hand to her forehead.

"Come on, forget about it for the moment," Sophie said, taking her grandmother's arm. "Let's get changed for the meeting."

Sophie had pictured the Silver Spouts as four or five grandmotherly ladies with knitting bags, but that was not the case. Laverne had come back to Auntie Rose's and brought her niece, Cindy, with her, as well as her elderly father, Malcolm. The Hodge Seneca heritage was strong in Malcolm's face, the straight, long nose and downturned mouth giving no hint of the quiet, mild-tempered gentleman he was. Sophie greeted him affectionately—he was an old friend—with a hug he returned with surprising strength for a man in his nineties.

The rest, other than two old friends of Nana's, were strangers to Sophie.

"Sophie, come, let me introduce you to everyone," Nana said. "You know Annabelle and Helen," she said, stopping at each old friend.

They made the usual noises of welcome and Helen, the sharper of the two, asked, "We're all so pleased for Cissy, catching such a promising young man as Francis Whittaker. When will we hear wedding bells for *you*, Sophie dear?"

"You do still need someone else in your life before you can get married, right?" she asked. "Or has that changed?"

One fellow chuckled under his breath, and she eyed him with interest. He was dressed very nicely, but with an old-fashioned air. He was slim and tall, she noted, with a sports jacket and bow tie; that alone in Gracious Grove set him apart, as most men wore polo shirts and khakis, or a T-shirt and jeans. His thinning fair hair was combed back and parted in the middle, like a banker in an old photo.

"Sophie, this is a newer member of the club, Forsythe Villiers," Nana said, leading her over to the fellow, who leaned against the archway that separated the tearoom from The Tea Nook. "He just started collecting a year ago but already has a fine collection of art deco teapots. You two are sure to hit it off."

His pale-gray eyes bright with interest, he bowed over her hand. "And why is that, Mrs. Freemont, other than the obvious, that Miss Sophie is as lovely as her grandmother?"

"I collect art deco and art nouveau teapots and accessories," Sophie said, watching him place an air kiss a correct one inch above the back of her hand. It could have seemed affected but he played it naturally, so she believed the formal manners were just a part of his character. "I've actually got a couple to show the group tonight."

"We'll compare notes later, shall we?" he asked, squeezing her fingers and releasing.

"Certainly."

Next was an elderly gentleman, Horace Brubaker. He was the only member, Nana said, who had more teapots than she did. He had been collecting for a very, *very* long time. Nana then led her to a teenage boy who stood blushing and eyeing Cindy. "This young fellow is Josh Sinclair; he's Lina Sinclair's grandson. You remember Lina, Sophie. She owned the big green house three doors down when you were a teenager."

Sophie remembered Lina Sinclair quite well . . . *too* well. That woman was as crabby as Thelma Mae Earnshaw, but without the charm.

"Lina moved into assisted living almost a year ago now. Josh and his folks were cleaning up the house to sell—it still hasn't sold—and they all came here to lunch one day. He came over to help out with the yard work, got interested in teapots and started collecting! We've never had a full-fledged member this young, but Josh collects English teapots, and has a couple of rare ones!"

"Josh, hi. So . . . why teapots?" Sophie asked.

With a quick glance over at pretty green-eyed Cindy, who sat with her hands folded on her lap, watching, he swept his unruly reddish-brown hair out of his eyes and said, "My *great*-grandma gave me a teapot the last Christmas before she died. Everyone laughed—thought she was nuts . . . uh . . . senile—but I understood why she did it. She knew it would mean something to me. We used to talk about English history and I told her I was going to research the family background in England, so she gave me a teapot with the Sinclair crest on it."

"That's really interesting," Sophie said. He was so well spoken for a sixteen-year-old boy! She cocked her head and listened as he went on.

"I . . . uh . . . I write a blog on English history, and do the minutes for the Silver Spouts meetings."

"That's great!"

Nana took Sophie's arm and moved her on to the last member present that evening, a young Asian-American woman with straight, dark hair perfectly cut to shoulder length, and wearing skinny blue jeans with a patterned chiffon blouse. "And this is SuLinn Miller. She's new to Gracious Grove and new to the Silver Spouts. She collects Chinese and Japanese tea vessels."

"Where did you live before GiGi?" Sophie asked after commenting on the tea information.

"New York," she said. "My husband and I had an apartment on the Lower East Side. I loved it so much!"

"Sounds like you miss it." Sophie examined the other woman with interest; here was someone to talk to about New York!

"I really do. I've never lived in a smaller town, and it's a little hard to get used to. You know, I've actually eaten at In Fashion. I was so sad to hear it had closed!"

Sophie shrugged, but murmured a "*thank you*." That was the last thing she wanted to talk about this evening, but fortunately her grandmother called the meeting to order before she needed to respond further. Sophie took a seat by Laverne, who proceeded to gossip in her ear about each of the members.

Nana talked about a proposed bus trip to Wadmalaw Island, in the low country of South Carolina, to visit the last remaining American tea plantation. She then asked for members' opinions on an alternate trip, to Trenton, Tennessee, where the world's largest collection of teapots was housed. Many were the *veilleuses-théières* type, or night-light tea-warmer teapots, very old and very valuable. It was decided to put it to a vote during the end-of-the-month meeting, when all twenty-one members would hopefully attend. Josh took notes and promised to make up a ballot for the vote.

Laverne chattered on; Sophie learned that Josh was sweet on Cindy, whom he had met a couple of times before at meetings, but that Laverne, as much as she liked the boy, did not want them to get too friendly. Cindy was only fourteen and too young for all that "love nonsense." Cindy could hear her aunt and looked like she wanted to sink through the floor. Sophie tried to quiet her friend down, but Laverne seemed to be purposefully raising her voice just enough that Cindy heard.

Sophie changed the subject to the other Silver Spouts she had never met before. Laverne proceeded to tell her about SuLinn Miller and Forsythe Villiers.

"That SuLinn . . . she's a real nice girl, but shy, I think. Got the most amazing teapots, though! She brought a couple of them for her talk to the Silver Spouts . . . you know,

everyone who wants to join has to do a little talk. Her ma
came from Japan and taught SuLinn the tea ceremony. She's
going to show us sometime."

"What does she do here in Gracious Grove?"

"Well, now, I don't know if she does anything. They don't
have any kids yet. Her husband is an architect at Leathorne
and Hedges, the same place where Francis Whittaker works,
but I don't know if SuLinn has a job of her own. That Forsythe fellow, he works at the same place. He doesn't seem
to be friends with Francis—I asked him outright—but
they're in different departments, so maybe that just stands
to reason in a big company like that."

"What does *he* do there?" Sophie asked, trying to keep
everyone straight. It was starting to get confusing.

"He's an accountant."

Nana, who spoke about tea growing in general after pro-
posing the bus trip, had been sending them quelling looks
for a while, so they both hushed up.

It was Sophie's turn. She retrieved her two teapots from
a table behind them. "I've chosen a couple of my favorite
teapots." She talked about the metal teapot first. "You'll
notice the design . . . it's shaped like an art deco light
sconce, flared upward in a fan shape, with an oversized black
Bakelite handle and finial on top. It is highly collectible and
reasonably valuable, but still not my favorite."

She had their attention; this was good. Her nerves began
to ease. "This beauty is my favorite," she said, holding up
a teal-blue Fiestaware teapot. She gave them a brief history
of Fiesta dinnerware, the beginning of the Homer Laughlin
company in 1936 and through the various designs. "I love
the colors of Fiesta," she said. "The solids are so gorgeous—
bright and bold—and they combine utility with beauty. I
like it so much I collect and use the dinnerware!"

The Silver Spouts applauded politely, with Horace
Brubaker clearing his throat and thanking her for an infor-
mative talk, and inviting her to come see his Fiesta collection anytime. The meeting was over, Nana announced, and

the social part of the evening commenced. "I want you all to enjoy the treats this evening," Nana said, "since my granddaughter, the famous chef, made most of them!"

Sophie blushed and had to restrain herself from rolling her eyes. There must be some middle ground between her mother's resolute ignoring of her career choice and her grandmother's unwavering fawning over it. Okay, maybe fawning was a little harsh, but Nana sometimes went overboard in her praise. "I didn't do much," Sophie said, straightening her sleeves. "I visited the patisserie downtown today and made some pastries inspired by what I ate there. I baked what I'm calling Baklava Scones, sweetened with honey and studded with walnuts." She and Cindy brought out the trays of goodies while Laverne and Nana made tea, a smoky Earl Grey for some, a strong, black, orange pekoe for the others.

SuLinn approached Sophie after most had their plates and were munching enthusiastically. "You're so brave, standing up there impromptu and speaking! I find it hard to speak to groups. Just after I joined I had to bring a couple of *my* teapots to show folks and tell them what they were." Joining the Silver Spouts meant the member had to agree to display and talk about their teapot collection. "I just read off index cards. I don't think I looked up once."

"It wasn't easy for me at first. Speeches in school were awful! But I've been hardened to it. As a chef it was part of my job to go out on the floor and talk to the guests, see if they're enjoying the food."

"Yes, I remember. My husband and I had the A-Line Skirt Steak at In Fashion. You stopped by our table to ask how it was. My husband told you it was wonderful!"

A-Line Skirt Steak, so named merely to fit their fashion district theme, was a simple marinated, grilled skirt steak with caramelized onions and a balsamic reduction. Sophie sighed. "It *was* good, wasn't it? Simple is sometimes best."

Forsythe joined them and greeted SuLinn with a chaste peck on the cheek. "So, Miss Sophie, I understand you were at the heart of the excitement, the murder of Mrs. Vivienne Whittaker!"

She found his ghoulish interest a little unsettling, as she looked into his glittering gray eyes. Why did it excite him so? "I was there. It was awful."

SuLinn gave him a look and said, "It must have been. You poor thing! Did she . . . did she suffer?"

"Yes, did she?" Forsythe prodded. "I heard her tongue was protruding."

"I think we can safely assume she suffered," Sophie said, feeling ill. "Could we change the subject, please?"

"Francis was in to work for a moment today," Forsythe said. "He looked terrible. We're all getting together to send a bouquet."

"I understood you didn't know him?" Sophie said, reflecting on what Laverne had told her.

Forsythe gave her a sharp look. "That *was* true; I didn't know him except to see him, but last week we had a budget meeting concerning his coup. I had to be there to take notes for the accounting department head, who was away."

"What exactly *is* his coup?" Sophie asked.

He didn't answer, but SuLinn jumped in. "My husband says that Francis is going to be the architect for some of the model homes and maybe more in that new development. They're talking big: housing, condos, commercial, the whole thing. No one quite knows what Francis did to get the job."

"I saw the signs when I was out on the highway today. It's probably good for Gracious Grove, as long as it doesn't gut the downtown. I've heard of that happening to small towns."

Forsythe gave SuLinn a look. "No one was supposed to say anything about Francis *getting* the job. Yet. I don't know why it's such a big secret. I think that's only because there is some venom over the fact that young Francis was given such a plum assignment. Your *husband* can't be pleased."

SuLinn looked hurt, and Sophie rushed to say, "So . . . housing and commercial? Like, new stores and malls, maybe?"

Forsythe nodded. "Huge! Especially by Gracious Grove terms. The planned development spans hundreds of acres outside of town limits, but it's an area planned for annexation. The residential units already are designed with a higher density than allowed by Gracious Grove bylaws. If annexation goes through, something is going to have to change, either the plans or the bylaws."

"It depends on who is greasing whose palms," spoke a deep voice. It was Horace Brubaker, who was sitting placidly nearby.

That made Sophie think of the other headlines she had seen in the newspaper that day and the implication of a kickback scheme. She hadn't read the piece. "Do you really think there is bribery going on, Mr. Brubaker?"

His leathery face creased in a grimace. "I think wherever there is big business, there is corruption. I've lived long enough to believe that the corruption that is noticed and acted upon legally is only about ten percent of the reality."

Laverne came over just then to help the elderly man to a table where her father sat. He bowed, and tottered off to have his tea and muffins.

Sophie digested what Mr. Brubaker had said. "It's amazing they gave the design job to Francis, since he's a junior member of the company."

"Randy—that's my husband—said it's only fair Francis gets the job," SuLinn commented, giving Forsythe a look. "He's the one who snagged the development for Leathorne and Hedges."

Sophie considered that and wondered how he did it. "He brought it in, so he gets the job?"

Forsythe's brow wrinkled. "That's not how *I'd* run a company. Whoever will do the best job should get the assignment."

SuLinn shrugged. "That's the way Leathorne and Hedges works, Randy says."

"Maybe Randy is kissing up to Francis to get a piece of the action," Forsythe said, his tone dry.

SuLinn clamped her mouth shut and looked away. It was not a very polite thing to say right to the fellow's wife, Sophie thought. Forsythe had a sharp tongue but little company loyalty.

"It'll be tough for Francis to concentrate on work for a while, with his mother gone," Sophie said, to deflect the topic away from the disagreement between the two. "They were close, weren't they?"

SuLinn shrugged. "I guess. Say, I hear you're doing a bridal shower for Cissy here at Auntie Rose's; it's weird that it's not going to be at her grandmother's place."

"Not so weird if you know the history. It goes back to when we were teenagers. Cissy told me she wants it just like my Sweet Sixteen birthday party that was held here. I guess that's what the engagement tea at Belle Époque was all about, to placate Mrs. Earnshaw."

"Too bad a dead body ruined it," Forsythe said.

On that less than diplomatic remark, the conversation turned away from the topic, and SuLinn and Forsythe started talking about Leathorne and Hedges business again, but more mundane stuff than the controversial material they had been discussing. Sophie drifted over to talk to Josh. He seemed to be feeling a little out of place now that the meeting was over and the social part of the evening had commenced.

"You'll have to write down your blog name for me, so I can look it up," she said, after greeting him.

"I can give you my card," he said, pulling out a card with his name, e-mail and various social handles, as well as his blog URL. "So, is it true?" he blurted out. "Was Mrs. Earnshaw arrested?"

"No! Not at all. She just had to go and give her statement to the police, you know, like on the cop shows."

"I don't watch cop shows," he said.

"Oh. Well, that's all it was, and there was a misunderstanding with the police officer."

Josh rolled his eyes. "I'll bet. The only woman on this street crabbier than Mrs. Earnshaw used to be my grandmother. Now that Grandma has moved . . ." He trailed off and shrugged.

Sophie chuckled then sobered. "Is that the rumor that's going around? That Mrs. Earnshaw was arrested?"

"It's 'cause everyone knows how much she hated the Whittakers and didn't want Cissy marrying Francis."

"I still don't get why."

The boy shrugged again, but didn't comment.

"But surely she's not the only one who would have wanted Vivienne Whittaker gone," Sophie continued. Odd to be discussing this with a sixteen-year-old boy, but the kid was an old soul, mature beyond his years.

"It's not just her, it's her grandson, too. Everyone knows that Phil Peterson hated Mrs. Vivienne," Josh said. "He made it real clear. And the woman who works there . . . *she* had a grudge against Mrs. Whittaker, too."

"Gilda had something against Mrs. Whittaker?"

He nodded, his expression solemn. "I deliver the local paper, and one afternoon a few months ago I was coming for my pay. Miss Bachman was always the one who gave me the money. No one answered at the side door, so I went in and heard her crying. I asked her what was wrong and she told me that Mrs. Whittaker had been having tea with a charity group when Miss Bachman spilled it all down her blouse and skirt. I guess the woman had a fit and demanded Gilda be fired."

"Really? I didn't know that. Are you sure that was Mrs. *Vivienne* Whitaker?"

He nodded. "And Dana Saunders . . . do you know her? She works at the bookstore. She wasn't too fond of her, either."

"*Dana* didn't like Vivienne Whittaker? Why is that?"

"I don't know, it was some stuff from a hundred years ago about Mrs. W. breaking her and Frank Whittaker up."

How odd that Dana hadn't seen fit to mention that when she was talking about Vivienne Whittaker breaking up Francis and Belinda's romance! But it did explain why she had sounded so sour when talking about Vivienne breaking up Francis's love affairs. "How do you know all this?"

He quirked a smile. "I listen. People don't think teenage guys do, but . . . well, I do. If you're gonna be a writer, you have to listen."

He was going to be a reporter someday, or an exposé writer.

"So do you know anything about Gretchen Harcourt, or her husband, Hollis?"

But the boy's attention had drifted elsewhere by that point. Laverne was deep in a conversation with Nana and her two old friends, Helen and Annabelle, as Malcolm sat nearby sipping his tea and chatting with Horace Brubaker. Instead of answering Sophie's question, Josh took the chance to scoot over to Cindy, who was making shy eyes at him. Sophie drifted over to the foursome of older ladies who sat in a semicircle, in time to hear Helen say, "That Thelma . . . she sure is in a heap of trouble."

Nana replied, "Just because she phoned in her suspicion that Francis did something to his mother, that doesn't automatically mean she's the guilty party!"

Laverne grumbled, "I wouldn't put anything past that woman. Nothing! The hell that she puts poor Gilda through . . . it's too much!"

"But surely she wouldn't actually *hurt* anyone, would she? Not on purpose." Annabelle, a soft-spoken and timid lady who was never seen without her knitting bag, making something soft and pink or blue for one of her innumerable great-grandbabies, looked horrified at the thought. She dropped a stitch, tsk-tsked to herself, and concentrated on picking it up.

"I heard that they figured out the poison was in a cupcake, the *very* one that was made in their kitchens!" Helen interjected. "And just last week Thelma was saying the world would get along very nicely without the Whittaker family, and Vivienne in particular."

Nana, with a troubled look on her softly wrinkled face, shook her head. "I've known Thelma Mae almost my whole life. She can be cantankerous and downright impossible at times, but I have never known her to harm a soul, unless it was with a cutting word. There's no reason to think the deadly cupcake was made in their kitchen."

"Who else could have done it?" Sophie asked, thinking

aloud. "I'm not saying I think she did it, but I'm just wondering how many *other* folks could have done it."

"I wouldn't put it past Florence. Those two never did get along!" Helen said.

"Would *you* get along with the hussy who bedded your husband?" Laverne said.

"You told me that story the other day," Sophie said to Laverne. "But was it true? I mean . . . was it more than an accusation on Vivienne's part?"

"Who knows?" Nana said.

"Who knows if it's true? Vivienne accused Florence of it right there in the country club in front of all their friends!" Laverne said.

"But that was a long time ago, right?" Sophie pointed out. "What happened *after* that?"

"There was a lot of talk in Gracious Grove, I can tell you," Laverne said. "I heard that Francis Senior bought Vivienne a big diamond ring soon after, and Florence and Jackson Whittaker separated."

Helen nodded and leaned forward. "Jackson Whittaker had a terrible temper and was a drinker and gambler. It wasn't a good marriage from the start. He lost all his share of the Whittaker family money they made from the grocery stores, but they never did divorce."

Nana said, "I guess through the years and after both brothers died in that car crash the gossip has died down. Vivienne didn't cut Florence out of her family's life, anyway. You'd think she would have if the gossip was true."

"But Mrs. Earnshaw is really unhappy about Cissy marrying a Whittaker," Sophie commented. "I guess she believes all the gossip. Phil sure seems angry about Cissy marrying Francis, too."

"I was terribly troubled when I heard someone saying it must be Phillip Peterson who did it," Annabelle said. "He wasn't even there that afternoon, I said. Imagine, blaming poor Cissy's brother!"

Annabelle didn't want it to be anyone. Sophie sympathized, but if there was a murder, there was a murderer right there in sleepy, comfortable, wonderful Gracious Grove. "Why was this . . . this *person* saying it was Phil?"

"Well, it was that trouble a few years back," Helen said, trading glances with Nana. "I really shouldn't say anything."

"Are you talking about the trouble between Phil and Francis?" Sophie had both Cissy's and Phil's view of the traffic stop that resulted in Phil's legal troubles. What did others think?

"Well . . . kind of," Helen said.

"And then there was something about him damaging Vivienne's car, right?" Sophie asked.

The women exchanged looks but stayed silent. Just then Sophie heard something banging in the kitchen. She dashed back and noticed a figure silhouetted in the glass insert of the kitchen door. She looked out the sidelight and saw, standing shivering, Gretchen Harcourt. She hurried to open the door. "Gretchen! What are you doing here tonight?"

"I've been trying to call you for hours, but your phone just keeps going to message," she griped, squeezing past Sophie into the kitchen and pulling her cashmere sweater close around her shoulders. "Gosh, it's freezing out there! It's May, for heaven's sake. Supposed to be almost summer."

Sophie was tempted to say that it was May in upstate New York, so you had to expect the unexpected. It was not unheard of for there to be light snow showers in May. Where had Gretchen been living? "What can I do for you?" Sophie asked, her tone cold, not even willing to ask someone *that* rude in for a cup of tea.

The young woman stiffened and crossed her arms over her body in a combative stance. She glared at Sophie, her face pale in the fluorescent light of the kitchen, and said, "I want you to tell Cissy Peterson that you're not going to plan her bridal shower. It just isn't right! I'm the maid of honor; it's supposed to be *my* job!"

"You and I are working together on it, right?" Sophie said, slowly, taking in how angry Gretchen was. The woman's face was set in a pout. "Look, Gretchen, why is this such a big deal to you? Cissy knows what she wants, so why shouldn't I help her get it? She wants a party like my Sweet Sixteen, and you weren't even *here* then."

To her dismay Gretchen plunked down right there in the middle of the kitchen floor. "This wretched ole town! Of *course* I wasn't here then! I grew up in Tuscaloosa and I've worked durned hard to make myself over as a northerner, but y'all are so . . . just so . . . aw, *heck*! You're a bunch o' crabby, stiff-necked, know-it-all Yankees!" Then she burst into tears.

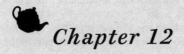 *Chapter 12*

After getting the woman calmed down and sitting at the table with a hot cup of tea in her frozen fingers—Pearl helped soothe the weeping belle, coming to the rescue with a throaty purr and comforting "body kiss"— Sophie got the whole story. Gretchen Mayweather Harcourt, daughter of the South, had been trying to fit in up North for as long as she had been married to Hollis Harcourt. That was why the country club and all its purviews were so important.

"Instead of trying to change, you should have realized that to most of us there is nothing so charming as a Southern accent. We find it disarming!" Sophie smiled across the table at her.

Gretchen hugged Pearl and sniffed. "But y'all think we're a bunch of dumb bunnies if we talk like this, dontcha?"

"Some folks, maybe. But I've met people from all over, and there isn't an accent around that indicates anything about a person other than where they're from," Sophie said, with all sincerity.

"Thank you for that! I've had a devil of a time tryin' to

change pretty much everything about me. Hollis's momma, Marva Harcourt, says I sound like a hick."

"She's rude to say that. I don't pay attention to what rude people think."

Gretchen cocked her head to one side. "Y'know, you're right."

"So we'll work on the shower together," Sophie said. "I do know what Cissy wants as far as the tea part of the shower and the colors, but you probably know a lot better than I do what to do about games and stuff like that."

Gretchen sighed heavily, the weight of the world on her narrow shoulders. "If this was one o' my friends back home, I'd know exactly what she wants. But this is different!" She ruffled Pearl's fur with agitated movements, and the elegant cat leaped down with a *mrow* of disapproval. She started grooming to right the flow of her luxurious fur. Again Gretchen sighed deeply. "Fact is, I'm not Cissy's first choice; that woulda been Dana. She'd even of preferred *you* over me, no offense."

"None taken," Sophie murmured, amused by Gretchen's blundering impolitic remarks. "So why did you agree to do it?"

"Hollis. Him'n Francis Whittaker . . . why, they're thicker'n fleas on a redbone! Francis is gonna be a big-shot businessman. He's got him a ten-year plan to make partner at Leathorne and Hedges. And my Hollis . . . he plans to be governor of New York one day. Or a senator. Or something. I don't pay too much attention when his family starts talking politics, which means I don't pay attention most of the time at family gatherings. Hollis is gonna start with a run at city council in Gracious Grove, and from there the sky's the limit!"

"He'll have to get some hidden sex scandals first, though," Sophie joked. Gretchen's face paled and Sophie realized she had gone much too far. "I was joking, Gretchen, just a stupid comment about politicians," she said, touching the other woman's arm. "I didn't mean it. I'm *so* sorry!"

Gretchen stared at her. "I swear, I do not get y'all's sense of humor. As *if*!"

"Speaking of city politics . . . you must know Belinda Blenkenship, right? The mayor's wife?"

Gretchen sniffed. "I know her." Her shortness spoke volumes.

"But you don't like her."

"In my town we woulda called her lowlife white trash. No better'n she ought to be."

"That's harsh."

"If you knew what I know . . ."

"And what is that?"

She looked conflicted, but then said, "She made a dead set at every man in this town. She only married old Blenkenship because she couldn't find anyone else to make an honest woman of her after all the messin' around she done. Hollis told me that." A sly expression settled on her face and she leaned forward, her eyes wide. "Y'all know she hated Vivienne Whitaker, right?"

Sophie nodded. "I've heard that Vivienne broke up her romance with Francis."

"Darn tootin'. She told a friend of mine that someone oughta put Vivienne out of her misery like a mad dog."

"Holy cow! That's a little pointed," Sophie replied.

With a malicious grin, Gretchen said, "That's just the kinda gal she is. Anyway, my Hollis, he's gonna be mayor someday, then move on to state politics. Far's I know."

"It's an expensive game, though, politics. Does Hollis's family have money?"

If Gretchen noticed how indelicate it was to ask about someone's financial situation, she didn't flinch. "Enough to make a splash in Gracious Grove and Ithaca. But he's gonna need more. Him and his daddy are gettin' into real estate development with some o' Papa Holly's good-ole boys. Francis is gonna be their pet architect, he says." She sighed. "It all sounds boring as heck! If I'd'a known Hollis was serious about politics, I woulda run in the other direction at the Southern Ladies' League Cotillion."

Papa Holly. Why did that name . . . ah! Sophie remembered now that Vivienne had called the older man she was sitting with *Holly*. So that must have been Hollis Harcourt Senior. And they were arguing about Francis's involvement in something, and now she found that Mr. Harcourt and his son were involved in the development that Francis was head architect on. Interesting. Gretchen had been at the engagement tea, but she couldn't have had anything to do with the poisoning. Could she?

"Does Mr. Harcourt know Vivienne Whittaker?" she said, fishing for more information.

"Well, sure. They all belong to the country club, you know."

"Did they have any business together? Or was there anything between Mr. Harcourt and Francis Whittaker?"

Gretchen stared at her. "I do not have a clue what y'all are talkin' about!"

From the lessening babble of voices in the tearoom, it seemed that the tea was winding down, but Laverne and Nana could handle it. Cindy and Laverne had already pledged to stay a few minutes after the meeting to tidy up. Sophie was interested in Gretchen's take on the tragedy, and curious about one more thing. "After the tragedy, when you all were corralled here in the tearoom, I saw you texting someone while we were waiting for the police to interview us. Who were you texting, if you don't mind me asking?"

"Hollis, of course. I just wanted him to know I might be late."

It seemed like she was texting a lot more than that, but Gretchen seemed suddenly evasive, so Sophie left it alone for the moment. "What exactly happened, anyway? I haven't been able to get an independent view of the tea."

Gretchen rolled her eyes. "It was boring, then it was awful. Old women are the most hateful . . ." She trailed off as Nana came into the kitchen.

"Well hello, Gretchen. How are you doing, dear?" she asked, as she put a pitcher of milk back in the glass-doored refrigerator.

"I'm very well, ma'am, thank you. And how are you

holding up?" Her Southern accent was gone, erased by careful diction.

"I'm fine." Nana paused on the threshold, and glanced back and forth between the two of them. "I'll just be in the tearoom with Laverne. A couple of the others will be coming through the kitchen and out the back door, Sophie, since they parked in back."

"Okay. Do you need any help?"

"We're fine. Josh is staying to help . . . the lure of Cindy, I think."

"I'm sure it didn't take that. He's a nice kid with good manners," Sophie commented.

"That he is."

At that moment Forsythe Villiers came through the door. He stopped as he caught sight of Gretchen. "Mrs. Harcourt, how divine to see you again!"

Gretchen flipped her long hair back. "Why, hello there, Mr. Villiers. Fancy seeing you here. And how are *you* doing this fine evening?" There was a flirtatious note in her voice.

"How do you two know each other?" Sophie asked.

"Mr. Villiers is a member of the country club, of course," she said, all of the snobby brittleness back in her tone.

"When I moved here, my family insisted. And we are well connected in other social ways, are we not?" He dropped a wink. "Good evening, Sophie," he continued, "and as for you, Mrs. Harcourt, I'll see *you* online."

Sophie felt like an outsider in her own home, with undercurrents between the two visitors that she didn't understand. Good-ole Southern gal or country club snob: Which was the real Gretchen?

"You were saying that old women were the most hateful . . . and then you had to stop. Were you talking about the Mrs. Whittakers?"

"Who else? I know y'all aren't supposed to speak ill of the dead, but my granny said if that was so, and we couldn't be nasty to one another when we're alive, where did that leave us?"

"True. Were the Whittakers behaving badly?"

"Just some sniping back and forth."

"About what?"

Gretchen shrugged. "I dunno. Something about money."

"Try to remember; what exactly was said?"

"I tell you, I don't *recall*! And then Mrs. Vivienne was asking what was in everything, putting up her nose like there was a funny smell in the room and she wasn't sure which of us dealt it."

Sophie snickered, surprised that the old *he who smelt it dealt it* rhyme from childhood had come back in such a strange guise. She sobered, though, and asked, "What did you all eat? What was there?"

Gretchen wrinkled her nose. "Why?" Sophie was silent for a moment, and Gretchen's expression changed. She bounced up and down in her chair. "Oh! Are y'all snoopin'? Tryin' to figure out whodunit?" Her eyes sparkled.

"Do I look like the kind of person who would do that?" Sophie asked, rather than answering directly.

Gretchen sighed. "Nah, I guess not. Sure would be a hoot, though, right? I mean, putting one over on that dumb ole Wally Bowman."

"You think Wally is dumb?" Sophie was surprised. She knew Wally from way back, and he was quiet but smart. It was easy to underestimate his kind of intelligence, though, Sophie supposed.

"Dumb as a box o' rocks. Why, any idiot can see that he's holdin' a candle bright as day for Cissy, but does he say anything? Nope. Suffers in silence instead. I just hate that *let the better man win* crap. Who says Francis is the better man?"

Gretchen's take on the dynamic between Wally and Cissy shocked Sophie. "Wally and Cissy? *Really?*" Maybe Sophie hadn't been back in Gracious Grove long enough, nor had she been looking for the signs.

"Yeah." Gretchen tilted her head to one side, her eyes holding a far-off look. "I know I just said Wally's dumb, but still . . . it's romantic, don't you think? My daddy used to sing a song to Momma . . . 'Young love, first love,'" she warbled.

"But Wally wasn't her first love. Was he?"

Gretchen gave her a look. "Boy oh boy, it's true, then. You really were full of yourself as a kid and clueless about anyone else. That's what Dana told me, but I didn't believe her."

Sophie didn't have an answer. None of *them* would ever realize it, of course, but Sophie had seemed so self-absorbed because she was working hard at fitting in, in Gracious Grove. "Every teenager in the world is self-centered," she finally said.

Gretchen thought about it and said, "I think you're prob'ly mostly right."

"So Wally was Cissy's first love?"

"Yup. And I don't think he's ever gotten over her."

Learn something new every day, Sophie thought. But back to the matter at hand . . . "I was asking about what was served at the tea party."

"Oh, yeah!" Gretchen wrinkled her nose. "Nothing worth eatin', that's my answer. Sandwiches. A whole bunch of 'em! Dry, tasteless . . . worse than I've ever had. Some filling that came out of a can. There were cookies. Biscuits, only they call 'em scones, another name for dry wedges of tasteless dough."

"And cupcakes, right?"

"Yup. Red velvet."

"*Only* red velvet?" Sophie asked, remembering the vanilla yellow-frosted cupcake Vivienne had eaten.

"Far as I know," Gretchen said, eyeing her. "Why do you wanna know?"

Sophie shook her head. She pondered what her grandmother had told her that Laverne discovered over at Belle Époque, about the commercial clamshell container with RED-VELVET CUPCAKES printed on it, against the woman's assertion that the cupcakes had looked homemade. Gilda wasn't the sharpest knife in the drawer, but she wasn't so out of it that she didn't know homemade from store bought. "You said Vivienne was asking what was in everything. Did it seem like she was suspicious of what had been put in her cupcake? I mean . . . did it seem like she was worried that someone was trying to poison her?"

"Gosh, of course not!" Gretchen picked up her cup and stared into it, then set it back down on the table. "She was . . . just being careful of her allergies. I'm like that. I can't eat shrimp, and folks put shrimp in the darnedest things. This one time—"

"Did she say what she was allergic to?" Sophie took Gretchen's mug over to the teapot, refilling it and setting it down in front of her as the girl answered.

"Well, no."

It didn't really matter, Sophie supposed, since it wasn't an allergic reaction that had killed her.

Gretchen took a sip of tea but set the cup aside. "I don't really even like tea. I drink it 'cause I have to, but . . . I think I'd best get going," she said, standing abruptly.

"There was something I wanted to ask you; why did you want to move the wedding shower to the country club?"

"That was my mother-in-law's idea."

"Why did *she* want it moved?"

"I don't know. Y'all will have to ask her."

Just then Josh Sinclair came through the door to the kitchen followed by SuLinn Miller. "Don't worry about it, Josh," she was saying. She patted his shoulder. "It'll all be okay."

"What's wrong?" Sophie asked.

Josh shook his head and stumbled out the back door, mortification expressed in his hunched shoulders and beet-red face. SuLinn stayed behind for a moment, though, and whispered, "He asked Cindy out to a movie. She said 'yes' but her aunt said 'no' in the most ferocious manner! She then told him that Cindy was only fourteen and wouldn't be going out any time in the near future. Poor Josh . . . he thought she was older."

Ah, the heartache of teenagehood. It came back to her in that moment, the longing looks young Wally Bowman used to cast toward pale, pretty Cissy Peterson. How could

Sophie have been so blind? But surely teen infatuation didn't last a decade or more, judging by Jason Murphy's measured response to *her.*

"Poor kid," Gretchen said, referring to Josh.

"I'm giving him a ride home," SuLinn said. "So I'd better move! I don't think he's in any mood to hang around."

SuLinn stood aside as Làverne and her gang came through the kitchen, her hand on her niece's shoulder. Laverne was ferrying the two older ladies home, as well as Cindy, who looked a little put out. Thinking back to being that age, Sophie realized how flattering it would be for a fourteen-year-old girl to have a sixteen-year-old boy ask you out. And then to be outed by your great aunt for being so young! Mr. Malcolm Hodge followed them out slowly, taking his time with the aid of a carved mahogany cane, nodding to each lady as he passed.

"I gotta . . . uh, have got to get going, too," Gretchen said, heading toward the back door. "I'll talk to you tomorrow, Sophie, and we'll coordinate details for the wedding shower. Will you come to Cissy Peterson's shower, SuLinn?"

The woman flushed, her olive skin burnishing with a hint of coral on her cheeks. "I'd love to! Is she listed anywhere?"

"Yes, of course," Gretchen said, slipping on her mantle of Yankee stiffness. "I can tell you where. Give me a call; Forsythe has my telephone number. Or check me out online. Cissy and Francis have a wedding site and registry link on The Knot, with a page for the shower details that I'm going to update as soon as we firm things up." She was all business.

Sophie felt a little left out; so *that* was how a girl was supposed to react when she heard about a shower, asking where the bride-to-be was listed? She had never been asked to be a bridesmaid and had only rarely even been asked to a wedding. The last five or six years had been spent with her nose to the grindstone, working so hard to get and keep In Fashion afloat that she rarely came up for air and went home every night to a cold apartment and no messages on her phone.

Sometimes she got wedding invitations in the mail, but

she sent back "no" to them all, preferring to mail a check as a gift. Before that, school had consumed her, with part-time catering jobs and restaurant positions fit in between. Well, that was what coming home to Gracious Grove was supposed to be about, figuring out how she wanted to live the next decade or so of her life.

Once everyone had gone and she had sent Nana up to bed once again with a cup of tea, a purring Pearl and a good mystery novel, Sophie restlessly moved around the tearoom, putting things to rights. Most of it had been done, but it wasn't quite the way she thought it should be. She had done the same at In Fashion, drifting through the dining room after the cleaners and waitstaff were gone, putting things exactly as she wanted them.

Then she settled in the front window, pulled back the curtain and gazed out on the deserted street. Why did it feel like nothing here was the same as it used to be? Had she been gone too long, or was she coming back to it all with different eyes? She was seeing it now, her beloved idyllic summer retreat, with an adult's clear gaze.

The last time she had spent longer than a few days in Gracious Grove she was just seventeen. She had graduated from high school and come to spend the summer, as usual, with Nana. But the old gang had broken up, or maybe she just wasn't a part of it anymore. Cissy had a job at a youth camp on the lake and Jason had left town. She'd heard that after hitchhiking around Europe for a year he joined the army, but some medical condition forced him to leave. He then went to college, got his undergrad degree, then his master's, and became an English professor.

Her separation from all things Gracious Grove saddened her. It was the one place on Earth—other than New York as a whole—where she felt at home. As evening crept up Seneca Street, she decided that so far she had been coasting along, just thinking ahead a few weeks or a month at a time. But she missed having a commitment to something. She needed to figure out if what she had been missing all these years was this town, her true home, Gracious Grove.

Vivienne Whittaker's murder was a dark cloud over everything right now, though. The poor woman had died just feet away from where Sophie stood; it was unnerving to imagine someone creeping around in Belle Époque planning the heinous deed. And worse to think Sophie had looked into the face of a killer, perhaps, and hadn't even known it. Wouldn't that kind of evil show in someone's expression, in their eyes? It *had* to, surely. But maybe that was naive.

One thing she knew for sure: In the last hour she had come to a couple of momentous decisions. She was staying in Gracious Grove for as long as she wanted; no time limits, no restrictions of *any* kind, no matter what her mother said. And she was truly going to try to find out, from her outsider's perspective, who murdered Vivienne Whittaker.

Chapter 13

The next morning she descended to the tea-room kitchen to find Nana and Laverne yakking over a cup of tea as they had almost every morning for umpteen years. Here was the rock-solid foundation she had craved in her own home but never gotten, and so appreciated when she visited her grandmother. If she could go back and change things, Sophie would insist that she be allowed to spend her senior year living with Nana and going to GiGi High as she had secretly wanted, and she wouldn't have broken up with Jason Murphy.

However, though she couldn't go back, she *could* start fresh. "Good morning," she chirped, then dropped a kiss on each cheek, relishing the softness of aging skin.

Nana and Laverne exchanged a look.

"Well, aren't we the bright little birdie this morning?" Laverne said.

"I've decided that for the foreseeable future, I'm staying in Gracious Grove."

Nana and Laverne again shared a look. "Do you mean that was in question before now?" Nana asked.

Sophie realized she had stepped wrong. She didn't want to hurt her grandmother's feelings. Pouring a cup of coffee from the carafe on the counter, she turned and carefully said, "Well, I *knew* I was staying for a while, but I wasn't sure how long. Then I looked around last night and said to myself, 'Where else would I rather be?' So here I am!" She hugged both women, being careful not to spill, then she went for a walk, coffee cup in hand. The morning seemed bright and shiny and full of promise until she looked over at Belle Époque, and felt the dark blight on the town that was the murder of Vivienne Whittaker. It needed to be solved, the sooner the better.

As she walked uphill past Belle Époque toward the old cemetery, she contemplated the awful event. It would take a lot of desperation to kill someone. In the first black days after the investors had told her they were folding In Fashion, she had certainly *felt* like killing someone. But if she was ever going to do it, no matter how angry she was, it sure wouldn't be in a public place in such a public manner.

What kind of person killed someone the way Vivienne had been done in? You'd have to have nerves of steel to plant a poison cupcake. You'd have to not really care if the plan fell through and someone else died instead. You'd have to be desperate. Find someone with all those qualities and you might just catch a murderer. Or you could do it the old-fashioned way and follow the clues: who bought poison, who procured or baked the poison cupcake, that kind of thing. That, however, was the province of the police. The amateur had to ask questions, make surmises, test theories.

When she returned to the kitchen of Auntie Rose's, a depressed-looking Wally Bowman sat with Laverne, his large, square hands wrapped around a mug of coffee. "What's up, Wally?" She sat down opposite him as Laverne excused herself to go help in the tearoom.

"This whole thing is driving me crazy," he admitted, looking up at Sophie. "Why did Mrs. Earnshaw have to make such a muck of things? Why'd she call the station and say that Francis killed his mom?"

"I was wondering the same thing," Sophie said. She hesitated; was she talking to Wally her old pal, or Officer Bowman? "I'm worried about how it's affecting Cissy, too. She loves her grandmother, even if the woman is difficult."

Wally's cheeks pinked but he stayed silent, gloomily staring down into his cup.

"So you and Francis are cousins, right? Did you spend a lot of time together growing up?"

"Technically we're not cousins. Aunt Flo is my dad's sister, and Francis is Vivienne Whittaker's son, so there's no blood relation."

"But did you spend any time together as kids?"

"Just like anyone else going to the same school. Not a whole lot. But I sure do feel for him right now, losing his mother like he did, right in front of him. He's really broken up over it."

Sophie was silent for a moment. "I'm surprised they haven't made an arrest yet," she finally commented, watching him. "I would think that there were a very limited number of people who could have tampered with the cupcakes."

"How did you know the poison was in the cupcake?" he asked, then clamped his mouth shut.

"You know this town, Wally," she chided. "You can't keep anything a secret in Gracious Grove. I hope Detective Morris knows that."

"Probably does. She may be an outsider, but she's good at her job," he admitted grudgingly. "She busted a theft ring last year when one of the fences ended up dead in an alleyway behind those shops in the middle of town. The murderer already pled guilty and is in prison."

"This is a different kind of murder, though, isn't it?"

"What do you mean?"

She thought for a moment. "Well, a murder that happens as a part of a crime ring . . . that leaves traces among the criminal elements, such as they are in a town like this. But this is a murder among friends and relatives. Or rather, among frenemies."

"Frenemies," he said, rolling the world around on his tongue like wine. "You talking about that old stuff between Aunt Flo and Vivienne Whittaker?"

"I keep hearing about it."

He shrugged. "It's old history, isn't it?"

Was it, though? Some wounds dug deep and left a mark forever. She pondered everything she had learned recently, but realized it may have sounded like she was implying that Florence Whittaker was involved. "How *is* your aunt?"

"She's taking it hard. People think they were enemies, but she told me once that Vivienne was good folk. Said she'd bailed her out of a sticky financial situation, and Aunt Flo appreciated it. She wasn't left much money when her husband died."

"I've heard that Mrs. Vivienne got the responsible Whittaker, the one who didn't squander his money."

"Aunt Flo feels . . ." He shook his head and shrugged.

"Bereft?"

"Yeah. That's the word."

"It's got to be tough for Francis, so much good stuff happening, with the new development and his promotion, and then his mom is murdered."

"I heard he got a promotion. Good for him!" Wally said, with a smile that swiftly died. "We'll find out who killed his mother, then he can move on, get past it. He's got lots of great stuff to look forward to other than just work."

There was an edge to Wally's tone. Sophie watched his face, the resolute line of his jaw, the sadness in his eyes. "You mean getting married to Cissy."

His jaw flexed. "Yeah, that." He moved the coffee mug around in circles, watching the liquid slosh over the edge.

So what she had heard from Gretchen was true, he was still pining for Cissy. The big dummy. Why didn't he say something to her? Sophie sighed. After being out of the social scene of Gracious Grove for so many years, it was not up to her to correct the path of true love, and Cissy seemed to be content to marry Francis. If she felt anything at all for Wally, it was not evident to Sophie. "I don't know how it will go on. The wedding is supposed to be in just a month or so, right?"

"Four weeks and three days," Wally croaked.

"A murder investigation in the middle of it isn't going to help. Some folks think that maybe Vivienne wasn't the intended victim, that maybe Francis or Florence was."

He glanced at her, thick brows knit in thought. "I don't think so. Why would someone want to kill either one of them?"

"But why Vivienne, then? Who would want to kill *her*?"

He was silent, his expression blanking to one of professional neutrality.

"Look, I know you can't talk about official police business, but I already know a lot of this stuff, so there's no harm in telling me. You *know* I don't talk to anyone! Have you tracked down the origin of all the cupcakes?"

"I don't know, Sophie. I shouldn't even be talking to you about this."

"I know. But Wally, I promise it won't go any further than me. And Nana and Laverne. I *promise*!" She crossed her heart, like they had as kids.

He took in a deep breath and let it out, eyeing her. "Okay. We've interviewed the bakeshop owner, but she didn't know anything, didn't recognize any of the photos she was shown, other than just knowing they were locals who may have been into her shop," Wally admitted.

"I know they found a container that was labeled RED-VELVET CUPCAKES, but if it was labeled, it was probably from the grocery store."

"Yup. The old Whittaker Groceries, now Triple G."

"It's been sold a couple of times since the Whittakers owned it, right?"

"Yeah. It's some locals who bought it this time, I hear. But the detective says we have to keep an open mind, that just because the container says it came from the grocery store it doesn't mean the cupcakes in it were the original ones."

Exactly what she had thought. "And we know the cupcake that killed Vivienne was not a red-velvet cupcake anyway because of the color of the frosting right?" He nodded. Sophie's wandering thoughts caught on another troubling problem. "Wally, I keep hearing that there is something fishy about this promotion Francis got. Do you know anything about that?"

He put his palms flat on the table and shook his head. "Far as I know there's nothing fishy about it, just business as usual. Florence Whittaker knows folks in the building industry, so she pulled a few strings behind the scenes with those folks—"

"Folks like Stanfield Homes and Hammond Construction?"

"Yeah, I guess. When the contract for the model homes was given to Leathorne and Hedges, Frankie got credit and the promotion."

Put that way it seemed clear cut enough. Happened all the time in business; it was *you scratch my back, I'll scratch yours.* It certainly didn't have anything to do with the murder at Belle Époque. Or at least . . . if she hadn't overheard that quarrel between Vivienne Whittaker and Holly Harcourt, she'd be able to dismiss it. A few things began to come together in her mind, but nothing she wanted to share. In fact, nothing that even made any kind of coherent sense yet.

Holly Harcourt and others were going into the "development business" to fund Hollis Junior's political ambition. Was that the development just outside of town? Must be. Florence Whittaker had helped Francis get the promotion at Leathorne and Hedges. Vivienne Whittaker was upset about something to do with Francis, and she was talking to Hollis Senior about it. Gretchen Harcourt was at the tea where Vivienne had died. So was Belinda Blenkenship, whose husband, the mayor, had been mentioned a lot lately. It was a jumbled mess in her brain.

"I'm worried for Mrs. Earnshaw," she said, suddenly. "What was she thinking, calling and throwing Francis under the bus like that?"

He relaxed, just plain Wally Bowman for a moment. "I know, right? She's a piece of work; always was. Detective Morris said maybe *she* accidentally did it, and is trying to cover up."

"Mrs. Earnshaw? Detective Morris doesn't actually think that, does she?"

"I *think* she was joking. It's hard to tell with her. She's got kind of a dry sense of humor." He drained his coffee cup. "Poor Cissy. She's more worried for her grandmother than for Francis."

"Well, some of the food was made in Thelma's kitchen, and there were accusations flying around Nana's tearoom after the whole awful event. I heard them! Mrs. Whittaker and even Gilda were blaming Mrs. Earnshaw, but that was before anyone knew it was deliberate poisoning."

Wally nodded, his brows knit.

"I guess, though . . . I mean, it had to be someone who had access to the kitchen, and that kind of limits the field to those few people," Sophie said, struggling to explain what she meant. "If Vivienne was the intended victim, then it was likely someone who was at the tea that afternoon."

He nodded again, watching her eyes. "I can't officially say, but that makes sense. Go on."

"If she was *not* the intended victim, then the real intended murderee had to be there, too."

He frowned. "Yeah, of course. What are you saying?"

She paused, lining up the salt and pepper shakers on the table, as she ordered her thoughts. "Just that I guess we can't focus *only* on people who may have wanted Vivienne Whittaker dead. What if it was a misfire? Then the murderer could be someone who had no beef with Vivienne, but was trying to kill someone else." She frowned and shook her head. "I don't know. I'm just thinking out loud."

"The old saying in police work is, *Look around the victim to find the killer*, you know?"

"Of course. I'm just worried and afraid for everyone. If Vivienne wasn't the one they meant to kill, then whoever it was is still in danger." Silence fell. Wally was clearly not going to discuss his own suspicions or feelings. He was a police officer, after all. On to something else, then. She paused, watching his face, then said, "Do you ever think about the old days, Wally?"

"You mean when we were teenagers? Sure, all the time."

"If you could go back, would you do anything differently?"

"What do you mean?"

She searched his eyes, wondering if it was true that he still loved Cissy. Maybe it was just a lingering softness toward her, a kind of affection. "Is there anything you would do differently, about *anything*? Life, work, school . . . love . . . anything at all."

"No one gets through life without regrets, right? I wish I'd done better in school and police college so I could take the detective's test right now instead of having to upgrade. I'm doing correspondence courses to bring up my grade average from college." His smile died, as he added, "I sure would like to be the one who busts whoever killed Mrs. Whittaker. For Cissy's sake. And Francis's, of course. Look, I gotta go. It's been nice talking to you."

"Okay. Be careful out there."

"Sure, 'cause the mean streets of Gracious Grove are so darned dangerous." He was being facetious.

"But someone has killed, and once that happens . . ." She shuddered, as it passed through her, the chill of knowing that someone she had met was a killer. Maybe even someone she knew very well.

As Wally left, Nana entered the kitchen and put the kettle on the stove. "I need a cup of tea. I'm kind of tired today. Did you and Wally have a nice visit, honey? I saw him leave."

"Yes," she said, absently. "Nana, who do *you* think killed Vivienne Whittaker? You must have an opinion."

"Oh, must I?" She sat down opposite her granddaughter. "I just can't credit that any one of those folks would set out to poison someone. Did it have to be someone at the party?"

"Well, not necessarily, I suppose. But if you were going to

kill someone that way, you'd want to be there to make sure it went according to plan, right? I'm assuming that only one cupcake was poisoned. No one would risk killing a whole party of folks with random poisoned cupcakes, and no one else keeled over, even though some of the cupcakes were eaten."

"Even if you were there it wouldn't be easy," Nana said. "How would you make sure, if you only had one poisoned cupcake, that the right person got it?"

"But *did* the right person get it? Or did the wrong person die? Is there a killer out there even now plotting to knock off the person they originally intended? I just can't get that thought out of my head."

"Honey, if Vivienne died, isn't it likely that she's the one they intended to die?"

"I know you're right. That's what Wally said. Okay, so going back to your question, how would I make sure the right person got the one poisoned cupcake? Well, I'd be the one to hand it to her."

Nana nodded thoughtfully as the kettle whistled. She poured the steaming water in the teapot and clapped the lid on, then sat down in Wally's vacated chair. "That's the best way to be sure, I guess. But what if people remembered that? Wouldn't it be risky to be the one who poisoned the cupcake *and* passed it to Vivienne?"

"How else could you be sure she got the right one? Unless . . ." Sophie's brain finally kicked into gear. "Of course! Nana, if you made up a plate of cupcakes and wanted to be sure I picked a certain one, what would you do?"

The older woman considered the question for a moment. Her lined brow furrowed in thought. "For *you*? I'd make sure only one was chocolate. You love chocolate, so you'd probably pick that one."

"Right!" She paused and thought some more. "There's another way, though; if you wanted to be sure I didn't pick any other, you could be even more certain if *every other cupcake had coconut on it*," she said, leaning forward and emphasizing each word by tapping on the table.

Nana's bright blue eyes widened. "Of course, because you don't like coconut."

Sophie nodded. "I loathe coconut *on* things. Don't so much mind it *in* things, but I hate it just sprinkled over the top of something. So if there was a plate full of cupcakes, and only one did *not* have coconut, I would be sure to pick that one."

"Honey, I think you've got something there," Nana said, her eyes sparkling with excitement. "You should tell the police."

"Oh, right, go to the detective and say I have a way to break the case?" Sophie snorted in laughter. "I'm sure they've already thought of this. And it doesn't really prove anything. Maybe they already know who did it and are just waiting for forensic evidence, or something." Sophie got up and made her grandmother a cup of tea and set it down in front of her.

"Thanks, honey. It would be interesting to know if Vivienne had strong preferences, though. Did you notice anything about the cupcakes when you were over there?"

Sophie shuddered. "I don't think I'll ever be able to look at yellow frosting the same way again, after seeing it smeared all over Vivienne's face."

"Okay, so she was eating one with yellow icing?"

Sophie nodded. "A vanilla cupcake with yellow frosting, judging by the smooshed remains on the floor. And the other ones on the platter—the ones that were left—were all red-velvet cupcakes."

"So . . . maybe she didn't like red-velvet cupcakes."

"Interesting idea. Kind of weak, though." She looked over at her grandmother, who sipped her tea and sighed in contentment. "How do I find out Vivienne Whittaker's preferences?"

"I'd say ask Francis or Florence."

Sophie nodded. "You're right. Maybe I should talk to them before I worry the police about any of this. I might be barking up the wrong tree."

* * *

With her new goal in mind—helping however she could to figure out who had tainted the lives of people she cared about—Sophie raced upstairs and called Cissy. Pearl jumped up on her lap as she leaned back in one of the cushy chairs and waited as the phone rang.

"Hello?" Cissy sounded out of breath.

"Cissy, it's Sophie. I hope I haven't caught you at a bad time." Dumb thing to say. Her fiancé's mother had been murdered; could there be a good time?

"No, it's fine."

It occurred to Sophie in that moment how difficult Cissy's path was, and that she'd had little or no help lately, especially with a grandmother as nutty as Thelma Mae Earnshaw. On impulse, she said, "I was just wondering, can I do anything? More than just with the shower, I mean. But now that I've mentioned it . . . do you still want that to go off as scheduled?"

"Why not?" she said. "Francis still wants to have the wedding, so yes, the shower is on."

"But can I help you out in any other way? You're dealing with so much right now."

She hesitated. "I need to go to Ithaca for a couple of hours; there's a mix-up with a book shipment. Could you come over and sit with Francis? Florence went down to the police station to ask about any breaks in the case—she's desperate for them to solve this—and I hate leaving Francis alone right now. He's distraught."

"I'll be there in fifteen minutes." It was the least she could do.

"Would you? Thank you so much, Sophie! I really appreciate it."

Feeling a little guilty because what she really wanted was information, Sophie said, "Don't mention it."

"No, I *really* appreciate it. I don't have anyone else I can ask. Dana would, but I need her in the store. And Gretchen . . ." She fell silent.

"She's not so bad, you know," Sophie said. "I talked to her last night and it seems like she's just trying too hard to fit in."

Cissy said, "So she got to you with her *ah'm just a sweet Southern belle among all o' y'all nasty-ole Yankees* routine, did she?" Her mimicry of Gretchen's Southern drawl was perfect.

Taken aback, Sophie stammered, "Yeah, I guess maybe she did. She came to our door last night all upset."

"Let me guess: She was mad that I asked you to help with the shower. Sophie, I believed her sweetness and light routine the first time I heard it, too. Then after I heard her trash-talking me to some of her country club friends, I decided I'd keep her at arm's length. I'm only nice to her for Francis's sake and because of his friendship with Hollis."

"I was taken in, hook, line and sinker," Sophie admitted. "I thought maybe we could work together after all."

"Don't let it stop you from working her over to get what I want for the shower, but don't be suckered in and end up doing everything yourself."

Cissy actually sounded much more focused today than Sophie had ever heard her, and Sophie was grateful. Tragedy had that sharpening effect on some people, Sophie had observed before. "I'll be right over."

Ten minutes later she parked her grandmother's SUV behind the bookstore and trotted up the steps to Cissy's upstairs apartment. She didn't even have a chance to knock on the door before Cissy pulled it open, as she tugged on a Windbreaker and grabbed her purse.

"Cissy!" Francis yelled from somewhere in the depths of the apartment. "Will you be gone long? What if I need something? Where are you going?"

Cissy rolled her eyes and disappeared back into the apartment. Sophie entered and listened to the indistinct soothing murmur of Cissy's voice in what must be a bedroom, since she could see the empty living room from the kitchen. Arriving like this felt almost like the babysitting assignments she'd had as a teenager during the summer in Gracious

Grove. She'd arrive just as the parent was putting the kid to bed and telling them to be good.

Cissy reappeared. "Here," she whispered, holding out a piece of paper. "This is my cell-phone number in case Francis needs something."

"Is he going to be okay with you gone?" Sophie matched her voice level to Cissy's whisper.

She sighed, her pale, thin face wan with exhaustion. "I think so. It's just hit him hard . . . harder than I expected it would."

"It's his mother, after all; I guess we never know how it's going to hit us until it does. You probably know that better than anyone."

Cissy surprised Sophie by reaching out and hugging her. "You're right, I do know how he feels. Maybe that's why I'm trying to be there for him, but it's not easy. Look, thanks for this," she murmured. "I need to go to Ithaca and sort this book shipment out, but I'll be back in an hour or so."

"Okay."

She was gone swiftly. Sophie stood for a moment, gathering her wandering thoughts, and heard Francis say something. She headed toward the other room, about to ask him what he had said, when she heard him speak again. This time he said, louder, "I need to talk to you, and soon!"

She came around the corner of the door and said, "I'm right here."

He was on the phone and started, gasping, "What the heck?" He slammed the phone down and glared at her, then lay down on the bed and turned away.

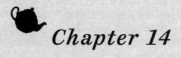

Chapter 14

In the brief glance she had of him, Francis looked dreadful; scruffy, beard coming in, eyes hollow and bags under them.

"I'm sorry, did I startle you?"

"I . . . I didn't know you were here," he mumbled, over his shoulder.

"Cissy didn't want you to be alone. I thought she told you I was here."

"No, she didn't bother. I'm not a baby, for God's sake. You can go."

Sophie hesitated. On the one hand, with his rudeness there was nothing more she'd like to do. On the other hand, if she was honest with herself, she had come with ulterior motives, and so she'd stay. "Don't let me stop you from phoning whoever you were phoning. How about I make us some tea? My grandmother always says there is nothing like it to make you feel better."

He didn't say anything, so she went back to the kitchen and busied herself with making a pot of tea. Cissy had a complete setup . . . teapot, diffuser ball, loose-leaf tea, strainer, everything. She had Earl Grey, English breakfast, oolong, green and even maté, an Argentinean tea with a bit of a kick to it. Plain-old English breakfast was safest, so she brewed a pot while pondering how to get Francis to talk.

He ambled into the kitchen. His haunted expression tore at Sophie's heart, and she wordlessly pushed him into a chair and gave him a cup of tea with sugar. He was suffering shock, as any person who witnessed a loved one murdered before their eyes would, and sugar could help, or so she'd heard.

"I'm sorry I snapped at you," he said, glancing at her, then frowning down into his cup.

"Don't mention it," she said, sitting opposite him at the little dinette table. "I know you don't need babysitting, but Cissy is so worried about you she just didn't want to leave you alone. When I happened to call about the wedding shower, she asked me to come over. Have you eaten today?"

He shrugged.

She jumped up. "Let me fix you what Nana used to make when I didn't feel like eating." She rummaged around and came up with some eggs, milk, sugar, vanilla and a blender, and whipped up a frothy eggnog, poured it into a tumbler and grated some nutmeg over it. "Drink up."

As she ran water and squirted some dish soap into the sink, she said, over her shoulder, "Go ahead and call the person back, the one you were calling when I interrupted." Curiosity was eating her alive; to whom did he say, *We need to talk*? And what did it mean?

"It's not important. I just left a message on the voice mail of a friend of my mom's who lives out of state. I really don't want her finding out about . . . about the thing on the news."

"Oh. Of course!" Sophie immediately felt bad for what she had been thinking. She sat down opposite Francis again. "Drink! You need to keep up your strength."

"I miss Mom so bad," he said, his voice thick with tears. "Who would do that to her? She was such a good woman! I just don't understand."

"Me neither," Sophie said. "And I can't imagine what you're going through. It must be awful."

"It was terrifying to be right there and yet not be able to help her," he said, wrapping his hands around the tumbler. "I didn't know what to do! If I could go back, if I could . . . I don't know, do things differently . . ."

Sophie waited, but when he didn't continue, she asked, "Like what?"

He shrugged, and took a gulp of the eggnog. "I don't know."

She hesitated, but then said, "Did she seem ill before it happened?"

"No, not at all! Everything was fine. She gave a nice speech before lunch. We ate that god-awful food and dessert, then she looked . . . I don't know. Dizzy, or something. She got up, then collapsed."

"Is there any news on the investigation from the police?"

"They don't seem to be doing a damn thing!"

"Have you asked them what's going on?"

"Yesterday I talked to Wally, but he's no good. I'm so frustrated!" He clutched his head and scrunched his tousled hair in his fingers.

"It's so awful. Someone would have to plan well ahead of time to do that, to poison your mother, right?"

He scruffed his fingers along his jaw, where a dark beard was beginning to bristle. "That's true, isn't it?" he said, frowning down at the tabletop. "I mean, poison? It's not a spur-of-the-moment kind of thing."

Sophie could see the wheels turning as he considered it. It was good that he was focused on something other than his own pain, so she decided to encourage his thought process. "Who could have wanted to kill your mother? I haven't been back to town long, but everyone says she was a great woman, just like you said."

He nodded, his mouth compressed in a firm line against the onslaught of emotion Sophie could see welling up in his eyes. "*Nobody* would want to kill her! That's the thing. It doesn't make any *sense*." He hammered the table on the last word.

She didn't state the obvious, that someone must have

wanted her dead because she had been murdered. "Was she involved with anyone? Or did she have any friends?"

"Involved . . . do you mean, was she dating anyone? No. When she went to country club dances, she would go with a couple who are her best friends."

"Who are they?"

"Marva and Holly Harcourt. They're the parents of my buddy Hollis Harcourt Junior; everyone just calls Hollis Senior 'Holly.' "

"Oh. What about . . ." She paused, surprised to learn that Hollis and Marva Harcourt were Vivienne's particular friends. The meeting she had witnessed between Vivienne and Holly did not seem friendly. She tried to figure a way to ask about the meeting. "Uh, Francis, was your mother worried about anything to do with your, uh . . . your recent promotion?"

He stared at her, brow crinkled. "No, of course not. Why would she be?"

Sophie didn't know how to respond, and she didn't want to talk about the meeting she had witnessed. Not yet, anyway. "What about anyone else at the tea? Was there anyone there that someone might have a grudge against? Like . . . you, or your aunt?"

He looked startled and his eyes widened, but he shook his head and said, "You mean maybe my mom wasn't the target? That's just not possible!"

But Sophie would swear there was something or someone. His mind went elsewhere, even as he stared at her, his eyes glazing and his brows furrowing in thought. "Francis, are you sure?" she urged. "I mean, if there is no one who would want to kill your mother, then maybe someone *else* at that tea party was the intended target." She worried that if he had thought of something, he'd try to tackle it himself. That could be terribly dangerous with someone out there willing to kill. But it was such a limited array of possibilities, motives and murderers; who among those few killed Vivienne Whittaker, either on purpose or accidentally?

There was a tap at the back door; Florence Whittaker,

looking older and less well kept than usual, came in without waiting for an answer. She frowned as she stared at Sophie. "What are you doing here? Where's Cissy? Who . . . ?" She looked over Sophie's shoulder. "Francis!" She pushed past Sophie and flew at her nephew. "My dear boy! You should be lying down, getting rest. Come on, right now." She grabbed his shoulder.

"I'm okay, Aunt Flo!" he said irritably, hunching his shoulder out of her grip. He glared up at her. "I wish every-body would just leave me alone."

"We were just having some tea and I made him an egg-nog. To keep his strength up, he needs food."

The woman's sharp gaze softened as she looked down at her nephew. "You're right about that."

"Would you like a cup of tea? Cissy had to go out to take care of a misdirected book shipment in Ithaca, but she'll be back in a half hour or so."

Florence Whittaker slumped down in a chair and seemed grateful when Sophie set in front of her a warm mug of tea, then pushed a sugar bowl and cream pitcher toward her. She dribbled a little milk in the mug and took a long draft. "Oh, that's good. I don't think I've stopped for a cup of tea in the last twenty-four hours, much less something to eat."

"Mrs. Whittaker, the same goes for you as goes for Fran-cis," Sophie said, examining the woman's face. She seemed to have aged a decade in the last day or so, her strong jaw softened by sagging skin and her dark eyes clouded. "You need to keep your strength up, too."

"I just don't think I could eat." She stared down into the cup, her gaze pensive. "I miss everything about Vivienne. I used to call her most mornings and we'd meet at the coffee shop. I know everyone drags out the old gossip, the stuff about us being enemies, but that just wasn't the case. When we lost our husbands, it was . . . it was a bonding experience, I guess you'd call it. With Jackson gone, Vivienne and Fran-cis were all the family I had left." She put her hand across the table and rested it on Francis's. "Now you're it, my boy, you're all I have left!" She squeezed and released.

He didn't seem comforted and moved his hand. He'd probably rather have his mom back, Sophie thought. "We were trying to figure out who at the party would have wanted to harm Vivienne."

Florence's mouth tightened. "That's just . . . that's *gruesome*, to speculate like that about our friends!"

"I didn't mean it that way, Mrs. Whittaker. Don't *you* want to figure out who killed your sister-in-law?" Sophie sat down opposite Florence, who she had thought of as an enemy of Vivienne's until now. What about all the scandal, the accusation of adultery? Sophie considered it for a moment; was it possible that the whole thing had been blown out of proportion? Could it have been one of those mistakes that the two then got past and even laughed about later? Both women were widows, and neither had remarried; they had a lot in common. She wished she could just ask the woman outright about her legendary feud with Vivienne, but Sophie just wasn't hard-nosed enough to ask, *So, did you really have an affair with Vivienne's husband?*

Florence Whittaker stood, tugging her beige jacket down over her stomach. "I think you need look no further than that—that miserable old interfering—" She stopped and shook her head. "How *could* she call the police and tell them that Francis had anything to do with the death of his own mother? It was unthinkable."

"So you think Mrs. Earnshaw did it?"

She looked undecided. "Well, not on purpose," she said, backtracking. "I'm not saying that." She paced over to the kitchen sink and stared out the little window that overlooked the back lawn. "But there was probably some rat poison out in that kitchen, or something, and she thought it was flour. I wouldn't put anything past that busybody. She's nutty as a fruitcake."

There were so many holes in that theory that Sophie didn't even address it. But she was curious about Florence's poor opinion of Cissy's grandmother. "Everyone is saying that Mrs. Earnshaw is upset that her granddaughter is marrying Francis. What does she have against your family? I'd think she'd be thrilled that her only granddaughter was getting married."

Francis shook his head. "I was *floored* when I heard what she'd done, turning on me like that. To call the cops? I haven't exchanged more than two words with the woman since . . . well, since we were all teenagers!"

"You hung around with Phil, though, right?"

"And Phil is her grandchild and therefore perfect," Florence said bitterly, turning to face them. "That skunk has had more second chances than a lucky Las Vegas gambler. Heck, if he was at the tea, I'd say maybe *he* did it. He hated Vivienne and he hates me."

"Why would he hate *you*, either of you, for that matter?"

"Aunt Flo!" Francis said, with warning in his tone. He gave her a look, then eyed Sophie. After a moment he seemed to make up his mind and said, "You won't pass this on, right? If I tell you something?"

Sophie knew she shouldn't promise. Carefully she said, "Who would I tell? I mean, really, I have never lived in GiGi, and I've only been back for a week after being away for the better part of ten years! I don't know *anyone*."

Francis nodded, took another drink of the eggnog, then set the glass aside. "Mrs. Earnshaw always blamed my mom for that trouble Phil was in a few years back, when he was caught bringing booze into Gracious Grove. She thought, for some reason, that my mom had called the cops and turned Phil in. He told his grandma that he and I were brewing moonshine in my dorm room at Cornell, and that's why the booze was in his truck."

She knew the story already, but didn't say so. "Was it true?"

"Of course not!" he barked, glaring at her. "Would I risk my college career on a bootlegging business? That's *crazy*! I was past all that kid stuff and was focused on getting my architecture degree. But she has always given Phil a pass for every dumb thing he ever did."

Sophie let that sink in; some of it was true. Phil, by the evidence of her own eyes, was *still* trying to smuggle booze into Gracious Grove. Also, Cissy had said much the same thing about Phil's run-in with the police. It was true that Thelma Mae Earnshaw was *still* making excuses for him. However . . . "You aren't suggesting that Mrs. Earnshaw took out her grudge against your mother by killing her?"

"I didn't *say* that." He scruffed his hair and sighed. "I guess that's ridiculous. I just don't know who else . . . I mean, there's no one!"

"Okay, say Phil *was* there . . . do you think he hated your mom enough that *he'd* try to kill her?" She wasn't about to say Phil *was* in Belle Époque that afternoon.

"I didn't say that, either," he said, on a deep sigh, giving his aunt a look. "I was just explaining why Aunt Flo is suspicious of the woman, and what grudge Mrs. Earnshaw might have against me . . . why she doesn't want me marrying Cissy."

"I get what you're saying." Sophie thought for a long moment. "But you know, someone who truly *did* want Mrs. Whittaker dead could have used Mrs. Earnshaw's old grudge to put the blame on her."

Francis's eyebrows went up and he straightened in his chair. "That's possible! But who? Everyone at that tea was a friend." He swallowed hard and collapsed in on himself again, his shoulders slumping. "I just can't *believe* that we're talking about my mom's death like this!" he moaned. "What did she ever do to deserve this? She was the best, most loyal, most loving . . ." He put his head down on the table, cradled in his arms, and his shoulders shook.

Florence patted his back, her expression one of sadness. She looked at Sophie and said, "You can see how this has affected him. I wish they'd just find whoever did it so we can begin to heal. Could you leave us alone? I appreciate all you've done, Sophie, and you got him to drink a bit of the eggnog, but I think he needs more rest."

"You're right about that." It didn't look like either one of them wanted to discuss the tragedy any more, and who could blame them? Sophie jumped up, washed the few things in the sink and put them in the drainboard to dry. "Are you staying here?" she asked Florence, and when that woman nodded, she made a quick decision. She grabbed her purse and said, "I'll get going, then. Tell Cissy I'll call her later, okay?"

Florence Whittaker nodded.

Sophie exited and stood on the top step, pulling in a big breath of fresh May air. It felt good to be out of that cloying atmosphere of mourning, though she felt awful for even thinking it. She descended and went into Peterson Books 'n Stuff, letting her eyes adjust to the dimmer lighting. The store was set up so pin spot halogen lights highlighted some of the glittering ornaments that Cissy had strewn around to sell. Crystals were hung from hooks between the bookshelves and over a branch mounted in the window overlooking the lane, catching the May sunshine and sending prisms of rainbow colors across the walls. It was a beautiful place that Cissy had created; restful, calming and peaceful. Today the music playing was some kind of violin concerto.

Beauty greeted Sophie at the door, winding around her feet to welcome her. Dana looked up from a book and said, "Surprised to see *you*. Cissy said you were upstairs with darling Francis."

Her derisive tone didn't set well with Sophie. "Dana, he just lost his mother. You might show a little respect."

"You just can't help being Miss Goody Two-Shoes, can you? Slipping back into your old ways."

Sophie stiffened. "Okay, so maybe that's just who I am, take me or leave me. Call me Goody, from now on, I don't care. Can you tell Cissy I left because Florence arrived and took over babysitting her fiancé?" She turned to leave.

"Hey, Soph, don't go! I was kidding." Dana stood and leaned on the counter. "You've gotten feisty sometime in the last ten years. Good for you. Used to be you just laid back and took the ribbing."

Sophie returned and looked Dana over, from her carefully tousled streaked locks to her emerald blouse and white linen capris; she looked gorgeous, as always. The capris and blouse theme seemed to be almost like a uniform, and she had many variations.

Dana was one of those people who had a sarcastic under-tone to almost everything she said. Sophie never knew when she was being genuine, or if that congratulations she'd just offered was yet another layer of mockery. It was a way to put people off, Sophie guessed, to keep them uneasily at arm's length. Approaching the desk, she said, "Dana, I know you and I never got along when we were teenagers, but let's cut to the chase. We're both adults now. I won't apologize for my family having money and you don't need to apologize for being a sarcastic bitch."

Dana laughed out loud and stuck her hand out; when Sophie took it, they shook. "Deal," Dana said. "So how is Baby Francis doing, anyway? Now that Auntie Flo is there, probably a lot better."

"Were he and his aunt always so close?"

The woman shrugged and patted the counter. Beauty gracefully leaped up and began to walk back and forth, curling her tail around Dana's shoulder like an expensive shawl. "Ever since he got out of college, anyway. Florence has used all her influence—and she's sucked up to a lot of rich people—to help him get where he is today."

"You mean at Leathorne and Hedges and this new, mys-terious development deal?"

She nodded. "Enter the fabulous Gretchen and Hollis Harcourt, Gracious Grove's own royal couple."

"You don't like Gretchen?"

"I don't like *Hollis*. He's a jerk. Went down south to find a bride 'cause those girls are trained up early to be subservi-ent, then made her change everything about herself. I knew her just after they were first married and she was a nice enough little thing, down-home accent and all. Now she's a bigger snob than any of them. She had plastic surgery, I tell people; she got her nose turned up."

"Cissy seems to think she's faking the 'aw shucks' South-ern girl deal—you know, slipping back into it—for whenever she wants to get her way, or worm her way into someone's confidence."

"Hmm, could be, I guess, but I don't think so. I think

being two people at once, a Yankee snob and a Southern good-ole gal, is breaking the poor kid."

"Kid? She's about the same age as we are, or older. You do realize that you've always acted like you were twenty going on fifty?"

"Just an old soul, I guess," she said, with a quirky grin that darkened. "I didn't have much time to be a kid, so I've always felt older than the rest of you."

"Why?"

She shook her head. "Nothing important." Her expression shuttered.

"I hear from *them*," Sophie said, looking upward, "that Vivienne was a friend of Hollis's parents. Do you know anything about them?"

"Marva and Holly 'Give 'em Hell' Harcourt? They have an estate near Ithaca as befits their social status. Holly Harcourt is a big deal in business, but now he goes in mostly for investment."

"Like real estate investment?" Sophie asked. "I heard Hollis Junior and Senior are investors in the new development."

"Could be. Anyway, Francis and Hollis Junior met at Cornell. He's no idiot, our Frankie. He knew to suck up to the rich folks, probably trained by his aunt. Ever since her husband lost their money, she's been good at that. Clawed her way back to financial stability, it seems."

"So this development deal Francis brought to Leathorne and Hedges . . . do you think the Harcourts had anything to do with him being able to do that?"

"Probably. I don't *really* know."

And it didn't seem to have a single thing to do with Vivienne's poisoning. "Cissy still wants to go ahead with the shower, so I'm going to track down Gretchen and start the planning. Apparently the shower date is already set for the third Sunday of the month, about two weeks before the wedding."

"Yeah, well, the whole thing has been mishandled because Miss Gretchen doesn't really give a care for it, fiddle-dee-dee," she said, flipping her hair and lightly drawling the last word. "She should have worked all this out two months ago, giving folks time to shop and access the gift registries at some local stores, like Libby Lemon's Kitchen Boutique. That's what I would have done if I was the maid of honor."

"Libby Lemon's what?"

"Downtown . . . a new kitchen shop. It's cool; you should go. That's where Cissy is registered for her kitchenware."

"I didn't know that."

"Not sure if Gretchen does, either."

"I hear she does have a gift registry and a site on The Knot."

"Sure, but it only lists the usual things, you know . . . Bloomie's is great, but Lord & Taylor? It would have been nice to support some local businesses so folks don't have to go all the way to Syracuse. And lots of the people who need to buy gifts don't have the Internet. She didn't even give a passing thought to the old folks."

"I'll see if I can do anything to correct that." Sophie glanced around. "Wish I had time to look through the cookbook section." She paused, as a wave of weariness passed over her. "What I *really* wish is that this whole thing had never happened."

"I'm sure Francis is with you on that," Dana replied.

Sophie paused, then said, "Dana, I heard that you and Francis were a couple once, but that Vivienne split you up. Is that true?"

"Technically. We did date for a while. Are you asking if I had a motive to kill Vivienne?"

Sophie smiled. "You weren't even there, at the engagement tea, so no, not really."

"It's true that old Viv split us up. She never failed to point out to Frankie that I couldn't help his career in any way. But my head was pretty messed up at that point. I was a party-hearty girl, and when Francis drifted out of my life, I don't think I even noticed."

That explained that. "I guess I'd better call Gretchen and try to meet up with her. She sure seems to be in the know with a lot of folks at Leathorne and Hedges," Sophie said, explaining about the Silver Spouts meeting the night before, and Forsythe Villiers and SuLinn Miller.

"Watch out for Forsythe," Dana said, her tone and expression suddenly serious.

"Why? He seemed nice enough when we talked."

"Oh, he *seems* that way, all right, but he's a snake in the grass. Watch out, that's all I'm saying."

"Come on, you *have* to explain more than that."

"No, I don't; just know I met him in questionable circumstances once, and I'll say no more. You'll see. Now scoot, I have some serious reading to catch up on."

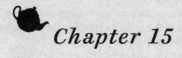

Chapter 15

Outside, Sophie sat down on the front stoop and pulled out her phone, calling Gretchen's number. The girl answered.

"It's Sophie Taylor, Gretchen. Cissy wants to go ahead with the shower as planned despite the tragedy, so there's no time to lose. Do you have a half hour?" There was silence for a moment, but Sophie could hear the other girl's breath puffing into the phone, and she mumbled something. "Gretchen?" Sophie prompted.

"Well, sure. Okay. Where would you like to meet?"

So, no invitation to Gretchen's home. "I had coffee with Cissy downtown at a little patisserie the other day. How about there?"

"I know where you mean. Give me half an hour to . . . to take care of some things."

Sophie agreed. In the meantime, she called home to talk to Nana. "I'm still working on the wedding shower tea for Cissy," she explained, telling her grandmother that she was meeting with Gretchen.

"Why didn't you have her come here?"

"I didn't think of that. But I wanted to go downtown to check out this kitchen shop Dana Saunders told me about, anyway, so I'm on my way." Something else had occurred to her, and she asked, "Nana, you've known Gilda Bachman a long time, right?"

"Well, yes. I've known her a long time, but I don't know her well. Laverne knows her better than I do, especially since Gilda started going to the church Laverne attends."

"Do you think she would ever do something strange?"

"Like poisoning Vivienne Whittaker to get her boss in trouble? Or to get back at the Whittakers for being rude to her in the past in a million little ways? Honey, I've been on this earth for a long time and I know better than to put anything past anyone."

So it was possible that Gilda may have done something, either for the motives her grandmother mentioned, or one more obscure. "I'll be back in an hour or two, early enough to help with that busload you have late this afternoon."

"Thanks honey. Don't get into any trouble, and don't ask the wrong people the wrong questions. Or even the right people the wrong questions!"

Once again her grandmother had proved to be a touchstone of good sense in a weird world. Sophie retrieved the SUV and drove off toward the center of town. Libby Lemon's was a revelation. She had been in lots of kitchen stores, especially as she was stocking In Fashion, but she never expected to find one in Gracious Grove, nor had she ever been in one that combined professional-grade kitchen equipment with the cute, the handmade and the extraordinary from around the world. She wandered through the kitchenware emporium, enjoying handling all the tools of her chosen trade. Sophie soon had a basketful of citrus zesters, pasta cutters, a gnocchi board, a cupcake corer and icing sugar stencils. Some handmade kitchen towels that looped over drawer pulls called out to her—handy and pretty—since they had teacups and teapots all over them. She also checked

Cissy's listing on their wedding registry, and added a practical set of three graduated sizes of springform pans to the pile at the cash register.

She turned around to check out the last aisle, which had paper goods, like fancy cupcake papers and sleeves, and saw Belinda Blenkenship browsing the retro aisle that had baking dishes in funky 1950s colors. It was too good an opportunity to miss.

Sophie hustled over and browsed the same aisle, "accidentally" bumping into her. "Oh, I'm sorry, I just . . . oh! I know you." She tempered her expression to one of appropriate sadness. "You were at the engagement tea the other day, the one where Vivienne Whittaker died!"

The young woman's dark eyes widened. "Y-yes, I was there."

"I hope you're doing okay?"

"I . . . I'm fine, thank you very much." She was dressed in a pastel skirt suit, pale mauve, over a patterned blouse with lilacs strewn over it. Her blonde pouf of hair was topped by a pillbox hat, and she clutched a yellow purse. The color scheme was a little Easter egg and a lot 1950s homebody.

"I understand congratulations are in order," Sophie soldiered on, "for your marriage to the mayor. How wonderful!" The young woman's expression was one of fear and her gaze darted this way and that, like she was looking for an escape hatch. "Oh, by the way, my name is Sophie Taylor," she said, sticking her hand out. "My grandmother owns the tearoom you were taken over to."

"Oh. Yes." Belinda brightened. "I liked that tearoom better than the other one. It was prettier."

"You should come for tea one day." Sophie was starting to think this was a waste of time and actually feel sorry for the girl, but she had a purpose. "It must be exciting to be married to the mayor, right? All those formal parties and luncheons, kind of like being the First Lady of Gracious Grove!" Sophie was swinging for the fences, hoping her instincts were right and Belinda saw herself as a modern-day Jackie Kennedy.

"Do you think so?" she asked, pathetically eager. "I want to be a credit to Gracious Grove, you know, and to do a good job."

So she saw being the mayor's wife as a job; interesting. "Your husband is a lucky man," Sophie said. "He must be popular. My godmother says he runs unopposed almost every time, except this last time. I guess Oliver Stanfield ran against him in the last election. I wonder why?"

"Oh, it was just a misunderstanding. Mikey went and had a talk with Oliver and he withdrew."

"But he said there was a family reason?"

She colored. "Mikey said he reminded Oliver that his son was in jail, and that wouldn't look good to the town for the mayor to have a son in jail."

Hmm . . . blackmail. Lovely quality in a mayor. She bit back her first response, which would have been that Mikey ought to watch what skeletons he had in his own closet before rattling those in someone else's, and instead she said, "That was so smart! I'm sure Mr. Stanfield appreciated the warning."

"Mikey says that sometimes you just have to be honest with people and warn them when they're about to do something stupid, like talk about something they ought not, or do something that is bad for their friends."

Sounded faintly ominous. "So does he know Vivienne? Is that why you were at the engagement tea?"

She looked nervous and picked a tea towel off the rack, a completely impractical tea towel that was glitzed up with beads and embroidery. "Do you think Cissy Peterson would like things like this for her shower?"

She just didn't seem bright enough to pull off the cupcake switcheroo necessary to kill Vivienne Whittaker. Or was she cleverly hiding intelligence behind a facade of stupidity? In any case, she seemed to be avoiding the question. "Who *did* invite you to the tea, Belinda?"

"Uh, I don't remember."

"Oh. Francis Whittaker told me he did, but maybe he misspoke."

She looked relieved. "Yes, that's it, it was Francis Whittaker! He came to see us at the house once. Mike and him and friends."

Mike Blenkenship, Francis Whittaker and "friends." "So you and Cissy and Gretchen must all get along well, right? I mean, you're almost the same age, have a lot in common . . ." Sophie let that trail off as Belinda's face held a confused expression.

"I don't know Cissy very well, but Gretchen doesn't like me much. I don't know why."

That confirmed the guess she'd made based on the chilly exchange in the tearoom after the murder. Sophie said, "You should definitely get those tea towels. I'd buy a half dozen if I were you. Cissy will love them!"

The mayor's young wife lunged at the remaining ones on the peg and bundled them in her arms. "Thank you so much! I just didn't know, and it's always best to get advice when you don't know, right? Excuse me now. I'll go buy these."

For a second Sophie felt bad for suggesting the hideously impractical tea towels, but in the grand scheme of things it didn't matter much. Everyone got gifts they regifted or quietly donated to charity. But the test had served its purpose; Belinda was the kind of girl who could be depended upon to do exactly what you told her to do. That was probably how she had been coerced into making a sex tape and why she'd ended up at a drug den. Belinda would be a useful pawn in someone's scheme, Sophie thought, following her to the checkout. As she lined up behind her, she said, "So, what did you take to the shower . . . what food, I mean?"

Belinda whirled, her eyes wide. "Uh, I don't remember. Gotta go! Ta-ta!" She grabbed her bag and exited swiftly.

Couldn't remember? Interesting. Sophie took her bags to the SUV and stowed her purchases in the back. As she locked up, Sophie noticed Gretchen on a street corner deep in a conversation with Forsythe Villiers. Sophie was about to start over to meet her, but the conversation evidently took a serious turn and the two embraced. Not hugged . . . embraced. It was more personal and lasted too long for a casual, friendly hug. The gentleman then strolled off down the street, hands in his trouser pockets, his fedora jauntily tipped to one side. He disappeared into an old brick repurposed office building.

Trouble in paradise? Sophie wondered. Did this mean Gretchen was tired enough of Hollis's political ambitions that she had embarked on an affair, or was it just a basically harmless but a little too cuddly flirtation? Dana's warning about Forsythe echoed in her memory; a snake in the grass, she called him. That implied that he would strike out when one least expected it. But how? And why?

She headed toward the patisserie wondering how to handle what she had seen. She got a table for them, and when Gretchen entered, looking adorable in a pale-blue jacket over skinny jeans and a white blouse, she waved to her.

"Well, hey there, Sophie," Gretchen said, bending over and giving her a quick, brief "girlfriend" hug. She plunked down in the seat opposite Sophie and looked around. "Now, what to have that's totally bad for me? I'm ravenous."

"Talking to Forsythe probably made you that hungry," Sophie said, watching the young woman. "He does seem to specialize in arch drollery, which can be so tiring!"

Gretchen cocked her head to one side. "Whatever do you mean?"

"What do I mean about Forsythe? I just saw you two on the street hugging. I assumed you'd just had lunch with him or . . . or something." Gosh, she was no good at this. She hadn't wanted to make it sound accusatory, because . . . because she just didn't.

"Yes, we . . . well, we didn't have lunch, we just bumped into each other and were talking."

"Oh." She couldn't very well say what it had looked like, and she didn't want to get into it, so she just dropped the subject. "So, let's grab a coffee and some pastries. I tried a few things here with Cissy, and now I want something different, something gooey and chocolaty!"

"Sure. Uh . . . Forsythe and I . . . we're just friends, you know."

Sophie glanced over at the worried young woman. "Okay. Don't sweat it." She paused, but then said, "I ran into Belinda Blenkenship at Libby Lemon's just a few minutes ago. She seemed so out of place at the engagement tea the other day, but she says Francis invited her."

"He did not!" Gretchen snapped. "As if he would invite that white trash—" She shut up then, and shook her head. "I don't know who invited her, but it couldn't have been Francis."

"She wouldn't have just shown up out of the blue. Maybe she's friends with Cissy?"

"I'm sure I don't know," Gretchen said, retreating to frosty politeness.

Time to let it go. After sharing a slab of brownie and sipping their coffees, Sophie took a notebook out of her purse and laid it on the table in front of her. "We know the color scheme of the shower now; Cissy wants it yellow and white." She shuddered, the memory of the yellow icing on Vivienne Whittaker's face, as she died, like a bad dream that just wouldn't go away.

"What is it with those folks and yellow?" Gretchen said, picking up the last crumbs on the brownie plate with the moistened tip of her finger. She licked her finger. "Vivienne Whittaker leaped on that yellow cupcake like it was manna from Heaven." She paused, and her eyes widened. "Oh my gosh! The cupcake . . . was the poison in that? Do you know?"

"Maybe," Sophie said, unwilling to give away anything that she had learned from Dana or Wally. "How many vanilla cupcakes with yellow frosting were there on the tea table?"

Gretchen shrugged and rolled her eyes. "I'm supposed to remember that?"

Sophie paused, watching her. She seemed nervous. "No, I guess you wouldn't be watching anything like that, would you?"

"I was bored to tears," she huffed. "Especially after my mother-in-law got in a snit and left. Then I—"

"Your mother-in-law? That's Marva Harcourt, right? *She* was at the engagement tea?"

Gretchen frowned at Sophie's tone. "For a little bit, yeah. Is that a big deal?"

"No . . . no, of course not. But nobody had mentioned it." Sophie's mind was reeling as she ran through the implications. Hollis Harcourt Senior was involved in the development deal. Somehow Francis got the rights to design for the development for Leathorne and Hedges and was rewarded with a big promotion and first dibs on the designing. Hollis and Vivienne were arguing at Auntie Rose's. And now she learned that Marva Harcourt was indeed at the tea that fateful afternoon. "I'm just surprised, I guess. I didn't know Cissy knew your mother-in-law."

"Everybody who is anybody knows each other in this town, but . . . well, I don't know if Cissy knows Mama Harcourt or not."

"Why did Mrs. Harcourt leave early?"

"Oh, that awful old woman insulted her. Florence tried to smooth things over, but Marva got in a fight with Cissy's grandma—or as much of a fight as a clubwoman ever engages in—and stormed out. Does it matter in some way?"

"No," Sophie assured her. "Like I said, I'm just surprised. If Cissy doesn't know Mrs. Harcourt, why was she invited?"

"Vivienne and Florence know her. Marva and Holly Harcourt are solid-gold members of the country club, like the two Mrs. Whittakers."

Sophie digested that for a moment. Had Vivienne Whittaker threatened some kind of status quo when she tackled Mr. Harcourt? Had she threatened to disclose something about the new development? Was she upset about how her son got his advancement? Maybe she was worried it would come back to haunt him. But still . . . that was an awful lot of supposition, and it didn't give any proof that Marva Harcourt was the one to plant the lethal cupcake. "So, just to get this straight, Vivienne and Florence invited her to Mrs. Earnshaw's engagement tea for her granddaughter?"

"Well, yeah, I guess. When you put it that way, it sounds

kind of . . . interfering. Is . . . is there something wrong, Sophie?"

She ignored the question. "But both Florence *and* Vivienne wouldn't have invited her to the tea. Which one actually did the inviting?"

"Florence, I think."

"So what was the fight between Marva and Thelma about?"

Gretchen sighed wearily. "Oh lord, it was stupid. First off, I think Thelma was in a snit because she didn't know Marva and was put out that Florence had invited her. Then something happened in the kitchen; I guess Marva insulted the place—"

"Wait, in the kitchen? *Marva* was in the kitchen? Why?"

"How should I know?"

Sophie remembered what Gilda had been complaining about, the folks milling around in the kitchen "helping." What a great opportunity to arrange the cupcake platter with the one poisoned cupcake. But it still didn't say how the killer directed that cupcake to Vivienne, unless they knew her preference for yellow, or vanilla, or something like that. If Marva had left before the tea, then she couldn't have been the one who made *sure* Vivienne got the poisoned cupcake. A dedicated risk taker might have planned it that way, though, and then skedaddled to get out of there so she wouldn't be under suspicion. That insult and the resulting fight and her storming out could have been just the cover Marva wanted. "So you weren't in the kitchen when all this was happening?"

"Gosh, no! I don't go in any kitchen unless I have to."

"You can't cook?"

Gretchen looked smug. "I didn't say I couldn't, I just don't. Honey, every Southern girl with a proper mama is taught how to make biscuits and gravy, grits, greens, the whole bit. I can cook a ham hock with the best of 'em, but I'll deny it if you ever tell anyone!" She laughed, a lovely tinkling sound.

Sophie could see how one could be charmed by Gretchen

Harcourt, and wondered how much of the Southern girl act was fake, as Cissy seemed to think it was. "So you don't know for sure what the argument was over and why Marva left?" Gretchen shook her head, so Sophie asked, "Do the police know Marva was there?"

"Good lord, I don't know. And I am not going to be the one to tell them. Hollis would have my head on a platter if I told the cops his mother was at that tea party."

Then I will, Sophie thought. She was also going to have to track Cissy down, with the excuse of talking about the party, and pump her for information about a number of things, including whether she had invited Belinda Blenkenship to the engagement tea. Of course, Cissy would *want* to know the truth about the murder because she sure would not want her grandmother accused of the crime. "Okay, let's figure out where we are with this bridal shower. I'm going to do a brief tea talk, and the presentation of the tea-a-ra." She explained what that was to Gretchen, who clapped her hands and said it sounded darling. "Cissy will wear it while she opens her gifts."

Sophie took notes as they talked. Gretchen was going to take care of the invitations that very day and because of the late date would hand deliver them, except to the out-of-town folks.

"Can you give me a list later of all the invitees?" Sophie asked. "I need to know food allergies, et cetera."

"I never thought of that, though I should have after that dreadful engagement tea. Vivienne made such a big deal out of her allergies."

"I heard that," Sophie said, looking up from her notes. "Did she say what she was allergic to?"

"There was a list. Shellfish. Peanuts. Red dye. MSG."

"Red dye?" That pinged in Sophie's mind, as she considered the plate of red-velvet cupcakes.

"Just one of many."

"Was it common knowledge, her allergies?"

"Well, sure. She made it known at the country club, anyway. I can't say more than that."

"Uh, Gretchen, who put out the cupcakes? Do you remember?"

"Well, that helper, Gilda, brought them out."

"But who arranged the platter?"

She paused for a long moment, looking uncomfortable. "I haven't a clue. I *told* you, I wasn't in the kitchen. We had already eaten the awful finger sandwiches and hard-as-a-rock biscuits or scones, or *whatever* you call them, by then. I wasn't going to risk a cupcake. Why, is it . . . is it important?"

"I don't know. Probably not."

"I have to go," Gretchen said, suddenly. She stood and fussed for a moment with her cuffs and purse, but then said, "Look, you're not going to tell anyone that Forsythe and I were out there talking, are you?"

"Why would I?"

"Oh, I don't know. It's just . . . it might look bad. Lots of folks don't like Forsythe. He can be . . . mischievous, in what he says."

"Mischievous?"

"You know . . . imply things, make comments, snarky, but funny."

That was the second person who had warned her about Forsythe. "I see. I have no reason to mention that you were both on the street talking," Sophie said.

She looked relieved, but simply twiddled her fingers in farewell and sailed out the door into the May sunshine.

Something was off there, but Sophie couldn't put her finger on what it was. Gretchen had looked uneasy, certainly, at the mention of the cupcakes, but she didn't look guilty.

Back at Auntie Rose's Sophie barely had time to unload her purchases from Libby Lemon's and make a quick call to the police to give them the info that in case no one had mentioned it, Marva Harcourt had been at the engagement tea party before the deadly cupcake incident. Then she was thrown into the afternoon's schedule. It was a busy day, with a Red Hat luncheon, a bridge club outing and two bus tours, as well as lots of other drop-in customers.

One table in particular intrigued Sophie. The group was a gathering of Gracious Grove businesswomen, among them Libby Lemon proprietor Elizabeth Lemmon, a middle-aged woman with fluffy, dark hair drawn back with a yellow headband. It was the same group that the proprietor of GiGi's French Pastries belonged to, though she was not present. Sophie introduced herself, and mentioned how much she had enjoyed going in to the kitchenware store. Then she asked about joining their women's group, since the tearoom was run by her and her grandmother, Rose Freemont.

"We'd be pleased to have you both!" Elizabeth said. She glanced over at one of the other women at the table, who nodded. "We also have a political action group many of us belong to. Some of the older women in Gracious Grove think we're a little *too* active in that way. Would you be interested in joining that?"

"Not right now," Sophie said, glancing around the room. She'd need to get back to checking on tables and bussing them. "I'm not a very political person, actually."

"And you haven't been back in Gracious Grove long. I'll bet once you see how this town has changed in the last ten years, the way the good-old-boy network is using the town like its personal fiefdom, you may decide to join."

Sophie let that sink in a moment. "Do you mean the mayor and council might not be acting in the best interests of the town?"

Most of the women nodded and one snickered. Elizabeth said, "I won't say all that I believe, but yes, we think there is money changing hands inappropriately for things like land zoning and bylaw changes. We feel that conflict-of-interest laws aren't being followed and we're worried about the future of Gracious Grove."

Someone on the other side of the room was waving her hand and asking for another pot of tea; Sophie acknowledged them as her mind spun, thinking about the newspaper headlines and all she had heard of annexation and development deals and the network of businessmen running it all.

"Ms. Lemmon, what would happen if someone stood in the way of their plans?"

"What do you mean?" She looked alarmed, her lined face pinched in a worried expression.

"Never mind." She didn't want to be precipitate and say something she ought not to say. "I have to excuse myself, ladies," she said. "Let me think about this some."

"Certainly. But regardless, we would welcome you and your grandmother to sit in on a meeting of the Gracious Grove Businesswomen's Association. No pressure."

Sophie smiled and nodded, then went to the aid of her customer.

When they closed up, she shooed her grandmother and Laverne out and cleaned up the place herself, vacuuming, wiping down the tables and chairs, dusting, doing a load of linens in the professional washer and dryer tucked away in the corner of the kitchen, and setting up the tearoom for the next day. Cut tulips and daffodils would be delivered first thing in the morning, and the tables would look lovely, as always.

Occasionally she glanced over at Belle Époque and noticed the lonely-looking light in one window of the upstairs apartment. How had Thelma Mae Earnshaw gotten the way she was? She was grumpy, yes, but surely not a killer? Nana said there was no way the woman had killed anyone, and her grandmother knew peoples' hearts. But why the heck had Thelma turned in Francis Whittaker when she had not a shred of evidence that he'd done anything wrong?

Or did she *have* evidence she just wasn't sharing? No, that was impossible, or Francis would be under arrest by then, surely. On an impulse, she took out a container of the Zuppa Maritata she had made and skipped across the alleyway to the back door of Mrs. Earnshaw's home and knocked.

"C'mon in," she heard from above. She tried the door; it was unlocked! That was trust or living dangerously, to leave the door unlocked when there was a murderer around.

"Mrs. Earnshaw?" she called out. "It's Sophie Taylor.

Can I come up?" She peeked up the stairs just as the elderly woman came to the top.

"I thought it might be Phil or Cissy."

"No. I just . . . I made too much soup and I was wondering if you would try some and tell me what you think?" She ascended the steps and followed the woman to her small kitchenette.

"All right," she said, slowly. "I'll try it."

Sophie heated up the soup, found a bowl on the drying rack and filled it, then set it in front of Mrs. Earnshaw. She peered at it suspiciously, then took a spoonful. Soon, she was scooping it into her mouth quickly and finished, with a sigh. "That was real good, young lady. So you really are a cook?"

Whereas from the snooty doctor, Sebastian, on that date her mother had arranged, being called a cook had been an obvious insult, it certainly wasn't coming from Mrs. Earnshaw. "I am. Trained and everything. Are you all alone? Don't you have any guests staying?"

"Nope. Tell you the truth, it's getting a bit much to run this place as an inn. I sure could use the money, but looking after 'em is too much."

"You should have someone move in and pay room and board. That way there would be someone here, but you wouldn't have to cater to them."

The woman looked thoughtful, but didn't answer.

"Mrs. Earnshaw, the day of the engagement tea, did anyone else come to the kitchen besides the folks at the tea?"

"No. Why?"

"No reason. Just curious. I heard today that Marva Harcourt was here, but you and she argued and she stormed out. What did you argue about?"

Her sagging jowl wobbled as she grimaced. "She said I had stuff in the fridge way past its due date, and I asked her what she was doing snooping in my fridge."

"Had she been fussing with anything else, like the cupcakes?"

"Not so's I noticed, but everyone was everywhere that day. Gilda was whining that Mrs. Harcourt and her daughter-in-law were fussing about something; Florence Whittaker was acting snooty, saying the sandwiches weren't fresh enough; Vivienne Whittaker was giving orders like it was her own place . . . it was a mess. Why?"

"Just an idea I had." Sophie noticed the weariness on the older woman's face, and the lines of pain on her forehead and bracketing her mouth, and her heart went out to her. "I'll let you go on to bed, ma'am."

Sophie went back to Auntie Rose's, made a cup of tea, sat down at the kitchen table and pulled her notebook out of her bag. Instead of bridal shower tea party plans, though, she began to make notes about who could have killed Vivienne Whittaker. It pretty much had to be someone at the engagement tea party, though Phil, by virtue of having been in the kitchen just minutes before, was a possibility.

So . . . Phil Peterson, Florence Whittaker, Francis Whittaker, Gilda Bachman, Thelma Mae Earnshaw, Marva Harcourt, Belinda Blenkenship and even Gretchen Harcourt, though she claimed she wasn't in the kitchen. Oh, and Cissy Peterson! She couldn't completely eliminate Cissy, though it was clearly impossible that sweet, reserved Cissy Peterson could have murdered her mother-in-law-to-be.

Tapping at the back door startled her. She got up and looked through the glass, then opened the door. "Jason! It's so good to see you!" She threw her arms around him and hugged him—he was taller than she remembered—then, suddenly shy, backed away. "Uh, I'm having a cup of tea. Would you like tea or coffee?"

"Whatever you're having."

"Sit! I'll get you a cup." When she returned to the table, Jason was looking at her list with a quizzical expression.

"What's up with this?" he asked.

She shrugged and eased into the chair next to him. "It's unnerving to have a murder happen right next door. I saw Vivienne dying. It was . . . awful." Her voice trembled and she cleared her throat, trying to get ahold of her emotions.

"So this is a list of everyone at the party, or maybe a list of who could have done it. But it was poison, right? Was the killer necessarily right there?"

She told him her reasoning so far.

"And you know for certain that the poison was in the cupcake?"

"I'm pretty sure, yes. Look, I have an idea. Tell me if this makes sense."

Chapter 16

It had all started with the conversation she had with her grandmother about how you could make sure a person would choose a certain cupcake from a plate, she told him. Then she paused for a moment, gathered her thoughts and went on. "Someone who knew about Vivienne Whittaker's allergy to red dye would know she wouldn't touch red-velvet cupcakes, nor any cupcakes with red or pink icing. Of course, it seems like pretty much everyone knew about her allergy, so that doesn't narrow the field. But if you wanted to poison her, and you knew there were going to be red-velvet cupcakes at an event, then all you had to do was make sure there was one non-red-dye cupcake on the platter."

"But how could you be sure she would even eat that one?" Jason asked. "Maybe she doesn't like sweets, or maybe she was full. How would you know that someone else wouldn't snatch it up before she got it?"

"True. It was an awful risk. Unless someone knew her habits, and maybe knew she would never refuse a sweet. That would indicate someone really close to her, right? Like

Francis or Florence." She chewed her lip and frowned down at the paper, then looked up to find Jason's gaze steady on her. "What?"

"I was just recalling that expression. When you were working hard on an algebra problem, you'd look like that."

She flushed, remembering school vacations in Gracious Grove when she and Jason would work on their homework together, sometimes in this very room, while Nana cooked. "I remember," she said, softly. She stared back down at the sheet, but it blurred in front of her eyes. "Jason, if I could go back in time—"

"But nobody can, right?" he said. "So, why are you trying to figure this out?"

Snapped back to reality by his no-nonsense comment, she replied, "I just don't want the wrong person railroaded. Like Phil Peterson; he's such a screwup, but he wouldn't kill someone."

"He wasn't even there, was he?"

Knowing it would go no further, she told him what she'd seen, Phil sneaking out the back door as the others were arriving in the front. "If I was the police, I'd be wondering if Mrs. Earnshaw called them with Francis's name because she's protecting someone, and the only people she would try to protect would be Phil or Cissy."

"You have a devious mind," Jason said.

"I lived in New York for seven years working in the food industry. You have to be devious to navigate your way through the restaurant world, especially when you're dealing with food critics." She thought more about the cupcake conundrum. "I need to figure this out. Maybe Nana will know something." She would talk to Cissy, too, the next day, and see if she could get a sense of what all had happened in the kitchen before the tea started.

There were a few things she could investigate. First, who knew Vivienne Whittaker had a red-dye allergy before the event? It seemed to be common knowledge and something she had spoken of openly in the past. Second, who had the chance to not only bring the poison cupcake, but place it on the plate? Third, who had access to cyanide, or knew some-one else who did?

"Sophie?"

She looked up. "Mhmm?"

"I'm glad you're back in Gracious Grove. I was won-dering . . ."

She held her breath, waiting for an invitation to go out to dinner. Or something else!

"You obviously know a lot about starting a restaurant; do you think there's a market in our town for a fine dining establishment?"

That was not what she was expecting. She scrambled to think. "Uh . . . well, maybe. It's a popular tourist area. The problem is that they wouldn't be able to serve alcohol if they were in Gracious Grove proper, and for those accustomed to a wine list that could be a problem. Why do you ask?"

"A colleague of mine is talking about sinking a lot of money into starting a restaurant and I'm concerned."

"Colleague?"

"Yes, you met Julia."

"She's starting a restaurant?"

"I guess it depends somewhat on that new development and the plans for it, but she has promised to invest her 401(k) in it."

"If it's in the new development, then liquor laws in Gra-cious Grove won't affect her." Sophie stared down at the paper in front of her. Jason seemed quite tied up with the other professor's intentions. "Are you investing, too?"

"No way. Investing in a restaurant is like throwing your money in the garbage, one of my financial friends says." His eyes widened and he stared at her. "Uh, I'm sorry, Soph, I didn't mean—"

"It's okay. It's nothing I haven't heard before." She frowned, as something he said sank in. "So, it depends on the new development, you said; where did she hear about it?"

"It's no secret. You've seen the signboards, right?"

She nodded.

"I guess it's been in the works for a while, and some folks have heard about it and started making plans."

"I just didn't know anyone was already talking about building or leasing the commercial space." To change the subject, she said, "You're pretty good friends with Francis, right?"

He shrugged. "Lately he's been hanging out with me more than he used to, I don't know why."

"He's been trying to clean up his image for a long time," Sophie said. "Did you hear about Phil's trouble a few years back, when Francis was in architecture school at Cornell?"

"I heard *something* about it."

"Phil says Francis was making moonshine in his dorm room, but Francis claims Phil was lying to get him in trouble."

"Out of the two, I know which one I'd believe."

"Francis."

Jason nodded.

"Phil thinks Vivienne Whittaker turned him in to protect her son."

"Do you believe Phil?"

Sophie tapped her pencil on the notebook page. "I don't know. Just speculating."

"Clarify."

"Say Francis really was in partnership with Phil to make booze and sell it in Gracious Grove, and say Francis's mom wanted to shut the guys down, and yet keep her son out of trouble. For a determined mother like Vivienne Whittaker, it would make sense to turn *Phil* in to the cops, knowing that the police were unlikely to believe much of what he said. Her position as an important woman in the community would make it easier to pin it all on screwup Phil, rather than college kid Francis. All Francis would have to do is deny, deny, deny when they asked him about Phil's accusation. It would serve the purpose of shutting Francis down *and* making sure he didn't suffer the blame *and* separating the two guys."

"That's Machiavellian! It would take a lot of guts to turn in the guy who could squeal on your son, though."

"I think both those Whittaker women have a lot of guts."

"But that's all water under the bridge and now Vivienne Whittaker is gone. Those two things don't have anything to do with each other."

Yet hatred was a powerful motive for murder, and Phil must have hated Vivienne for getting him in trouble.

Jason stood and stretched. "I'd better get going."

"One sec . . . you said Francis has been hanging out with you more lately. You've been invited to the wedding, right?"

"Francis has asked me to be a groomsman."

"Let me guess: Hollis Harcourt Junior is best man, right? Did you agree?"

"Of course. I mean, what was I going to say?"

"But you used to call Francis an idiot," she said, eyeing him with a sly smile.

"That was a long time ago," he said severely. "He's changed his life and now he's marrying Cissy."

Sophie was ashamed of herself. "I was with him today, and this has really hit him hard."

"He was close to his mom. I should go."

Sophie stood and walked with him to the back door. "Jason, about your friend, the professor . . ."

After a moment, he prompted her, "Yes?"

She chickened out of asking him what their relationship was, and simply said, "I would tell her to wait and find out more before investing too much money in a restaurant in the new development. If the town does annex the land, and the no-alcohol bylaws stay in place, it could be pretty tricky to open a fine dining establishment. It's a tough business, and the only people who should gamble on it are those who have the money to lose if it goes belly-up."

"Thanks, Soph. I'm glad you're staying in GiGi." He dropped a kiss on her cheek and headed out, hands in his pockets, whistling.

She watched him go, hand to her cheek.

* * *

As Jason Murphy left Auntie Rose's, Thelma, watching out her kitchen window, kept her eye on Sophie Taylor, who stood in the back door and looked after him. Anybody with half a brain could see that girl was regretting dumping the fellow. He wasn't good enough for her when he was bumming around Europe and then going into the army, but now that he was a professor he was suddenly good enough again. Hmph.

Her conscience stirred. The girl was a nice child, though, to bring her soup like that. Why she was wondering about Marva Harcourt being in the kitchen was a mystery, though. Thelma was just about to lock up when she heard rustling in the bushes that lined the parking lot of Auntie Rose's.

"Who's there?" she shouted nervously. "I got the cops on speed dial, you know!" She was about to skedaddle inside and slam the door shut when her grandson emerged from the bushes.

"I thought Jason'd never leave," Phil hissed and sidled past her into Belle Époque. "Can you put me up for the night, Grandma?" he asked.

"Who are you hiding from, the police?"

He shrugged and loped into the kitchen; as she locked the door, he stuck his head in the fridge and came out with a hunk of cheese in his hand. She watched him eat hungrily, her heart softening. She had planned on giving him a good talking to, but instead said, "You want something to eat? I'll make you scrambled eggs."

He nodded and sat down at the table by the window, gloomily staring over at Auntie Rose's. "What was *he* doing there?" he asked.

"I don't know, but he was there for a good half hour or so. That girl is sweet on him again, I can tell."

"I always liked Sophie. She's pretty," Phil said. "But man, she is so stuck up!"

"The whole family is," Thelma grumbled, moving from

the fridge to the stove and cracking a couple of eggs into a hot pan. She cooked them for a while, made some toast and slid it all onto a plate. The eggs were browned real good, just like Phil always wanted them. He loved her cooking, which was more than she could say for Cissy. Thelma sat down opposite him and drank a cup of cold tea while he ate. "Phil, why were you in here that afternoon, the day that Vivienne Whittaker keeled over?"

He shrugged, hunching one shoulder as he mopped up the last bit of ketchup with his toast. "Free country, right?"

She waited, knowing he would feel compelled to say something more. He always did, even as a youngster, when he was in the wrong.

"Look, I'm not supposed to tell anyone," he said, glancing around, "but someone asked me to put something in the punch you were serving."

Thelma's heart did a flip-flop dance. "You put something in the punch? Are you crazy? What did you put in it?"

"Just a little hooch, that's all."

She reached over and smacked the side of his head. "What is wrong with you?"

"Ow! Nothing's wrong with me! I have a plan, is all."

"A plan to end up in jail? What kind of plan?"

"It's all up here," he said, sitting back and tapping the side of his head. "But I need money, and lots of it!"

She closed her eyes and counted; ten might be enough, but if not, then twenty or thirty would do. Plan? Phil Peterson never had a plan in his life. He was as shiftless as his father and twice as dumb, and she had to admit that even though she loved him. Why hadn't he taken after his mother, like Cissy had? She opened her eyes after a twenty count and glared at him. "So, who asked you to liquor up the punch?" She hadn't noticed anything, but then she hadn't drunk it. Neither had Vivienne, as a matter of fact, because it was red fruit punch made with that tropical blend Thelma liked, and served to her patrons, and the picky woman made a big deal about all the dyes in punch mixes.

Phil smirked. "I'm not saying."

"Okay, have it your own way," she said, weary to the bone. "You staying the night?"

"Yeah. I'm beat."

"The cops know you're here?"

"Nope."

"You trying to stay away from them?"

"No more than normal," he said. He got up, stretched and hugged her hard. "You're the best, Grandma."

"I know," she grumbled, but hugged him back. As long as there was breath in her body, she would look after Phil and Cissy. No one was going to hurt them, or use them bad. No one!

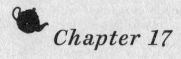

Chapter 17

Sophie made a quick call to Cissy to ask that they meet the next day, then went to bed. After morning coffee and a quick shower, she headed out. It was Dana's day off, so Cissy was tied to the store. She was at the computer that was in a corner behind the counter when Sophie came in, carrying a white pastry bag of cranberry lemon scones and a little pot of homemade strawberry preserves. "Let's have a feast," she said to her new/old friend.

As they wiped their fingers clean on paper napkins after their repast, Sophie took a sip of coffee and said, "Cissy, who do *you* think did it, poisoned Vivienne Whittaker?"

Pale-blue eyes wide, Cissy shook her head. "I just don't know! I've had nightmares, and in my dreams it's . . ." She stopped and shook her head. "Never mind."

"No, go on," Sophie said, crumpling the paper bag into a ball and tossing it into the recycling bin. Beauty dashed after it and sniffed the bag, then returned to hop up on the counter, using a stool nearby as a step.

"In my dreams it's Florence who died, not Vivienne." She shot a quivery look at Sophie. "That sounds bad, right?"

"You can't help wishing Vivienne hadn't died—she was your fiancé's mother—and even if you subconsciously wish it was Florence instead, that doesn't make it bad, either. I know you wish *no one* had died."

"That's true." She took a deep breath, and let it out. "Thanks, Soph."

"I've heard so many stories about the engagement party," Sophie said, carefully. "What really happened?"

"What do you mean?"

"Okay, can we start at the beginning? I don't mean to be nosy, but it's so confusing! The engagement tea was your grandmother's idea, right?"

"No, not at all. Where did you hear that?"

"I don't exactly remember . . . I think it was your grandmother who said it. So, if it *wasn't* your grandmother's idea, whose was it?"

"Well, it was Vivienne's, really," Cissy said, frowning into her coffee mug. "I was telling her that Grandma complained that she felt left out, since I wanted my bridal shower at Auntie Rose's. Vivienne said, why didn't Grandma have a tea to celebrate the engagement?"

"Okay." Sophie readjusted her thinking. "But your grandmother was happy about it?"

"She grumped about it a lot. You know what she's like."

"I did wonder about that. It was a lot of work, and meant she had to close the tearoom for that one day."

Cissy nodded. "She complained about it being just her and Gilda doing everything, so I told her I'd have people bring stuff, you know, to help out. Like a potluck."

"And *did* they bring stuff?"

"Sure. I wasn't supposed to bring anything, but I brought red-velvet cupcakes."

Sophie was stunned. "*You* brought the red-velvet cupcakes?"

"Sure. Why?"

"Uh . . . no reason." This changed everything. "Did you buy them or make them?"

"Oh, bought them. I don't bake."

"Who put them out on a plate?"

"I did," Cissy said.

Sophie stared at her friend, trying to rein in her ideas. She had been wondering where the cupcakes had come from, but not once did she consider Cissy as a possible source. "Why red-velvet cupcakes?"

Cissy shrugged. "Someone suggested them, so I brought them."

"Someone said to bring red-velvet cupcakes?"

"Not specifically." She paused and furrowed her brow. "What was it . . . ? Oh, I don't remember!" she cried, shaking her head. "This has all been so difficult . . . it's chased thoughts right out of my head."

"If you plated them, where did you get the one non-red-velvet cupcake?"

"I don't understand," Cissy said. "I only put six red-velvet cupcakes on that plate."

"Six?" There had been at least that many left on the plate when Sophie saw it, but they were just arranged in a sporadic semicircle. "And then what? Did you take it out to the tearoom?"

"No, I left the plate where it was; we weren't ready for dessert. We hadn't even had lunch. Besides, the plate wasn't full. I thought I'd put something else on it to fill it up."

What else had been on the platter? She had pictured a plate with a full ring of red-velvet cupcakes and one non-red-velvet cupcake in the center. But was that the case? It didn't make any sense. If Cissy's were store bought, then who provided the homemade ones? "You sure you didn't notice if someone else put more red-velvet cupcakes out?"

Cissy said, "I didn't see if they did, but I got distracted and didn't think about it after that. It was about then that Vivienne took me aside to talk for a moment. She was worried about something."

"Worried? What about?"

"I don't know. It was too busy and there were too many people milling around, so we never got to finish our talk." She clicked on her cell phone, checked her text messages, then looked back up. "How are you and Gretchen doing with the shower plans?"

"You're not supposed to fret about that," Sophie said absently, while she considered all that she had heard. If she was right, then someone, between the time Cissy had put her red-velvet cupcakes on the plate and went to talk with Vivienne, had finished filling it. It was then brought out to the tearoom with that one poisonous vanilla cupcake with yellow frosting. *If* she was right. But who did it?

"Cissy, how well do you know Belinda Blenkenship?"

"Not very."

"So who invited her to the engagement tea? There seems to be some confusion about that."

"I don't know."

Cissy's vagueness could be so frustrating at times! "Who is likely to have?"

"Maybe Vivienne? Or Florence?"

"Why didn't they leave it up to your grandmother?"

Cissy sighed and rubbed her forehead. "I don't know. Vivienne probably thought Granny would invite Phil and his girlfriend and no one else. She'd have been right." She paused. "What you need is the Gracious Grove Whisperer."

"What?"

"It's this social site where rumors and gossip are traded. I'll bring it up for you; give me your phone."

Sophie handed over her cell phone and Cissy tapped in some searches and came up with a social network called Whisperer. She handed it back to Sophie, explaining that towns, cities, social groups, all kind of units had Whisperer sites.

"There is one voice in particular on the GiGi Whisperer site that seems to have all the dirt on everybody. You can privately ask prominent Whisperers or post a public message asking for whispers, or you can do a search."

Sophie did a quick search on Belinda Blenkenship and came up with all the old scandals, but also saw some interesting photos. There was Belinda with a man who must be her husband, the mayor, and a bunch of men all by the development sign going into the ground. Everything she looked into came back to the new development, and it all started with Vivienne's concern that Francis was going to be connected to it and it was going to backfire. Why? And could that actually have led to her murder? Or did it just mask a more personal reason for her killing?

How frustrating investigation must be for the police, all the innuendo and confusing paths that led nowhere. But maybe they had already figured it all out. Maybe even now they were planning an arrest.

Sophie hoped so; she wanted to stop worrying about it, but she just couldn't while it was unresolved, such a terrible crime and right next door to her grandma's establishment. She watched her friend, who was now just staring out the store window and petting Beauty, who did not seem as friendly with Cissy as she did with Dana. "I'm curious, Cissy; how did you and Francis get together?"

She cocked her head to one side. "It just kinda happened, you know? There aren't many guys in Gracious Grove. Most of them leave for college and never come back, so I haven't dated a whole lot. Grandma always fussed that I'd be an old maid. But one day Vivienne came into the bookstore and we got talking. She invited me over to the house for dinner. Francis was there, too, and he asked if I wanted to go out for coffee. We talked, and he was so nice to me. Then he asked me out to dinner, and I went. He had changed a lot from when we were teenagers and he listened to me as I talked about the store, and what I wanted to do with it; it was nice to be listened to for once. That was a year ago."

It almost sounded like an arranged marriage with Vivienne as the matchmaker, and Sophie couldn't help but remember the women who had been chased off to make way for her. Belinda was only the latest, Sophie would bet, and Dana one of the earliest. It was likely no coincidence that Vivienne *happened* to come into the bookstore and *happened* to invite Cissy to dinner on the same night Francis *happened* to be there. Jason said Sophie had a devious mind, but it wasn't devious to see the careful planning behind so-called happenstance, was it?

Cissy Peterson would make the ideal ambitious and successful fellow's wife, intelligent, gentle, reserved. Even clothes-wise she was perfect; no shocking outfits or risqué head turners on Cissy. No scandalous past, and no tattoos or piercings to frighten the conservative in Gracious Grove political and social circles. Today she was dressed in a pretty butter-yellow twin set with real pearls and a blue-floral skirt, very ladylike and proper.

"You must love Francis," Sophie said.

"Of course," Cissy said calmly, and went back to checking her messages.

"Are you waiting for something?" Sophie asked, watching her thumb through her list. "If I'm holding you up . . ."

"No, not at all," Cissy said, looking up from the phone. "I ran into Wally last night and he said he'd let me know if he found out anything about Vivienne that he can share with me."

"Ran into him? Where?"

"At the grocery store."

Sophie was silent, wondering about all she'd heard about Wally still caring for Cissy. "What made you decide to get married?"

"Francis asked," she replied, with a surprised expression.

"That doesn't mean you had to say yes," Sophie said.

"But I want to be married. Don't you? I want . . ." She paused and sighed, wrapping her arms around herself and looking up at the display of twinkling crystals overhead. A prism of color kissed her cheek. "I want a home; a *real* home. And kids. I want . . . I want . . ." She stopped, tears gleaming in her eyes.

"Oh Cissy, I'm sorry!" Sophie said, tears welling in her own eyes. Of course all that would mean a lot to Cissy; she'd lost her mother at sixteen, just when a girl needed her mom the most. "But we're young; we've got time. Besides, marrying doesn't necessarily mean you'll get it all. Is Francis the right guy?"

Cissy, her eyes glittering, said, "Yes, he *is*. He's a good man; he loves me and we want the same things. That's what's important, you know, not all this other pie-in-the-sky, love-forever-after stuff. People think I'm a little flighty, but I'm really very practical."

"More than I am," Sophie admitted, thinking that she really wanted the *love-forever-after stuff*, as Cissy called it. "It's too bad for him his mom died, and so close to the wedding."

"Vivienne was going to be the mom I lost," Cissy said, turning her engagement ring round and round on her finger. "I miss her already. She brought a gift to the engagement tea, you know, a really nice one!"

"You told me that, but you didn't know then what it was. Do you know now?"

She nodded. "I finally opened it. She would have wanted me to," she said, her voice soft.

"You said before that she was worried; are you *sure* you don't know what about?"

"I really don't. She said she didn't know how much she could trust people, and she looked toward the tearoom, then she thrust the box into my hands and asked me to open it later and tell me what I thought when we talked."

"What you thought? About what? What did that *mean*?"

"What I thought of the gift, I guess."

Sophie asked, "So what did you think? What *was* the gift?"

"A vintage teapot. Really pretty, but not very practical. It looked like it was out of her own collection, you know?"

"I didn't know she *had* a collection."

"Oh yes, she did; she has . . . had . . . a *lovely* collection. That's why Grandma tried to get her to start a collector's group with her, The Teapot Society. The one Vivienne gave me is a Haviland Eglantine-pattern teapot; I looked it up on the Net to see if it was special in some way. Pretty, but a strange choice. Like I said, I'm not a collector. I'll cherish it, though, just because she gave it to me."

"Eglantine . . . I've heard that flower name before. I wonder what it means? Do you remember when we were kids and Nana set us down with a book on the language of flowers, and told us to write a poem?"

Cissy smiled. "I do! Mine was awful, like 'roses are red' awful. Wait . . . let me see what it does mean." She took out her phone and went to a browser, then tapped in EGLANTINE—LANGUAGE OF FLOWERS. She frowned, her mouth twisted in puzzlement. "It means *a wound to heal,* " she said, softly.

A wound to heal. But then again, few people knew about the language of flowers, and it was probably a random pick. Sophie said so to Cissy, who relaxed.

"You're right."

"Still, it's nice that she thought of you," Sophie said. "At least you'll have had a gift from your husband's mother to remember her by."

Cissy nodded, but there was still a puzzled look on her face. "Why did she want me to tell her what I thought? I don't understand. It's just a teapot."

"Can I see it?"

"Sure, I'll go get it. Can you watch the store for a minute?"

"If I can use your computer." Cissy invited her to help herself, and Sophie did some research on cyanide. She really would have to see about getting her grandmother's house wired for Internet access and get her laptop out of storage. Maybe she'd set the place up for Wi-Fi and advertise it as the first hot-spot tearoom! She could do a lot on her cell phone, but she didn't have unlimited usage.

Cyanide was not the easiest material to get. Or was it? She tripped over a suicide site where many offered suicide pills bought in other countries. Tears pooled in her eyes as she read the hopeless messages of those wanting the pills to leave this world. Or . . . her cynical mind kicked in again. Were some of the so-called suiciders really just looking for pills to get rid of someone *else* in their life?

Maybe it was easier than she had thought to get hold of cyanide, or maybe some of the cyanide for sale was just sugar pills offered by con-artist sellers. She deleted her search, left with an uneasy sense that she had stumbled across something more she needed to share with the police.

Cissy came back bearing a pale-blue box. She set it down on the counter and lifted the lid, setting it aside, then took out a butter-yellow tissue-wrapped item, which she carefully unwrapped and put down on the counter.

The pattern was an old-fashioned open type of rose in a pale pink, but the teapot was nothing spectacular, just a deeply fluted china six-cup teapot. The lid was stuck on. Nana did that in the tearoom to thwart the occasional touchy-feely type who just had to lift a teapot down and sometimes broke loose lids. But this was a gift, and the lid should have been wrapped separately in tissue to keep it from clanking, rather than sticking it onto the pot. "Why is this stuck?" Sophie murmured, and tugged on it. It released with a bit of a clatter to reveal some sticky putty holding the lid on. Inside the teapot she could see a piece of paper folded. She hesitated, but then said, "I think Vivienne may have left you a note."

"I didn't see that!" Cissy took it and unfolded it. "I don't understand," she murmured, scanning it as another loose piece of paper fell out of the fold.

Sophie held out her hand and Cissy gave her the first sheet. It was a list of names, some she recognized, some she didn't. "Marva Harcourt, Florence Whittaker, Julia Dandridge, Nuñez Ortega, Forsythe Villiers, Mike Blenkenship, Francis Whittaker, Oliver Stanfield, Shep Hammond. Is this Vivienne's handwriting?"

"It is."

"Who are these people? I mean, I know some of them . . . Marva Harcourt is Hollis Harcourt's mother, and of course I know Francis and Florence, and I've met Forsythe Villiers; he's in Nana's teapot-collecting group, actually, and I know he works at Leathorne and Hedges." She paused, as another name rang a bell. "Julia Dandridge . . . that's a professor at Cruickshank, head of Jason's department, actually. But who are the others?"

Cissy took the paper back and said, "Well, Nuñez Ortega

is a partner at Leathorne and Hedges, Mike Blenkenship
you already know is the mayor of Gracious Grove, and both
Oliver Stanfield and Shep Hammond are local builders."

Aha! Both names were on the sign announcing the new
development, Stanfield Homes and Hammond Construction.
If she remembered right, GG Group was the investors'
group. Gracious Grove Group? Maybe. Sophie pondered the
list, but couldn't make any sense of it and why Vivienne had
passed it on to Cissy. "What's on the other piece of paper?"

"It's just a series of numbers," Cissy said, handing it to
Sophie.

"It looks like a combination," Sophie said. "It's a numeri-
cal code to something, maybe an alarm code. But it also
says, 'In case something happens.' What does that mean?"

"I don't know. Why would she give me something like
that?"

Sophie didn't have an answer. A tone indicated someone
coming into the store, and both women looked up.

"Well hello, ladies!" Gretchen Harcourt cried. "How are
y'all?"

Sophie folded the piece of paper and stuck it in her
pocket, not sure why she wasn't comfortable letting Gretchen
see it.

"Hey, Gretchen," Cissy said.

"What's that?" Gretchen asked, coming up to the counter
and examining the teapot.

"It was a gift Vivienne gave me."

"Isn't it all just tragic? I'm actually here about poor Mrs.
Whittaker. Mama and Papa Harcourt are hosting a memorial
service at the country club tomorrow morning at eleven, and
I'm supposed to make sure you're coming, Cissy. Francis
has already said he'll pick up his Aunt Florence."

"Of course I'll go," Cissy said, her cheeks paling.

"Why Marva and Holly? I mean . . . why are *they* putting
on a memorial?" Sophie asked.

"Well, they are just incensed that Gracious Grove's finest,
meaning that awful detective woman and dumb-as-a-stump
Wally Bowman, haven't arrested anyone yet, you know?"

"Wally is not dumb," Cissy declared, her cheeks flaming. "And I'm sure the detective is doing the best she can."

"*Anyway*, Marva and Holly think we need to honor poor Vivienne's life while folks still remember the tragedy of the whole thing."

"I don't think people are going to forget this any time soon," Cissy demurred.

"I agree; Vivienne Whittaker was a pillar of local society." Sophie was puzzled by the Harcourts' interest.

"You know what I mean. They don't want anyone to think they've forgotten her, I guess."

"So this is about them, really," Cissy said, with uncharacteristic sharpness.

Gretchen stiffened. "They're just trying to do the right thing!"

Sophie put a hand on Cissy's knee; she could feel the tension in her friend. "Cissy, why don't I pick you up? I know Nana will want to go, and Laverne too, probably, so I'll bring them and swing by to get you. "

With a brittle smile, Gretchen said, "Well, I'm glad that's settled. I'll tell Mama Marva that *you'll* be there, too, after I explain who you are." She whirled and left the shop.

"I'm *really* starting to dislike her," Cissy said, with a sigh.

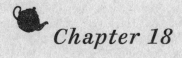

Chapter 18

"I know exactly what you mean. She seems to rocket between sweet and snobbish at the speed of light. Hollis is going to be Francis's best man, right?" Sophie asked.

"That's why I ended up with Gretchen as my matron of honor, and now I'm stuck with her." Cissy rolled her eyes. "I can tell she isn't really into it, so I don't expect much from her in the way of support." She paused, then said, "Thanks for offering to take me to the memorial service, though God only knows why Marva and Holly Harcourt are putting it on. It's got to be just for show. Marva and Vivienne did *not* get along!"

Sophie really wanted Cissy's entrée into the country club circle so she could meet the people named on the note from Vivienne, but it didn't hurt to let Cissy think she was trying to be helpful. "Why didn't they get along?"

"I'm not sure. They were friends once, but something happened lately, and Vivienne was pulling away from that group. She said something about that whole country club crowd, as she called them."

"What did she say?"

Cissy frowned, concentrating. "What did she say? Something like, if the only purpose of having money was to make money, then . . . oh, I can't remember!"

Sophie pulled out the paper and pondered the names. Marva's was right at the top of the list. What could all these people have in common? There were employees at Leathorne and Hedges, builders and the mayor of the city. *And* Jason's department head, who Sophie knew was talking about investing in a business that was going to be in the new development. The new development; that was the tie that bound all of the names. "So, how *did* Francis get such a great promotion, to be the designer in charge of this new hush-hush development?" She had her suspicions, but nothing solid, and wondered how much Cissy knew.

"He's a good architect, I guess. Isn't that enough?"

"Not at his age. I'm sure there are others in the company with more seniority, and seniority usually wins out. I heard that he somehow got a design contract for the development for Leathorne and Hedges, and that's why he got the promotion; was that true?"

"Maybe," Cissy said.

"The names on this note . . . they mostly have to do with the new development. It sounds like Vivienne was worried about something to do with it, don't you think? Something she wanted to talk to you about?"

Cissy just shrugged and looked mystified.

How little did she know about her fiancé's life? It was odd, Sophie thought. "Where did Vivienne live?"

"She has . . . had a house," Cissy said. "Actually, I've been over there to feed her poor cat. Sweet Pea is just *lost*. I feel so bad for him!"

"What's going to happen to him?"

"I don't know. Francis doesn't like cats, nor does Florence. She's more a dog person. Poor woman lost her dog recently, and she was heartbroken! But cats . . . not so much. I can't take him because the last time I tried to adopt another cat, Beauty just about killed it. She does *not* share."

"Are you going over there to feed him today?"

"No, not today. I only planned to go over every other day."

Sophie considered for just a moment, then said, "I could do it for you, if you like. I hate to think of the poor cat cooped up all day, waiting for Vivienne."

"Would you do that?" Cissy said, relief registering on her pale face. "To tell you the truth, I'm not *really* such a big fan of cats myself. I love kittens, but cats . . . Beauty is okay because she stays in the store, and Dana looks after her mostly. She's really more Dana's cat than mine. But Sweet Pea . . . he kind of intimidates me."

"I'd be happy to do it. Francis won't mind, will he? I mean, me going into his mother's home?"

"No, not at all! He was so grateful that you made that eggnog for him yesterday. I'm really going to have to learn to cook; I know how to boil water, but that's pretty much it. Would you teach me the basics?"

"Sure." Sophie stood. "Look, I have to get going, but would you like me to go now to feed Sweet Pea?"

"Would you? Thank you so much, Sophie!" She retrieved a key out of her purse, along with a card that had a numeric alarm code on it, and an explanation of how the alarm worked.

So the numeric code on the piece of paper in the teapot was not to the security system. Sophie had a feeling it was for a safe, and the curiosity that thought provoked was like an itch, especially when paired with the words on the paper. *In case you need it.* If it was a safe code, why would Vivienne think Cissy might need it? Was she afraid of something happening to her? Didn't she trust the people closest to her? Of course, just because she had passed this on to Cissy didn't mean she hadn't left the same thing for her son.

"Could you photocopy this stuff for me to mull over?" Sophie said, flapping the two pieces of paper that came out of the teapot. "If Vivienne gave you a teapot with this stuff in it, it must be important, so I'd like to think about it some more."

"Sure, if you really want to," Cissy said, and went over

to the computer printer on a table by the cash desk. "It can't hurt, I guess."

As she photocopied the two pieces of paper, Sophie casually said, "So what exactly is Phil doing these days? Besides still trying to smuggle booze."

"He works in construction sometimes. Shep Hammond was a friend of dad's, and keeps saying he made some promise to keep his eye on us." She shivered. "I don't like him at all. He's . . . creepy, you know, like, handsy? He's always touching me. But he does give my brother roofing work from time to time. That's where Phil is right now."

Hammond . . . that name kept cropping up with the others. Though she already knew the answer, Sophie asked, "Did Phil approve of you and Francis marrying?"

"Phil doesn't approve of anything." She scribbled an address on the reverse of one of the photocopies and handed both sheets to Sophie, with the explanation of how to get to Vivienne's home. "My brother drives me nuts. He seems to think the world owes him something. Grandma doesn't help matters; he can go to her with any sad story and she always gives him money, or a place to stay or whatever. I keep telling him he has to stop mooching off of her. She's not getting any younger and she worries about him."

"I'd better get going." Sophie hugged Cissy. "You make sure you're taking care of yourself."

Vivienne Whittaker's home was a faux-Victorian mansion on a hill above the town proper. The winding road that led to it twisted and turned enough that the lavish homes had no view of one another, only of the town and valley over which they looked. Sophie parked the SUV behind a line of cedars—not that she was hiding, exactly, but she did not want to excite interest in such a wealthy enclave, where they might call the police at the drop of a hat—and went up to the front door. She let herself in and set about using the code to disable the alarm.

"Sweet Pea?" she called, her voice echoing back to her. Nothing. The entry had soaring thirty-foot ceilings, with an enormous dining room to one side and a parlor or sitting room on the other. The dining room was furnished with a heavy dining table—it squatted on thick legs and was topped by a crimson-velvet runner—ten chairs, and a sideboard that groaned under the weight of a silver tea service and matching candelabras.

She turned to examine the parlor; the style was ornate and very formal, with Louis XIV–style gilt mirrors and a settee with low ladies' chairs by a marble fireplace. A couple of bow-front display cases held Vivienne's collection of teapots. Sophie went closer to examine them. They were mostly eighteenth- and nineteenth-century Staffordshire china: blue willow, hand-painted country scenes and even a couple of Toby-style figurals. Everything was antique, whispering of wealth and prestige. It saddened her that she had not known the woman who appreciated items of such rare beauty and historical significance, and now never would.

Sophie felt eerily like someone was watching her. She turned and found that a stocky chocolate-point Siamese was glaring at her, poised in perfect position on the dining table, statuelike in his stillness. He had silently hopped up there in the few moments Sophie's back had been turned. "Hey, Sweet Pea. You hungry, fella?"

He yowled at her, then leaped from the dining table to the floor and trotted away. Sophie followed to the kitchen, where he sat on the marble work area by huge windows that overlooked a ravine. Spellbound, Sophie strolled over to the windows and gazed out over the lush green gardens, and then down to the town below.

The cat yowled and she whirled. "Okay, all right. Food first, view after." She found the food exactly where Cissy had told her, and gave him a full bowl of canned food, which he gobbled down as she took his empty bowl to the sink. She felt a little like the housekeeper, because Sweet Pea was clearly the lord of the manor. She filled another bowl with kibble, scooped his litter, depositing the clumps in the litter locker Vivienne had used to keep the odor from the kitchen, then washed the dishes.

Dishes done and dried, she was free to wander. She had

permission to be in the house, but that probably didn't extend to cracking a safe, if that's what the series of numbers really was. Still . . . oh, *darn* her conscience. If she found a safe, she should ask Cissy what she ought to do. That was a big *if*, she realized, as she explored the house, followed by the snoopy Siamese.

The house was huge. There was a gallery above the dining room, parlor and entrance, off which most of the main rooms were situated. But there was another wing, she soon discovered, with a home office furnished in leather and decorated in wood paneling and brass. It was all too heavy and ornate for Sophie's tastes. She'd been in many nice homes, some of them her own, but she appreciated the clean, the stark and the simple best.

Sighing, she turned in the big room as Sweet Pea sat gazing at her from the desk. "Kitty, there is no way I'm going to find a safe in this house. I should leave it alone and turn this stuff over to the police to handle. So I'll just go and let you get on with your day, whatever that consists of, and . . ." She trailed off as she caught sight of something not quite right.

There was a painting ajar on the wall behind the desk. *Couldn't be*, she thought, shaking her head. That was so cliché, like every safecracking movie she had ever seen. But then she glimpsed a sliver of gray steel just beyond the edge of the painting. She slipped behind the desk and lifted the painting off the wall to reveal a safe. Now, her moral dilemma: To open or not? To call Cissy or not?

Sweet Pea followed and leaped up to the desk in one fluid bound. "Mrow!" he said, abruptly.

"You know, I'm going to take that as permission from the lord of the manor to open the doggone safe," she said. "There's probably not a thing in there; telling the police would just be a distraction to them and require a long explanation. If there *is* anything in there, I'll close it up and get Cissy to come back with me. Or Wally. Or someone!" She found a short key on the house keychain, and it fit in the lock. She turned it and heard a click, but it still wouldn't open. She got out the piece of paper with the combination. "Here goes me embarking on a life of crime." She punched in the number on the keypad.

Thelma Mae Earnshaw was *sorely* troubled, and in her hour of need she turned to the Lord for guidance. "I've been a miserable old woman at times, and I am not gonna deny it. But I've had my trials, now you know that's true! Losing my only child was awful, and raising two high-strung teenagers was hard. But Cissy has always made me proud. Not so much Phil, but he'll straighten out, I just know he will. There's no harm in the boy." She paused, then added, "No, I won't hear of it! There is no harm in him, and he would not kill that woman no matter how much he hated her and no matter how much he put something in the darned punch that she never did drink, anyway."

Even with the Lord, Thelma had a tendency to become argumentative. She didn't mean to, but it was part of a running conversation in her head, as if she knew exactly what he would say to her. As always, communing with God gave Thelma the free space in her noggin to think, and what she thought was, if she could just figure out who did it—who killed that woman in her beautiful tearoom—then she would have peace and Phil would be safe. Besides, if someone killed Vivienne Whittaker, then it might be her next!

She glanced up at the clock. Gilda would be there any minute, and she would set her employee on the task . . . not that Gilda had the brains of a pigeon, but if directed the right way, she could at least follow orders. Thelma, with her bum hip and cranky knees, found it rough to do more than get out of bed in the morning and stay upright.

At that very moment, as if summoned by her employer, Gilda slipped in the back door, her wiry, graying hair covered in a silk(ish) kerchief, and dark sunglasses perched on her beaky nose. *Still looking like she fancies herself an international spy*, Thelma thought, snickering to herself. The woman carefully undid her trench coat and hung it up on the coat tree by the door, then untied her kerchief, took it off, folded it in a neat square and placed it in her coat pocket. Then the sunglasses came off, were folded and joined the kerchief.

"You about done with your fiddling?" Thelma barked.

Gilda leaped and whirled, one hand over her heart. "I did not see you there! You about scared me right out of my skin."

Her powers of observation were not those of a spy, for sure. But she was all Thelma had in the way of gofer. "Sit down. We need to talk."

Gilda made them a cup of tea, first, and thawed some muffins. She ate her buttered muffin, and then finally wiped the crumbs off her fingers and stood, dusting them from her lap, as well. She heaved a sigh, shoulders slumped. "I suppose I ought to go make sure the tearoom is ready to open."

"Didn't I say we needed to talk?" Thelma griped. "You have the attention span of a gnat. I was just waiting for you to finish stuffing your gullet. I know you can't eat and think at the same time. Those cops are going to try to pin that murder on me or Phil, I just know it. They've always had it out for my poor Philly-boy, but I won't let them."

"No ma'am." When nothing more came, Gilda said, "So what can we do about it?"

"I want you to do some snooping for me. Go over to talk to Laverne . . ."

Gilda perceptibly brightened; it sounded like a bit of gossip and a cup of tea.

"*Not* to gossip, but I want you to find out who Rose and Sophie and Laverne think did it. I want to know if they saw anything, especially that granddaughter of hers. That girl is sharp. More so'n Cissy, I have to say. Not as pretty, though."

"Okay . . . find out who they think did it," Gilda repeated, dutifully.

"And find out if they know who brought in the cupcake that killed that woman."

Gilda looked frightened. "A c-cupcake did her in?"

Sounded like a title from one of the old black-and-white movies Thelma loved. She grimaced. "I think so. Lord

knows I have no clue who done it. With all of 'em yammer-
ing and milling around, any one of 'em could have slipped
the cupcake onto the plate. But someone was trying to pin
it on Cissy or me, 'cause *someone* suggested she bring red-
velvet cupcakes to the party. The little ninny says she can't
recall who."

Gilda's mouth formed an *O* of astonishment. "Who would
do such a thing?"

"If I knew that, I'd have a handle on this whole thing,"
Thelma snapped. "Now, get moving, and then come back
here and get a start on the tearoom. I got baking to do."

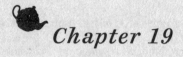

Chapter 19

The safe looked empty. Sophie peered into the dark cavity, then turned on a desk light and picked it up, directing it to shine into the depths. Sweet Pea leaped up onto the back of the chair with an inquisitive *mrow?* It was practically punctuated with a question mark at the end.

"I wish I knew, Sweet Pea," Sophie said. It paid to talk to animals; one never knew where the conversation would lead. "If I knew who killed your owner, I'd turn him in to the cops this minute."

"Yow!" The cat took one flying leap from the chair up into the safe.

"Sweet Pea!" Sophie cried, and reached up to get him. As she grabbed him, her hands brushed against something that crackled; there was some paper stuck to the side of the safe wall with a strip of tape. She took the cat out and carefully set him down on the desk, then peeled the tape from the wall, releasing the folded-over note and an envelope. "What in the world is this?"

She sat down at the desk and unfolded the paper. This

time there were names, some of them the same as in the first note—the mayor, Shep Hammond, Marva Harcourt, as well as a couple of new ones, including Harvey Leathorne, a founding partner of Leathorne and Hedges—but there was also a list of questions. In an elegant scrawl, Vivienne—it was the same handwriting as the note in the teapot—had written:

> *Who bought the property?*
> *Why did Francis get promotion?*
> *GG Group . . . Marva, Hollis, and . . . who else?*
> *Who influenced the rezoning? Mike.*
> *Who is pushing for annexation? Mike*
> *Why did Olly back off when Mike was running*
>   *again? Payoff?*
> *Who paid who?*
> *Where did my money go????*

Sophie sat and stared at the paper. Did this have anything to do with Vivienne's death, or was it just things she was worried about? It was in the safe, and she had given the safe combination to Cissy. Not Francis, not Florence, not Marva Harcourt, and not any one of her other friends. Not even a lawyer.

There was no avoiding one thing: This must have to do with her son's promotion and new job at Leathorne and Hedges and the development outside of town. If there *was* something dirty about Francis's promotion, then did he kill his own mother to keep her quiet? It was possible, Sophie supposed, though it horrified her to even imagine that. It wouldn't be the first time a son had plotted and carried out his parent's death, though.

She looked at the envelope, wondering about the contents. It was sealed. Opening the safe was one thing, but opening a sealed envelope now that she knew the safe contents must have some bearing on the case . . . she just couldn't. She held it up to the desk lamp as Sweet Pea sniffed the envelope.

It looked like a wad of paper with a list of numbers . . . maybe a bank statement or something? That would fit with *Where did my money go?*

She had enough to wonder about, anyway, that was for sure, even without knowing the contents of the envelope. She needed to talk about this with her grandmother and Laverne, both of whom knew more about Gracious Grove politics and society than she did. She picked up the phone and called information, wrote down a phone number and called the police.

In ten minutes, Wally Bowman and Detective Morris were there. She had already compromised the scene, the woman told Sophie. Sophie wasn't about to apologize; after all, her first thought had been to just lock it all up, or call the cops without confessing what she had found, but her prints would be everywhere if she'd done that and she'd have to explain why. She pointed out that they wouldn't have even known to look in the safe if she hadn't followed the teapot clues, and after all, she didn't know she'd find anything. "What's done is done," she told them.

Wally guided her down to the kitchen, sat her at the table and told her to wait, and the detective joined her there a few minutes later. They took her through everything she did and thought. Sophie held Sweet Pea on her lap while telling them her conjectures and musings, everything she had talked about and pondered. This was not a time to hold anything back.

Detective Morris eyed her with interest. "You, young lady, have taken an awful risk, asking so many questions, coming here like this and exploring."

"It didn't feel like a risk at the time. I didn't expect to find anything."

"Just so you know, we were in the process of getting the safe combination from her attorney. You should have called us first."

Sophie hung her head and thought. "You're right," she said. "I just . . . I didn't think it through. I really only came here because of the cat. I wanted Sweet Pea here to have

someone check on him, someone who loves cats, not someone who's afraid of him, like Cissy is." She snuggled him
and he began to purr. "What's going to happen to him?" she
asked.

"I don't know," the detective admitted, her expression
softening as she reached out and stroked his head. "No one
seems to want him. We asked both Florence and Francis,
and even Cissy Peterson, but no one volunteered to take him
home."

"I can't without asking my grandmother, but maybe I can
find him a home."

"You let us know if you can." She stood and said, "You
can go now, but don't talk about this with anyone."

"Okay," she said, but in her mind made an exception for
her nana and Laverne.

On her way home, she called Cissy to confess what she
had done, though she didn't reveal the contents of the safe.
Cissy took it stoically, simply saying it was probably for the
best, and that she would let Francis know about the safe and
why cops were at his mother's house, though she wouldn't
tell him it was Sophie who had discovered it unless she had
to. It was still relatively early in the day, so neither Auntie
Rose's nor Belle Époque was open yet. Sophie let herself in
the back door to find Gilda and Laverne deep in conversation. Thelma's factotum looked weary and worried, but that
was her usual expression, and who could blame her, working
for such a fractious employer?

"How is everything going over at Belle Époque?" Sophie
asked Gilda.

The woman shrugged. "As good as usual, I guess," she
said.

Sophie had always felt sorry for long-suffering Gilda, but
really, the woman needed to grow a backbone and maybe
she wouldn't be treated like a human cleaning rag. "No more
murders, right?"

Gilda looked horrified.

"Now honey, you know you shouldn't joke about things
like that," Laverne said, dropping a wink at Sophie.

"Sorry, Miss Bachman," Sophie said, with a prim politeness that made Laverne smirk into her napkin. "I didn't mean to be cheeky."

Gilda harrumphed and sat up straight. It was amazing what a little coddling did for her sense of self-worth. "I forgive you, child. No, no murders, but I swear, with Phil creeping around the place I worry the cops are going to come down on us again."

Sophie got a cup of tea and sat down at the table. "Phil has been around? What does *he* want?"

"Exactly my thought," Gilda said, her tone acid. "Thelma lets him get away with murder, but me . . . one broken cup, and I'm docked on my pay."

Lets him get away with murder. Sophie was sure Gilda didn't mean that literally. She decided not to point out the not-so-subtle difference between family and employees. Of course, Nana treated Laverne more like family than an employee, so Gilda had a difficult pattern to follow. "That afternoon, the day of the party . . . what all went on over there? I get the sense there were a lot of folks in the kitchen, at some point in the afternoon." Laverne gave her a look, but Sophie shook her head slightly.

"There sure were. Every single person was in the kitchen at one point or another."

"Except Gretchen Harcourt," Sophie corrected.

"Are you kidding? She was in there, too! Nosing around in the fridge, lifting the covers on food tubs, putting her finger in the frosting . . . she was the worst of the bunch and in there first, last and in between. She was in there before anyone else, even when I was trying to shoo the rest of them out."

Sophie was taken aback. Gretchen had been so definite that she had not been in the kitchen at any point, and now it turned out that she had been there during just the right time frame to have put the poisoned cupcake on the tray. "Did you see her near the, uh . . . sweets?"

"Didn't I just say? Fingers in everything."

"Was she ever in there alone?"

"I wouldn't know that, would I?"

"Well, were you ever out of the kitchen?"

Gilda looked around, as if there were spies in the walls, then leaned forward and whispered, "I had a touch of tummy upset—nervous bowel syndrome, you know—and I had to sneak off to the ladies' room for a moment or two." She cleared her throat. "Or three."

Leaving the kitchen unattended. "When would that have been? I mean, had the luncheon started?"

"Well, yes, yes it had. It was during the speeches, you know. Mrs. Whittaker—Mrs. Vivienne Whittaker, that was—was quite the orator."

Interesting . . . Sophie wondered what she had spoken about. She eyed Gilda and asked, "So, Mrs. Vivienne Whittaker made a speech. What all did she say?"

"I don't know. Do you think I had time to listen, with Thelma telling me to hurry up, bring this out, bring that out, don't be so slow, don't be so stupid?"

Sophie was reminded of what people had told her. "You carried out the food, that's right. You carried out a platter with the cupcakes on it, right?"

Gilda's eyes widened. "Y-yes. But . . . but I didn't know, that is—"

"You didn't know then what we know now. I understand that. Was the platter full? What did it look like? How many red-velvet cupcakes were there on it?"

"I-I-I . . . uh, well, now, I don't quite remember."

Sophie eyed the older woman. Beads of sweat had broken out on her temples among the sprouting gray hairs. "More than six red-velvet cupcakes?"

"Oh yes, more than six."

"And the vanilla cupcake in the center. Who put that one there?" Sophie asked, holding her breath.

"The police asked the same thing and I'll tell you what I told them," she said sharply, restlessly moving in her seat. "I have no idea. Not a single one."

Well, if Gilda was the one who had put the lone poisoned cupcake on the platter, she would certainly not volunteer that information.

Gilda sighed dramatically. "I suppose I had better go back soon," she said. "Thelma will be telling me how much time I waste if I don't."

"I honestly don't know why you put up with it," Laverne said.

"You need to tell her that you deserve respect," Sophie said. "And if you don't get it, you'll have to find another job."

"Oh, I couldn't do *that*!" Gilda exclaimed, one hand over her heart. "I'd never find another job in this town. With *my* health?"

"Health?" Sophie was puzzled. Gilda always seemed as strong as an ox.

"I have so many problems," Gilda said. "Nervous bowel is only one." She listed off a host of illnesses that all sounded vaguely the same and had to do with her fragile digestive system.

"Eating too much of your own cooking?" Laverne said.

Sophie shot her a shocked look. Laverne was never purposely mean.

"You are *so* right!" Gilda said. "I've been eating too much at Belle Époque, and Thelma buys the cheapest stuff she can find, and mostly frozen processed food at that. Other than that, I live at Mrs. Stanislowski's boarding house, and her cooking is . . . well, foreign. Goulashes and such. Other stuff I can't even pronounce. She means well, but it's not good, plain American cooking."

"American cooking? Like what?"

Gilda sighed. "I'd love spaghetti, pizza, macaroni, chicken chow mein . . . that kind of thing."

Sophie bit her lip; good American cooking, indeed! They discussed food for a few minutes, and Sophie put together a grab bag of her homemade treats for Gilda and Thelma as Nana ambled into the kitchen. Gilda started up and said she'd better get back to Belle Époque. It was odd how nervous she suddenly seemed, Sophie thought.

"S-so, I've been wondering and wondering," Gilda said, as she fussed with her hair, "who do *you* all think k-killed poor Mrs. Whittaker?"

It was such an abrupt change of subject that Sophie exchanged glances with Nana and Laverne. This was the work of Thelma trying to pick their brains, and why Gilda had been allowed to come over and visit, as both tearooms were getting set up for the day. But it was odd how nervous Nana seemed to make her.

"I sure hope the police don't keep wondering if Mrs. Earnshaw did it," Sophie mused, with a wink at Laverne.

Gilda gabbled, "They don't . . . you don't think—"

Nana sent her a disapproving frown. "Now, I'm sure they are doing no such thing! Don't you worry about it, Gilda."

She stopped clucking and just gasped, quietly, catching her breath. Sophie felt sorry for the woman, so under Thelma's thumb and so afraid to do anything. She could not be the killer; there was just *no* way. It was a crime of desperation and planning, the latter not being something Gilda would be able to pull off.

"Are you and Mrs. E. going to the memorial at the country club for Mrs. Whittaker, Gilda?"

The woman's protuberant eyes widened. "I didn't know there was one!"

"Mr. and Mrs. Harcourt are hosting it, and I said I'd take you both and Cissy," Sophie said, to her grandmother and Laverne.

"Yes, of course," Nana said. Laverne agreed.

"I'd better tell Thelma," Gilda said, heading to the back door. "When is it?"

"Tomorrow morning at eleven," Sophie said, impatient for Gilda to leave. She was bursting to share what she had been up to, with Laverne and Nana.

Gilda hustled out the door and over to Belle Époque. Sophie turned back to her grandmother and friend, relating her discovery of the list in the teapot and the safe code. She told them that with Cissy's permission she had gone over to Vivienne Whittaker's home, and what she had found in the safe.

All three women were silent for a good long time as their tea cooled.

"Why would Vivienne Whittaker be so shady?" Laverne mused, spreading her arthritic fingers out on the tablecloth and turning the gold topaz ring she wore on her index finger. "Why not just come right out and ask Cissy what she thought, rather than write down some names on a note and her safe code? I don't understand."

"It's odd, isn't it?" Sophie said. Laverne had a point; why not come right out and talk to Cissy? "And the safe code had written on it, 'In case you need it.' It's almost like she was afraid something was going to happen to her. Nana, you look like you have an idea or two about that."

"I do," she said. She fiddled with the potted plant in the center of the table. It was a simple yellow primula—a primrose—centered on a hand-quilted placemat with Birman cats as the pattern. She turned the pot around and around, then said, "If I was unsure of myself, if I was afraid of stating too clearly what I thought for fear of accusing the wrong person, I would be obscure."

"Vivienne was afraid of something, or feared something was going on. She wasn't sure, though, and she wanted someone else's input, but . . ." Sophie trailed off, trying to connect the dots in her mind.

"But she was afraid to come right out and say what worried her," Nana finished.

"Or she didn't want to taint Cissy's mind," Laverne said. "You know, put thoughts in her head."

"But why the note and the safe combination. And why Cissy?" Sophie said.

Nana said, "If what she was worried about had to do with her son, then Cissy would be concerned. Maybe she didn't trust anyone else."

"That's what I was thinking." Sophie thought for a moment about the predicament the poor woman had been in. If she was afraid of what might happen, and even thought someone was out to get her, how lonely she must have been! "But why not talk to Francis directly?"

"If I thought someone was sabotaging *you*, my Sophie, I'd try to fix the problem before I involved you, for fear it would only get worse. I'd be afraid if I said anything, you'd tackle it on your own."

"I would never have thought about it from that perspective. What about the names on the lists? Do you know anything about those folks?" She had learned some but not enough.

"Let's see, Mayor Blenkenship ran on a platform of Progress for Gracious Grove," Nana said. "He said we needed to expand or suffocate. New business needs room to develop."

Laverne wryly added, "But some said he was in the pockets of developers, and that they contributed under the table to his campaign fund."

"Developers like the other guys on the list?" Sophie asked.

"I suppose," Nana said.

"Those same builders are listed on that new development sign on the highway. I feel like it's all tied in together: the new development; the recent articles about kickback schemes; talk about annexation; Leathorne and Hedges getting the contract to design the houses and commercial buildings for the new development; and their promotion of Francis." She thought back to the story Phil had told, of Vivienne being the one who turned him in when he was carrying booze for Francis. If it was true, she had a history of intervening when she thought her son was getting into trouble. Is that what was happening this time? But were the players involved a lot more dangerous than Phil Peterson? She shared what she had been pondering.

Sophie knew her grandmother was thinking, but she went ahead and asked, "Running for mayor in Gracious Grove . . . that's never been a big deal, right?"

Nana nodded and smiled. "Mayor Blenkenship usually runs unopposed. This last time, though, he had opposition from another candidate, one who was very popular."

"Oliver Stanfield," Sophie said. "And he's on the list."

"He is."

"And he ran for mayor."

"*But* he withdrew from the race just before the election,

and Mayor Blenkenship ended up unopposed again, except for the usual oddballs, like the spaceship lady and the guy who stands on the corner downtown spouting poetry."

"Does anyone know why Stanfield withdrew?" Sophie asked.

Nana frowned and glanced at Laverne. "Do you remember what was said?"

"He had a family crisis to deal with, didn't he?" Laverne said.

From her conversation with Belinda Blenkenship, Sophie now knew that the "family crisis" for Oliver Stanfield was being reminded by the incumbent that he had a son in prison, the implication being that Blenkenship would raise that subject if necessary and remind the public. She didn't share that; there was no point. Why had Stanfield decided to run against Blenkenship in the first place? "What about the others? What could they have to do with Vivienne's death?"

Nana said, "I don't know."

"That's a good reason to go to the memorial tomorrow; we're bound to meet some of these folks. I'm especially interested in Marva and Holly Harcourt. Cissy said that Marva and Vivienne did not get along at all, which makes it odd that they are hosting the memorial service." She considered telling Nana about what she had overheard between Holly and Vivienne right there in the tearoom, but it didn't mean anything to her yet. Maybe she'd find out more the next day.

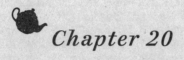

Chapter 20

On a lovely spring morning, with robins warbling and sparrows quarreling, Sophie pulled the SUV up to the portico by the main entrance of the Seneca Golf and Country Club, just outside of Gracious Grove. The parking lot was jammed with cars, most of them elegant luxury models. She helped Nana from the SUV, while Cissy and Laverne climbed out of the backseat. Thelma pulled up behind them in her harvest-gold 1973 Lincoln Town Car. Gilda clambered out and ran around, opening Thelma's door for her. The elderly woman took several minutes to heave herself out, while the valet staff gathered around the car, eyes wide. One young parking valet whistled and asked if she ever wanted to sell it.

"Get your hands off my car and drive it carefully," Thelma snapped, handing him the keys, then joining Sophie and her group on the sidewalk in front of the country club entrance.

As they entered, Sophie took in the facility. The entrance was illuminated with muted lighting, a glittering crystal chandelier over a waterfall that trickled, the sound echoing with the murmurs of the crowd filing into the ballroom where the memorial was being held. By the double doors there was a big sign on an easel; it had Vivienne's photo and her name, with MEMORIAL SERVICE written under it.

As they entered together, an usher guided them to seats, and murmured that after a brief nondenominational service there would be a meet and greet and refreshments provided by the country club and the Harcourts. Sophie watched an usher guide in a soberly dressed Francis Whittaker, on whose arm Florence Whittaker leaned. Cissy hurried to join them. She had closed the bookstore for the morning, so Dana was there, too, and she followed her friend and employer to the front. Gretchen and a young man Sophie took to be her husband, Hollis Harcourt Junior, stood near the dais. Gretchen stalked over to Dana and whispered in her ear; the young woman flushed bright red and moved away from the seat near the front she was about to take.

Nana pointed out Mayor Blenkenship, a pompous-looking fellow with a sturdy build; Belinda Blenkenship stood by him looking terribly out of place in her skirt suit— navy blue this time—and a black fascinator veil springing from a black-velvet bow in her pouffy hair. The young woman appeared to gird her loins, and she approached Gretchen Harcourt. A fake smile on her face, Gretchen greeted her and the two moved off, chattering as if they were lifelong friends. A tall florid fellow with a booming voice strode up the aisle, eschewing the usher by saying, "Don't you think I know my way around this joint? I built it, fer chrissake!"

"*That* is Shep Hammond," Laverne, seated on the other side of Sophie, muttered.

"He looks every bit as creepy as Cissy said he was," Sophie murmured back, as Shep moved to the front, shook the mayor's hand, then went directly to Gretchen and the mayor's wife, kissing both soundly on the cheek close to the lips. He put his arms over each of their shoulders, his hands eventually roaming down their back to their bums. Gretchen giggled and batted at his arm, but Belinda held herself rigidly in place with a look of distaste on her pale face. Why didn't she hit him? Sophie wondered.

The mayor went to Shep—he swiftly released the two young women, who no doubt put up with him because of their husbands—and shook his hand, then led him away to talk in hushed, secretive tones, glancing around the room as he did. They were joined by Holly Harcourt, but it appeared that the conversation became less secretive. This was a coven of men who worked together to benefit themselves, no doubt finding ways to exclude others, as the Libby Lemon owner had suggested. It seemed to happen all too often in government, but Sophie was disappointed to see it working, politics as usual, even in Gracious Grove. Did they manage to keep it legal? Or were there rules flouted, correct ways of dealing circumvented? And did Vivienne Whittaker find out about it and threaten the status quo?

Sophie glanced around the room and noticed Wally Bowman lingering at the back, his eyes scanning the space, as Detective Morris, dressed in a black skirt suit, roamed the perimeter, her gaze focusing on some of the folks named in the note Vivienne had written. Sophie wondered if they had cracked what Vivienne's cryptic messages meant, and if the contents of the envelope had helped.

The last few folks filtered in, the doors were closed and the memorial began. A local pastor spoke, then many others gave speeches praising Vivienne for her civic pride and philanthropy. Some complained about the police department's lack of movement on the case, and took the opportunity to deride the police chief. Then Francis got up to speak. A hush fell over the crowd that had been getting a little restless at the length of the politicians' and businessmen's speeches.

"My mother would have enjoyed seeing you all here today," he said, scanning the crowd. "But she would have been puzzled, too."

Some murmured, as Sophie wondered where he was going with this.

"She would have wondered, why are so-and-so here," he

said, jabbing his finger at the crowd, "when they talked so cruelly about me in the past? And why is *she* here, the woman who snubbed me before I got in the country club, then pretended to be my best friend? She would have wondered, why is *he* here, when he told everyone what a bitch I was for turning him down for a date?"

The murmur grew. Sophie was fascinated. Francis was angry, she could tell even from a distance. Detective Morris was not watching Francis, instead scanning the crowd, pausing on certain folks whose expression made her think, Sophie supposed.

"But most of all, she would have wondered why the one who killed her was here!"

Gasps whispered through the crowd, and the murmur became a babble. Marva Harcourt rushed onto the stage, grabbed the microphone from Francis and exclaimed, "Now, Francis, we know you are suffering, poor, dear boy, as are we all, but there is no call—"

"Let him talk!" someone yelled.

Sophie turned and was amazed to see Phil Peterson standing in the aisle. Wally Bowman accosted him, but not before Phil also yelled, swaying on his feet, "You think my grandma did it—why dontcha come right out and say it, you scumbag!"

Detective Morris, Sophie saw in a glance, was taking notes and watching.

But Wally Bowman, whether in his capacity as police officer or friend, grabbed his arm and said, "Come on, Phil, you know this is not the time or place—"

Phil shook him off and staggered up the aisle, shouting incoherently. Wally sighed, squared his shoulders, then grabbed him and wrestled him to the floor. "Phil, what is wrong with you?" Wally yelled.

Thelma, seated beside Gilda a few rows back of the principals, struggled to her feet and hollered, "Wally, you let go of him!"

"Grandma, let Wally do his job!" Cissy said. She had been heading toward her brother and Wally but she veered away from the drama in the aisle to take her grandmother's arm and coax her to sit back down. Then she looked her brother in the face, as Wally held him upright. "You should be ashamed of yourself, Phillip Peterson!" she said, her voice choked with emotion. "Go home. Sober up. Then start behaving like an adult, instead of an idiot!"

Applause broke out, and Francis, up on the stage, said into the mic, "That's my girl!"

Weeping echoed through the ballroom; Sophie soon realized it was Florence Whittaker, sitting with Marva Harcourt. "Vivienne would have hated all this fuss!" she wailed, as Marva patted her shoulder, ineffectually trying to comfort her.

Sophie caught Wally's grim expression as he half led, half hauled Phil down the aisle and out the door, where a uniformed police officer grabbed him by the hoodie, bent his arm behind his back and dragged him away. The big double doors closed behind them. The memorial service broke up soon after. Francis's momentum had been shattered by the interruption; if he had anything more to say, he kept it to himself.

"I sure wish Wally hadn't stopped Phil and Francis," Nana said.

"Actually, I wish Phil hadn't interrupted Francis," Sophie said. "Phil assumed he was talking about Mrs. Earnshaw, but I don't know if that's true. I don't think it can be. I wonder who he was *really* pointing out as the murderer?"

"Good question," Laverne said. "And I'll bet it's one Missy Detective over there is asking him right now."

Sophie looked in the direction of Laverne's gaze and saw Detective Morris talking to Francis off away from everyone else. He was gesticulating and shaking his head, while she calmly watched and nodded.

Marva Harcourt took the microphone and announced that there would be food and coffee served in the smaller conference room, and that Cissy, Francis and Florence would be there to accept condolences.

As Sophie, Nana and Laverne filed into the conference room behind Cissy, leading Thelma, Sophie whispered,

"Well, that was interesting! Why do you think Phil chose to come and make such a scene?"

"Grandstanding, as usual. That boy has a sense of the dramatic, I will say that." Laverne shook her head and compressed her lips.

Laverne was right, Sophie thought. Phil had always dramatized himself, and maybe in that way he was like Cissy, but at least Cissy had a head on her shoulders. In the conference room, Sophie noted several Silver Spouts members in attendance. Surprisingly, Josh Sinclair was there with his mother, who Nana said had long been acquainted with the Whittaker family. Forsythe Villiers and SuLinn Miller were also there in their capacity as Leathorne and Hedges employee and, in SuLinn's case, the wife of an employee. She had her arm through that of a chubby bespectacled fellow with slicked-back dark hair who must be her husband, Randy.

Just thinking of Leathorne and Hedges made Sophie's mind return to the thorny issue at hand. "Nana, if what we think is correct, then Vivienne suspected something wasn't right with her son's promotion, and/or the deal for the development," Sophie whispered. "She was afraid it would come back to bite Francis later. She has always protected him, even from girls she thought were below him and friends that were trouble."

"She would be worried that her son was going to suffer in the whole deal if it came to light," Nana said. "*I'd* be worried, too, and I'd be trying to figure out how to expose it all without implicating him, if that was my child."

That was an aspect she hadn't considered thoroughly, but it was an excellent point. Sophie needed to look at the list of people in that light. Who could have been endangered by Vivienne's quest to protect her son? And who, among them, had the ability to cause her death? "I need to meet some of these folks. I'm hoping Cissy will introduce me."

"You go ahead, child. Laverne and I are going to find a quiet place and some tea. We'll let information come to us!"

"We'll be like Miss Marple and Ariadne Oliver," Laverne said, with a snicker.

"And which of you is Ariadne?" Sophie said, remembering her grandmother's stack of Agatha Christie novels, and the recurring village spinster and mystery-author character. She had read many of them herself on school vacations spent at Nana's.

"Well, I know I *must* be Miss Marple," Nana said.

"That leaves me as Ariadne," Laverne said. "I won't eat apples in the bathtub, though. Draw the line there."

Sophie spotted Cissy, looking alone and vulnerable despite being on the periphery of a crowd around Francis and Florence. "I gotta go," she said, and slipped away. She approached and touched Cissy's arm. The girl whirled, crying out in alarm, then calmed, taking a deep breath. "You've been through the ringer," Sophie said, holding her arms wide for a hug. "And then Phil has to go and make it worse!"

Cissy fell into her open arms and they embraced. "Thanks, Soph. I don't know what to do about Phil. If Grandma wouldn't coddle him so much, maybe he'd straighten up, but she just keeps giving him 'second' chances. He'll second-chance himself right into jail someday."

"Was he drunk? He looked it."

"He was totally wasted! Grandma is trying to tell everyone he has a chemical imbalance, and that was why he was swaying and slurring. I wish she'd just let him take the fall, for once!"

"So, who are all these people?" Sophie said. "I recognize Forsythe Villiers, because he belongs to my grandma's teapot-collector group, and that's SuLinn Miller, the pretty one with the straight dark hair; she's also a member. Her husband works with Francis, right?"

"Forsythe is such a pill," Cissy said. "He is sucking up to every member of the company like crazy! I heard him tell Harvey Leathorne—one of the founders—that Francis will need a break after this, so he might need to appoint someone else head of the development project."

"What business is it of his?" Sophie asked, remembering Forsythe's name on the teapot list. "He's just in the accounting department, right?"

"Exactly!" Cissy exclaimed. "It's not as if he could be trying to horn in on the project."

But he could be trying to help someone else, Sophie thought. She eyed Randy Miller with interest. That didn't make sense, though, because Randy didn't have a chance to murder Vivienne. Unless he had enlisted a partner in crime. She sighed. She had too many suspects already and didn't need one more. The architect was a long shot, so she dismissed him from her mind.

Cissy then pointed out others and named them. Some were the people on the lists, and she knew them or knew of them already, but wanted more info. "Cissy, I keep meaning to ask . . . I heard that Vivienne made a kind of speech at your engagement tea. Did she say anything odd?"

"Not that I recall," Cissy said.

"What *did* she talk about?" Sophie asked, exasperated. Cissy was less than no use when it came to noticing anything.

Cissy frowned and looked down at her polished nails. "She said . . . let's see . . . that she was so happy I was coming into the Whittaker family, but that she hoped I would find everything in my life easier, not harder, after marriage. She said Francis was . . . what did she say? Francis was a good man who deserved a good wife, and she hoped I would be his mainstay in the difficult days to come."

"Wait . . . she predicted difficult days to come?"

Cissy shrugged. "I think that's what she said." Her eyes widened. "Do you think she had, like, a psychic vision of her death?"

Sophie didn't think Vivienne Whittaker was prescient. It had to be that, as she and Nana and Laverne had speculated, Vivienne worried that Francis would be implicated in some kind of scandal to do with the development deal. Did Francis innocently or not-so-innocently help the bigwigs push something through? Or did he just know something, and so had to be shut up with a promotion ahead of more-senior staff? And did Vivienne threaten the status quo so much she had to be taken out, either to stop her from talking, or as a warning to Francis?

"Cissy, what did Francis mean when he said the murderer was in the room?"

"I asked him and so did the detective, but he just said it stood to reason; everyone Vivienne knew was in the room, so whoever killed her must be there."

Sophie didn't believe that for a minute, but if he wouldn't tell Cissy or the detective who he suspected, then he sure wouldn't tell her. "I'd better circulate," Sophie said. "Could you introduce me around? I'd like to meet some of the folks from Leathorne and Hedges and the others."

Cissy did so, taking Sophie around and introducing her as a very old, very dear friend from her childhood. She took a deep breath as Shep Hammond, his eyes wide with delight, slung his arm over Sophie's shoulders. "Well, aren't you a special treat! Didn't know sweet little Cissy had another friend as pretty as herself!"

Sophie gritted her teeth as Cissy floated away, and said, "I'm pleased to meet you, Mr. Hammond. Cissy must be so grateful to you for finding work for Phil all the time." His arm was heavy over her shoulders, but she resisted the urge to duck away. "What did you think of his display at the memorial service?"

He shook his head and squeezed her shoulder, rubbing it with one massive mitt. "Awful. Just awful. That boy . . . well, I do give him work from time to time, but he's unreliable."

"What kind of work?"

"Odd jobs."

"On building sites?"

"Sometimes, sometimes personal errands. He's like family, you know."

Personal errands? "I hear a lot about this new development . . . has he been helping you with that?"

"No, not that," Shep said, with a hearty laugh that had folks eyeing him with distaste. No one likes big laughter at a memorial for the recently deceased. "I got other folks for

that in my pocket, you know," he said, patting his sport-
jacket pocket with one giant paw.

That phrase had unsavory political implications to
Sophie, but she smiled up at him like a fatuous idiot. "I'll
just bet you do! I'll bet you can pull all kinds of strings if
you want. Maybe you could even get town council to strike
the bylaw against liquor in Gracious Grove?"

"Oho, don't think it hasn't crossed my mind, little lady,
but we're just gonna wait on that, you see, until we have the
annexation all right and tight and . . . well, now, I don't mean
to bore you with business talk."

Just then a gentleman strolled over, one she had just met.
It was Harvey Leathorne. He said, "Shep, we need to talk."
He glanced at Sophie. "You don't mind, do you, missy?"

"No, not at all," she said, as she slid from Shep Hammond's clutch. It was bad timing because she would have
liked to worm more information out of Mr. Hammond. The
talk of annexation and his willingness to discuss erasing the
anti-liquor bylaw from the books was interesting. He must
feel he had access to and the will of the right politicians to
accomplish that.

But she didn't take off as the two men started talking;
instead she drifted close to them, as Leathorne began with,
"We have to contain this, and soon. He's your problem,
Shep—you swore you could handle him—and I won't see
him ruin everything."

He who? Phil, likely, but could *he* be Francis, instead?
Probably had nothing to do with the murder, but . . .

"Look, he wouldn't listen to me."

"I know, but that damn detective has been sniffing around
all of us involved in GGG, and the last thing we need is the
public getting wind of all we've had to do to get this thing
done. All I wanted was for him to suggest that . . ." Leathorne
glanced around, and Sophie felt his gaze settle on her. "Let's
talk about this elsewhere," he finished.

They moved through the crowd away from her, and Sophie
saw that the two men were joined by two others, the mayor

and, surprisingly, Marva Harcourt. What did they have in
common? Well, they were all on Vivienne Whittaker's
second list. And maybe they were all involved in the
development deal. Gretchen had said that Holly Harcourt
was involved, but maybe Marva was behind that.

Dana edged over to her through the crowd and whispered,
"You look like you wish you could follow that crew," she
said, indicating the departing foursome. "What is up with
that? I can't stand Shep Hammond. He's a real creepola."

Sophie eyed Dana; she was way smarter than Sophie had
given her credit for, and a little devious, too. "There is something going on in this town, something to do with the new
development. It stinks of political payoffs." She explained
her thought process, that the developers, namely Shep Hammond, Oliver Stanfield, the GG Group (whoever that was)
and even Harvey Leathorne, had been paying off someone
in high places, quite probably Mayor Blenkenship himself,
to facilitate an eventual annexation bid—which would surely
increase the value of the development land—and maybe
even a change to the town's "dry" status.

"And you think it's tied up with Vivienne's murder?"
Dana asked, eyes wide. "How do you know all this?"

Sophie quickly filled Dana in on the notes naming the
developers and others, though she didn't tell Dana *all* the
names. "You have to keep this to yourself, though, and I
mean it. I shouldn't even have told you that much."

The young woman's eyes danced with mischief. "Want
me to follow them and find out what they're saying?"

"That would be awesome!" Sophie gasped.

Dana chuckled. "I used to work here as a server, so I
know all the tricks. A lot of the walls in this place are thin
as paper, meant to move aside to throw rooms together. Talk
to you later!" She sauntered out after them.

Sophie turned her attention to her grandmother, but Nana
and Laverne had cornered Forsythe Villiers, and Randy and
SuLinn Miller. Maybe they were finding something out that
very minute. That left . . . Jason and Julia, who stood nearby

chatting with another group of folks. What was Julia Dandridge's name doing on one of the lists, and what did she have to do with the new development?

"Sophie!" Jason said, as she wandered over to join them. "You met Julia the other day, but you haven't met her husband, Nuñez Ortega. He's an architect and partner at Leathorne and Hedges!"

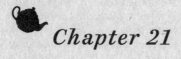

Chapter 21

Sophie blinked rapidly. Julia Dandridge was married, and Nuñez Ortega was her husband *and* a partner at Leathorne and Hedges? Was he the reason Julia's name was on the lists? She realized they were staring at her, Jason with an odd look on his face. Nuñez had his hand thrust out toward her, and Julia was watching with a frown on her face. "I'm sorry. I've been a little shaken by everything today," she said, taking the man's hand. He was a dark, good-looking fellow in his forties. As he released her hand, he slung his arm over his wife's shoulders.

"We all have been," Nuñez said, his expression and tone somber. "Vivienne Whittaker was a guiding light in this town, a woman of impeccable social conscience. I served on the board of a couple of charities with her."

"Really? Which ones?"

"We were forming an exploratory committee to create a local Habitat for Humanity group. Even in relatively affluent Gracious Grove there are those who could use a hand finding a home for their family. We were on one that may interest you, too, Miss Taylor. We were founding members of Foodies for Families, a group that gleans for the needy."

"My husband is talking about the Bible verses, you know, about gleaning the fields . . . but we glean from local restaurants to give the unused foods to shelters and hostels," Julia said, sending a warm glance at her husband.

"That is a *great* cause."

"Would you, as a chef, be interested in helping?" Nuñez said. "Jason has told us all about your career in New York. We were thinking of putting together a recipe book as a fund-raiser and would be honored by your input."

"I would love to help, and perhaps in a more practical way, too, Mr. Ortega. At Auntie Rose's Victorian Tea House we often have leftover scones and other goodies. Nana does her best in sending them to folks who can use them, but maybe we can offer some to Foodies for Families." She paused a beat. "I, uh, I understand you are thinking of investing in a fine dining establishment in Gracious Grove," Sophie said, turning to Julia. She needed to process the fact that Nuñez knew Vivienne so well. His name was on the first list, but not the second. What did that mean?

"I asked her professional opinion, as a chef, about opening a fine dining establishment here in town," Jason said, shifting uncomfortably.

Maybe he hadn't told Julia he was going to ask Sophie her opinion. Too bad. It was out there now.

Julie exchanged a look with her husband and said, "Nothing so formal as thinking about it, even. I know someone who is tossing around the notion, and we would invest if it came to that. But things will have to change in this town, first."

"You mean, like it being a dry town?" Sophie asked, glancing from face to face.

"Well, yes," Julia said. "It's ridiculous, in this day and age, that we can't go out to a restaurant in this town and order a glass of wine, or buy alcohol at a store. It is simply *ridiculous*."

"I know a lot of folks think as you do," Sophie said, feeling the condescension in the professor's manner as a slight against her beloved town. "But I wouldn't count on it chang-ing. I think even Vivienne Whittaker was opposed to a change in that way, was she not?"

"But she was only one person," Nunez said. "Town coun-cil seems more progress-minded."

Progress-minded . . . that was one way of looking at it. Crooked and bought was another way. In developers' vest pockets yet another.

"I guess you could avoid that completely by placing the restaurant outside town limits, right? In the new develop-ment, say?"

Nuñez was watching Sophie with a puzzled look. Julia glanced at her husband, then said, "That is one option, to be sure, but my concern is that if it was annexed, would the new development be subject to the same liquor laws as the rest of Gracious Grove?"

"True . . . that would be a concern." This was a waste of time. Though both Nuñez and Julia were on Vivienne's list, neither one of them had had a chance to poison the woman. Julia had not been at the engagement tea, nor had she been at the tearoom at all that day, as far as Sophie knew. There was no random chance in Vivienne selecting the one poi-soned cupcake on that plate, so the killer just *had* to be someone at the party. That didn't mean one or both of them couldn't be a coconspirator, and/or might know more than they were saying. She'd have to keep that in mind, but for the moment they were low priority. She spotted Gretchen standing with the older Harcourts, and excused herself, tell-ing Jason she'd love to talk to him in the next couple of days, if he had some free time.

So, Marva was back from her discussion with the mayor and the builder. Sophie slid through the crowd and tapped Gretchen on her shoulder. "Hi, Gretchen. How are you doing?"

Her face frozen in a polite smile, Gretchen murmured that she was fine.

"Why don't you introduce me?" Sophie said, smiling at Marva and Holly Harcourt.

With great reluctance, Gretchen did just that.

"Your grandmother runs that charming establishment, Auntie Rose's," Marva said. "I've been there many times. Much better run than Belle Époque, I must say. That Earnshaw woman has no business sense, and her food is atrocious."

Gretchen appeared uneasy.

"Are you saying that because poor Mrs. Whittaker was poisoned there?" Sophie asked, eyes wide.

"Hey now," Holly Harcourt said, jovially. "That was an accident, pure and simple. I'm sure that poor old woman didn't mean to poison anyone. Right? Am I right?"

"Mrs. Earnshaw didn't poison anyone on purpose *or* by accident," Sophie said, trying to quell her anger. "It was someone at the engagement party, but not Mrs. Earnshaw."

"Why do you say that, little lady?" Holly's tone was indulgent.

"She didn't really have any motive, did she? And she'd be foolish to do it in her own place. Right?"

Marva Harcourt's face was white. "Enough about the death. This is hardly the time or place to be talking about all of this!"

Where and when better? Sophie wondered. It occurred to her suddenly that the murder could have been a two-person job: Marva could have planted the poison cupcake, and Gretchen could have been delegated the task of making sure she ate it. It was an interesting thought.

"C'mon, chill, Marva honey," Holly Harcourt said, with another chuckle. "I like this girl; she's cheeky."

"What did you all think of Phil Peterson's display? I guess he can be forgiven for worrying about his grandmother." Sophie watched Marva's eyes. There was a lot of white around the irises, like she was nervous or frightened.

"It was appalling," Gretchen said, in her snootiest tone. "He had no right to bust in here and say that everyone was gunning for his grandma."

His expression sober, Harcourt said, "Vivienne was a

grand lady. That lack of decorum would have upset her greatly."

She was aching to mention seeing him at Auntie Rose's with Vivienne, but she didn't want to upset the apple cart just yet. "Poor Cissy is right in the middle, with her grandmother and Phil on one side, and the Whittaker family on the other."

"If she's smart, she'll side with the Whittakers. That's where the money is," Marva said, her tone nasty. "That Earnshaw-Peterson family doesn't have two nickels to rub together. Thelma Mae Earnshaw goes around with her nose in the air acting like Francis isn't good enough for her precious granddaughter, but I can tell you, Vivienne felt like it was the opposite way around."

Where the money was . . . and yet Vivienne had said something about those whose only use of money was to make more money. "But Mrs. Whittaker got Francis and Cissy together in the first place," Sophie said.

"That was before she knew what a mess that family was! She was regretting it, I can tell you," Marva said.

From what Sophie had learned, it seemed that Vivienne was reaching out to Cissy, trusting her over her country club friends. Or maybe she just wasn't sure who she could trust. "Did the police give you any sense of what they were thinking when they interviewed you about being at the engagement tea that day?" Sophie asked, watching the older woman's face.

Her eyes widened and she shook her head, but she remained mute.

"Why did you leave so early?"

"She is an impossible woman to get along with, that Thelma Earnshaw," Marva said, moving her clutch purse from under one arm to the other.

Holly Harcourt was more emphatic. "She told my wife she had no business mucking about in the food. Imagine that! Marva was just trying to help her out."

"That's too bad. Mrs. Earnshaw can be a bit touchy at

times. Did you bring something special?" she asked, still
watching the woman.

"I brought whole-wheat wraps; nutritious food instead of
the garbage she serves. I *thought* she'd be grateful, but
instead, when I just tried to plate them, she got upset. She
said it was the last straw, that folks had better stop rooting
around in her cupboards or she was going to call the police."

Holly patted his wife's shoulder in a vague attempt to
soothe her. From what Mrs. Earnshaw had said, it seemed
like Marva Harcourt was doing a little investigating and
then commenting on past-date items in the fridge or
cupboard—bad form for an invited guest, no matter how
true it was.

Right now everything was a jumble in Sophie's mind.
Phil Peterson could not be the murderer, that she was sure
of, and the same reasoning applied to Thelma Mae Earnshaw. Whoever did it had made sure that there was one
poisoned vanilla cupcake, and that it would be the only one
Vivienne Whittaker would choose from a plate of red-velvet
cupcakes.

Though Cissy certainly had the opportunity, perhaps
more than anyone else, given that it was her grandmother's
establishment, she didn't seem to have a motive. Cissy had
no feelings of ill will toward Vivienne, and she was not the
type of girl to plan a murder, certainly not at her own
engagement tea in her grandmother's tearoom.

But Marva . . . Sophie could see Marva happily poisoning someone she didn't like or resented. However, there was
no evidence that she felt that way toward Vivienne. And that
brought Sophie back to Holly Harcourt. "Mr. Harcourt, I
happened to see you at my grandmother's teahouse one day
with Mrs. Whittaker just before her death. I was clearing
the table next to you. You were talking about Francis, if I
overheard correctly?"

Gretchen gasped and Marva blanched, stretched face as
pale as could be under beige matte foundation. But Holly
looked Sophie over for a long moment and then replied,

"Vivienne and I, uh . . . we were talking about Francis, it's true. She'd heard that folks were gossiping about his promotion, saying that it was fishy." His gaze was censorious. "I think I see now what she meant by gossips. Is this some kind of inquisition?"

That was intended to put Sophie in her place, but she was not cowed by his booming voice and grave manner. It was an explanation, she supposed, but not a particularly good one. What she found interesting was that it had seemed to take an awfully long time for him to say anything. Had he been trying to remember word for word what Vivienne had said, so he could respond in a way to deflect suspicion?

"I think we ought to go mingle, Holly," Marva said, taking his arm and tugging him away. Gretchen followed, throwing worried glances over her shoulder toward Sophie.

Sophie spotted Dana slinking along the periphery of the crowd. Marva had been first to return, but now all the principals from that impromptu meeting were back in the ballroom. She caught up with Dana and pulled her into a private alcove away from the crowd. "So what did you overhear?"

"I don't know if any of this has anything to do with anything," Dana said, with a frustrated shrug. "It was a lot of babble."

"Like about what?"

"Well, Leathorne kept talking about 'value for dollar spent,' and fussing about the 'deal' going sour. Those are the only words he used, over and over, 'deal' and 'development deal.' Marva Harcourt griped about her 'investment.'"

"Investment . . . hmm. I wish I'd known that a few moments ago when I was talking to the Harcourts." Sophie ducked her head out of the alcove; Marva and Holly were now over in a corner with a couple of the others, the same folks together time and time again. What had been so crucial for them to talk about at such an event? "So what did the mayor have to say?"

"Typical politician; he said a lot, but most of it was gabble. He kept talking and talking . . . he said he wanted the

best for Gracious Grove and truly believed that development
would help the town prosper and grow, giving their eco-
nomic future just the shot in the arm it needed . . . and blah,
blah, blah . . . whatever. He said something about 'changes
needed before annexation can be considered.' A lot more
stuff like that."

"Annexation . . . I keep hearing that word. Interesting.
What about Shep Hammond?"

"That guy is a piece of work!" Dana exclaimed. She
waved and smiled at someone who drifted by their private
nook and paused, waiting for that person to go out of earshot
as Sophie fidgeted impatiently. "He said, and I quote, 'We
need to contain the tearoom talkers 'cause they're gonna
cause trouble. I say we send out a stern warning not to get
their knickers in a twist.' Don't even ask me what the hell
he's talking about, but there are only two tearooms involved,
your grandmother's and Cissy's grandmother's."

"*Tearoom talkers*," Sophie mused. "That could mean
anything, though! It might be a group who meets at one of
the tearooms. Nana has several groups that meet once a
month, or once every other week, and I know for a fact that
Forsythe Villiers has a group of Leathorne and Hedges
young professionals who meet at Auntie Rose's. As a matter
of fact, the Gracious Grove Businesswomen's group met at
Nana's tearoom, too." And those women, with their action
committee in the works and their critical view of the Gracious Grove political climate, just might be the "tearoom
talkers" Hammond was so concerned about.

"Like I said, I have no clue what he's talking about. I just
report!" Dana eyed Sophie. "Have *you* been asking questions? Nosing around?"

"Not much before today, or not so anyone would notice,
anyway."

"So they don't mean you!"

"I hope not. Thanks for your snooping, Dana, I really
appreciate it." Sophie watched her drift away. Dana joined
the group that surrounded Francis and touched his sleeve,
then put her arm over his shoulders. Sophie had kind of

forgotten about Francis and Dana once being an item, but was vividly reminded.

"She'd love to push little Cissy out of the running," Gretchen Harcourt said.

Sophie snapped around, surprised to find the young woman so close. "No. Dana and Francis are still friends, but anything else was over a long time ago."

"You sure about that?" Gretchen watched them for a long minute. "I say she still has the hots for him, or at least for old Whittaker money. And *new* Whittaker money!"

"*New* Whittaker money?"

"Well, sure! He's been promoted and given a handsome raise, and I heard that he got his mama to invest in the new development pretty heavy, so her estate—and Francis, I suppose—stands to make a bundle."

Where is my money? Vivienne had written on the note in the safe. Did she *know* she had invested in the development? Or was that where her money had gone without her being aware of it?

Money, the root of all evil, it had been said. Or rather, the *love* of money was the root of all evil. But did Francis really love money so much? He didn't drive a flashy car, didn't appear to have a lavish lifestyle, and his mom seemed inclined to be generous to her son and daughter-in-law-to-be. No reason for Francis to want her dead.

She turned to the girl, remembering something she wanted to ask her. "Gretchen, I was wondering about something. You told me adamantly that you were never in the kitchen, but Gilda said you were in there poking about in the fridge and checking out the sweets. What's up with that?

Gretchen was silent for a long moment. "I did go in there. Guess I just plumb forgot."

Eyes narrowed, Sophie watched her. "Did you bring something to the tea?"

She swallowed. "I did. Red-velvet cupcakes, homemade from my mama's recipe. It's a down-home tradition."

"Why didn't you say that before?"

"It just didn't seem important."

"Why red velvet?"

She shrugged. "Someone mentioned them, and I said I had a good recipe, that's all."

"Who mentioned them?"

She licked her lips. "I . . . I can't remember."

"Oh, come on . . . was it your mother-in-law, maybe?"

"I told you," Gretchen cried. "I don't remember!"

"Did you put the cupcakes out?"

"Well, sure. I put 'em on the same plate as those awful store-bought ones."

"And yet you didn't think that was important enough to mention?"

The young woman shook her head with a self-conscious look. "I . . . I gotta go," she mumbled, and headed away, across the room.

Sophie stared at her for a long moment. Was there anything else Gretchen Harcourt was concealing?

Chapter 22

The crowd was breaking up and folks were drifting off. Sophie had a lot to think about, but just as she was considering gathering her group and leaving, she saw Jason heading toward her. He made her nerves flutter, but that ship had sailed long ago. The somber thought steadied her nerves.

"Hey, Jason. How are you doing?"

"I'm good. I thought I'd talk to you before I left, but I didn't want to do it in front of the others." He hesitated, frowning, and looked over his shoulder toward his group of friends. "Nuñez seems antsy about this development everyone is talking about, worried somehow. Is Leathorne and Hedges involved?"

She nodded. "They've apparently got the design contract. Must be a big one. Francis has been appointed lead architect on the project, so I'm assuming it's a done deal. I've heard that there is jealousy in the firm over his promotion; some thought that he was pushed ahead of more-senior architects, but maybe there's a reason for that."

"What do you mean?"

Sophie shrugged.

"You're not saying there's anything fishy about it, are you?"

Sophie sighed. "I'm no hard-nosed cynic, Jason, but I've been up close and personal with business, and I've seen how it works. I've been offered great jobs if I was willing to cozy up to the right people. I've been *denied* jobs I was qualified for because someone's nephew or daughter got it, with less experience."

"Francis always did take the easy way, when he could," Jason mused.

Sophie thought about that for a long moment, wondering if Phil had been telling the truth after all about Francis's involvement in the bootlegging. Not that that had anything to do with anything, now, but it was an interesting thought. "So, did Nuñez think *he* ought to have gotten the job, rather than Francis?"

"I didn't say that; he's a partner, so I would imagine he's way beyond that. From what I understand he mostly deals with higher-end commercial buildings and some out-of-town properties. He's lead architect on an office tower in Ithaca. He just acted . . . a little odd. When someone tried to talk to him about the development, he kind of hushed them."

"Who tried to talk to him?"

"Uh . . . I think it was that Hammond guy. He's got a booming voice and Nuñez looked uncomfortable. Maybe it was just that he didn't think it was appropriate to be talking about work at a memorial service. Anyway, Julia doesn't like Hammond. Nuñez had him over to dinner a few times, but she told me she thinks he's a creep."

"Along with every other female in Gracious Grove." Sophie pondered the implications and a question popped into her mind. "So why would Nuñez have Hammond over to dinner?"

"I don't know. Why wouldn't he?"

"Because the guy's a creep."

"If we only associated with people we wholly approved of, we'd never socialize," Jason said.

"Thank you for that lesson; I didn't know." Sophie knew immediately that she had gone too far, and saw the hurt look on his face. "I'm sorry, Jason, but that just sounded—"

"Pompous? Sententious?" He gave a quirky grin. "I think becoming a college professor makes you that way. Sometimes I listen to the stuff that comes out of my mouth, and I'm appalled at how pedantic I sound."

"I didn't mean it," she said, one hand on his sleeve. "I think I'm a little . . . sensitive. Coming back to Gracious Grove has been great, but I'm a different person than I was when I last stayed here for any length of time. I'm constantly being reminded that I was kind of standoffish and seemed snobby, when all that time I just longed to be a part of the group. I'm older and I've grown up, but it's hard for people here to see that."

"*I* see it," he said, warmly. He pulled her in for a hug. "Time hasn't stood still for any of us."

It was good to be in his arms, but he was different, too, a man now. He had been a boy the last time he had hugged her this way.

Julia Dandridge approached. "Are you ready to go, Jason?" She gave Sophie an apologetic look. "I wouldn't interrupt, but Jason is our ride and I have a million things to do back at work. Nuñez needs to get back to the office, too."

"That's okay," she said. "I have to get Nana and friend back to the tearoom. We're opening late today." She and Jason said a brief good-bye, and Sophie crossed the room to her grandmother and Laverne. They were deep in conversation with Josh Sinclair.

"No one could have known what they intended to do with the property, Josh. I know your mom's upset, but it's not her fault." Nana looked worried, and had one wrinkled blue-veined hand on the boy's shoulder.

"What's going on?"

"Sneaky doings in Gracious Grove, that's what is going on," Laverne said, with a *hmph* of disapproval.

"It's a free world, Laverne," Nana said. "Don't you worry about it, Josh. Everything will be all right."

"Anyone want to clue me in?" Sophie asked.

Nana said, "Josh's grandma's house, just down the street, finally sold. He just found out it was bought by a group that's going to turn it into another tearoom. He's worried that will cut into business."

"Not yours," Sophie said, though it was a bit of a shock. "People will still come to Auntie Rose's Victorian Tea House for the Auntie Rose experience. Bookings are up this year, right?"

The boy looked relieved. "That's good. I was so mad when I heard, I just thought it was a jerky thing to do."

"It's business," Sophie said. "Business is never personal."

"But you don't expect someone you like to do something you think is jerky, you know? I *like* the professor. I'm taking a college-level preparatory English Lit course from her as a part of my accelerated program," he explained. "I'm going to Cruickshank for a year before going to an out-of-state college; my mom thinks I'm too young to leave home yet. But she's a nice lady, so I guess I'm just surprised."

"Professor? She? *She* who?" Sophie said, still a little confused.

Nana said, "Oh, that's right. You weren't here for the whole conversation. The house was bought by a college professor and her husband. They're going to convert it into a New Age tearoom, so Josh tells me."

"Are you talking about Julia Dandridge?" Sophie blurted out.

"Yeah. She's a great teacher, actually," Josh said. "But why would she buy an old house to make it into a tearoom on a street where there's already two tearooms?"

Sophie was stunned, and she watched as Jason and his group left. Julia caught her eye and waved. Sophie didn't wave back.

Thelma sat in an alcove hidden from view and thought over the day. Poor Phil had been troublesome, as usual. That boy . . . he needed a whooping, but it was kind of late in his life for that. She couldn't help worrying that despite what folks were saying—she had heard that the poison was in a cupcake, of all places—that Phil's little addition to the punch had been lethal for Vivienne Whittaker. Did she drink it? She couldn't have drunk it. But what if she *did* drink it? That thought kept rattling around in her brain like a hamster in a wheel, over and over. All this worry was going to make her sick, if she didn't watch it.

Where was Gilda? She was supposed to be nosing around and reporting back. Thelma's feet hurt, and she wasn't about to trot around asking questions and snooping like she'd like to, even if she did resemble Margaret Rutherford as Miss Marple, from the old movies. Cissy was off who knew where, catering to Francis Whittaker, no doubt, the big baby. You'd think he was a kid, not a grown man, the way he went on about losing his mother. Cissy had lost hers at sixteen and you didn't hear her whine about it.

Not now, anyway.

She slipped her shoes off and rubbed one foot against the other, hoping her elastic hose didn't develop a hole in the toe. These things were darned expensive and the way things were going at Belle Époque, she'd have to start subsisting on her pension. If they didn't solve the murder soon, she'd be out of business. Bookings had slowed once the initial curiosity about the "Killer Tearoom," as the local TV station had called it, was over. They got a great video of her waving her fist and calling the reporter names, too, just as the fool was trying to do a spot right outside her door. Invasion of property, that's what it was!

"It's getting dicey," a voice remarked, just around the corner from her little alcove.

"I know," said a second speaker. "But we need to just keep our noses to the grindstone, so to speak, and keep on. Now that Vivienne's gone, we oughtn't to have any more trouble, right?"

"Yeah, she was the only one who was really onto the plan," the first fellow said. "Or at least the only one inclined to squawk about it."

"We'd better get moving," the second guy said. "That tearoom girl is giving us an odd look. I don't like the way she's been snooping around."

"You think she's suspicious?"

"I do," second guy replied. "She's been asking a lot of questions. But there are ways to make sure she doesn't cause us any trouble."

The first guy made a sound of surprise.

"No, not that way!" second guy said. "Nothing drastic, just something to scare her. We need a little more time, and it'll be a done deal."

The rustling sound of men in suit jackets moving away told Thelma they were leaving; she ducked her head around the corner to see who had been talking. *Well, fancy that*, she thought, recognizing one of the men. What were they up to? From their words she couldn't be sure if they were involved in Vivienne Whittaker's murder or not; she hadn't thought of the possibility that whoever planned it might not have even been at the party.

She was going to have to go home and think about this. It sure seemed shady. But those cops, especially that woman detective, wouldn't look kindly on Thelma calling them with a tip again, not after the last little trouble. It was important that she actually have a solid lead this time.

Gilda hobbled over with a plate full of food and sank into a seat on the bench next to Thelma. "Gosh, my feet hurt so bad!"

"Bet mine hurt worse. You're gulping down a platter of free food and yet you didn't even think to bring me a cup of tea? A fine helper you are," Thelma grumbled.

Gilda shrugged. "You didn't ask me for tea, you just asked me to snoop around."

Thelma decided to ignore the back talk in favor of information. "And?"

"And what?" Gilda asked, her protuberant eyes holding a puzzled expression. She chewed and swallowed.

"*And* did you find anything out?"

"Not really. Folks were mostly talking about Francis and Phil and what they said."

"Who said what?"

Gilda's eyes widened and she processed the question. She took another bite of a brownie and chewed, thoughtfully. "Well," she said, after she swallowed. "The mayor said that Francis ought not to have to put up with abuse from the likes of Phil Peterson."

"Humph. I knew I never liked him. I sure didn't vote for him!" She hadn't voted for anyone, but Thelma didn't share *that* information. "What else?"

"Oh! The most interesting bit . . . old lady Sinclair's house that just sold? Some college professor bought it and they're going to put in a new tearoom, all modern, fang shooey, or something like that, with the latest of everything!"

Thelma's hand flew to her bosom and she couldn't breathe. Another tearoom on their street? More like another nail in her coffin! "How—who—" Her voice came out as a croak. Now what?

"Sophie looked real worried, I can tell you that. She said it would be all right, but she sure looked worried."

Thelma took a deep breath. Sophie Taylor was a smart young girl. If *she* was worried, it didn't look good. Would the misery never end for Belle Époque?

I t was late, and darkness had crept across the sky, shading from mauve to deep purple. Sophie was up in her room trying to plan Cissy's wedding shower tea party, even though her mind was in a million other places. She was tired of thinking the same things. Vivienne's murder had something to do with the new development; she was worried about Francis being held responsible for some kind of illegal activity, and had threatened the wrong person, but who?

Marva's behavior was suspect, and Gretchen seemed frightened. Could the two have worked together to kill Vivienne? Neither seemed like the type to commit such a heinous act.

Belinda Blenkenship would make the ideal tool, and could have been used to place the cupcake without even being aware of what she was doing until it was too late. That would explain why she now looked so frightened, Sophie thought.

Florence Whittaker had the nerves for that kind of plot, but how did she benefit from killing Vivienne unless it was motivated by the long-existing enmity between them, which seemed to have mostly evaporated?

Francis was there and could have done it, but since his mother had only ever acted with his best interests at heart and there didn't seem to be any problems between them, his motive was murky at best.

Sophie heard a clatter and looked out her kitchenette window toward the street; her grandmother was dragging a garbage pail to the road. Darn it! Why hadn't she known it was garbage night? She had to pay more attention to duties around Auntie Rose's to make Nana's life easier.

She slipped on a pair of tennies and, followed by Pearl, galloped down the steps and wound her way through the kitchen, hoping she'd be in time to help, or at least scold Nana for doing the labor herself. But when she got to the street, all she could see was the garbage can and no Nana. How the heck . . . ?

"Nana? Where are you . . . oh!" Sophie saw a pair of slippered feet sticking out from behind the garbage can. As she raced toward her grandmother, someone ran up behind her and scooped up Pearl, who yowled indignantly and struggled to get free.

The hooded figure, face shadowed in darkness, muttered, "Keep your nose out of everyone else's business, or you'll suffer. We'll start with the cat."

Sophie shrieked, "Let her go!"

He tossed Pearl down and raced off. Torn between following and taking care of her grandmother, Sophie chose to scoop up Pearl and go to help Nana, who was now clambering to her feet, quivering all over with fear.

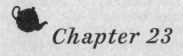

Chapter 23

"**W**ho do you think did it?" Laverne asked Sophie the next morning.

Sophie shook her head, staring out the window toward Belle Époque. The attack was deeply troubling. She feared that even the police, who had come rapidly when she called 911, couldn't stop a determined killer. Wally Bowman and the detective agreed that given the attacker's words, it had to be related to the murder next door. Their officers scoured the neighborhood, but the attacker was nowhere to be found. Sophie spent the night in her grandmother's apartment, not content to be even one floor away.

"I don't know," Sophie said, in response to Laverne's question. "But I know who I suspect." She related her conclusions of the night before.

Nana limped into the kitchen, looking exhausted. "I'll be glad when all of this is over," she moaned, getting a mug from the mug tree on the counter.

"You sit!" Sophie said, jumping up. "I'll get your tea. After what you've been through . . ." She shook her head and grabbed the teapot, as Pearl ambled in and wound around her feet, none the worse for the trauma of the night before.

Nana slumped down in a chair and Pearl jumped up on her lap. Nana hadn't argued with Sophie about getting her own tea, and she normally would have. Laverne cast her a worried glance, brows raised.

"Don't go fussing about me just because I'm letting someone else get my tea," Nana said, hugging the cat to her in a fierce embrace. "I'll be fine, but at my age aren't I entitled to take it easy sometimes?"

"You sure are," Laverne said, promptly. "It's just that we've been telling you that for a while, but you never let us take care of you."

"Maybe I've decided I should. Anyway, you were talking about the crime, the *real* crime, poor Vivienne Whittaker's death." She shifted the cat and pulled a paper out of her housecoat pocket. "I tried to figure out a list of suspects. Like Sophie said, it ended up being everyone at the tea the day Vivienne was killed!"

"I know," Sophie said, putting the steaming mug in front of her grandmother. "But surely we can eliminate some."

"Like Gilda?" Laverne said. "That woman couldn't poison anyone unless it was with bad cooking."

"And Mrs. Earnshaw," Sophie agreed, taking her grandmother's list and drawing a line through them both.

"It's her bargain hunting that'll kill someone. She never saw day-old anything she wouldn't buy and pass off as fresh!" Laverne said.

Nana frowned at the paper. "I just can't see that Belinda, the mayor's wife, as doing anything. She seems like such an inoffensive little thing! My bets are on Florence Whittaker, Marva Harcourt, Gretchen Harcourt, or Francis himself."

"You think he would kill his own mother?" Laverne's dark face wrinkled in a troubled frown. They had gone over it again and again, but still, it was shocking to consider.

Nana shook her head. "I just don't know anymore. I can't believe he would, but you really never know."

Sophie was alarmed by her grandmother's weary willingness to consider Francis the villain. "I just can't believe he'd do it!"

Laverne shrugged. "If you'd said two weeks ago that there would even *be* a murder next door, I would have said you were crazy. We can't rule anyone out!"

Nana said, "I'm just *afraid* to rule anyone out."

"So we're back to square one, with everyone who had access on the list of suspects, including Phil Peterson."

"Poor Thelma. If he's guilty . . . just imagine how she'll feel!" Nana shook her head.

"I'm really angry. I've never been so afraid in my life as when I saw you lying on the ground, hurt," she said to her grandmother. "And to threaten poor Pearl? That sweet cat never did anyone harm in her life! I want this over, and I want it over soon. I know the police are doing their best, but I almost feel like we have a better shot of figuring this out than they do. We should have some kind of a gathering and invite all of the people who had opportunity or motive to do it, even if they weren't on the scene."

"Then what?" Laverne said.

"Then we watch, listen and make comments. Maybe one of them will reveal something if we put them all together."

"It works in the movies!" Laverne said. "But I don't know about real life."

"It might be worth a try." Nana sat up straighter. "We'll only have one chance with all the suspects together."

"I was thinking about how we could get them all here," Sophie said. "Maybe we could make it a memorial tea to honor Vivienne's charity work?"

"Good idea!" Laverne said. "Bigwigs can't resist making it look like they're committed to charitable causes, even if they only do it to network. Probably never heard of the widow's mite," she grumbled, referring to the biblical parable.

"It's a good thought, Sophie, and I hope I have another one," Nana said. "I want to hold it over at Thelma's."

"At Belle Époque, right where the murder happened?" Sophie asked.

Nana nodded. "Make the guilty squirm."

"Do you think Mrs. Earnshaw will go along with the plan?"

"Old fool ought to, with you two trying to help her!" Laverne said.

"She'll do it if Cissy says it's a good idea," Nana commented.

"So I'd better get Cissy on our side," Sophie said. "But I don't know whether to tell her everything or not."

"Do you know, I never once thought of Cissy as a suspect?" Nana said.

"I considered it," Sophie admitted. "But not seriously. Is that strange?"

"Not at all," Laverne said. "It just means we know that child better than to believe her capable of it."

The two older women set to planning the menu for the memorial tea, and Sophie promised to design invitations and hand deliver them. Her mind was still working furiously on the problem of who killed Vivienne Whittaker, but she was also wondering who would have the nerve to attack Nana. Everyone in Gracious Grove adored Rose Freemont.

She hadn't recognized the voice, nor the figure, but the person—probably a man—had been growling and was hunched over. She must have been asking the wrong questions and had endangered Nana, and that just wouldn't do.

So it was imperative that they figure it out. First things first: Get Cissy on board with the charity memorial, without letting her in on the secret motive behind it. She thought for a moment, then called her friend. "Cissy, how are you? How is Francis today?" she asked. Cissy replied that they were both all right, and Sophie launched into an explanation of their intent to put on a charity memorial on a more personal scale to honor Vivienne Whittaker. "I think we could do a better job to honor her than the country club, I mean the true essence of who she was. What do you think?"

"I think it could be a good idea," she said, slowly, sounding unsure.

Sophie immediately continued, saying, "We were wondering, though, if you could talk your grandmother into having it at Belle Époque?"

There was a pause, then Cissy said, "Why would you want to have it there? Why not Auntie Rose's, away from the . . . uh, the scene of the crime?"

Sophie was ready for that. "Nana is concerned for your grandmother, Cissy. Business has fallen off at Belle Époque since the murder, right? If we have the event there, it will signal the public that the tearoom is open and ready for business, and that it's safe to go there."

"Ah, I get it! Public Relations 101 . . . appearance is everything."

"Right!"

There was silence for a minute. "I guess we can try it, but it'll mean convincing Grandma to go ahead. She's kinda difficult."

No kidding, Sophie thought. "I'm sure you could get her to agree if you tell her that it will be good for business. I'm still working toward resolving that old feud between our grandmothers. Maybe this will help, if we're all working together? We'll take care of the menu, all she has to supply is the venue."

"Okay, so when do you want to do this?"

"Is this Sunday afternoon all right? I'm going to have the invitations printed and hand deliver them myself." She paused for a beat, then added, "Oh, and Cissy? Please don't invite anyone yourself. I'd rather do this with the invitations so we can be sure to get the right folks there."

"Okay," she said. "Are you inviting Gretchen?"

"Yes, of course."

"What about Dana?"

"Uh, I don't know." Sophie thought quickly. Dana was a good coconspirator and one of the few people who could not have committed the crime. "Do you want her there?"

"She could be helpful."

"Helpful?" For a moment Sophie thought Cissy had caught on to their plot to uncover the murderer of Vivienne Whittaker, but then she continued.

"She's great at pitching in to serve food, and all that. Gretchen would have a fit if I asked *her* to help, and we can't leave it all up to Gilda, poor old dear, on her day off!"

Sophie wondered how Dana would appreciate being volunteered to help, but she made a swift decision to appeal to their friend's sneaky side. "I'll invite her myself," she said. "Don't you worry about it."

The quick copy place out near the college did a great job with the invitations Sophie carefully designed on her laptop, and Cissy called late that night to let her know that her grandma had acquiesced, after a lot of grumbling and a promise from Cissy to help her get ready for the memorial.

So the next day Sophie, envelope of invitations on the seat beside her, checked the list she and Nana and Laverne had made.

- *Gretchen and Hollis Harcourt*
- *Marva and Holly Harcourt*
- *Mayor and Mrs. Michael Blenkenship*
- *Nuñez Ortega and Julia Dandridge*
- *Shep Hammond*
- *Harvey Leathorne*
- *Oliver Stanfield*
- *Forsythe Villiers*
- *Randy and SuLinn Miller*
- *Francis Whittaker*
- *Florence Whittaker*

She was inviting a couple more folks, of course, like Jason—she just liked having him around—and even Phil Peterson, who she could not eliminate from her list of suspects.

One of the people on the list was a killer; someone, with malice in their heart, had laced a cupcake with poison and arranged it so that Vivienne would eat it and die in agony.

That was easier to imagine in some of the invitees than others.

Sophie had begun to like Gretchen Harcourt after she showed up and acted like she was a plain-ole country girl out of her depth. But after seeing her sneaking around with Forsythe Villiers, who seemed to have his finger in the whole Leathorne and Hedges development pie, she had moved to distrust. Was the girl devious and vindictive enough to kill Vivienne Whittaker, though? And if so, why? Did it have something to do with her mother-in-law, who seemed to be tied in with the development coalition?

Then there was the mayor and his sly conference with Marva, Shep Hammond and Harvey Leathorne . . . they had chosen an odd place to talk, at the memorial service for a woman they swore was a Gracious Grove benefactor. What had come up that made a confab so important? Was it Phil's appearance, as it seemed to be by Leathorne's words about the "boy"? But why? Phil couldn't be in on any of it, could he?

Or . . . were they worried that he was about to spill something he knew? If she could only get ahold of Phil, she'd ask him herself, but he seemed to have dropped off the edge of the world after being released from jail, where he had been briefly held until he sobered up, according to Cissy. She'd need to find Phil, because she wanted him at the memorial tea at his grandmother's.

Shep Hammond she out and out did not trust; who could trust a lech?

Maybe by getting them all together Sophie, Nana and Laverne could figure it out. The event had to be managed carefully to make sure everyone she invited came to the tea, and that no stragglers snuck in.

The invitation read:

You are cordially invited to a memorial tea and charity event dedicated to the memory of the late Mrs. Vivienne Whittaker. Time: Sunday, 2–4 P.M. Venue: Belle Époque Inn and Tearoom. Please bring

a cash donation or check made out to Foodies for
Families and be prepared to speak briefly on what
Mrs. Whittaker did for the charities of Gracious
Grove. ***Note:** The media have been alerted, and we
hope that they will attend and report on the event
to highlight the primary benefactors in our
beautiful town!

That was to guarantee the media hogs among the group
would attend, but she had no notion of including reporters.
Nope, this was a private shindig. Sophie had carefully
worded it so that everyone invited would attend, for fear that
others would appear more charitable than they. She set off
to deliver the invitation to the easiest guest first. Where
would be the best place to accost the mayor of Gracious
Grove?

L ater that day, weary and sick of smiling, Sophie pulled
up to the bookstore. She slumped into the store, the
cheery bell tinkling overhead, and was greeted by Beauty,
who thumped down off the cash desk and wound around
her feet, welcoming her back as a frequent visitor. "Hey,
Dana," Sophie said, throwing her purse down on the floor
and stooping to pet the gorgeous cat.

"Hey, you," Dana said.

Sophie straightened and stretched. "And I thought coming back to Gracious Grove would be restful."

Dana laughed, then said, "Well, arranging a memorial
charity tea in two days for all of the leading lights of town
must be tiring. I don't like those folks at the best of times,
and you've had to personally invite each and every one of
them."

"I know. And that's why I'm here."

"Not to invite me, is it?" Dana said, eyes wide and hand
pressed to her bosom. "*Moi?* Why . . . I'd be delighted," she
said, fluttering her eyelashes.

Sophie laughed uneasily, not sure if Cissy had already

gotten to Dana and blown things. "Look, Dana, not to butter you up, but you are simply the smartest person I know who I can trust."

Dana paused, then said, her brows arched, "Go on. For someone who's not trying to butter me up, you're doing a decent job of buttering me up."

"You've heard about the tea, and know I've been inviting people."

"Mhmm," Dana said, eyeing her as Beauty leaped gracefully up to the counter and waved her tail like a fan.

"I would like you to be there."

"But you're not going to hand me an engraved invitation, are you?"

"No. I'm going to ask you to help us with the setup and serving." She said it straight, not wanting to sugarcoat it for the astute brunette.

Dana leaned on the counter, her scoop-necked aqua tank top offering a good look at her respectable décolletage. "You want me to *serve* these . . . people?"

"Yup. Right alongside me."

"Unlike Cissy, I assumed there was some ulterior motive behind coming up with this plan apart from wanting to memorialize a woman you barely knew. You'd like me to keep my eyes and ears open so we can try to figure out who murdered Mrs. Vivienne Whittaker in that very spot, right?"

"*Exactly!* Nobody hears and sees more than the servers, and it gives you access to places that are concealed, and no one pays attention to you. Though with you there, I would bet every man in the place will be paying attention."

Dana smirked. "I can play it down, too, you know . . . more small-town girl, less femme fatale."

Sophie nodded. Dana knew exactly what she needed. "I wish you were at that darned engagement tea. We probably would have solved the murder by now."

"You bet! However, if I was there, you would have to consider me a suspect, wouldn't you? People keep assuming I'm still ticked over Vivienne breaking up my young love affair with Mr. Francie-pants."

"That's true. So I'm glad you weren't there!" She paused. "You know, if you want people to stop thinking you're still angry, you could stop being so rude about Francis." And clinging to him in public, Sophie was tempted to add.

"He's a weenie. He totally deserves it," she said, with a sniff. "But we're still friends and he knows where we stand. On a more serious note, I heard your grandmother was attacked night before last. Is she okay?"

"Yeah, but spitting mad."

"And that precipitated this sneaky little party?"

"You got it. We are going to figure out who did it or die tr . . . ah, maybe that's not a good thing to say."

Grimly, Dana nodded. "Let's not have any of that kind of talk. I'll be there, and I'll be early. You going to invite the police?"

Sophie cocked her head to one side. "Do you know what? Wally Bowman just might want to be there. He is Florence's nephew, after all, so I can justify an invitation that way."

"Oh, he'll come, even if it's just to stare longingly at Cissy," Dana replied. "I'll see you on Sunday."

Chapter 24

Sunday, the one day of the week that the tearoom was closed, dawned gorgeous, and Sophie couldn't help but think of spending it by the lake with a picnic lunch. She remembered long-ago summer vacations in GiGi with Jason and the others, down by the lake all day. It had been idyllic and far removed from the rest of her life. And yet after most of a year split between boarding school, Christmas vacation in Switzerland or Acapulco, and her parent's condo in Manhattan, it was summer in Gracious Grove that really felt like home.

Poor little rich girl, her GiGi friends had called her. Jason and Cissy were the only ones in their group who had never taunted her. Maybe now, with the experience of the past ten or twelve years, she had grown up enough to shed that image.

Sunday brunch with Nana was a frittata she made using heirloom tomatoes and local herbs. It was a recipe she thought would work in the tearoom for the lunch menu, especially when the local produce started hitting the farmers' markets. They talked about the afternoon and shared their thoughts. Nana believed they ought to go into it with an open mind, but feared they wouldn't learn anything new. Sophie was determined to figure out once and for all who killed Vivienne Whittaker. After what had happened to Nana, she couldn't countenance any other outcome.

Sophie retreated up to her own apartment while her grandmother had a nap. First thing on her agenda was a phone call to Wally, who she found out was off duty. She invited him, since he was in a way related to Vivienne Whittaker, and he agreed to come, though he seemed puzzled by the purpose of holding the tea. It was mostly for Cissy's grandmother's sake, she emphasized; folks needed to stop being afraid to come to Belle Époque.

She was nervous, looking ahead, like she had been on the opening night for In Fashion. Lounging in one of the comfy chairs in her living room, Sophie decided that not only did she need to psych herself up for this experience, she should also write down her thoughts on paper, to clarify what she knew and what she suspected so she wasn't going into it blind.

Pearl sat on the arm of the chair, and Sophie said, "Okay, Pearlie-girl, we need to figure this out." She jotted down:

- *Whoever put out the poisoned cupcake had to have been at the tea party to be sure it was delivered to the right person.*
- *But that didn't mean necessarily that the cupcake deliverer was the only killer; there could have been one or more conspirators behind the murder.*
- *The kitchen was left unattended on occasion because of Gilda Bachman's digestive troubles.*
- *It appeared that most of Gracious Grove knew Vivienne Whittaker was allergic to some foods, including red dye.*

It was all interesting and suggestive, but she still didn't have a clear idea of who may have killed Vivienne Whittaker, and she was tired of thinking about it.

At one P.M. she met Nana in the kitchen. Sophie had spent every spare moment in the last two days making food for the memorial tea. Nana had offered the usual Auntie Rose specialties, scones, tea biscuits, muffins and the like. A tea party of any kind *had* to have those. Sophie had whipped up a couple of batches of mini quiche florentine, lemon curd tartlets and some savory snacks. They would make tea and coffee on the spot, in the Belle Époque kitchen.

Just as they exited the back door of Auntie Rose's, Dana pulled up and got out of her car. Sophie eyed her in surprise; the usually flamboyant Dana had definitely dressed down in tan capris and a white blouse, with a black sash belt. Her hair was neatly pinned into a bun, and she wore . . . gasp . . . glasses!

"Don't look at me like that!" Dana said, slinging her purse over her shoulder. "I told you I could tone it down. This is how I dress when I go to the bank for a loan . . . *if* I'm going to have a female loan officer."

Nana said, "I think you look very pretty, Dana."

"Thank you, Mrs. Freemont," Dana replied primly.

Sophie laughed, and gave Dana the trays to carry, while she hustled back to Auntie Rose's, got the rest of the stuff, and met them at the back door. Gilda Bachman let them into the kitchen, then fluttered around nervously getting in the way until Sophie took charge. It felt like any catering job she'd had while she was still in culinary school and directly after, so she followed the same routine: Familiarize yourself with the kitchen, make sure supplies are in place, and get organized. She had learned a lot by working her way up in the catering business, doing any job large or small.

"Okay, let's set up the tearoom appropriately for this kind of gathering." She eyed the dithering Belle Époque employee. How to keep her busy? "Gilda, we'll need your expert opinion as to . . . uh, table placement, so if you would

like to go into the tearoom and have a look around, we'll
consult in a few minutes."

The woman trudged through the door looking like she
had lost her only friend.

Sophie turned to Dana. "I've got some brochures I picked
up from Foodies for Families, and some donation pouches.
I talked to them yesterday and they were more than happy
to supply all kinds of promotional material. The director of
the charity will be attending to welcome and thank donors.
I didn't meet her, but she sounds like a great person." She
explained what she wanted and set Dana on *that* job, since
she was the only one Sophie trusted to do it right.

Cissy was supposed to be there early to help out, but
couldn't guarantee anything, she said, since Francis seemed
even more depressed than he was before the memorial service for his mom and could hardly be coaxed out of the
house. Nana and Laverne made themselves at home in
Thelma's kitchen, a fact that set that woman to grumble
moodily in the corner. She had agreed to the memorial being
held at Belle Époque, but now loudly complained about folks
"running around like they owned the place."

Sophie noticed she parked herself in a spot in the kitchen
where she could easily see the alleyway and over to Auntie
Rose's. Was that the secret behind how she always seemed
to know what was going on, who was coming and going?
She had been obsessed with Rose Freemont for decades,
since young Rose had supposedly stolen her beau, Harold
Freemont, at a church picnic.

Maybe hoping for a cessation of hostilities was too much
wishful thinking.

It was ten to two when the first guests started to arrive.
Cissy, Francis and Florence pulled up the lane in a dark
Lexus and parked in back, as Thelma faithfully reported.
They entered through the back door, but Sophie ushered
them straight through to the front, where Dana took them
in hand and sat them down at a table along the wall. Sophie
watched from the door into the kitchen. Francis looked as
distraught as he must *be*, given that he had watched his

mother die at the hand of a poisoner, but no one as yet had been apprehended. It was the scene of her death, too; that had to be painful. He had dark circles under his eyes and stared off, seemingly oblivious to the others around him.

She thought of her own glamorous mother, right now drifting on the calm Mediterranean Sea with her friends on a "girls" week of relaxation. First of all, *girls*? They were in their sixties. When did women stop being *girls* to one another? And second . . . relaxation from what? She had asked her mom that question. "From being a wife and mother," Rosalind Taylor had returned tartly. But with all her chicks grown and flown, what effort did that entail, Sophie wondered. Hers was not a particularly close family, and she had regularly chosen Gracious Grove over vacations with her parents and brothers once she was old enough to make her wishes heard.

Now that she had seen her mom's teenage pictures and heard about her difficult youth, Sophie had some compassion for her; however, didn't growing up mean leaving behind the drama of youth in favor of a more mature outlook? Sometimes she felt more like the mother in their relationship, but she was disengaging from that now to retreat to a more neutral stance. Her mother was her mother, and she did the best she could. Unfortunately her best was not a whole lot beyond plaguing Sophie to marry soon and marry *well*, which meant rich. But still . . . Sophie loved her and yearned for a deeper relationship; she just didn't think that would ever happen.

"What are you thinking, my Sophie?"

Sophie turned and smiled down at her teeny-tiny Nana. "I'm thinking how lucky I am to have you. And how scared I was when I saw your little slippered feeties sticking out from behind the garbage can." Tears blurred her vision. "I want to help Francis find out who killed his mother. I want it resolved today."

T he event was now in full swing, with everyone who had been invited in attendance, plus a couple of stragglers and minus Phil Peterson, who no one had yet gotten ahold of, though Cissy said she had left a message on his cell phone. Shep Hammond had brought with him a glamorous young woman he explained was his "assistant." Harvey Leathorne had brought his wife, as had Oliver Stanfield. Sophie had let a special secret guest into the kitchen, and that person was listening to what was going on.

The director of Foodies for Families had arrived right on time. Sophie was delighted to learn that Felice Delorme, a tiny five-foot-nothing fireball, was a chef, like Sophie, who had come back to Gracious Grove after a career in New York. She was several decades older than Sophie and had been a chef at a time when females were not so accepted in the kitchens of the big city. During their brief talk, Felice rolled her eyes when Sophie asked her about how male chefs had treated her over the years.

"I'm grateful women like you paved the way," Sophie said.

Felice said, "I've had far too many young'uns say things could not have been *that bad*. They always act like I'm exaggerating when I tell them how it was. I'm happy that not all young female chefs feel that way."

Sophie turned to the group, and cleared her throat. "Hello, everyone. Thank you so much for coming out today. Mrs. Earnshaw wanted to hold this gathering," she said, indicating Thelma, who sat nearby, "to honor poor Mrs. Whittaker and give back to the program she held so dear to her heart."

Julia Dandridge and Nuñez Ortega, arms linked, nodded soberly.

Felice was the first to speak. "I hadn't known Vivienne Whittaker for long before she was taken from us in such an untimely manner," she said, sweeping her gaze around the room. "But I did know how committed she was to charitable enterprises. One conversation we had just a couple of weeks ago still stands out to me. She said, 'Felice, I've been poor and I've been wealthy, and through it all I've learned a lot about human nature. Some of what I've learned along the way has broken my heart. I want to die poor. I want to know that I have given every cent I have to help those who deserve it, instead of dying with riches that did no one any good.'"

Sophie experienced a jolt of alarm. Vivienne had certainly not gotten that wish. Was this whole thing as simple as the woman's plan to give away too much money that others were counting on using or inheriting? She looked over at Francis, who had tears welling in his haunted eyes. Surely Vivienne wanted to leave some of her wealth for her son and his future wife and possible grandchildren to enjoy? Francis wouldn't have killed her simply to keep her from giving away all her money, would he?

"But though she did not live to see her hopes achieved, we can honor her today by raising money toward our Foodies for Families goal of instituting a hot-lunch program at Gracious Grove Junior High School. This is a lovely little town and I feel blessed to be a part of this community, but too many people overlook the less fortunate in our midst. So, in Vivienne's name, give."

Sophie stepped forward after Felice was done and looked around the group. Had she been kidding herself that anything would come of this? She took a deep breath and said, "I would love folks to come up and say a word or two about Vivienne, and why her charitable interests were such an important part of her character. I didn't know her well, but everything I've heard lately makes me wish I did. Mayor Blenkenship, would you start us off?"

He raised his eyebrows and looked around. Sophie had the sudden thought that he was looking for the reporters she had implied would be on hand to breathlessly record every moment of the important folks' speeches. But he was on the spot now and nodded, stepping forward and turning to address the small crowd.

He tugged his suit jacket down over his paunch and took a deep breath. "Vivienne Whittaker was a grand lady. We will all miss her grace, her wit, and her dedication to this fine town and all of the citizens of it, which is why we are gathered here today. I urge every one of you to think of her as you make out a check to Foods for Families in her name." No doubt if there had been reporters he would have been more inclined to speak on.

He wasn't really the one she was interested in hearing from, anyway, since he wasn't at the engagement tea and Belinda was not a serious suspect.

Felice stepped forward and said, with a tight smile, "By the way, the organization is *Foodies* for Families, just to be clear."

"Mrs. Harcourt, as one who knew her better than many— you both belonged to the country club and served on the board together—would you like to say a few words?" Sophie asked, directing her gaze at Marva. "You were at the fatal tea party, and can speak about her final hours."

Marva Harcourt, her face frozen in an expression of distaste, murmured, "I don't think I . . . no, I really couldn't."

"We'd all love to hear about your special relationship with Vivienne," Florence Whittaker said, her eyes alight with malice.

Sophie eyed her with interest. What was that all about?

Marva shot Florence a look of dislike, but perhaps realizing that resistance was futile and would attract too much attention, she stood and moved to the front of the room. "I don't know exactly what to say," she began.

"As a special friend you must have had many conversations about the upcoming wedding of her son. I keep thinking how pleased she must have been to be celebrating his engagement with you all. How about you tell us about the last time you saw Mrs. Whittaker," Sophie suggested. "You were at the engagement tea, but left *early*?"

"Well, yes, but that was because that woman insulted me," she said, pointing at Thelma.

"Liar! You and I got into it, but that wasn't what got you really lathered up. I may be old but my memory's not gone yet. We had our tiff, sure, but that was before you and Mrs. Vivienne Whittaker got into a catfight, and *then* you stormed out." All heads swiveled toward Thelma Mae Earnshaw, who squatted like a malevolent gnome in a chair by the door into the kitchen. She glared at Mrs. Harcourt and continued. "You and her were talking in real quiet tones, but I could tell you were arguing about something. Then you jumped up and hollered, 'It's not true!' and stormed off."

Sophie glanced at Wally, whose eyes had narrowed, but he remained quiet. It looked like he was going to let things play out as they would.

Marva looked around, then caught her husband's steady gaze. She calmed and raised her chin. "It wasn't an argument."

"Then what did you say wasn't true?" Sophie asked. When confronting tension or fights between employees, she had learned that putting them on the spot in front of each other with a pointed question often resulted in the truth coming out more than it would in a private conversation, during which each could lie and falsely accuse with impunity.

"Vivienne said I was conspiring with . . . with others to get Francis in trouble," Marva whispered, looking scared.

Holly Harcourt said, his tone steely, "What does any of this have to do with anything? Say, why are we here, after all? Is this really about charity?"

Felice Delorme answered, "Yes, Mr. Harcourt, this is certainly about Foodies for Families, as far as I know, anyway." She glanced at Sophie, brows raised.

"I thought y'all wanted us to talk about Mrs. Whittaker," Gretchen said, staring at Sophie with dislike in her eyes, her Southern showing just a little.

"I was asking Mrs. Harcourt that very thing, to speak about her friendship with Mrs. Whittaker," Sophie said.

Thelma harrumphed. "*Friend*ship," she muttered.

"It was just a misunderstanding," Marva said, her voice on the edge of hysteria. "Dear Vivienne was mistaken!"

Nuñez Ortega stood, and said, "I'd be happy to say a few words, if Mrs. Harcourt is unable." He strode to the front of the room. "As a board member of Foodies for Families, I have worked alongside Mrs. Vivienne Whittaker. Our friendship is not old but it was active. I felt that we were kindred spirits. She was a very good woman, committed to the cause we shared."

Felice Delorme, who had been watching the activity with puzzlement, now smiled. "I can attest to that. Mrs. Whittaker was passionate about feeding the hungry. But her overwhelming passion was her family. I know she was looking forward to her son marrying Cissy Peterson. She told me she never had a daughter, but would very soon."

"Doesn't anyone have anything *else* to say about Vivienne Whittaker?" Sophie asked, hoping to make the situation uncomfortable enough that someone would speak rashly.

Thelma sniffed. "Bunch of phonies; all of you kowtowed to her like you did *all* those lowdown Whittakers."

"Grandma, that's enough!" Cissy cried out.

"You know it's true. After what she did to your brother, I'd think you'd be a little more careful who you married!"

"That is *enough*!" Francis yelled, standing up, his fist balled at his sides, but Cissy grabbed his jacket sleeve and tugged him down.

Julia Dandridge, wide eyed, looked on, and Jason, standing next to her, sighed. He knew Thelma Mae Earnshaw from way back, and knew how irascible the old lady was.

"Oh come on, Francie-pants, have your say," came a voice from the archway near Thelma. It was Phil, but this time he wasn't drunk. He was clear-eyed and had his hand on his grandmother's shoulder. "Were you going to beat up on an old lady? You've *never* been good enough for my sister, and we both know that. You always let mommy dearest do your dirty work for you. Isn't that how you got where you are today? Or was it your auntie who helped you out this time?"

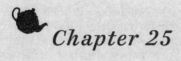

Chapter 25

"**W**hat do you mean, Phil?" Sophie asked.
Shep Hammond cleared his throat, stood, and held up one meaty paw. "Now, Philly, you have got no call to speak that way to the man who will soon be your brother."

"He'll never be my *brother*. My sister is a freakin' idiot if she marries a guy who would kill his own mom to get ahead."

Sophie would later remember it as a collective gasp, that sound she heard, just before Francis Whittaker launched himself at Phil Peterson.

"You son of a bitch!" Francis yelped, dragging Phil down to the floor and rolling around with him, both men flailing, taking ineffective shots at each other. They almost knocked Thelma Earnshaw off her chair, but Felice Delorme raced to the elderly woman and helped her out of the way.

Jason leaped forward and collared Phil as Wally grabbed Francis Whittaker's arm and hauled him off. "Enough!" Jason said, his tone husky with anger, shaking Phil. "What the hell do you think you're doing, Phil? How can you accuse Francis of something that disgusting?"

"Don't ask *him*!" Florence said, her voice trembling with emotion.

"Now, Phil, you sure have bungled it up this time, son," Shep Hammond said, grabbing a handful of Phil's denim shirt in his fist.

"He was there, he coulda done it!" Phil yelped, pulling away from everyone and rounding on his older friend. "Why don't you tell the truth, Shep, huh? Why'd you want me to put alcohol in the punch at that stupid tea party? For a week I was afraid you gave me some kind of poison that killed Mrs. W., until I heard it was a stupid cupcake that did her in."

Shep slammed his hand on Phil's shoulder and clenched; the younger man buckled.

Jason grabbed Phil's arms and pulled him away, saying, "Hey, now, don't hurt him!" to the older man.

Wally had released Francis and was examining them all, his eyes narrowed. But he didn't speak up.

In the sudden silence, Sophie asked, "Why did Shep *say* he was giving you something to put in the punch, Phil?"

"You're not actually listening to this fool, are you?" Marva Harcourt said. Her husband stared down at her, puzzlement and distrust in his eyes.

Harvey Leathorne stood and hammered his fist on the table in front of him. "This has turned into a farce. Vivienne would be horrified if she heard this little slimebucket accuse her son of killing her."

"Unless he did it," Thelma said. "Then she'd be applauding that we finally caught on."

"All I know is, it wasn't me who put that poison cupcake on the plate, and as God is my witness, I want the guilty to pay!" Gilda Bachman, tears in her eyes, had moved to the middle of the floor. "I know how some of you joke about this place," she went on. "But Mrs. Earnshaw tries real hard to make it a nice place that folks will be happy to come to, and I just think it is the lowest thing on earth to use food to kill that woman here."

Sophie was amazed to hear Gilda speak up like that.

Mrs. Florence Whittaker said, "*You* are saying that? You

who *hated* her? Oh, don't think I didn't know. She was nasty to you once, and you never forgave her. Why should we believe it wasn't you who made sure she had the poisoned cupcake?"

Gretchen, trembling, stood up. "No . . . no, I know she didn't do that. Mrs. W., it was *y'all* who tole Mama Harcourt to tell me to bring red-velvet cupcakes to the tea party. You told her that Mrs. Vivienne loved 'em."

"And you're the one who suggested that I bring red-velvet cupcakes, too. Now I remember!" Cissy said.

"But Vivienne was allergic to red dye and never ate anything that looked like it had red dye in it," Sophie said, eyeing Florence, as the pieces of the puzzle fell into place. "You needed to be sure there were only red-velvet cupcakes other than the one poisoned one *you* brought in your big, huge handbag."

"That is a lie!" Florence stated, her tone calm and tinged with hauteur. "I would never do anything to harm my family. Why would I?"

An agonized groan cut through the babble. "It wasn't *supposed* to be poison, it was—" All eyes turned to Francis, who had spoken. His face blanched and he shook his head. "I mean, Aunt Flo wouldn't kill Mom. There's no *way*."

"Despite the fact that your mother was afraid you had cheated your way into the promotion with bribery? And exposing that would overturn all you had already accomplished." Sophie glanced toward the mayor, who was slinking toward the door, his weeping wife in tow. "Wait, Mayor, isn't it true that some money changed hands in the development deal that now sees Francis Whittaker as the chief architect of the housing complex? And that a good portion of it came to you?"

"That is a very serious charge, young lady," Mayor Blenkenship said, his voice high and loud with tension. He waggled his finger, then pointed it at her. "You had better be able to back that up, or I will see you in court on a libel charge."

"Slander," Jason said, watching him, eyebrows knit in a

puzzled furrow. "You couldn't charge her with libeling you because it's spoken word, not published."

"Mayor, just tell her it isn't true," Nuñez Ortega pleaded, his tone hollow. "She doesn't know what she's talking about. Right?" He looked toward Harvey Leathorne, his face pale. *"Right?* Come on Harvey, *tell* them! Tell them our company had nothing to do with any bribery to get the contract. For God's sake, Harvey, how is this going to look?"

Hollis Harcourt said, "I suggest everyone just *shut up!*"

"Is that your legal opinion, counselor?" Sophie asked.

Gretchen had gone silent and was shivering, tears welling in her eyes. She was shooting glances at Francis and Florence, sobs catching in her throat. Something was seriously wrong. Sophie sidled over to her as her husband was talking about sorting things out in the legal system and the difference between libel and slander.

"Gretchen, are you okay?" Sophie murmured.

Gretchen shook her head, then whispered something to Sophie.

"Good grief!" Sophie muttered. She stood and loudly talked over Hollis. "Wally, I think Gretchen Harcourt has something she needs to say to you."

"No!" the young woman screeched, her whole body trembling. "No, I can't . . ." She trailed off and dissolved into weeping, hands over her face.

Wally knelt beside her and looked up into her face. "Gretchen, you told us you didn't know anything about what happened. Do you have something to add to your statement?"

"What the hell is going on here?" the mayor said, angrily.

"I will not stay in this place where my dear sister died and be a witness to this insanity!" Florence said, standing. She tugged her jacket down around her hips and grabbed her purse. "And if I were all of you, I would not listen to this craziness. I will not look kindly on anyone who stays to listen to the words of an idiot girl who doesn't know what she's up to, I can tell you that!"

SuLinn Miller stood, too, and spoke, her voice trembling.

"I think we ought to do whatever it takes to clear up this terrible tragedy. We've *all* heard the whispers about that development deal and corruption at city hall. If it has anything at all to do with the murder—" Her husband shushed her, but she went on. "Gretchen, what do you have to say?"

Hollis Harcourt barked, "Don't anyone say anything!" He shot his wife a look, but she still had her head hung low.

When Gretchen looked up, gone was any hint of cunning; her blue eyes held nothing but puzzlement. "Y'know what? Y'all are crazy as bedbugs, and crooked as a barrel of fishhooks. My granny told me all o' y'all up here were nuts . . . Yankees, she meant. But poison in a little-ole innocent cupcake?" she said, and she was staring directly at Florence Whittaker. "That's just—well, it ain't nice. It ain't nice at *all*!" Then she collapsed back in her chair in a genteel faint.

Cissy, on her feet and breathing heavily, turned to her fiancé and said, "What is going on here, Francis? What did you mean when you said that it wasn't supposed to be poison?"

Francis, tight-lipped, said nothing, but there were tears in his eyes. He stared at his aunt, eyebrows knit. Florence headed toward the door, but Wally had hastened in that direction and barred it with his body, as Sophie struggled to help Gretchen, who was recovering consciousness even as Hollis was whispering in a corner with his father and mother. Forsythe Villiers came to Gretchen's rescue and helped her sit up, fanning her and muttering tender words in her ear.

Belinda Blenkenship pulled her arm from her husband's grip and said, "I've been wondering and wondering about something for a while. See, Gretchen picked up the platter of cupcakes and took it to Mrs. Vivienne Whittaker first. When Mrs. Whittaker said she didn't want one, Gretchen told her she just *had* to, since the vanilla cupcake had been made *just for her*!"

All eyes turned toward Gretchen, but she was weeping and didn't look up.

Sophie, heart pounding and stomach churning, glanced

around the room. Most were silent, but a couple of people talked in hushed tones to each other. Francis was staring at his aunt, whose face was beet red. "Gretchen, it's time for the truth," Sophie said, turning to the young woman. "Why did you tell me you hadn't been in the kitchen here at all that day?"

"I was plumb s-scared! I thought anyone who was in the kitchen . . . the poison had to be somethin' she ate, raght?" Her Southern accent was getting stronger. "And then . . . and then I wondered about Mrs. Whittaker askin' me to put the cupcake on the plate, sayin' it was a li'l surprise for her sister. She gave me one vanilla cupcake with yeller frosting to put on the plate with my nice, normal yummy red-velvet ones and the bakery shop ones that was already there. That's why I handed it to Miz Vivienne . . . I thought it was real nice, a sweet *s-s-surprise!*" She started weeping, big, gulping, gusty sobs. "Ever since I heard it was poison I bin just sick to mah stomach. That horrible woman made me into a . . . a murderer!"

Wally's shrewd gaze swept over the room, and he touched Mrs. Whittaker's arm gently and said, his expression grim and pained, "Aunt Flo . . . uh, Mrs. Florence Whittaker, I think we ought to go down to the police station to have a little talk."

"Don't you lay your hands on me, Wally!" she said, clutching her handbag to her bosom. "I'll have a strong word to say to my brother about your behavior today."

"You haven't spoken to Dad in years; he never was good enough to be your brother, was he, especially after you married a Whittaker? Look, Aunt Flo, I'm sorry, but if you won't go, I'll need to detain you."

"Francis, you tell them!" Florence said, her voice wavering. "You tell them it was all your idea! I *can't* go to jail. I'm a member of the country club."

"I never wanted Mom dead, I just wanted . . ." He shook his head.

"You wanted her to shut up. She was worried about the

money you had been filtering out of her bank account, wasn't she?" Sophie said, the idea coming to her suddenly.

He covered his face. "I tried explaining to her, that last day, but she said I had to return it or . . ."

Sophie watched him and the room was silent now, even Florence was quiet. "Or she was going to go to the police? She was done covering for you? She was tired of rescuing you from situations that you got yourself into, like selling moonshine out of your dorm room at college?"

"Yes!" Phil said, dancing around in circles. "*Yeah*! Vivienne turned me in 'cause she was protecting Francis."

"But you really didn't want her dead, did you?" Sophie asked. She spotted Detective Morris edging out from the kitchen, where she had been listening to the whole exchange. The detective nodded once to Sophie, their signal that she had called for backup, and it was on its way. No one had noticed the detective yet except Wally Bowman, who looked relieved. Sophie hadn't wanted to put Wally in a difficult position by including him in her plans, given that his family was involved. Besides, she wasn't sure he would believe her theories. But Sophie felt he had a right to be there, and the detective had agreed. It had just seemed simpler to keep him out of the loop, given what she suspected about his aunt.

Francis groaned. "I didn't want her dead. I never agreed to that! Aunt Flo said she was going to scare her, that's all, then get her to talk more rationally. I never would have agreed if—" He stopped and stared at his aunt. "I guess you didn't want to take the risk that Mom was going to turn us in."

"This is ridiculous," Florence said, holding herself rigid against Wally's detaining arm. "I am Florence Whittaker, and I will not stand for—"

"But you were born just plain-old Florence Bowman." Thelma crossed her arms over her bosom and cackled. "Maybe in jail you'll meet up with some of your other country club folks! Like that one that's trying to sneak out the back door!"

Marva Harcourt, caught in the collective gaze of the crowd, turned, her pinched, immobile face expressionless. "I do *not* know what this is all about," she rasped, her voice guttural with fear, "but I know I didn't do anything to poor Vivienne."

"Maybe not," Sophie said. "But that's not the only crime that's happened in Gracious Grove lately, is it? Now I recognize the voice . . . you're in pretty good shape for a woman your age, aren't you, Marva? And you must have borrowed a hoodie, because *you're* the one who knocked my grandma down and threatened her cat."

"And Wally," Sophie continued, as Marva, weeping, sank down into a chair, her husband staring at her like he didn't know who she was. "I think you'll find that there has been bribery and maybe fraud in the new development everyone has been whispering about, and it's related to the motion being discussed in city council to lift the alcohol ban so that folks who own grocery stores and restaurants can sell booze."

Julia Dandridge gasped and grabbed hold of her husband. Nuñez frowned and glanced over at Mayor Blenkenship.

"Who do you think the new owners of the old Whittaker grocery store are?" Sophie said. "Right now one of them is being held firmly by Officer Wally Bowman. Florence Whittaker went in with some of her friends," Sophie continued, gathering in her glance Marva Harcourt, "to get back what she thought the Whittakers owed her. Her husband sold his interest in Whittaker Groceries, lost the money and died broke years ago. She's been climbing the social ladder back up ever since."

Francis stared at his aunt. "Is this true, Aunt Flo?"

"You're making a lot of accusations against a pillar of this community, young lady!" Mayor Blenkenship huffed.

"Is any of it true?" Belinda Blenkenship asked. "Mikey, you didn't take any bribes, did you?"

"It's *all* true," Sophie said, sad for the life lost and the lives ruined. "Vivienne Whittaker died because she would not stand by and let her son profit from the corruption and bribery taking place between the developers of Lakeview Enclave and the town council. They were plotting the upcoming annexation and the plan to lift the ban on alcohol to try and drive up property values."

"Oh crap, you mean we were that close to having booze in Gracious Grove, and I've helped stop it?" Phil Peterson said with a groan. "Just my luck!"

Detective Morris stepped out from the kitchen area just as the sound of sirens filled the air. "Mrs. Florence Whittaker," she said, "you are under arrest for the murder of Vivienne Whittaker. You have the right to remain silent and the right to retain counsel . . ."

Thelma, exhausted, slumped down in her chair by the window that looked toward Auntie Rose's Victorian Tea House. Sophie, Dana, Nana and Laverne had helped Gilda clean up the tearoom after the fractious and babbling crowd had broken up. In the end, a few hundred dollars had been raised for Foodies for Families, and Nana had offered her help to raise more. Felice Delorme, though shocked by the proceedings, had left reasonably satisfied.

Gretchen Harcourt was at the police station giving an amended statement about her actions at the tea party—she was "cooperating" with the police—with her husband by her side. Though Marva was the one who had told Gretchen to bring red-velvet cupcakes, she claimed to have done so at the direction of Florence Whittaker. Phil was taken in, too, just to clarify his part in adding alcohol to the punch. Why Shep had him do that was still a mystery, except as some misguided idea to get the gathering drunk and damage reputations. Shep seemed to be a loose cannon in the whole affair, going rogue on the tight-knit group that was trying to manage the town to their own benefit.

Marva Harcourt, the mayor, Harvey Leathorne and a few others were being questioned by a whole different cadre of detectives and police officers about the charges of bribery

and fraud involving the town of Gracious Grove, Leathorne
and Hedges, Hammond Construction and Stanfield Homes.
Thelma loudly claimed that she had overheard Harvey
Leathorne and Oliver Stanfield talking, at the country club
memorial, and though they didn't seem to know who killed
Vivienne Whittaker, they sure were fine about taking advantage of her death to hustle along their plans. Who knew what
and when would be the puzzle to figure out, and Sophie was
glad she didn't have to do it.

Nuñez Ortega had called an emergency meeting of all
employees in light of the breaking problem at Leathorne
and Hedges, so Randy Miller and Forsythe Villiers had
rushed off to attend. Belinda Blenkenship had unexpectedly
vowed to stand by her husband and help him get through
the political firestorm that was sure to follow such an event.

It had been a momentous afternoon, and late May sun-
shine was now slanting into the newly cleaned kitchen of
Belle Époque. Sophie made tea for the older ladies while
Dana finished drying the dishes and Gilda put them away.
Sophie heard a scratching at the back door and opened it to
Cissy, who practically fell into her arms, weeping.

"What am I going to do? What if . . . oh my lord, what if
Francis really *did* it? He says he didn't kill his mother, that
he had no idea what Florence was up to, but . . ." The torrent
became a flood and she collapsed into a chair, head in her
arms on the table, her shoulders shaking as she wept.

After the worst had subsided, Laverne said, "Honey, if
it helps any, I don't think he really did kill his mama."

"I don't either," Nana said.

Thelma just harrumphed, but at least didn't say anything
to make matters worse.

"But he had *something* to do with it. I know he did."

"He's admitted that much," Sophie agreed. To agree to
a plan to scare his own mother to keep her in line . . . it was
a terrible thing for a son to do. And there was still the question of the missing money Vivienne was worried about;
Sophie had gathered from a few hints Detective Morris
dropped that it was money from bank accounts only she and

Francis had access to. The detective hadn't been willing to say much, but had not denied Sophie's assertion that the missing money had probably been used to invest in the development land and bribe Mayor Blenkenship.

"I told the police anything I knew," Cissy said. Her eyes welled up. "Now that I think back, I believe Florence tested the poison on her own old dog! Poor old Samuel died last month, and Francis told me it looked like someone had poisoned him."

Sophie felt ill. That was exactly what would have happened if Florence wanted to be sure that she had honest-to-goodness cyanide pills, and not sugar pills. No doubt the police would be seizing her computer to see if she had ordered anything off the Internet, and maybe they'd even exhume the dog to see if it was cyanide that killed it.

"How do you feel about marrying Francis now?" Sophie asked. Dana stood by, watching her friend and employer.

Cissy, her tear-ravaged face ethereal in the thin sunlight streaming through the kitchen window, pushed her hair back behind her ears. "You know how you feel when you wake up from a nightmare? Like it was you in the dream, but you weren't *acting* like you? That's how I feel." She paused and shook her head, choking back another wave of tears.

Dana touched her shoulder. "Say it, Cissy. Say what you have on your mind."

"I don't love Francis. I don't think I ever did. Isn't that awful?"

"You liked Vivienne, though, didn't you?" Sophie asked. Cissy nodded.

"Did it feel kind of like having a mom again?"

She nodded, her breath catching on a sob.

Thelma moaned, "My poor girl! You always seemed so strong. I never gave you enough, did I?"

Cissy jumped up and went to her grandmother, kneeling by her side. "Grandma, you did all you could! I know that. Phil knows it, too. We both love you *so* much." She hugged her grandmother and put her head on her shoulder. "I'll be okay. And I'll spend more time here, I promise."

"We'll all look after each other better," Nana said. "Thelma, you and I have got to stick together. We're some of the last of the old crowd, and we'd all—Helen and Annabelle and me—would love it if you'd join the Silver Spouts."

"Me? Join the Silver Spouts?" Thelma harrumphed again, but said, "I'll think about it."

"I'd love to join!" Gilda offered, as she picked at a plate of the treats left over from the shortened charity memorial tea.

A murder arrest tends to put off even the heartiest appetites; no one had eaten anything.

"Come on, Thelma," Nana said, sitting down beside her nemesis and taking her hand as Cissy looked on, her arms around her grandmother's neck. "We have to stick together, old friend. We haven't always gotten along, maybe, but I know what it is to lose a child. When Harold Junior died in Vietnam, I just thought a black hole was going to open up, especially since it happened so soon after losing Harold Senior. When you lost Cassie, I felt for you, I really did, but I didn't know how to tell you. I *should* have just busted your door down and made you talk to me. I'm so sorry, Thelma. Cassie was a wonderful girl."

In that moment Thelma Mae Earnshaw did something she hadn't done in years. She burst into tears.

It was late. Sophie had tucked her grandmother in bed with a hot water bottle, Pearl, and a good Agatha Christie mystery, *The Body in the Library*. The benefit of having a bad memory, Nana said, was being able to read a book you'd already read, and have it feel like the first time. Tomorrow was another day at Auntie Rose's Victorian Tea House, with a Red Hat luncheon and a bus tour to prepare for. Sophie was going to make her frittata for the luncheon and see how it went over. She would hand print menu cards in the morning with her Frittata Primavera listed.

But she was restless. She looked out her window and

could see, over at Belle Époque, that Cissy was still at her grandmother's fussing around in the kitchen. After the bout of tears, Thelma had gotten gruff again, but Cissy said she was not leaving her grandma's place and would probably stay the night. Sophie had suggested to her friend that maybe Gilda should move into one of the rooms upstairs that Thelma didn't really want to rent out anymore. Cissy said it was a good idea, and she'd try to talk her grandma into it. Maybe they'd all have coffee in the morning and hash it out.

The phone rang; it was Sophie's mother. "Mom? I can hardly hear you!" Sophie said.

"Darling, your grandmother called me! Said she just wanted to hear my voice. What in heaven's name is that all about?"

"She misses you," Sophie said, simply.

"But she said someone was murdered and you figured out who did it. She hasn't had a stroke or anything, has she?"

"No, Mom, Nana is just fine and she was kind of right, except I didn't really figure out who did it until the last possible minute."

"What is going on in Gracious Grove?"

"I'll e-mail you and tell you all about it. It's easier than on the phone. How are things there?"

"Beautiful, as always. Dawn is just breaking on the Aegean . . . lovely! I'm sipping a mimosa . . . so civilized and European. I wish you'd fly over. My girlfriends are leaving in a day or two and your father is going to join me for a little vacation—as much as he ever takes—then we're coming back for summer in the Hamptons. Buffie Tidewater's son, Benjamin, is a concierge physician in East Hampton and he is single, darling! He'd *adore* meeting you. You could play golf together."

Buffie was one of her mother's oldest friends, but she was a snob in the worst sense, meaning, to Sophie, a sense of superiority without any claims to superior character or accomplishment. Sophie controlled her tone as she said, "I'm going to stay here and help Nana out. She can really

use me right now. I'm having fun, actually, coming up with
some ideas for the menu and—"

"Oh darling, I have to go. Suzette is calling me. We're
going to walk down on the dock and flirt with the Greek
men. Even the fishermen here are . . . well, European. So
gal*lant*!"

Sophie set the phone gently down on the cradle as her
mother hung up, and looked back out the window. A figure
strolled along the sidewalk and just then stopped under a
streetlight. It was Jason! She wondered if he could see her;
that moment he lifted one hand and waved. He motioned
for her to come out for a walk.

She waved back and slipped into her tennies and grabbed
a sweater, one of Nana's that still smelled like her lotion. As
she raced down the stairs, she thought of her mother on the
Aegean. Would she trade places with her mom? As Sophie
stepped out onto the sidewalk and locked the door behind
her she thought, *Not in a million years*. She was right where
she wanted to be, right where Providence had put her.

"Hey, Jason, what brings you to this neck of the woods?"

"I just couldn't sleep after that scene at the tearoom. Want
to take a little walk and talk about it?"

"Sure. Let's walk up to the old cemetery. I want to visit
my Uncle Harry's grave. I never knew him, but now I realize
how much Nana misses him and Grandpa Harold."

He put his arm over her shoulders and gave a little
squeeze, then released. She wished he'd left it there, but at
least he had felt comfortable enough to do that.

"Sure. Let's go."

She took his arm and sighed happily. Life in Gracious
Grove, New York, was better than she even remembered.

Cranberry Pecan Yogurt Scones

Makes eight generous-sized scones.

1 ½ cups all-purpose flour
¼ cup white sugar
1 tsp. baking powder
¼ tsp. baking soda
¼ tsp. salt
6 tblsps. or ⅓ cup cold butter—if you are using
    salted butter, you can omit salt from the recipe.
½ cup dried cranberries
½ cup chopped pecans
½ cup plain yogurt

Preheat oven to 425° F.

Sift together flour, sugar, baking powder, baking soda, and salt (if you are using it).

Add in butter, bit by bit, mixing as you go. Rub it in with your fingers, if you like, but leave small pebbles of the cold butter in the mixture.

Stir in the cranberries and pecans, and then the yogurt. Mix gently, but thoroughly. It may take a bit to get all the dry ingredients worked into the yogurt.

Form dough into a ball. Place on a greased or parchment-paper-covered baking sheet and pat into a circle about ½ inch thick.

Sprinkle with sugar—you could use turbinado or another decorative sugar for this, if you want, but plain sugar works just fine.

Cut into eight pie-shaped segments, but don't separate the wedges!

Bake for about 20 minutes, or until edges are slightly crisp and the top is lightly browned. It may need as little as 18 minutes, or as much as 22, but don't over- *or* underbake the scones!

The scones will break apart nicely into perfect wedges. These are delicious warm or cold, with butter or not, and also stand up well to preserves or jams like Cranberry Apple conserve or cherry jam. Perfect with tea of any kind!

How to Steep
the Perfect Cup of Tea

*Courtesy of the tea experts at The Tea Haus
(theteahaus.com), London, Ontario, Canada.*

Steeping tea involves a few processes, all equally important in producing the desired beverage. In the world of tea, we like to use the word *steep* rather than *brew* since it conveys more of the process involved.

Three things are required to make that perfect cup: water, good tea, and time. Depending on the origin of the particular tea, various tricks of the trade may be employed.

Black tea is the most common tea in the west. It is a tea that is fully fermented or oxidized and has the highest caffeine content. It requires water that is at a rolling boil. One level teaspoon or two grams of tealeaf is needed per cup.

Remember that in the world of tea, a teacup is a 120-milliliter, (approximately four-ounce) not a 250-milliliter (eight-ounce) measuring cup! You may wish to utilize a strainer or infuser, a way to keep the leaves from invading the cup. Many people desire a clean cup of tea. Add the boiling water and make sure the leaves are completely immersed. They will start to uncurl themselves and begin releasing flavor and aroma. This part of the steeping is often called "the agony of the leaf."

Allow 3–5 minutes for the full flavor to come out before removing the infuser or strainer, or if you have made the tea without the aid of one, you can begin to enjoy the subtleties of the tea. Many people add milk or sugar, but we recommend you try the tea without adding anything that will obliterate the flavors.

Green tea, white tea, and oolong tea are all prepared the same way, with one major difference; water temperature should be well *under* the boil, no more than 75 degrees centigrade or 167 degrees Fahrenheit. Green tea leaves should *not* be cooked, which the boiling water will do. All the tannins are shocked out of the leaf and you are left with a bitter cup of tea. Made properly, green tea, white tea, and oolong tea are not bitter but exude a smoothness that needs to be savored.

To summarize: bring freshly drawn water (filtered is preferred) to a boil, use 1 teaspoon or 2 grams of tea per cup, pour boiling water over the leaf, let stand or steep for 3–5 minutes. Enjoy the tea. For green, white, and oolong teas, you want to bring water to a boil and stand to cool down. A thermometer is helpful; once the water has cooled to 75–80 degrees centigrade or 167–176 degrees Fahrenheit, it is poured over the leaves, left to steep for 3 minutes and enjoyed!

From *New York Times* Bestselling Author
LAURA CHILDS

STEEPED IN EVIL
· *A Tea Shop Mystery* ·

Indigo Tea Shop owner Theodosia Browning is called in
to solve a murder at an upscale Charleston winery after
a body is found in a wine barrel.

They say *in vino veritas*, but everyone at the winery
seems to be lying through their teeth. It may look like
the killer has her over a barrel, but cracking tough cases
is vintage Theodosia Browning.

PRAISE FOR THE SERIES

"A love letter to Charleston, tea, and fine living."
—*Kirkus Reviews*

"Murder suits [Laura Childs] to a tea."
—*St. Paul (MN) Pioneer Press*

laurachilds.com
facebook.com/TheCrimeSceneBooks
penguin.com

M1385T0913

The Tea Shop Mysteries by
New York Times Bestselling Author
Laura Childs

DEATH BY DARJEELING
GUNPOWDER GREEN
SHADES OF EARL GREY
THE ENGLISH BREAKFAST MURDER
THE JASMINE MOON MURDER
CHAMOMILE MOURNING
BLOOD ORANGE BREWING
DRAGONWELL DEAD
THE SILVER NEEDLE MURDER
OOLONG DEAD
THE TEABERRY STRANGLER
SCONES & BONES
AGONY OF THE LEAVES
SWEET TEA REVENGE
STEEPED IN EVIL

"A delightful series."
—*The Mystery Reader*

"Murder suits [Laura Childs] to a Tea."
—*St. Paul Pioneer Press*

laurachilds.com
penguin.com

M314AS0913

Searching for the perfect mystery?

Looking for a place to get the latest clues
and connect with fellow fans?

"Like" The Crime Scene on Facebook!

- Participate in author chats
- Enter book giveaways
- Learn about the latest releases
- Get book recommendations
  and more!

facebook.com/TheCrimeSceneBooks

Obsidian

M884G1011

The delicious mysteries of Berkley Prime Crime for gourmet detectives

Julie Hyzy
WHITE HOUSE CHEF MYSTERIES

B. B. Haywood
CANDY HOLLIDAY MURDER MYSTERIES

Jenn McKinlay
CUPCAKE BAKERY MYSTERIES

Laura Childs
TEA SHOP MYSTERIES

Claudia Bishop
HEMLOCK FALLS MYSTERIES

Nancy Fairbanks
CULINARY MYSTERIES

Cleo Coyle
COFFEEHOUSE MYSTERIES

Solving crime can be a treat.

penguin.com

M7G0610